Duet

Carol Shields is the author of ten novels and three collections of short stories. *The Stone Diaries* won the Pulitzer Prize and was shortlisted for the Booker Prize. *Larry's Party* won the Orange Prize and *Unless* was shortlisted for the 2002 Man Booker Prize. Born and brought up in Chicago, Carol Shields has lived in Canada since 1957.

For more information on Carol Shields visit
www.4thestate.com/carolshields

THE WORK OF CAROL SHIELDS

POETRY
Others
Intersect
Coming to Canada

NOVELS
Unless
Larry's Party
The Stone Diaries
The Republic of Love
A Celibate Season (with Blanche Howard)
Mary Swann
A Fairly Conventional Woman
Happenstance
The Box Garden
Small Ceremonies

STORY COLLECTIONS
Various Miracles
The Orange Fish
Dressing Up for the Carnival

PLAYS
Departures and Arrivals
Thirteen Hands
Fashion, Power, Guilt and the Charity of Families
(with Catherine Shields)
Anniversary (with David Williamson)

CRITICISM
Susanna Moodie: Voice and Vision

ANTHOLOGY
Dropped Threads: What We Aren't Told
(Edited with Marjorie Anderson)
Dropped Threads: More of What We Aren't Told
(Edited with Marjorie Anderson)

BIOGRAPHY
Jane Austen

Duet

Carol Shields

FOURTH ESTATE • *London* and *New York*

Originally published as two companion novels:
Small Ceremonies (1976) and *The Box Garden* (1977)
This edition first published in Great Britain in 2003 by Fourth Estate
A Division of HarperCollins*Publishers*
77–85 Fulham Palace Road
London W6 8JB
www.4thestate.com

3 5 7 9 10 8 6 4 2

A catalogue record for this book is available from the British Library

ISBN 0-00-717167-6

Typeset by Palimpsest Book Production Limited,
Polmont, Stirlingshire

Printed in Great Britain by
Clays Ltd, St Ives plc

Introduction

I've always thought of my first two books as 'companion' novels, a term I seem to have invented. *Small Ceremonies* was published in 1976, and a year later, 1977, came *The Box Garden*. There is no sense of this second book being a sequel to the first, but a number of threads connect them. Above all, they are about two women, Judith and Charleen, who happen to be sisters.

The mother of the two women also appears in both novels. Mrs McNinn is an sour, disenfranchised housewife whose only relief is found in the manic redecorating of her small suburban house. Judith, a biographer, is scarcely touched by her mother's narrowness; Charleen, on the other hand, a poet, has been thwarted by her bitter mother.

These are both short novels, and the idea of publishing them together makes sense to me. Each enriches and fills out the other, and together they lead to the sisters' discovery of what their mother really is; an artist who, like themselves, stumbles toward that recognition.

Carol Shields

Judith

For Inez
1902–1971

September

Sunday night. And the thought strikes me that I ought to be happier than I am.

We have high tea on Sunday, very Englishy, the four of us gathered in the dining ell of our cream-coloured living room at half-past five for cold pressed ham, a platter of tomatoes and sliced radishes. Slivers of hardboiled egg. A plate of pickles.

The salad vegetables vary with the season. In the summer they're larger and more varied, cut into thick peasant slices and drenched with vinegar and oil. And in the winter, in the pale Ontario winter, they are thin, watery, and tasteless, though their exotic pallor gives them a patrician presence. Now, since it is September, we are eating tomatoes from our own suburban garden, brilliant red under a scatter of parsley. Delicious, we all agree.

'Don't we have any mustard?' my husband Martin asks. He is an affectionate and forgetful man, and on weekends made awkward by leisure.

'We're all out,' I tell him, 'but there's chutney. And a little of that green relish.'

'Never mind, Judith. It doesn't matter.'

'I'll get the chutney for you,' Meredith offers.

'No, really. It doesn't matter.'

'Well, I'd like some,' Richard says.

'In that case you can just go and get it yourself,' Meredith tells him. She is sixteen; he is twelve. The bitterness between them is variable but always present.

Meredith makes a sweep for the basket in the middle of the table. 'Oh,' she says happily, 'fresh rolls.'

'I like garlic bread better,' Richard says. He is sour with love and cannot, will not, be civil.

'We had that last Sunday,' Meredith says, helping herself to butter. Always methodical, she keeps track of small ceremonies.

For us, Sunday high tea is a fairly recent ceremony, a ritual brought back from England where we spent Martin's sabbatical year. We are infected, all four of us, with a surrealistic nostalgia for our cold, filthy flat in Birmingham, actually homesick for fog and made edgy by the thought of swerving red buses.

And high tea. A strange hybrid meal, a curiosity at first, it was what we were most often invited out to during our year in England. We visited Martin's colleagues far out in the endless bricked-up suburbs, and drank cups and cups of milky tea and ate ham and cold beef, so thin on the platter it looked almost spiritual. The chirpy wives and their tranquil pipe-sucking husbands, acting out of some irrational good will, drew us into cozy sitting rooms hung with water colours, rows of Penguins framing the gasfires, night pressing in at the windows, so that snugness made us peaceful and generous. Always afterward, driving back to the flat in our little green Austin, we spoke to each other with unaccustomed charity, Martin humming and Meredith exclaiming again and again from the back seat how lovely the Blackstones were and wasn't she, Mrs Blackstone, a pet.

So we carry on the high tea ritual. But we've never managed to capture that essential shut-in coziness, that safe-from-the-storm solidarity. We fly off in midair. Our house, perhaps, is too open, too airy, and then again we are not the same people we were then; but still we persist.

After lemon cake and ice cream, we move into the family room to watch television. September is the real beginning of the year; even the media know, for the new fall television series are beginning this week.

I know it is the beginning because I feel the wall of energy, which I have allowed to soften with the mercury, toughen up. Get moving, Judith, it says. Martin knows it. All children know it. The first of January is bogus, frosty hung-over weather, a red herring in mindless snow. Winter is the middle of the year; spring the finale, and summer is free; in this climate, at least, summer is a special dispensation, a wave of weather, timeless and tax-free, when heat piles up in corners, sending us sandalled and half-bare to improbable beaches.

September is the real beginning and, settling into our favourite places, Martin and I on the sofa, Meredith in the old yellow chair and Richard stretched on the rug, we sit back to see what's new.

Six-thirty. A nature program is beginning, something called 'This Feathered World.' The life cycle of a bird is painstakingly described; eggs crack open emitting wet, untidy wings and feet; background music swells. There are fantastic migrations and speeds beyond imagining. Nesting and courtship practices are performed. Two storks are seen clacking their beaks together, bang, slash, bang, deranged in their private frenzy. Richard wants to know what they are doing.

'Courting.' Martin explains shortly.

'What's that?' Richard asks. Surely he knows, I think.

'Getting acquainted,' Martin answers. 'Now be quiet and watch.'

We see an insane rush of feathers. A windmill of wings. A beating of air.

'Was that it?' Richard asks. 'That was courting?'

'Idiot,' Meredith addresses him. 'And I can't see. Will you kindly remove your feet, Richard.'

'It's a dumb program anyway,' Richard says and, rolling his head back, he awaits confirmation.

'It's beautifully done, for your information,' Meredith tells him. She sits forward, groaning at the beauty of the birds' outstretched wings.

A man appears on the screen, extraordinarily intense, speaking in a low voice about ecology and the doomed species. He is leaning over, and his hands, very gentle, very sensitive, attach a slender identification tag to the leg of a tiny bird. The bird shudders in his hand, and unexpectedly its ruby throat puffs up to make an improbable balloon. 'I'd like to stick a pin in that,' Richard murmurs softly.

The man talks quietly all the time he strokes the little bird. This species is rare, he explains, and becoming more rare each year. It is a bird of fixed habits, he tells us; each year it finds a new mate.

Martin, his arm loose around my shoulder, scratches my neck. I lean back into a nest of corduroy. A muscle somewhere inside me tightens. Why?

Every year a new mate; it is beyond imagining. New feathers to rustle, new beaks to bang, new dense twiggy nests to construct and agree upon. But then birds are different from human beings, less individual. Scared little bundles of bones with instinct blurring their small differences; for all their clever facility they are really rather stupid things.

I can hear Meredith breathing from her perch on the yellow chair. She has drawn up her knees and is sitting with her arms circled round them. I can see the delicate arch of her neck. 'Beautiful. Beautiful,' she says.

I look at Martin, at his biscuity hair and slightly sandy skin, and it strikes me that he is no longer a young man. Martin Gill. Doctor Gill. Associate Professor of English, a Milton specialist. He is not, in fact, in any of the categories normally set aside for the young, no longer a young intellectual or a young professor or a young socialist or a young father.

And we, I notice with a lazy loop of alarm, we are no longer what is called a young couple.

Making the beds the next morning, pulling up the unbelievably heavy eiderdowns we brought back with us from England, I listened to local announcements on the radio. There was to be a 'glass blitz' organized by local women, and the public was being asked to sort their old bottles by colour – clear, green and brown – and to take them to various stated depots, after which they would be sent to a factory for recycling.

The organizers of the blitz were named on the air: Gwen Somebody, Peg Someone, Sue, Nan, Dot, Pat. All monosyllabic, what a coincidence! Had they noticed, I wondered. The distance I sometimes sensed between myself and other women saddened me, and I lay flat on my bed for a minute thinking about it.

Imagine, I though, sitting with friends one day, with Gwen, Sue, Pat and so on, and someone suddenly bursting out with, 'I know what. Let's have a glass blitz.' And then rolling into action, setting to work phoning the newspapers, the radio stations. Having circulars printed, arranging trucks. A multiplication of committees, akin to putting on a war. Not that I was unsympathetic to the cause, for who dares spoof ecology these days, but what I can never understand is the impulse that actually gets these women, Gwen, Sue, Pat and so on, moving.

Nevertheless, I made a mental note to sort out the bottles in the basement. Guilt, guilt.

And then I got down to work myself at the card table in the corner of our bedroom where I am writing my third biography.

This book is one that promises to be more interesting than the other two put together, although my first books, somewhat to my astonishment, were moderately well received. The press gave them adequate coverage, and Furlong Eberhardt, my old friend and the only really famous person I know, wrote a long and highly flattering review for a weekend newspaper. And although the public hadn't rushed out to buy in great numbers, the publishers – I am still too self-conscious a writer to say *my* publishers – Henderson and Yeo, had seemed satisfied. Sales hadn't been bad, they explained, for biography. Not everyone, after all, was fascinated by Morris Cardiff, first barrister in Upper Canada, no matter how carefully researched or how dashingly written. The same went for Josephine Macclesfield, prairie suffragette of the nineties.

The relative success of the two books had led me, two years ago, into a brief flirtation with fiction, a misadventure which cost me a year's work and much moral deliberation. In the end, all of it, one hundred execrable pages, was heaved in the wastebasket. I try not to think about it.

I am back in the good pastures of biography now, back where I belong, and in Susanna Moodie I believe I have a subject with somewhat wider appeal than the other two. Most people have at least heard of her, and thus her name brings forth the sweet jangle of familiarity. Furthermore Susanna has the appeal of fragility for, unlike Morris Cardiff, she was not the first anything and, unlike Josephine, she was not aflame with conviction. She has, in fact, just enough neuroses to make her interesting and just the right degree of weakness to make me feel friendly toward her. Whereas I had occasionally found my other subjects terrifying in their single-mindedness, there is a pleasing schizoid side to Susanna; she could never make up her mind what she was or where she stood.

The fact is, I am enamoured of her, and have felt from the beginning of my research, the pleasant shock of meeting a kindred spirit. Her indecisiveness wears well after the rough, peremptory temper of Josephine. Also, she has one of the qualities which I totally lack and, therefore, admire, that of reticence. Quaint Victorian restraint. Violet-tinted reserve, stemming as much from courtesy as from decorum.

Decency shimmers beneath her prose, and one sense that here is a woman who hesitates to bore her reader with the idle slopover of her soul. No one, she doubtless argued in her midnight heart, could possibly be interested in the detailing of her rancid sex life or the nasty discomfort of pregnancy in the backwoods. Thus she is genteel enough not to dangle her shredded placenta before her public, and what a lot she resisted, for it must have been a temptation to whine over her misfortunes. Or to blurt out her rage against the husband who brought her to the Ontario wilderness, gave her a rough shanty to live in, and then proceeded into debt; what wonders of scorn she might have heaped on him. One winter they lived on nothing but potatoes; what lyrical sorrowing she might have summoned on that subject. And how admirable of her not to crow when her royalty cheques came in, proclaiming herself the household saviour, which indeed she was in the end. But of all this, there is not one word.

Instead she presents a stout and rubbery persona, that of a generous, humorous woman who feeds on anecdotes and random philosophical devotions, sucking what she can out of daily events, the whole of her life glazed over with a neat edge-to-edge surface. It is the cracks in the surface I look for; for if her reticence is attractive, it also makes her a difficult subject to possess. But who, after all, could sustain such a portrait over so many pages without leaving a few chinks in the varnish? Already I've found, with even the most casual sleuthing, small passages in her novels and backwoods recollections of unconscious self-betrayal, isolated words and phrases, almost lost in the lyrical brush-work. I am gluing them together, here at my

11

card table, into a delicate design which may just possibly be the real Susanna.

What a difference from my former subject Josephine Macclesfield who, shameless, showed every filling in her teeth. Ah, she had an opinion on every bush and shrub! Her introspection was wide open, a field of potatoes; all I had to do was wander over it at will and select the choice produce. Poor Josephine, candid to a fault; I had not respected her in the end. Just as I had had reservations when reading the autobiography of Bertrand Russell who, in passages of obsessive self-abasement, confessed to boyhood masturbation and later to bad breath. For though I forgive him his sour breath and his childhood excesses, it is harder to forgive the impulse which makes it public. Holding back, that is the brave thing.

My research, begun last winter, is going well, and already I have a lovely stack of five-by-seven cards covered with notations. It is almost enough. My old portable is ready with fresh ribbon, newly conditioned at Simpson-Sears. It is ten o'clock; half the morning is gone. Richard will be home from school at noon. I must straighten my shoulders, take a deep breath and begin.

Far away downstairs the back door slammed. 'Where are you?' Richard called from the kitchen.

'Upstairs,' I answered. 'I'll be right down.'

At noon Martin eats at the university faculty club, and Meredith takes her lunch to school, so it is only Richard and I for lunch, a usually silent twosome huddled over sandwiches in the kitchen. Today I heated soup and made cheese sandwiches while Richard stood silently watching me. 'Any mail?' he asked at last.

'In the hall.'

'Anything for me?'

'Isn't there always something for you on Mondays?'

'Not always,' he countered nervously.

'Almost always.'

Richard dived into the hall and came back with his air-letter. He opened it with a table knife, taking enormous care, for he knows from experience that an English airletter is a puzzle of folds and glued edges.

While we ate, sitting close to the brotherly flank of the refrigerator, he read his letter, cupping it toward him cautiously so I couldn't see.

'Don't worry,' I chided him. 'I'm not going to peek.'

'You might,' he said, reading on.

'Do you think I've nothing to do but read my son's mail?' I asked, forcing my voice into feathery lightness.

He looked up in surprise. I believe he thinks that is exactly the case: that I have great vacant hours with nothing to do but satisfy my curiosity about his affairs.

In appearance Richard is somewhat like Martin, the same bran-coloured hair, lots of it, tidy shoulders, slender. He will be of medium height, I think, like Martin; and like his father, too, he speaks slowly and with deliberation. For most of his twelve years he has been an easy child to live with; we absorb him unthinking into ourselves, for he is so willingly one of us, so generally unprotesting. At school in England, when Meredith raged about having to wear school uniforms, he silently accepted shirt, tie, blazer, even the unspeakable short pants, and was transformed before our eyes into a boy who looked like someone else's son. And where Meredith despised most of her English schoolmates for being uppity and affected, he scarcely seemed to notice the difference between the boys he played soccer with in Birmingham and those he skated with at home. He is so healthy. The day he was born, watching his lean little arms struggle against the blanket, I gave up smoking forever. Nothing must hurt him.

Absorbed, he chewed a corner of his sandwich and read his weekly letter from Anita Spalding, whom he has never met.

She is twelve years old too, and it was her parents, John and Isabel Spalding, who sublet their Birmingham flat to us when we were in England. The arrangements had been made by the university, and the Spaldings, spending the year at the English School in Nicosia, far far away in sunny Cyprus, left us their rambling, freezing and inconvenient flat for which we paid, we later found out, far too much.

To begin with our feelings toward them were neutral, but we began to dislike them the day after we moved in, interpreting our various disasters as the work of their deliberate hands. The rusted taps, the burnt-out lights, the skin of mildew on the kitchen ceiling, a dead mouse in the pantry, the terrible iciness of their lumpy beds; all were linked in a plot to undermine us. Where was the refrigerator, we suddenly asked. How is it possible that there is no heat at all in the bathroom? Fleas in the armchairs as well as the beds?

Isabel we imagined as a slattern in a greasy apron, and John we pictured as a very small man with a tiny brain pickled in purest white vinegar. Its sour workings curdled in his many tidy lists and in the exclamatory pitch of his notes to us. 'May I trust you to look after my rubber plant? It's been with me since I took my degree.' 'You'll find the stuck blind a deuced bother.' 'The draught from the lavatory window can be wretched, I fear, but we take comfort that the air is fresh.' Even Martin took to cursing him. (These days I find it harder to hate him. I try not to think of John Spalding at all, but when I do it is with uneasiness. And regret.)

If nothing else the Spaldings' flat had plenty of bedrooms, windy cubicles really, each equipped like a hotel room with exactly four pieces; bed, bureau, wardrobe and chair, all constructed in cheap utilitarian woods. It was on a bare shelf in his wardrobe that Richard discovered Anita's letter of introduction.

He came running with it into the kitchen where we stood examining the ancient stove. At that time he was only nine, not yet given to secrecy, and he handed the letter proudly to Martin. 'Look what I've found.'

Martin read the letter aloud, very solemnly pronouncing each syllable, while the rest of us stood listening in a foolish smiling semicircle. It was a curious note, written in a puckered, precocious style with Lewis Carroll overtones, but sincere and simple.

To Whoever is the Keeper of This Room,

Greetings and welcome. I am distressed thinking about you, for my parents have told me that you are Canadians which I suppose is rather like being Americans. I am worried that you may find the arrangements here rather queer since I have seen packs and packs of American films and know what kind of houses they live in. This bed, for instance, is rotten through and through. It is odd to think that someone else will actually be sleeping in my bed. But then I shall be sleeping in someone else's bed in Nicosia. They are a Scottish family and they will spend the year in Glasgow, probably in someone else's flat. And the Glasgow family, they'll have to go off and live somewhere, won't they? Isn't it astonishing that we should all be sleeping in one another's beds. A sort of roundabout almost. Whoever you are, if you should happen to be a child (I am nine and a girl) perhaps you would like to write me a letter. I would be delighted to reply. I am exceedingly fond of writing letters but have no connexions at the moment. So please write. Isn't the kitchen a fright! Not like the ones in the films at all.

Your obedient servant,
ANITA DREW SPALDING 9

It took Richard more than a month to write back, although I reminded him once or twice. He hates writing letters, and was busy with other things; I did not press him.

But one dark chilly Sunday afternoon he asked me for some paper, and for an hour he sat at the kitchen table scratching away, asking me once whether there was an 'e' in homesick; his or hers, we never knew, for he didn't offer to show us what he'd written. He sealed it shyly, and the next day took it to the post office and sent it on its way to Cyprus.

Anita's reply was almost instantaneous. 'It's from her,' he explained, showing us the envelope. 'From that Cyprus girl.' That evening he asked for more paper.

Once a week, sometimes twice, a thick letter with the little grey Cyprus stamp shot through our mail slot. At least as often Richard wrote back, walking to the post office next to MacFisheries at the end of our road in time for the evening pickup.

We never did meet the Spaldings. We left England a month before they returned. We thought Richard would be heartbroken that he would not see Anita, but he seemed not to care much, and I had the idea that the correspondence might drop off when he got home to Canada. But their letters came and went as frequently as ever and seemed to grow even thicker. Postage mounted up, draining off Richard's pocket money, so they switched occasionally to air-letters. Always when Richard opens them, he smiles secretly to himself.

'What on earth do you write about?' I asked him.

'Just the same stuff everyone writes in letters,' he dodged.

'You mean just news? Like what you've been doing in school?'

'Sort of, yeah. Sometimes she sends cartoons from *Punch*. And I send her the best ones out of your old *New Yorkers*.'

I find it curious. I don't write to my own sister in Vancouver more than four times a year. To my mother in Scarborough I write a dutiful weekly letter, but sometimes I have to sit for half an hour thinking up items to fill one page. Martin's parents write weekly from Montreal, his mother using one side of the page, his father the other, but even they haven't the stamina of these two mysterious children. Richard's constancy in this correspondence seems oddly serious and out of proportion to childhood, causing me to wonder sometimes whether this little witch in England hasn't got hold of a corner of his soul and somehow transformed it. He is bewitched. I can see it by the way he is sitting here in the kitchen folding her letter. He has read it twice and now he is folding it. Creasing its edges. With tenderness.

'Well, how is Anita these days?' My light voice again.

'Fine.' Noncommittal.

'Has she ever sent a picture of herself?'

'No,' he says, and my heart leaps. She is ugly.

'Why not?' I ask foxily. 'I thought pen-pals always exchanged pictures.'

'We decided not to,' he says morosely, wincing, or so I believe, at the word pen-pal. Then he adds, 'It was an agreement we made. Not to send pictures.'

Of course. Their correspondence, I perceive, is a formalized structure, no snapshots, no gifts at Christmas, no postcards ever. Rules in acid, immovable, a pact bound on two sides, a covenant. I can't resist one more question.

'Does she still sign her letters "your obedient servant?"'

'No,' Richard says, and he sighs. The heaviness of that sound tells me that he sighs with love. My heart twists for him. I know the signs, or at least I used to. Absurd it may be, but I believe it; Richard is as deeply in love at twelve as many people are in a lifetime.

The house we live in – Martin, the children and I – is not really my house. That is, it is not the kind of house I once imagined I might be the mistress of. We live in the suburbs of a small city; our particular division is called Greenhills, and it is neither a town nor a community, not a neighbourhood, not even a postal zone. It is really nothing but the extension of a developer's pencil, the place on the map where he planned to plunk down his clutch of houses and make his million. I suppose he had to call it something, and perhaps he thought Greenhills was catchy and good for sales; or perhaps, who knows, it evoked happy rural images inside his head.

We are reached in the usual way by a main arterial route which we leave and enter by numbered exits and entrances. Greenhills is the seventh exit from the city centre which means we are within a mile or two of open countryside, although it might just as well be ten.

Where we live there are no streets, only crescents, drives, circles and one self-conscious boulevard. It is leafy green and safe for children; our lawns stretch luscious as flesh to the streets; our shrubs and borders are watered.

As soon as the sewers were installed nine years ago, we moved in. The house itself has all the bone-cracking clichés of Sixties domestic architecture: there is a family room, a dining ell, a utility room, a master bedroom with bath *en suite*. A Spanish step-saving kitchen with pass-through, colonial door, attached garage, sliding patio window, split-level grace, spacious garden. The only item we lack is a set of Westminster chimes; the week we moved in, Martin disconnected the mechanism with a screw-driver and installed a doorknocker instead, proving what I have always known, that despite his socialism, he is 90 per cent an aristocrat.

It is a beige and uninteresting house. Curtains join rugs, rugs join furniture; nubby sofa sits between matching lamps on twin tables, direct from Eaton's show room. Utilitarian at the comfort level, there is nothing unexpected. This is a shell to live in without thought.

And in a way it is deliberate, this minimal approach to decorating. My sister Charleen and I, now that we are safely grown up, agree on one thing, and that is that as children we were cruelly overburdened with interior decoration. The house in which we grew up in Scarborough – the old Scarborough that is, before television, before shopping centres, the Scarborough of neat and faintly rural streets – that tiny house was in a constant state of revitalization. All our young lives, or so it seemed, we dodged stepladders, stepped carefully around the wet paint, shared the lunch table with wallpaper samples. Our little living room broke out with staggered garlands one year, with French stripes the next, and our girlish bedroom at the back of the house was gutted almost annually. Shaking his head, our father used to say that the rooms would grow gradually smaller under their layers and layers of paint and paper. We would be pushed out on to the street one day, he predicted. It was his little joke, almost his only joke, but straining to recall his voice, do I now hear or imagine the desperate edge? *Better Homes and Gardens* was centred on our coffee table, cheerful with new storage ideas or instructions for gluing bold fabric to attic ceilings. The dining table was in the basement being refinished, or the chesterfield was being fitted for slipcovers. The pictures were changed with the seasons. 'My house is my hobby,' Mother used to say to the few visitors we ever had; and even as she spoke, her eyes turned inward, tuned to the next colour scheme, to the ultimate arrangement, just out of reach, beamed in from *House and Garden*, a world the rest of us never entered. Nor wished to.

Still we have put our mark on this place, Martin and I. The floor

CAROL SHIELDS

tiles rise periodically, reminding us they are now nine years old. The utility room is so filled with ski equipment that we call it the ski room. The dining ell has been partitioned off with a plywood planter which looks tacky and hellish, though we thought it a good idea at the time. Hosiery drips from the shower rail in the *en suite* bathroom. In the cool dry basement our first married furniture glooms around the furnace, its Lurex threads as luminous and accusing as the day we bought it; Richard's electric train tunnels between the brass-tipped legs. The spacious garden is the same flat rectangle it always was except for a row of tomato plants and a band of marigolds by the fence.

The house that I once held half-shaped in my head was old, a nook-and-cranny house with turrets and lovely sensuous lips of gingerbread, a night-before-Christmas house, bought for a song and priceless on today's market. Hung with the work of Quebec weavers, an electic composition of Swedish and Canadiana. Tasteful but offhand. A study, beamed, for Martin and a workroom, sunny, for me. Studious corners where children might sit and sip their souls in pools of filtered light. A garden drunk with roses, criss-crossed with paths, moist, shady, secret.

This place, 62 Beaver Place, is not really me, I used to say apologetically back in the days when I actually said such things. 'We're just roosting here until something "us" turns up.'

I never say it now. If we wanted to, Martin and I could look in his grey file drawer next to his desk in the family room. Between the folders for Tax and Health, we would find House, and from there we could pluck out our offer-to-purchase, the blueprints, the lot survey, the mortgage schedule and, clipped to it, the record of payments along with the annual tax receipts. It's all there. We could calculate, if we chose, the exact dimensions of our delusions. But we never do. We live here, after all.

20

Up and down the gentle curve of Beaver Place we see cedar-shake siding, colonial pillars, the jutting chins of split-levels, each of them bought in hours of panic, but with each one, some particular fantasy fulfilled. The house they never had as children perhaps. The house that will do for now, before the move to the big one on the river lot. The house where visions of dynasty are glimpsed, a house future generations will visit, spend holidays in and write up in memoirs. Why not?

Something curious. One day last week, having been especially energetic about Susanna Moodie and turning out six pages in one morning, I found myself out of paper. There must be some in the house, I thought and, although I prefer soft, pulpy yellow stuff, anything is useable in a pinch, I searched Meredith's room first, being careful not to disturb her things. Everything there is so carefully arranged; she has all sorts of curios, souvenirs, snapshots, a music award stencilled on felt, animal figurines she collected as a very young child, cosmetics in a pearly pale shade standing at attention on her dresser. Everything but paper.

In Richard's room I found desk drawers filled with Anita Spalding's letters, each one taped shut from prying eyes. Mine perhaps? Safety patrol badges, a map of England with an inked star on Birmingham, a copy of *Playboy*, hockey pictures, but not a single sheet of useable paper.

Martin will have some, I thought. I went downstairs to the family room to look in his desk. Nothing in the top drawer except his Xeroxed paper on *Paradise Regained*, recently rejected by the *Milton Quarterly*. In his second drawer were clipped notes for an article on *Samson Agonistes* and offprints of an article he had had printed in *Renaissance Studies*, the one on Milton's childhood which he had researched in England. The third drawer was full of wool.

I blinked. Unbelievable. The drawer was stuffed to the top with brand new hanks of wool, still with their little circular bands around them. I reached in and touched them. Blue, red, yellow, green; fat four-ounce bundles in all colours. Eight of them. Lying on their sides in Martin's drawer. Wool.

It couldn't be for me. I hate knitting and detest crocheting. For Meredith perhaps? An early Christmas present? But she hadn't knitted anything since Brownies, six years ago, and had never expressed any interest in taking it up again.

Frieda? Frieda who comes to clean out the house on Wednesday? She knits, and it is just possible, I thought, that it was hers. Absurd though. She never goes in Martin's desk, for one thing. And what reason would she have to stash all this lunatic wool in his drawer anyway? Richard? Out of the question. What would he be doing with wool? It must be Martin's. For his mother, maybe; she loves knitting. He might have seen it on sale and bought it for her, although it seemed odd he hadn't mentioned it to me. I'll ask him tonight, I thought.

But that night Martin was at a meeting, and I was asleep when he came home. The next day I forgot. And the next. Whenever it pops into my mind, he isn't around. And when he is, something makes me stumble and hesitate as though I were afraid of the reply. I still haven't asked him, but this morning I looked in the drawer to see if it was still there. It was all in place, all eight bundles; nothing had been touched. I must ask Martin about it.

As Meredith grows up I look at her and think, who does she remind me of? A shaded gesture, a position struck, or something curious she might say will touch off a shock of recognition in me, but I can never think who it is she is like.

I flip through my relatives – like flashcards. My mother. No, no, no. My sister Charleen? No. Charleen, for all her sensitivity, has a core of detachment. Aunt Liddy? Sometimes I am quite sure it is my old aunt. But no. Auntie's fragility is neurotic, not natural like Meredith's. Who else?

She has changed in the last year, is romantic and realistic in violent turns. Now she is reading Furlong Eberhardt's new book about the prairies. While she reads, her hands grip the cover so hard that the bones of her hands stand up, whey white. Her eyes float in a concerned sweep over the pages, her forehead puzzled. It's painful to watch her; she shouldn't invest so much of herself in anything as ephemeral as a book; it is criminal to care that much.

Like my family she is dark, but unlike us she has a delicious water-colour softness, and if she were braver she would be beautiful. She is as tall as I am but she has been spared the wide country shoulders; there are some blessings.

It is an irony, the sort I relish, that I who am a biographer and delight in sorting out personalities, can't even draw a circle around my own daughter's. Last night at the table, just as she was cutting into a baked potato, she raised her eyes, exceptionally sober even for her, and answered some trivial question Martin had asked her. The space between the movement of her hand and the upward angle of her eyes opened up, and I almost had it.

Then it slipped away.

Last night Martin and I went to a play. It was one of Shaw's early ones, written before he turned drama into social propaganda. The slimmest of drawingroom debacles, it was a zany sandwich of socialism and pie-in-the-eye, daft but with brisk touches of irreverence. And the heroes were real heroes, the way they should be, and the heroines were even better. The whole evening was a confection, a joy.

During the intermission we stood in the foyer chatting with Furlong Eberhardt and his mother, out delight in the play surfacing on our lips like crystals of sugar. Mrs Eberhardt, as broad-breasted as one of the Shavian heroines, encircled us with her peculiar clove-flavoured embrace. A big woman, she is mauve to the bone; even her skin is faintly lilac, her face a benign fretwork of lines framed with waves of palest violet.

'Judith, you look a picture. How I wish I could wear those pant suits.'

'You look lovely as you are, Mother,' Furlong said, and she did; if ever a woman deserved a son with a mother fixation, it was Mrs Eberhardt.

Martin disappeared to get us drinks, and Furlong, by a bit of clever steering, turned our discussion to his new book, *Graven Images*.

'I know I can count on you, Judith, for a candid opinion. The critics, mind you, have been very helpful, and thus far, very kind.' He paused.

For a son of the Saskatchewan soil, Furlong is remarkably courtly, and like all the courtly people I know, he inspires in me alleys of unknown coarseness. I want to slap his back, pump his hand, tell him to screw off. But I never do, never, for basically I am too fond of him and even grateful, thankful for his most dazzling talent which is not writing at all, but the ability he has to make the people around him feel alive. There is an exhausted Byzantine quality about him which demands response, and even at that moment, standing in the theatre foyer in my too-tight pantsuit and my hair falling down around my rapidly ageing face, I was swept with vitality, almost drunk with the recognition that all things are possible. Beauty, fame, power; I have not been passed by after all.

But about *Graven Images*, I had to confess ignorance. 'I've been locked up with Susanna for months,' I explained. It sounded weak. It *was* weak. But I thought to add kindly, 'Meredith is reading it right now. She was about halfway through when we left the house tonight.'

At this he beamed. 'Then it is to your charming daughter I shall have to speak.' Visibly wounded that I hadn't got around to his book, he rallied quickly, drowning his private pain in a flood of diffusion. 'Public reaction is really too general to be of any use, as you well know, Judith. It is one's friends one must rely upon.' He pronounced the word friends with such a silky sound that, for an instant, I wished he were a different make of man.

'Meredith would love to discuss it with you, Furlong,' I told him honestly. 'Besides, she's a more sensitive reader of fiction than I am. You, of all people, know fiction isn't my thing.'

'Ah yes, Judith,' he said. 'It's your old Scarborough puritanism, as I've frequently told you. Judith Gill, my girl, basically you believe fiction is wicked and timewasting. The devil's work. A web of lies.'

'You just might be right, Furlong.'

When Martin came back with our drinks, Furlong issued a general invitation to attend his publication party in November. He beamed at Martin, 'You two must plan to come.'

'Hmmm,' Martin murmured noncommitally. He doesn't really like Furlong; the relationship between them, although they teach in the same department, is one of tolerant scorn.

The lights dipped, and we found our way back to our seats. Back to the lovely arched setting, lit in some magical way to suggest sunrise. Heroines moved across the broad stage like clipper ships, their throats swollen with purpose. The play wound down and so did they in their final speeches. Holy holy, the crash of applause that always brings tears stinging to my eyes.

All night long memories of the play boiled through my dreams, a plummy jam stewed from those intelligent, cruising, early-century bosoms. Hour after hour I rode on a sea of breasts: the exhausted mounds of Susanna Moodie, touched with lamplight. The orchid hills and valleys of Mrs Eberhardt, bubbles of yeast. The tender curve of my daughter Meredith. The bratty twelve-year-old tits of Anita Spalding, rising, falling, melting, twisting in and out of the heavy folds of sleep.

I woke to find Martin's arm flung across my chest; the angle of his skin was perceived and recognized, a familiar coastline. The weight was a lever that cut off the electricity of dreams, pushing me down, down through the mattress, down through the floor, down, into the spongy cave of the blackest sleep. Oblivion.

October

The first frost this morning, a landmark. At breakfast Martin talks about snow tires and mentions a sale at Canadian Tire. After school these days Richard plays football with his friends in the shadowy yard, and when they thud to the grass, the ground rings with sound. Watching them, I am reassured.

It is almost dark now when we sit down to dinner. Meredith has found some candles in the cupboard, bent out of shape with the summer heat but still useable, so that now our dinners are washed with candlelight. I make pot roast which they love and mashed potatoes which make me think of Susanna Moodie. In the evening the children have their homework. Martin goes over papers at his desk or reads a book, sitting in the yellow chair, his feet resting on the coffeetable, and he hums. Richard and Meredith bicker lazily. Husband, children, they are not so much witnessed as perceived, flat leaves which grow absently from a stalk in my head, each fitting into the next, all their curving edges perfect. So far, so far. It seems they require someone, me, to watch them; otherwise they would float apart and disintegrate.

I watch them. They are as happy as can be expected. What is the matter with me, I wonder. Why am I always the one who watches?

*   *   *

27

One day this week I checked into the Civic Hospital for a minor operation, a delicate, feminine, unspeakable, minimal nothing, the sort of irksome repair work which I suppose I must expect now that I am forty.

A minor piece of surgery, but nevertheless requiring a general anaesthetic. Preparation, sleep, recovery, a whole day required, a day fully erased from my life. Martin drove me to the hospital at nine and came to take me home again in the evening. The snipping and sewing were entirely satisfactory, and except for an hour's discomfort, there were no after effects. None. I am in service again. A lost day, but there was one cheering interlude.

Shortly before the administering of the general anaesthetic, I was given a little white pill to make me drowsy. In a languorous trance I was then wheeled on a stretcher to a darkened room and lined up with about twelve other people, male and female, all in the same condition. White-faced nurses tiptoed between our parked rows, whispering. Far below us in another world, cars honked and squeaked.

Lying there semidrugged, I sensed a new identity: I was exactly like a biscuit set out to bake, just waiting my turn in the oven. I moved my head lazily to one side and found myself face to face, not six inches away from a man, another biscuit. His eyes met mine, and I watched him fascinated, a slow-motion film, as he laboured to open his mouth and pronounce with a slur, 'Funny feeling, eh?'

'Yes,' I said. 'As though we were a tray of biscuits.'

'That's right,' he said crookedly.

Surprised, I asked, 'What are you here for?'

'The old water works,' he said yawning. 'But nothing major.'

Kidneys, bladder, urine; a diagram flashed in my brain. 'That's good,' I mumbled. Always polite. I cannot, even here, escape courtesy.

'What about you?' he mouthed, almost inaudible now.

'One of those female things,' I whispered. 'Also not major.'

'You married?'

'Yes. Are you?' I asked, realizing too late that he had asked because of the nature of my complaint, not because we were comparing our status as we might had we met at a party.

'Yes,' he said. 'I'm married. But not happily.'

'Pardon?' Courtesy again, the scented phrase. Our mother had always insisted we say pardon and, as Charleen says, we are children all our lives, obedient to echoes.

'Not happily,' he said again. 'Married yes,' he made an effort to enunciate, 'but not happily married.'

A surreal testimony. It must be the anesthetic, I thought, pulling an admission like that from a sheeted stranger. The effect of the pill or perhaps the rarity of the circumstances, the two of us lying here nose to nose, almost naked under our thin sheets, horizontal in midmorning, chemical-smelling limbo, our conversation somehow crisped into truth.

'Too bad,' I said with just a shade of sympathy.

'You happily married?' he asked.

'Yes,' I murmured, a little ashamed at the affirmative ring in my voice. 'I'm one of the lucky ones. Not that I deserve it.'

'What do you mean, not that you deserve it?'

'I don't know.'

'Well, you said it,' he said crossly.

'I just meant that I'm not all that terrific a wife. You know, not self-sacrificial.' I groped for an example. 'For instance, when Martin asked me to type something for him last week. Just something short.'

'Yeah?' His mouth made a circle on the white sheet.

'I said, what's the matter with Nell? That's his secretary.'

'He's got a secretary, eh?'

'Yes,' I admitted, again stung with guilt. This was beginning

29

to sound like a man who didn't have a secretary. 'She's skinny though,' I explained. 'A real stick. And he shares her with two other professors.'

'I see. I see.' His voice dropped off, and I thought for a minute that he'd fallen asleep.

Pressing on anyway I repeated loudly, 'So I said, what's the matter with Nell?'

'And what did he say to that?' the voice came.

'Martin? Well, he just said, "Never mind, Judith." But then I felt so mean that I went ahead and did it anyway.'

'The typing you mean?'

'Uh huh.'

'So you're not such a rotten wife,' he accused me.

'In a way,' I said. 'I did it, but it doesn't count if you're not willing.' Where had I got that? Girl Guides maybe.

'I never ask my wife to type for me.'

'Why not?' I asked.

'Typing I don't need.'

'Maybe you ask for something else,' I suggested, aware that our conversation was slipping over into a new frontier.

'Just to let me alone, to let me goddamned alone. Every night she has to ask me what I did all day. At the plant. She wants to know, she says. I tell her, look, I lived through it once, do I have to live through it twice?'

'I see what you mean,' I said, hardly able to remember what we were talking about.

'You do?' Far away in his nest of sheets he registered surprise.

'Yes. I know exactly what you mean. As my mother used to say, "I don't want to chew my cabbage twice." '

'You mean you don't ask your husband what he did all day?'

'Well,' I said growing weary, 'no. I don't think I ever do. Poor Martin.'

'Christ,' he said as two nurses began rolling him to the doorway. 'Christ. I wish I was married to you.'

'Thank you,' I called faintly. 'Thank you, thank you.'

Absurdly flattered, I too was wheeled away. Joy closed my eyes, and all I remember seeing after that was a blur of brilliant blue.

'You haven't read it yet, have you?' Meredith accuses me.

'Read what yet?' I am ironing in the kitchen, late on a Thursday afternoon. Pillowcases, Martin's shirts. I am travelling across the yokes, thinking these shirts I bought on sale are no good. Just a touch-up they're supposed to need, but the point of my iron is required on every seam.

'You haven't read Furlong's book?' Meredith says sharply.

'The new one you mean?'

'*Graven Images.*'

'Well,' I say apologetically, letting that little word 'well' unwind slowly, making a wavy line out of it the way our mother used to do, 'well, you know how busy I've been.'

'You read Pearson's book.'

'That was different.'

Abruptly she lapses into confidence. 'It's the best one he's written. You've just got to read it. That one scene where Verna dies. You'll love it. She's the sister. Unmarried. But beautiful, spiritual, even though she never had a chance to go to school. She's blind, but she has these fantastic visions. Honestly, when you stop to think that here you have a man, a man who is actually writing from inside, you know, from inside a woman's head. It's unbelievable. That kind of intuition.'

'I'm planning to read it,' I assure her earnestly, for I want to make her happy. 'But there's the Susanna thing, and when I'm not working on that, there's the ironing. One thing after another.'

'You know that's not the reason you haven't read it,' she says, her eyes going icy.

I put down the iron, setting it securely on its heel. 'All right, Meredith. You tell me why.'

'You think he's a dumb corny romantic. Flabby. Feminine.'

'Paunchy,' I help her out.

'You see,' her voice rises.

'Predictable. That's it, if you really want to know, Meredith.'

'I don't know how you can say that.'

'Easy.' I tell her. 'This is his tenth novel, you know, and I've read them all. Every one. So I've a pretty good idea what's in this one. The formula, you might say, is familiar.'

'What's it about then?' her voice pleads, and I don't dare look at her.

I shake a blouse vigorously out of the basket. 'First there's the waving wheat. He opens, Chapter One, to waving wheat. Admit it, Meredith, Saskatchewan in powder form. Mix with honest rain water for native genre.'

'He grew up there.'

'I know, Meredith, I know. But he doesn't live there now, does he? He lives here in the east. For twenty years he's lived in the east. And he isn't a farmer. He's a writer. And when he's not being a writer, he's being a professor. Don't forget about that.'

'Roots matter to some people,' she says in a tone which accuses me of forgetting my own. Nurtured on the jointed avenues of Scarborough, did that count?

'All right,' I say. 'Then you move into his storm chapter. Rain, snow, hail, locusts maybe. It doesn't matter as long as it's devastating. Echoes of Moses. A punishing storm. To remind them they're reaching too high or sinning too low. A holocaust and, I grant you this, very well done. Furlong is exceptional on storms.'

'This book really is different. There's another plot altogether.'

I rip into a shirt of Richard's. 'Then the characters. Three I can be sure of. The Presbyterian Grandmother. And sometimes Grandfather too, staring out from his little chimney corner, all-knowing, all-seeing, but, alas, unheeded. Right, Meredith?'

Stop, I tell myself. You're enjoying this. You're a cruel, cynical woman piercing the pink valentine heart of your own daughter, shut up, shut up.

She mumbles something I don't catch.

'Then,' I say, 'we're into the wife. She endures. There's nothing more to say about her except that she endures. But her husband, rampant with lust, keep your eye on him.'

'You haven't even read it.'

'Watch the husband, Meredith. Lust will undo him. Furlong will get him for sure with a horde of locusts. Or a limb frozen in the storm and requiring a tense kitchen-table amputation.'

'Influenza,' Meredith murmurs. 'But the rest really is different.'

'And we close with more waving wheat. Vibrations from the hearthside saying, if only you'd listened.'

'It's not supposed to be real life. It's not biography,' she says, giving that last word a nasty snap. 'It's sort of a symbol of the country. You have to look at it as a kind of extended image. Like in Shakespeare.'

'I'm going to read it,' I tell her as I fold the ironing board, contrite now. 'I might even settle down with it tonight.'

We've had the book since August. Furlong brought me one, right off the press one steaming afternoon. Inscribed 'To Martin and Judith Who Care.' Beautiful thought, but I cringed reading it, hoping Martin wouldn't notice. Furlong seems unable to resist going the quarter-inch too far.

Furlong's picture on the back of the book is distressingly authorly. One can see evidence of a tally taken, a check list fulfilled.

Beard and moustache, of course. White turtleneck exposed at the collar of an overcoat. Tweed and cablestitch juxtaposed, a generation-straddling costume testifying to eclectic respectability.

A pipe angles from the corner of his mouth! It's bowl is missing, the outlines lost in the dark shadow of the overcoat, so that for a moment I thought it was a cigarillo or maybe just a fountain pen he was sucking on. But no, on close examination I could see the shine of the bowl. Everything in place.

The picture is two-colour, white and a sort of olive tone, bleeding off the edges, *Time-Life* style. Behind him a microcosm of Canada – a fretwork of bare branches and a blur of olive snow, man against nature.

His eyes are mere slits. Snow glare? The whole expression is nicely in place, a costly membrane, bemused but kindly, academic but gutsy. The photographer has clearly demanded detachment.

The jacket blurb admits he teaches creative writing in a university, but couched within this apology is the information that he has also swept floors, reported news, herded sheep, a man for all seasons, our friend Furlong.

Those slit eyes stick with me as I put away the ironing; shirts on hangers, handkerchiefs in drawers, pillowcases in the cupboard. They burn twin candles in my brain, and their nonchalance fails to convince me; I feel the muscular twitch of effort, the attempt to hold, to brave it out.

Poor Furlong, christened, legend has it, by the first reviewer of his first book who judged him a furlong ahead of all other current novelists. Before that he was known as Red, but I know the guilty secret of his real name: it is Rudyard. His mother let it slip one night at a department sherry party, then covered herself with a flustered apology. We grappled, she and I, in a polite but clumsy exchange, confused and feverish, but I am not a biographer for nothing; I filed it away; I remember the name Rudyard. Rudyard.

Rudyard. I think of it quite often, and in a way I love him, Rudyard Eberhardt. More than I could ever love Furlong.

Meredith slips past me on the stairs. She is on her way to her room and she doesn't speak; she doesn't even look at me. What have I done now?

'Martin.'

'Yes.'

'What are you doing?'

'Just going over some notes.'

'Lecture notes?'

'Yes.'

It is midnight, the children are sleeping, and we are in bed. Martin is leaning into the circle of light given off by our tiny and feeble bedside lamp, milkglass, a nobbly imitation with a scorched shade.

'Do you know I've never heard you give a lecture?'

'You hate Milton.' He says this gently, absently.

'I know. I know. But I'd like to hear you anyway.'

'You'd be bored stiff.'

'Probably. But I'd like to see what your style is like.'

'Style?'

'You know. Your lecturing style.'

'What do you think it's like?' He doesn't raise his eyes from his pile of papers.

But I reply thoughtfully. 'Orderly, I'm sure you're orderly. Not too theatrical, but here and there a flourish. An understated flourish though.'

'Hummm.'

'And I suppose you quote a few lines now and then. Sort of scatter them around.'

'Milton is notoriously unquotable, you know.' He looks up. I am in my yellow tulip nightgown, a birthday present from my sister Charleen.

I ask, 'What do you mean he's unquotable. The greatest master of the English language unquotable?'

'Can you think of anything he ever said?'

'No. I can't. Not a thing. Not at this hour anyway.'

'There you are.'

'Wasn't there something like tripping the light fantastic?'

'Uh huh.'

'It's hard to see why they bother teaching him then. If you can't even remember anything he wrote.'

'Memorable phrases aren't everything.'

'Maybe Milton should just be phased out.'

'Could be.' I have lost him again.

'Actually, Martin, I did hear you lecture once.'

'You did? When was that?'

'Remember last year. No, the year before last, the year after England. When I was taking Furlong's course in creative writing.'

'Oh yes.' He is scribbling in the margin.

'Well, on my way to the seminar room one day I was walking past a blank door on the third floor of the Arts Building.'

'Yes?'

'Through the door there was a sound coming. A familiar sound, all muffled through the wood. You know how thick those doors are. If it had been anyone else I wouldn't even have heard it.'

'And it was me.'

'It was you. And it's a funny thing, I couldn't hear a word you were saying. It was all too muffled. Just the rise and fall of your voice. And I suppose some sort of recognizable tonal quality. But it was mainly the rise and fall, the rise and fall. It was *your* voice, Martin. There wasn't a notice on the door saying it was you in there teaching Milton, but I was sure.'

'You should have come in.'

'I was on my way to Furlong's class. And besides I wouldn't have. I don't know why, but I never would have come in.'

'I'd better just check these notes over once more.'

'Actually, Martin, it was eerie. Your voice coming through the wood like that, rising and falling, rising and falling.'

'My God, Judith, you make me sound like some kind of drone.'

'It's something like handwriting.' I propped myself up on one elbow. 'Did you know that it's almost impossible to fake your handwriting? You can slant it backhand or straight up and down and put in endless curlicues, but the giveaway is the proportion of the tall letters to the size of the small ones. It's individual like fingerprints. Like your voice. The rhythm is personal, rising and falling. It was you.'

'Christ, Judith, let me get this done so I can get some sleep.'

'The funny thing is, Martin, that even when I was absolutely certain, I had the oddest sensation that I didn't know you at all. As though you were a stranger, someone I'd never met before.'

'Really?' He reaches for my breasts under the yellow nylon.

'You were a stranger. Of course, I realized it was just the novelty of the viewpoint. Coming across you unexpectedly. In a different role, really. It was just seeing you from another perspective.'

'Why don't we just make love?'

But I am still in a contemplative frame of mind. 'Did you ever think of what that expression means? Making love?'

'They also serve who only stand and wait.'

'Milton, eh?'

'Uh huh.'

'Well, that's quotable.'

'Fairly.'

37

'Martin. Before you turn out the light, there's a question I've been wanting to ask you for weeks.'

'Yes?'

'I don't want you to think I'm prying or anything.'

'Who would ever suspect you of a thing like that?' His tone is only slightly mocking.

'But I notice things and sometimes I wonder.'

His hand rests on the lamp switch. 'Judith, just shoot.'

'I was wondering, I was just wondering if you were really happy teaching Milton year after year?'

The light goes out, and we fall into our familiar private geometry, the friendly grazing of skin, the circling, circling. The walls tilt in; the darkness presses, but far away I am remembering two things. First, that Martin hasn't answered my question. And second – the question I have asked him – it wasn't the question I had meant to ask at all.

I spend one wet fall afternoon at the library researching Susanna Moodie, making notes, filling in the gaps.

This place is a scholarly retreat, high up overlooking the river, and the reading room is large and handsome. Even on a dark day it is fairly bright. There are rows of evenly spaced oak tables, and here and there groupings of leather armchairs where no one ever sits. The people around me are bent over enormous books, books so heavy that a library assistant delivers them on wheeled trolleys. They turn the pages slowly, and sometimes I see their heads bobbing in silent confirmation to the print. Unlike me, they have the appearance of serious scholars; distanced from their crisp stacks of notes, they are purposeful, industrious, admirable.

What I am doing is common, snoopy, vulgar; reading the junky old novelettes and serialized articles of Susanna Moodie;

catlike I wait for her to lose her grip. And though she is careful, artfully careful, I am finding gold. The bridal bed she mentions in her story 'The Miss Greens,' a hint of sexuality, hurray. Her democratic posture slipping in a book review in the *Victoria Magazine*, get it down, get it down. Her fear of ugliness. And today I find something altogether unsavoury – the way in which she dwells on the mutilated body of a young pioneer mother who is killed by a panther. She skirts the dreadful sight, but she is really circling in, moving around and around it, horrified, but hoping for one more view. Yes, Susanna, it must be true, you are crazy, crazy.

Susanna Strickland Moodie 1803–1885. Gentle English upbringing, gracious country house, large and literary family, privately tutored at home, an early scribbler of stories. Later to emerge in a small way in London reform circles, a meeting with a Lieutenant Moodie in a friend's drawing-room, marriage, pregnancy, birth, emigration, all in rapid order. Then more children, poverty, struggle, writing, writing by lamplight, a rag dipped into lard for a wick, writing to pay off debts and buy flour. Then burying her husband and going senile, little wonder, at eighty, and death in Toronto.

It is a real life, a matter of record, sewn together like a leather glove with all the years joining, no worse than some and better than many. A private life, completed, deserving decent burial, deserving the sweet black eclipse, but I am setting out to exhume her, searching, prying into the small seams, counting stitches, adding, subtracting, keeping score, invading an area of existence where I've no real rights. I ask the squares of light that fall on the oak table, doesn't this woman deserve the seal of oblivion? It is, after all, what I would want.

But I keep poking away.

No wonder Richard seals his letter with Scotch tape. No

wonder Meredith locks her diary, burns her mail, carries the telephone into her room when she talks. No wonder Martin is driven to subterfuge, not telling me that his latest paper has been turned down by the Renaissance Society. And concealing, for who knows what sinister purposes, his brilliant hanks of wool.

And John Spalding in Birmingham.

Poor John Spalding, how I added him up. Lecturer in English, possessor of a shrewish wife and precocious child, querulous and slightly affected, drinking too much at staff parties and forcing arguments about World Federalism, writing essays for obscure quarterlies; John Spalding, failed novelist, poor John Spalding.

How was he to know when he rented his flat to strangers that he would get me, Judith Gill, incorrigibly curious, for a tenant. Curious is kind; I am an invader, I am an enemy.

And he is a right chump, just handing it over like that, giving me several hundred square feet of new territory to explore. Drawers and cupboards to open. His books left candidly on the shelves where I could analyze the subtlety of his underlining or jeer at his marginal notations.

All that year I filtered him through the wallpaper, the kitchen utensils, the old snapshots, the shaving equipment, distilling him from the ratty blankets and the unpardonable home carpentry, the Marks-and-Spencer lamp shades and the paper bag in the bathroom cupboard where for mysterious reasons he saved burnt-out lightbulbs. Why, why?

The task of the biographer is to enlarge on available data.

The total image would never exist were it not for the careful daily accumulation of details. I had long since memorized the working axioms, the fleshy certitudes. Thus I peered into cupboards thinking. 'Tell me what a man eats and I will tell you who he is.' While examining the bookshelves, recalled that, 'A man's sensitivity is indexed in his library.' While looking into the household accounts – 'A man's bank balance betrays his character.' Into his medicine cabinet – 'A man's weakness is outlined by the medicines which enslave him.'

And his sex life, his and Isabel's, strewn about the flat like a mouldering marriage map; ancient douche bag under a pile of sheets in the airing cupboard; *The Potent Male* in paperback between the bedsprings; a disintegrating diaphram, dusty with powder in a zippered case; rubber safes sealed in plastic and hastily stuffed behind a crusted vaseline jar; half-squeezed tubes of vaginal jelly, sprays, circular discs emptied of birth control pills – didn't that woman ever throw anything away – stains on the mattress, brown-edged, stiff to the touch, ancient, untended.

Almost against the drift of my will I became an assimilator of details and, out of all the miscellaneous and unsorted debris in the Birmingham flat, John Spalding, wiry (or so I believe him to be), university lecturer, neurotic specialist in Thomas Hardy, a man who suffered insomnia and constipation, who fantasized on a love life beyond Isabel's loathsome douche bag, who was behind on his telephone bill – out of all this, John Spalding achieved, in my mind at least, something like solid dimensions.

Martin was busy that year. Daily he shut himself inside the walnut horizons of Trinity Library, having deluded himself into thinking he was happier in England than he had ever been before. The children were occupied in their daily battle with English schooling, and I was alone in the flat most of the time, restless between biographies, wandering from room to room, pondering on John and Isabel for want of something better to do.

Gradually they grew inside my head, a shifting composite leafing out like cauliflower, growing more and more elaborate, branching off like the filaments of a child's daydream. I could almost touch them through the walls. Almost.

Then I discovered, on the top shelf of John's bookcase, a row of loose-leaf notebooks.

His manuscripts.

I had noticed them before in their brown-and-buff covers, but the blank private spines had made me disinclined, until this particular day, to reach for them.

But taking them down at last, I knew before I had opened the first one that I was onto the real thing; the total disclosure which is what a biographer prays for, the swift fall of facts which requires no more laborious jigsaws. That first notebook weighed heavy in my hands; I knew it must all be there.

I had already known – someone must have told me – that John Spalding had written a number of novels, and that all of them had been rejected by publishers. And here they were, seven of them.

Since I had no way of recognizing their chronology, I simply started off, in orderly fashion, with the notebook on the far left. In a week I had read the whole shelf, the work, I guessed, of several years. I swallowed them, digested them whole in the ivory-tinted afternoons to the tune of the ticking clock and the spit of the gas fire.

Before long a pattern emerged from all that print, the rickety frame upon which he hung his rambling stream-of-consciousness plots. Like ugly cousins they resembled each other. Their insights bled geometrically, one to the other.

The machinery consisted of a shy sensitive young man pitted against the incomprehensible world of irritable women, cruel children, sour beer, and leaking roofs. Suddenly this man is given the gift of perfect beauty, and the form of this gift varies slightly from novel to novel. In one case it appears in the shape of a poetry-reciting nymphet; in another case it occurs as a French orphan with large unforgettable eyes. And large unforgettable breasts. A friendship with a black man, struck up one day on a bus, which leads into a damp cave of brothels and spiritualism. Thus stimulated, the frail world of the sensitive young man swirls with sudden meaning, warming his heart, skin, brain, blood, bowels, each in turn. And then a blackout, a plunge as the music fades. The blood cools, and the hand of despair stretches forth. On the journey between wretchedness and joy and back to wretchedness, the young man is tormented by poverty and by the level of his uninformed taste. He is taunted by his mysterious resistance to the materialistic world or his adherence to fatal truths. Thousands and thousands of pages, yards and yards of ascent and descent, all totally and climactically boring.

Although, in fairness, the first book – at least the one on the far left which I judged to be first – had a plot of fairly breathless originality. I pondered a while over the significance of that. Had he lived this plot himself or simply dreamed it up? The rest of the books were so helplessly conventional that it was difficult for me to credit him with creativity at any level. Still, it seemed reasonable, since the least of us are visited occasionally by genius, that this book might have been his one good idea.

Later I was to ask myself what made me pry into another person's private manuscripts, and I liked to think that having discovered the bright break of originality in the first book, I read to the end in the hope of finding more. But it was more likely my unhealthy lust for the lives of other people. I was fascinated watching him play the role of tormented hero, and his wife Isabel too, floating in and out, bloody with temper, recognizable even as she changed from Janet, Ida, Anna, Bella, Anabel, Ada, Irene.

But more was to come. Besides the loose-leaf notebooks there was a slim scribbler which turned out to be a sort of writer's diary. I should have stopped with the novels, for opening and reading such a personal document made me cringe at his candour, my face going hot and cold as his ego stumbled beyond mere boyish postures, falling into what seemed like near madness. The passages were random and undated.

This constant rejection is finally taking its toll. I honestly believe I am the next Shakespeare, but without some sign of recognition, how can I carry on?

Constipation. It seems I am meant to suffer. An hour today in the bathroom – the most painful so far. It is easy to blame I. Fried bread every morning. I am sick with grease. I am losing my grip.

Have not heard from publishers yet and it is now three months. No news is good news, I tell I. She smirks. Bitch, bitch, bitch.

My hopes are up at last. Surely they must be considering it – they've taken long enough over it. We are ready to go to London or even New York the minute we hear. Must speak to Prof. B. about leave of absence. Should be no trouble as university can only profit by having novelist on staff.

Have been thinking about movie rights. Must speak to

lawyer. Too expensive though. Could corner someone in the law faculty.

I am frightened at what comes out of my head. This long stream of negation. Life with I. and A. has become unreal. I exist somewhere else but where?

Manuscript returned today. Polite. But not very long note. Still, they must think I have some talent as they say they would like to see other manuscripts. I expected more after six months. My first book was my best. A prophet in his own country. . . .

Stale, stale, stale. The year in Nicosia will do me good. Freshen the perceptions. Thank God for Anita, who doesn't know how I suffer. Had another nosebleed last night.

I read the notebook to the end although the terrible open quality of its confessions brought me close to weeping. Silly, silly, silly little man. Paranoiac, inept, ridiculous. But he reached me through those disjointed bleeding notes as he hadn't in all his seven novels.

That shabby flat. I looked around at the border of brown lino and the imitation Indian rug. Fluffy green chunks of it pulled away daily in the vacuum cleaner. Why did he save light bulbs? Did he believe, somewhere in his halo of fantasy, that they might miraculously pull themselves together, suffer a spontaneous healing so that the filaments, reunited, their strength recovered, were once again able to throw out light?

I put the notebook back on the shelf with the sad, unwanted novels. I never told anyone about them, not even Martin, and I never again so much as touched their tense covers. John Spalding and his terrible sorrowing stayed with me all winter, a painful bruising, crippling as the weather, pulling me down. I never really shook it off until I was back aboard the BOAC, strapped in with a dazzling lunch tray on my lap and the wide winking ocean beneath me.

November

Richard's friends are random and seasonal. There are the friends he swims with in the summer and the casual sweatered football friends. There is a nice boy named Gavin Lord whom we often take skiing with us but forget about between seasons. There is a gaggle of deep-voiced brothers who live next door. For Richard they are interchangeable; they come and go; he functions within their offhand comradeship. In their absence he is indifferent. And, of course, he has Anita.

Meredith's best friend is a girl named Gwendolyn Ackerman, an intelligent girl with a curiously dark face and a disposition sour as rhubarb. She is sensitive: hurts cling to her like tiny burrs, and she and Meredith rock back and forth between the rhythm of their misunderstandings; apology and forgiveness are their coinage. It is possible, I think, that they won't always be friends. They are only, it seems, temporarily linked together in their terrible and mutual inadequacy. After school, huddled in Meredith's bedroom, they minutely examine and torment each other with the nuances of their daily happenings, not only what they said and did, but what they nearly said and almost did. They interpret each other until their separate experiences hang in exhausted shreds. They wear each other out; it can't last.

For a quiet man, Martin has many friends. They exist, it seems to me, in separate chambers, and when he sees them he turns his whole self toward them as though each were a privileged satellite. A great many people seem to be extraordinarily attached to him. There are two babies in the world named after him. Old friends from Montreal telephone him and write him chatty letters at Christmas as though he really might care about their new jobs or the cottages they are building. His university friends often drop in on Saturday afternoons and, in addition, he hears regularly from his colleagues in England. He is not an effervescent man, but when he is with his friends he listens to them with a slow and almost innocent smile on his face.

His closest friend at the university is Roger Ramsay who teaches Canadian Literature. Roger has a fat man's face, round and red, with a hedge of fat yellow curls. But his body is long and lean and muscular. He is younger than we are, young enough so he is able to live with someone without marrying her, and he and Ruthie have an apartment at the top of an old Gothic house which is cheap and charming and only a little uncomfortable. Posters instead of wallpaper, ragouts in brown pots instead of roasts, candles instead of trilights, Lightfoot records instead of children. A growing collection of Eskimo carvings and rare Canadian books.

Ruthie St Pierre is small, dark and brilliant; assistant to the head of the translation department in the Central Library. They both smoke the odd bit of pot or, as Roger puts it, they're into it. We love them, but what we can't understand is why they love us, but they do, especially Martin. In this friendship I am the extra; the clumsy big sister who is only accidentally included.

My closest friend is a woman named Nancy Krantz. She is about my age, mother to six children and wife to a lawyer named Paul Krantz, but that is strictly by the way. Nancy is not really attached to anyone, not even to me, I admit sadly. I am an incidental here as well.

She generally drops in unexpectedly between errands, usually in the morning. She almost, but not quite, keeps the Volkswagen engine running in the driveway while we talk. She is in a rush and she dances back and forth in my kitchen with the car keys still jingling in her fingers. I cannot, in fact, imagine her voice without the accompaniment of ringing car keys. Our friendship is made up of these brief frenzied exchanges, but the quality of our conversation, for all its feverish outpouring, is genuine.

We talk fast, both of us, as though we accelerated each other, and there is a thrilling madness in our morning dialogues. Nancy has always just been somewhere or is on her way to somewhere – to an anti-abortionist meeting, to a consumers' committee, to a curriculum symposium. And into these concerns, which in the abstract interest me very little, she manages to sweep me away. I stand, coffee cup in one hand, wildly gesticulating with the other, suddenly stunningly vocal. The quality of our exchanges is such that she enables me to string together miles of impressive phrases; my extemporaneous self reawakened. I pour more coffee, and still standing we talk on until, with a loud shake of her key ring, Nancy glances at her watch and flies to the door. I am left steaming with exhaustion and happiness.

Today she has come from a committee which is fighting rate increases in the telephone service. It is her special quality to be able to observe these activities as though she were a spectator at a play. She can be wildly humorous. This morning, as a footnote to her recital, she delivers what I think to be a stunning theory of life, for she has discovered the mechanism which monitors her existence.

Every month, she tells me, the water bill arrives in the mail. The Water and Sewerage Office informs her how much money she must pay and, in addition, how many gallons of water her household has consumed during the month. But that isn't all. Underneath that figure is another which is even more fascinating, the number of gallons which she and her family have consumed on the previous billing.

She has noticed something: since she and her husband Paul have been married, the number of gallons has gone up every month. There have been no exceptions over eighteen years, not one in eighteen years, twelve billing each year. By thousands and thousands of gallons she has gone steadily up the scale. It is inexorable. She and the meter are locked in combat. She would like to fool it once, to be very thrifty for a month, use her dishwater over again, make everyone conserve on baths, flush the toilet once a day, just to stop the rolling, rolling of the tide.

It has become a sign to her, a symbol of the gathering complexity of her life. Tearing open her water bill she finds her breath stuck in her chest. Travelling from gallon to gallon she is inching toward something. Is there such a thing as infinity gallons of water, she has wondered.

But recently it has occurred to her that she will never reach infinity. One month – the exact date already exists in the future, predestined – one month there will be a very slight decrease in number of gallons. And the next month there will be a further decrease. Very small, very gradual. It will work its way back, she says. And it will mean something important. Maybe that she is reverting to something simpler, less entangled.

She doesn't know whether it will be a good thing or bad, whether she is frightened or not of the day when the first decrease comes. But she sees her whole life gathered around that watershed. It may even mean the beginning of dying, she confides to the rhythm of her chromium-plated key ring.

Winter is about to fall in on us. Early this morning when I woke up I could almost feel the snow suspended over the backyard. Outside our window there was a dense gathering of white, a blank absence of sun, and through the walls of the house the blue air pinched and gnawed.

Downstairs in the kitchen I made coffee, and I was about to wake Martin and the children when I heard a thin waterfall of sound coming from behind the birch slab door leading to the family room. I opened it and found the television on.

Richard and Meredith were sitting on the sofa watching. All I could see from the doorway were the backs of their heads, the two of them side by side, Richard leaning slightly forward, his hands on his knees. The sight of them, the roughed fur of their hair and the crush of pajama collars, and especially the utter attentiveness to the screen, made me weak for a moment with love.

'What's going on?' I asked hoarsely.

'Shhh,' Richard rasped. 'They're getting into the Royal Coach.'

'Who?' I asked, and then remembered. It was Princess Anne's wedding day.

'How long have you two been up?' I asked.

'Five o'clock,' Meredith said shortly, never for a moment taking her eyes off the picture. 'Richard woke me up.'

'Five o'clock!' I felt my mouth go soft with disbelief.

'It's direct by satellite,' Richard said.

'But it will all be rebroadcast later,' I said with sternness, feeling at the same time wondering amazement at their early rising.

'It's not the same though,' Meredith said.

'They leave out half the junk,' said Richard.

(Would Anita Spalding be watching too? In the Birmingham flat, linked through satellite with Richard? Probably.)

While the coffee breathed and burped in the kitchen, I sat on the arm of the sofa watching the glittering coach drive through London. A camera scanned the crowds, and the announcer reminded us how they had stood all night waiting. The London sky looked tea-toned, foreign, water-thin.

'I thought you didn't like Princess Anne,' I challenged Meredith. 'I don't,' she told me, 'but this is a wedding.'

Later, when Martin was up, we ate breakfast, and I told them about Princess Margaret's wedding. There was no satellite in those days, so we didn't have to get up at five o'clock to watch. Instead, a film of the wedding was shot in London and rushed into a waiting transatlantic jet.

We were at home in our first apartment; Martin was writing the final draft of his thesis. It was just after lunch, and Meredith, who was very young, had been put into her crib for a nap. Our television was old, a second-hand set with a permanent crimp in the picture.

The camera was focused on a bit of sky off the coast of Newfoundland and, while Martin and I and millions of others stared at the blank patch, a commentator chattered on desperately about the history of royal weddings.

Finally a tiny speck appeared on the screen. The jet. We watched, breathless, as it landed. A man leaped out with an attaché case in his hand – the precious reels of film. Fresh from London. Rushed to the colonies. I remember my throat going tight. Stupid, but this man was a genuine courier, in a league with Roman runners and, though Martin and I were indifferent even then to royalty, we recognized a hero when we saw one.

We watched him race, satchel in hand, across the landing field and then into a flat terminal building where the projector was oiled and waiting. There was a moment's black-out, and the next thing we saw was the Royal Coach careening around Pall Mall. Miraculous.

While I was telling Meredith and Richard this story over cornflakes and toast, their eyes were fixed on me; they never miss a word. The genes are true; my children are like me in their lust after other people's stories.

Unlike Martin, whose family tree came well stocked with family tales, I am from a bleak non-storytelling family. I can remember my father, a tall, lank man who for forty years worked as inventory clerk in a screw factory, telling only one story, and this he told only two or three times. It was so extraordinary for him to tell a story at all that I remember the details perfectly.

A single incident fetched from his childhood: a girl in his high school tried to commit suicide by leaping into the stairwell. My father happened to be coming down a corridor just as she was sailing through the air. On impact she broke both her ankles and promptly fainted. This brought my father to the point of the story, the point as he conceived it being that the act of fainting was a benefice which spontaneously blocked out pain. He didn't explain to us why the girl was trying to take her life or whether she managed to live it afterwards. He seemed oddly incurious about such a dramatic event, and it must have been his bland acceptance of the facts which restrained us from asking him for details.

It is one of my fantasies that I meet this suicidal girl. She would be about seventy now – my father has been dead for ten years – and I imagine myself meeting her at a friend's. She is someone's aunt or family friend, and I recognize her the moment she touches on her attempted school suicide. I interrupt her and ask if she remembers a young boy, my father, who rushed to her when she fell and into whose arms she fainted. Yes, she would say, it happened just that way, and we would exchange long and meaningful looks, embrace each other, perhaps cry.

From my mother I can recall only two frail anecdotes, and the terrible thin poverty of their details may well account for my girlhood hunger for an expanded existence.

Once – I must have been about four at the time – my mother bought a teapot at Woolworth's, carried it home, and discovered when she opened it on the kitchen table that it was chipped. It was quite a nice brown teapot, she later explained to us, and it might have been bumped on the door coming out of Woolworth's. Or, on the other hand, it might have been chipped when she bought it. Should she return it?

She never slept a wink that night. After a week she had still not made up her mind what to do, and by this time she had broken out in a rash. It attacked the thin pink meat of her thighs and I can recall her, while dressing in the closet one morning, raising the hem of her housedress and showing me the mass of red welts. But I don't remember the teapot. She kept it for a year and used it to water her plants; then somehow it got broken.

Her other story, frequently told, concerned a friend of hers who greatly admired my mother's decorating talents. The friend, a Mrs Christianson, had written to *Canadian Homes* suggesting they come to photograph our house for a future issue. For a year my mother waited to hear from the magazine, all the while keeping the house perfect, every chair leg free from dust, every corner cheerful with potted plants. No one ever called, and she came to the conclusion in the end that they were just too hoity-toity (a favourite expression of hers) to bother about Scarborough bungalows.

That was all we had: my father's adventure in the stairwell, which never developed beyond the scientific rationale for fainting, my mother's teapot and rash and her nearbrush with fame. And a sort of half-story about something sinister that had happened to Aunt Liddy in Jamaica.

My sister Charleen, who is a poet, believes that we two sisters turned to literature out of simple malnutrition. Our own lives just weren't enough, she explains. We were underfed, undernourished; we were desperate. So we dug in. And here we are, all these years later, still digging.

*   *   *

On Tuesday Martin felt a cold coming on. He dosed himself with vitamin C and orange juice and went to bed early. He turned up the electric blanket full blast and shivered. His voice dried to a sandy rasp, but he never complained. It is one of the bargains we have.

Years ago, he claims, I put him under a curse by telling him that I loved him because he was so robust. Can I really have said such a thing? It seems impossible, but he swears it; he can even show me the particular park bench in Toronto where, in our courting days, I paid allegiance to his health. It has, he says, placed him under an obligation for the rest of his life. He is unable to enjoy poor health, he is permanently disbarred from hypochondria, he is obliged to be fit. So he went off to the university, his eyes set with fever and his pockets full of Kleenex.

I know the power of the casual curse. I have only to look at my children to see how they become the shapes we prepare for them. When Meredith was little, for instance, she, like any other child, collected stones, and for some reason we seized on it, calling her our little rock collector, our little geologist. Years later, nearly crowded out of her room by specimens, she confessed with convulsions of guilt that she wasn't interested in rocks any more. In fact, she never really liked them all that much. I saw in an instant that she had been trapped into a box, and I was only too happy to let her out; together we buried the rocks in the back yard. And forgot them.

Another example: Furlong, reviewing my first book for a newspaper, described me, Judith Gill, as a wry observer of human nature. Thus, for him I am always and ever wry. My wryness overcomes even me. I can feel it peeling off my tongue like very thick slices of imported salami, very special, the acidity measured on a meter somewhere in the back of my brain. Furlong has never once suspected that it was he who implanted this wryness in me, a tiny seedling which flourished on inception and which I am able to conceal from almost everyone else. For Furlong, though, I can be deeply, religiously, fanatically wry.

Just as for me Martin is strong and ruddy, quintessentially robust. But by the end of the week he was ready to give in. 'Go to bed,' I said. 'Surrender.'

Three days later he was still there, sipping tea, going from aspirin to aspirin.

I brought him the morning mail to cheer him up. 'Just look at this,' I said, handing him a milky-white square envelope.

I had already read it. It was an invitation to Furlong's lunch party in celebration of his new book. A one-thirty luncheon and a reading at three; an eccentric social arrangement, at least in our part of the world.

I squinted at the date over Martin's shoulder. 'It's a Sunday, I think.'

'It is,' Martin said. 'And I think –' his voice gathered in the raw bottom of his throat, 'I think it's Grey Cup Day.'

'That's impossible.'

'I'm sure, Judith. Look at the calendar.'

I counted on my fingers. 'You're right.'

He muttered something inaudible from the tumble of sheets.

'How could he do it?' I said.

'Well he did.'

'He can't have done it on purpose. Do you think he just forgot when Grey Cup is?'

'Furlong's not your average football fan, you know.'

'Nevertheless,' I said, breathless with disbelief, 'to give a literary party on Grey Cup.'

'For "one who embodies the national ethos,"' Martin was quoting from a review of *Graven Images*, 'he is fairly casual about the folkways of his country.'

'What'll we do?' I said. 'What can I tell him.'

'Just that we're terribly sorry, previous engagement, et cetera.'

'But Martin, it's not just us. No one will come. Absolutely no one. Even Roger, worshipper though he be, wouldn't give up the game for Furlong. He'll be left high and dry. And there's his mother to consider.'

'It's what they deserve. My God, of all days.'

'And he's so vain he'll probably expect us to come anyway.'

'Fat chance.'

'I'd better phone him right away.'

'The sooner the better.'

'Right.'

'And Judith.'

'What?'

'Make it a firm no.'

'Right,' I said.

But I didn't have to phone Furlong. He phoned me himself late in the afternoon.

'Judith,' he said, racing along. 'I suppose you got our invitation today. From Mother and me.'

'Yes, we did but –'

'Say no more. I understand. It seems I've made a colossal bloop.'

'Grey Cup Day.'

'Mother says the phone's been ringing all day. And I ran into Roger at the university. Poor lad, almost bent double with apology. Of course, the instant we realized, we decided on postponement.'

'That really is the best thing,' I said, relieved that I would not have to admit we put football before literature in this house.

'We'll make it December then, I think. Early December.'

'Maybe you should check the bowl games,' I suggested wanting to be helpful.

'Of course. Mother and I will put our heads together and come up with another date. Now I mustn't keep you from your work, Judith. How is it coming, by the way?'

'Well. I think I can honestly say it's going well.'

'Good. Good. No more novel-writing aspirations?' he asked, and for an instant I thought I heard a jealous edge to his voice.

'No,' I said. 'You can consider me cured of that bug.'

'That's what it is, a wretched virus. I can't tell you how I envy you your immunity.'

'It was madness,' I said. 'Pure madness.'

'That was Furlong on the phone,' I told Martin when I took up his supper tray. Soup, toast, a piece of cheese. He was sitting up reading the paper and looking better.

'And? What did he have to say for himself?'

'All a mistake. He never thought of Grey Cup. So don't worry, Martin. It's been postponed. Way off in the future. Sometime in December.'

'We might even be snowed in with luck,' he said going back to his paper. 'Anyway, that's the end of that story.'

Story, he had called it. He was right, it was a story, a fragment of one anyway. A human error causing human outcry and subdued by a human retraction. A comedy miniaturized.

It's the arrangement of events which makes the stories. It's throwing away, compressing, underlining. Hindsight can give structure to anything, but you have to be able to see it. Breathing, waking and sleeping; our lives are steamed and shaped into stories. Knowing that is what keeps me from going insane, and though I don't like to admit it, sometimes it's the only thing.

Names are funny things, I tell Richard. We are having lunch

one day, and he has asked me how I happened to name him Richard.

'I liked the "r" sound,' I tell him. 'It's a sort of repetition of the "r" in your father's name.'

'And Meredith?' he asks. 'Where did you get that?'

'I'm not sure,' I tell him, for the naming of our babies is a blur to me. Each time I was caught unprepared; each time I felt a compulsion amidst the confusion of birth, to pin a label, any label, on fast before the prize disappeared.

Meredith. It is, of course, an echo of my own name, the same thistle brush of 'th' at the end, just as Richard's name is a shadow of Martin's. Unconscious at the time; I have only noticed it since.

'I'm not sure,' I tell Richard. 'Names are funny things. They don't really mean anything until you enlist them.'

Now he confides a rare fact about Anita Spalding, introducing her name with elaborate formality.

'You know Anita Spalding? In Birmingham?'

'Yes,' I say, equally formal.

'Do you know what she does? She calls her parents by their first names.'

'Really?'

'Like she calls her father John. That's his first name. And she calls her mother Isabel.'

'Hmmmm.' I am deliberately offhand, anxious to prolong this moment of confidence.

But he breaks off with, 'But like you say, names are funny things.'

'Richard,' I say. 'Do you know what Susanna Moodie called her husband?'

There is no need to explain who Susanna Moodie is. After all these months she is one of us, one of the family. Every day

59

someone refers to her. She hovers over the house, a friendly ghost.

'What did she call her husband?' Richard asks.

'Moodie,' I tell him.

'What's wrong with that? That was his name wasn't it?'

'His last name. Don't you get it, Richard? It would be like me calling Daddy, Gill. Would you like a cup of tea, Gill? Well, Gill, how's the old flu coming along? Hi ya, Gill.'

'Yeah,' Richard agrees. 'That would be kind of strange.'

'Strange is the word.'

'Why'd she do it then? Why didn't she call him by his first name?'

'I don't know,' I tell him. 'It was the custom in certain levels of society in those days. And there's her sister, Catherine Parr Traill. She called her husband Mr Traill. All his life. Imagine that. Moodie is almost casual when you think of Mr Traill.'

'I guess so,' he says doubtfully.

'I like to think of it as a sort of nickname. Like Smitty or Jonesy. Maybe it was like that.'

'Maybe,' he says. 'I suppose it depends on how she said it. Like the expression she used when she said it. Do you know what I mean?'

I did know what he meant, and it was a common problem in biography. Could anyone love a man she called by his surname? Was such a thing possible? I would have to hear whether it was said coldly or with tenderness. One minute of eavesdropping and I could have travelled light-years in understanding her.

It was Leon Edel, who should know about the problems of biography if anyone does, who said that biography is the least exact of the sciences. So much of a man's life is lived inside his own head, that it is impossible to encompass a personality. There is never never enough material. Sometimes I read in the newspaper that some university or library has bought hundreds and hundreds of boxes of letters and papers connected with some famous deceased person, and I know every time that it's never going to be enough. It's hopeless, so why even try?

That was the question I found myself asking during the year we spent in England. My two biographies, although they had been somewhat successful, had left me dissatisfied. In the end, the personalities had eluded me. The expression in the voice, the concern in the eyes, the unspoken anxieties; none of these things could be gleaned from library research, no matter how patient and painstaking. Characters from the past, heroic as they may have been, lie coldly on the page. They are inert, having no details of person to make them fidget or scratch; they are toneless, simplified, stylized, myths distilled from letters; they are bloodless.

There is nothing to do but rely on available data, on diaries, bills, clippings, always something on paper. Even the rare photograph or drawing is single-dimensional and self-conscious.

And if one does enlarge on data, there is the danger of trespassing into that whorish field of biographical fiction, an arena already asplash with the purple blood of the queens of England or the lace-clutched tartish bosoms of French courtesans. Tasteless. Cheap. Tawdry.

That year in England I was restless. I started one or two research projects and abandoned them. I couldn't settle down. Everything was out of phase. My body seemed disproportionately large for the trim English landscape. I sensed that I alarmed people in shops by the wild nasal rock of my voice, and at parties I overheard myself suddenly raucous and bluff. It was better to fade back, hide out for a while. I became a full-time voyeur.

On trains I watched people, lusting to know their destinations, their middle names, their marital status and always and especially whether or not they were happy. I stared to see the titles of the books they were reading or the brand of cigarette they smoked. I strained to hear snatches of conversations and was occasionally rewarded, as when I actually heard an old gentleman alighting from his Rolls Royce saying to someone or other, 'Oh yes, yes. I did know Lord MacDonald. We were contemporaries at Cambridge.' And a pretty girl on a bus who turned to her friend and said, 'So I said to him, all right, but you have to buy the birth control pills.' And then, of course, I had the Spalding family artifacts around me twenty-four hours a day, and on that curious family trio I could speculate endlessly.

It occurred to me that famous people may be the real dullards of life. Perhaps shopgirls coming home from work on the buses are the breath and body of literature. Fiction just might be the answer to my restlessness.

'I think I might write a novel,' I said to Martin on a grey Birmingham morning as he was about to leave for the library.

'What for?' he asked, genuinely surprised.

'I'm tired of being boxed in by facts all the time,' I told him. 'Fiction might be an out for me. And it might be entertaining too.'

'You're too organized for full-time fantasy,' he said, and later I remembered those words and gave him credit for prophecy. Martin is astute, although sometimes, as on this particular morning, he looks overly affable and half-daft.

'You sound like a real academic,' I told him. 'All footnotes and sources.'

'I *know* you, Judith,' he said smiling.

'Well, I'm going to start today,' I told him. 'I've been making a few notes, and today I'm going to sit down and see what I can do.'

'Good luck,' was all he said, which disappointed me, for he had been interested in my biographies and, in a subdued way, proud of my successes.

Notes for Novel

Tweedy man on bus, no change, leaps off

beautiful girl at concert, husband observes her legs, keeps dropping program

children in park, sailboat, mother yells (warbles) 'Damn you David. You're getting your knees dirty.'

letter to editor about how to carry cello case in a mini-car. Reply from bass player

West Indians queue for mail. Fat white woman (rollers) cigarette in mouth says, 'what they need is ticket home.'

story in paper about woman who has baby and doesn't know she's preg. Husband comes home from work to find himself a father. Dramatize.

leader of labour party dies tragically, scramble for power. wife publishes memoirs.

hotel bath. each person rationed to one inch of hot water. Hilarious landlady.

Lord renounces title so he can run for House of Commons, boyhood dream and all that.

My random jottings made no sense to me at all. When I wrote them down I must have felt something; I must have thought there was yeast there, but whatever it was that had struck me at the time had faded away. There was no centre, no point to begin from.

I paced up and down in the flat thinking. A theme? A starting point? A central character or situation? I looked around the room and saw John Spalding's notebooks. That was the day I took them down and began to read them; my novel was abandoned.

After that I was too dispirited to do any writing at all. I spent the spring shopping and visiting art galleries and teashops and waiting for the end to come. I counted the days and it finally came. We packed our things, sold the Austin, gave the school uniforms away and, just as summer was getting big as a ball, we returned home.

Martin is better. Still on medication, but looking something like his real self. Today he went back to the university, and the house is quiet. For some reason I open his desk drawer, the one where the wool is.

It's gone. Nothing there but the wood slats of the drawer bottom and a paper clip or two. I look in the other drawers. Nothing.

I hadn't thought much about the wool while it was still there. I'd wondered about it, of course, but it was easy to forget, to push to the back of my thoughts. But now it has gone.

It has come and gone. I have been offered no explanations. Was it real, I wonder.

My hands feel cold and my heart pounds. I am afraid of something and don't know what it is.

December

The first snow has come, lush and feather-falling.

As a child I hated the snow, thinking it was both cruel and everlasting, but that was the hurting enemy snow of Scarborough that got down our necks, soaked through our mittens, fell into our boots and rubbed raw, red rings around our legs. It is one of the good surprises of life to find that snow can be so lovely.

Nancy Krantz and I skied all one day, and afterwards, driving home in her little Volkswagen with our skis forked gaily on its round back, we talked about childhood.

'The worst part for me,' Nancy said, 'was thinking all the time that I was crazy.'

'You? Crazy?'

'It wasn't until I hit university that I heard the expression *déjà vu* for the first time. I had always thought I was the only being in the universe who had experienced anything as eerie as that. Imagine, discovering at twenty that it is a universal phenomenon, all spelled out and recognized. And normal. What a cheat! Why hadn't someone told me about it? Taken me aside and said, look, don't you ever feel all this has happened before?'

'Hadn't you ever mentioned it to anyone?'

'What? And have them know I was crazy. Never.'

'You surprise me, Nancy,' I said. 'I would have thought you were very open as a child.'

'Not on your life. I was a regular clam,' she said, shifting gears at a hill. 'And scared of my own shadow. Especially at night. At one point I actually thought my mother, my dear, gentle, plump, little mother with her fox furs and little felt hats was trying to put poison in my food. Imagine! Well, thank God for second-year psychology, even though it was ten years too late. Because that's normal too, a child's fear that his parents will murder him. And if they didn't, someone else would. Hitler maybe. Or some terrible maniac hiding out in my clothes cupboard. Or lying under my bed with a bayonet. Right through the mattress. Oh God. It was so terrible. And so real. I could almost feel the cold, steely tip coming through the sheet. But I never told anyone. Never.'

'I wonder if children are that stoic today? Not to tell anyone their worse fears.'

'Mine are pretty brave. I can't tell if they're bluffing or not, though. Weren't you ever afraid like that, Judith?'

'Of course,' I said, 'I was a real coward. But it's funny looking back. Do you know what it was that frightened me most about childhood?'

'What?'

'That it would never end.'

'What do you mean?'

'I was frightened, but it wasn't so much the shadows in the cupboard that scared me. It was the terrible, terrible suffocating sameness of it all. It's true. I remember lying in bed trembling, but what I heard was the awful and relentless monotony. The furnace switching off and on in the basement. Amos and Andy. Or the kettle steaming in the kitchen. Even the sound of my parents turning the pages of the newspaper in the living room while we were supposed to be going to sleep. My mother's little cough, so genteel. The flush of the toilet through the wall before they went to bed. And other things. The way my mother always hung the pillowcases on the clothesline with the open end up, leaving just a little gap so the air could blow inside them. With a clothes peg in her mouth when she did it, always the same. It frightened me.'

'I always thought there was something to be said for stability in childhood.'

'I suppose there is,' I agreed. 'But I always hoped, or rather I think I actually knew, that there was another world out there and that someday I would walk away and live in it. But the long, long childhood nearly unhinged me. Take the floor tiles in our kitchen at home. I can tell you exactly the pattern of our floor in Scarborough, and it was a complicated pattern too. Blue squares with a yellow fleck, alternating in diagonal stair-steps with yellow squares with brown flecks. And I can tell you exactly the type of flowers on my bedspread when I was six and exactly what my dotted swiss curtains looked like when I was twelve. And the royal blue velvet tiebacks. It was so vivid, so present. That's what I was afraid of. All those details. And their claim on me.'

'And when you finally did get away from it into the other life, Judith – was it all you thought it would be?' She was driving carefully, concentrating on the road which was getting slippery under the new snow.

I tried to shape an answer, a real answer, but I couldn't. 'Oh, I don't know,' I said with a hint of dismissal. 'The trouble is that when you're a child you can sense something beyond the details. Or at least you hope there's something.'

'And now?' she prompted me.

'And now,' I said, 'I hardly ever think about the kind of life I want to live.'

'Why not?'

'I suppose I'm just too preoccupied with living it. Much less

CAROL SHIELDS

introspective. And one thing about writing biography is that you tend to focus less on your own life. But I think of Richard and Meredith sometimes, and wonder if they're taking it all in.'

'The pattern on the kitchen floor?'

'Yes. All of it. And I wonder if they're waiting for it to be over.'

'Maybe it's all a big gyp,' Nancy said. 'Maybe the whole thing is a big gyp the way Simone de Beauvoir says at the end of her autobiography. Life is a gyp.'

I nodded. It was warm in the car and I felt agreeable and sleepy. My legs and back ached pleasantly, and I thought that the snow blowing across the highway looked lovely in the last of the afternoon light. The motor hummed and the windshield wipers made gay little grabs at the snow.

'It can't all be a gyp,' I told her. 'It's too big. It can't be.'

And we left it at that.

'Judith.' Martin called to me one evening after dinner. 'Come quick. See who's being interviewed on television.'

I dropped the saucepan I was scraping and peeled off my rubber gloves. Probably Eric Kierans, I thought. He is my favourite politician with his sluggish good sense so exquisitely smothered in rare and perfect modesty. Or it might be Malcolm Muggeridge who, nimble-tongued, year after year, poured out a black oil stream of delicious hauteur.

But it was neither; it was Furlong Eberhardt being interviewed about his new book.

I sank down on the sofa between Martin and Meredith and stared at Furlong. We were tuned to a local channel, and this was a relaxed and informal chat. The young woman who was interviewing him was elegantly low-key in a soft shirtdress and possessed of a chuckly throatiness such as I had always desired for myself.

68

'Mr Eberhardt –' she began.

'My friends always call me by my first name,' he beamed at her, but she scurried past him with her next question.

'Perhaps you could tell our viewers who haven't yet read *Graven Images* a little about how you came upon the idea for it.'

Furlong leaned back, his face open with amusement, and spread his arms hopelessly. 'You know,' he said, 'that's a perfectly impossible question to ask a writer. How and where he gets his ideas.'

Smiling even harder than before, she refused to be put down. 'Of course, I know every writer has his own private source of imagination, but *Graven Images*, of all your books, tells such an extraordinary story that we thought you might want to tell us a little about how the idea for the book came to you.'

Furlong laughed. He drew back his head and laughed aloud, though not without kindness.

The interviewer waited patiently, leaning forward slightly, her hands in a hard knot.

'All I can tell you,' he said, composing himself and assuming his academic posture, 'is that a writer's sources are never simple. Always composite. The idea for *Graven Images* came to me in pieces. True, I may have had one generous burst of inspiration, for which I can only thank whichever deity it is who presides over creative imagination. But the rest came with less ease, torn daily out of the flesh as it were.'

'I see,' the interviewer said somewhat coldly, for plainly she felt he was toying with her. 'But Mr Eberhardt, this new novel seems to have an increased vigour. A new immediacy.' She had recaptured her lead and was pinning him down.

Furlong turned directly into the camera and was caught in a flattering close-up, the model of furrowed thoughtfulness. 'You may be right,' he nodded in response. 'You just may be right. But on the other hand, I wouldn't have thought I was exactly washed up as a writer before *Graven Images*.'

'If I may quote one of the critics, Mr Eberhardt –'

'Furlong. Please,' he pleaded.

'Furlong. One of the critics,' she rattled through her notes, cleared her throat and read, 'Eberhardt's new book is brisk and original, as fast moving and exciting as a movie.'

'Ah,' he said, his hands pulling together beneath his beard. 'You may be interested to know that it is soon to become a film.'

Her eyes widened. '*Graven Images* is to be made into a film?'

'We have only just signed the contract,' he said serenely, 'this afternoon.'

'Well, I must say, congratulations are in order, Mr Eberhardt. I suppose this film will be made in Canada?'

'Ah. I regret to say it will not. The offer was made by an American company, and I am afraid I can't release any details at this time. I'm sure your viewers will understand.'

Her eyes glittered as she leaned meaningfully into the camera. 'Wouldn't you say, Mr Eberhardt, that it is enormously ironical that you, a Canadian writer who has done so much to bring Canadian literature to the average reader, must turn to an American producer to have your novel filmed?'

He was rattled. 'Look here, I didn't go to them. They came. They approached me. And I can only say that of course I would have preferred a Canadian offer but –' an expression of helplessness transformed his face – 'what can one do?'

'I'm sure we'll all look forward eagerly to it, Mr Eberhardt. American or Canadian. And it has been a great pleasure to talk to you tonight.'

The camera grazed his face one last time before the fadeout. 'An even greater pleasure for me,' he said with just a touch too much chivalry.

Meredith sitting beside me looked flushed and excited, and Martin was muttering with unaccustomed malice, 'He's got it made now.'

'What do you mean?'

'Your friend Furlong has just struck it rich.'

I shrugged. 'He's never been exactly wanting.'

'Ah, Judith, you miss the point. A movie. This is no mere trickle of royalties. This is big rich.'

'Well, maybe,' I said, not really seeing the point.

'The old bugger,' Martin said. 'He's going to be really unbearable now.'

'Tell me, Martin. Have you read it yet? *Graven Images*?'

'No,' he said. 'I keep putting it off.'

'His party is next week. Sunday.'

'I know. I know,' he said despairingly.

'It may not be too bad.'

'It'll be bad.'

'Do you really despise him, Martin?'

'Despise him. God, no. It's just that he's such a perfect asshole. Worse than that, he's a phoney asshole.'

'For example?' I asked smiling.

'Well, remember that sign he had in his office a few years ago? On his desk?'

'No. I never saw a sign.'

'It was a framed motto. *You Shall Pass Through This Life but Once*.'

'Really? He had one of those? I can't imagine it. It seems so sort of Dale Carnegie for Furlong.'

'He had it. I swear.'

'And that's why he's an asshole?'

'No. Not that.'

'Well, why then?'

'Because, after he got the Canadian Fiction Prize, and that big write-up in *Maclean's* and the New York *Times*, both in the same month –'

'Yes?'

'Well, right after that happened, he took down his sign. Just took it away one day. And it's never been seen since.'

'He'd never own up to it now,' I said.

'When I think of that sign and the way he stealthily disposed of it, another notch of sophistication – I don't know. That just seems to be Furlong Eberhardt in a nutshell. That one act, as far as I'm concerned, encapsulates his whole personality.'

Meredith leapt from the sofa, startling us both. 'I think you're both being horrible. Just horrible. So middle-class, so smug. Sitting here. It's character assassination, that's what. And you're enjoying it.' She flew from the room with her breath coming out in jagged gasps.

For a moment Martin and I froze. Then he very slowly picked up the newspaper from the floor, reached for the sports page, and gave me a brief but hurting glance. 'I don't understand her sometimes,' was all he said.

It was then that I noticed Richard sitting quietly in a corner of the room, unobtrusive in his neat maroon sweater. He was watching us closely.

'What are you doing, Richard?' I asked.

'Nothing,' he said.

Frantically, neurotically, harried and beleaguered, I am addressing Christmas cards. Richard, home with a cold, sits at the dining table with me; he is checking addresses, licking stamps, stacking envelopes in their individual white pillars; the overseas stack that will now have to be sent expensively by airmail, the unsealed ones with nothing but a rude 'Judith and Martin Gill' scrawled inside them, the letters to old friends where I've crammed a year's outline into two or three inches – 'A good year for us, Martin busy teaching, the children are getting ENORMOUS, am working on a new book, not much news, wish you were closer, happy holidays.' And Martin's stack, the envelopes which Richard and I will leave unsealed so that tonight, after he gets home from the university, he can sit down and quickly, offhandedly write the funny, intense little messages he is so good at.

The afternoon wears on, and outside the window snow is falling and falling. Since noon we have had the overhead light on. Richard in striped pajamas looks pale.

This is a long, tedious task, and it irritates me to separate and put in order the constellations of our friends and to send them each these feeble scratched messages. But for the sake of the return, for the crash of creamy envelopes blazing with seals that will soon spill down upon us, I push on. For I want to hear from the O'Malleys who lived across the hall from us in our first apartment. I want to know if the Gorkys are still together and where the best man at our wedding, Kurt Weisman, has moved. Dr Lawrence who supervised Martin's graduate work and his wife Bettina always write us from Florida and so do the Grahams, the Lords, the Reillys, the Jensens. What matter that they were often dull and that we might have drifted apart eventually? What matter that they were sometimes stingy or overly frank or forgetful? They want to wish us a merry Christmas. They want to wish us all the best in the New Year. I can't help but take the printed card literally; these are our friends; they love us. We love them.

Richard is studying the airmail stamp which goes on the letters to Britain. It is a special issue with a portrait of the Queen, an enormous stamp, the largest we have ever seen. The image is handsome and the background is filled in with pale gold. On the corners of the tiny Rustcraft envelopes, all I could find at this late date, it gleams like a gem.

I write a brief note to the Spaldings, a spray of ritual phrases. 'We often remember the wonderful year we spent in Birmingham. The children have such happy memories. Hope your family is well and that you are having a mild winter, best wishes from the Gills.'

Richard seals it and affixes the great golden stamp. 'He's writing a book,' he says.

'Who?' I ask absently.

'Mr Spalding. He's writing a novel.' Richard seldom mentions the Spaldings, but when he does, it is abruptly, as though the words lay perpetually spring-loaded on the tip of his tongue.

'I suppose Anita wrote you about it?' I say inanely.

'Yes.'

'And is it going well? The novel?'

'I don't know,' he says. 'But she says that sometimes he stays up all night typing.'

'Well, I wish him luck,' I say, thinking of his row of rejected manuscripts.

Richard makes no reply, and after a minute I ask him, 'What's it about? The novel Anita's father is writing?'

'How should I know?' he says, suddenly querulous.

I snap back. 'I only asked.'

But I really would like to know what John Spalding is writing about. Maybe he's incorporating some new material from the year in Cyprus. Or perhaps reworking one of his old plots. He might even have resurrected his one good one.

I think of him typing through the night in the chilly, gas-smelling flat while the frowsy Isabel snores in a distant bedroom. I imagine his small frame, tense, gnatlike, concentrating on the impossible mass of a novel, and for a moment I see him as almost touchingly valiant.

74

Then guilt attacks me; a pain familiar by now, a spurt of heat between my eyes, damn.

The Magic Rocking Horse was the name of the novel I wrote the year we came back from England. I intended, and for a while even believed, that the title would convey a subtle, layered irony – a childlike innocence underlying a theme of enormous worldliness.

But the novel never materialized on either level. Instead it simply stretched and strained along, scene after scene pitiably stitched together and collapsing in the end for want of flesh. For, unlike biography, where a profusion of material makes it possible and even necessary to be selective, novel writing requires a complex mesh of details which has to be spun out of simple air. No running to the public library for facts, no sleuthing through bibliographies, no borrowing from the neat manila folders at the Archives. That year the most obvious fact about fiction struck me afresh: it all had to be made up.

And where to begin? For two or three months I did nothing at all but think about how to begin. Dialogue or description? Or a cold plunge into action? Once or twice I actually produced a page or two, but later, reading over what I had written, I found the essential silliness of make-believe disturbing, and I began to wonder whether I really wanted to write a novel at all.

I discussed it with everyone I knew and got very little support. Roger and Ruthie told me, flatteringly, that it was a waste of my biographical skills. Nancy Krantz, sipping coffee, pursed her lips and pronounced, in a way which was not exactly condemning but almost, that she seldom read novels. Martin said little, but it was obvious that he viewed the whole project as somewhat dilettantish, and the children thought it might be a good idea if I wrote something along the line of Agatha Christie but transferred to a Canadian setting.

Furlong Eberhardt was the only one who volunteered a halfway friendly ear, and when he suggested one day that I might want to sit in on his creative writing seminar, it seemed like a good idea; a chance to sit down with a circle of other struggling fiction writers, sympathetic listeners upon whom I might test my material and who, in turn, might provide wanted stimulation or, as Furlong put it, might 'prime the old pump.'

Looking back, I believe the idea of again being a student appealed to me too. I bought a notebook and a clutch of yellow pencils, and each Wednesday afternoon I dressed carefully for the class which met in an airless little room at the top of the Arts Building; my fawn slacks or my bronze corduroy skirt, a turtleneck, something youthful but never going too far, for what was the point of being grotesque for the sake of ten undergraduates ranging from eighteen-year-old Arleen whose black paintbrush hair fell to her hips, all the way to Ludwig, aged about twenty-four, horribly pimpled, who stared at me with hatred because I was married (and to a professor at that), because I lived in a house, because I was a friend of Furlong's, and possibly because my fingernails were clean.

No, I didn't fool myself that I was going to be one of them. And how could I since, despite my urging them to call me Judith, they always referred to me as Mrs Gill. And when I read my short weekly contributions, always a quarter the length of theirs, they listened politely, even Ludwig, and never ventured any remarks except perhaps, very deferentially, that my sentences were a bit too structured or that my situations seemed a little, well, conventional and contrived.

Somewhat to my surprise I found that Furlong ran his creative writing seminar in a highly organized manner, beginning with what he called warming-up exercises. These were specific weekly assignments in which we were to describe such things as the experience of ecstasy or the effect of ennui, a dialogue between lovers one week and enemies the next

I sweated through these assignments, typing out the minimum required words and, when my turn came, I read them aloud, feeling like a great overblown girl, red-faced and matronly, who should long since have abandoned such childish games.

The rest of them were not the least reticent; indeed they were positively eager to celebrate their hallucinations aloud. Arleen dragged us paragraph by paragraph through her thoughts on peace and mankind, and a girl named Lucy Rimer was anxious to split her psyche wide open, inviting us to inspect the tortured labyrinth of her awakening sexuality. Joseph, an African student, disgusted and thrilled us with portraits of his Ghanian grandparents. Someone called George Riorden dramatized his feeling on racial equality by having two characters, Whitey (a Negro) and Mr Black (a white) dialogue over the back fence, reminding us, in case we missed it, of the express irony implied by their names. Ludwig poked with a blunt and dirty finger into the sores of his consciousness, not stopping at his subtle and individual response to orgasm and the nuances of his erect penis. On and on.

They were relentless, compulsive, unsparing, as though they had waited all their lives for these moments of catharsis, these Wednesday afternoon epiphanies. But looking around, when I dared to look around, I watched them wearing down, week by week exhausting themselves, and I wondered how long it could go on.

Eventually Furlong, who until then had merely listened and nodded, nodded and listened, called a halt and announced that it was time to begin the term project. Each of us was to write a short novel, about ten chapters he suggested, a chapter a week, which we were to bring to class to be read aloud and discussed. I breathed with relief. This was what I had hoped for, a general to command me into action and an audience who, by its response, might indicate whether I was going in the right direction.

I began at once on my first chapter, carefully introducing my main characters, providing a generous feeling of setting, and observing all the conventions as I understood them. It was all quite easy, and when my turn came to read, the class listened attentively, and even Furlong beamed approval.

And then I got stuck. Having described the personalities of my characters, detailed where they lived and what they did, I didn't know what to do with them next. The following week when my turn came, I apologized and said I was unprepared.

The others in the class seemed not to suffer from my peculiar malady which was the complete inability to manufacture situations, and I envied the ease with which they drifted off into fantasies, for although they strained my credulity, their inventiveness seemed endless.

A second week went by, leaving me still at the end of Chapter One. A third week. Furlong questioned me kindly after class.

'Are you losing interest, Judith?'

'I think I'm losing my mind,' I said. 'I just can't seem to get any ideas.'

He was understanding, fatherly. 'It'll come,' he promised. 'You'll see.'

I waited but it didn't come, and I began to lie awake at night, frightened by the emptiness in my head. In the small hours of the morning, with Martin asleep beside me, I several times crept out of bed, padded downstairs, made tea, sat at the kitchen table and felt myself overcome by vacancy, barrenness, by failure.

A Wednesday afternoon came when I phoned Furlong before

class pleading a violent toothache and a sudden dental appointment. The following Wednesday I went one step further: I absented myself without excuse. I was in descent now, set on a not-too-painful decline. There were days when I seldom thought about the novel at all.

I went skiing. I had my hair restyled at a place called Rico's of Rome and I shopped for new clothes. I painted the upstairs bathroom turquoise and joined a Keep Fit class. I went to the movies with Martin and Roger and Ruthie. I fringed and embroidered Richard's jeans, wrote a long letter to my sister Charleen. Everyone was kind; no one said a word about my novel. No one inquired about the seminar I was attending. No one except Furlong.

He kept phoning me. 'You made a brilliant start, Judith. Your first chapter showed real strength. Head and shoulders above the rest of the little brats.'

'But I can't seem to expand on that, Furlong. And not for want of trying.'

'You say you really have been trying?'

'I have rings under my eyes,' I lied.

'How about just letting your mind go free. Conduct a sort of private brainstorming. I sometimes find that helps.'

'You mean you've felt like this too? Bereft? Not an idea in your head?'

'If you only knew. The truth is, Judith, I can be sympathetic because I haven't had a good idea in almost two years. And that, my old friend, is strictly entre-nous.'

'And you've no solutions? No advice?'

'Try coming back to class. I know you think you can't face it at this point, but steel yourself. Most of what they write is garbage, but it's stimulation of a sort.'

I promised, and I did actually go back for one or two sessions.

And at home I forced myself to sit down and type out a paragraph every morning, but the effort was akin to suffering.

And then one day, just as Furlong had said, it came. In the middle of a dazzling winter morning, ten o'clock with the sun bold and fringed as a zinnia, it came. I would be able to save myself after all.

I would simply borrow the plot from John Spalding's first abandoned and unpublished novel, the one I had so secretly consumed in Birmingham. Such a simple idea. What did it matter that his writing was banal, boyish, embarrassingly sincere; the plot had been not only clever – it had been astonishingly original. Otherwise I wouldn't have remembered it, for like many rapid readers, I forget what I read the minute I close the covers. But John Spalding's plot line, even after all these months, was surprisingly vivid.

What I couldn't understand was why I hadn't thought of it before now. It was so available; what a waste to leave it stuck in a buff folder on a dusty shelf in an obscure flat in Birmingham, England. A good idea should never be orphaned. Luxuriously, I allowed the details to circulate through my veins, marvelling that the solution to my dilemma had been so obvious, so right, so free for the taking; it had an aura of inevitability about it which made me wonder if it hadn't been incubating in my blood all these months – germination, growth, now the burst of blossom.

I thought of the Renaissance painters, and happily, gleefully, drew parallels; the master painter often doing nothing but tracing in the lines, while his worthy but less gifted artisans filled in the colours. It had been a less arrogant age in which creativity had been shared; surely that was an ennobling precedent. For I didn't intend anything as crude as stealing John Spalding's plot outright. I already had my line-up of characters. My setting had been composed. All I needed to borrow was the underlying plot structure.

I woke the next day feeling spare, nimble, energetic, sinewy with health and muscle, confident, even omnipotent. I felt as though the blood had been drained out of me and replaced with cool-flowing Freon gas. My fingers were lively little machines exciting the keys; my eyes rotated mechanically, left to right, left to right; the carriage rocked with purpose. My brain ticked along, cleanly, accurately, uncluttered. The first day I wrote fifty pages.

I telephoned Furlong, shrilling, 'I've finally got started.'

'All you needed was an idea,' he said. 'Didn't I tell you.'

The second day I wrote thirty pages. Somewhere I had lost my miraculous clarity; my idea had softened, lost shape; everything was blurring.

The third day I wrote ten pages and, for the first time, sat down to read what I had written.

Appalling, unbelievable, dull, dull. The bones of my stolen plot stuck out everywhere like great evil-gleaming knobs, accusing me, charging me. The action, such as it was, jerked along on dotted lines; there was no tissue to it. It was thin; worse than thin, it was skinny, a starved child.

Always when I had heard of writers destroying their manuscripts or painters shredding their canvases, I had considered it inexcusably theatrical, but now I could understand the desire to obliterate something that was shameful, infantile, degrading.

But I didn't tear it up. Not me, not Judith Gill, not my mother's daughter. I wrote a quick concluding chapter and retyped the whole thing before another Wednesday afternoon passed. I even made a special trip to Coles to buy a sky-blue binder with a special, newly patented steely jaw. And I carried it on the bus with me and delivered it to Furlong's office.

'But I don't want to read it to the class,' I told him firmly.

'Just do me a favour and read it yourself. And let me know what you think.'

He nodded gravely. He consoled me with his tender smile. He understood. He would take it home with him. I got on the bus and came home and started cooking pork chops for our dinner. And it was then, with hot fat spattering from the pan and the pale meat turning brown that I lurched into truth.

Six-thirty; the hour held me like a hand. Doors slamming, water running, steam rising, the floor tiles under my feet squared off with reality. The clatter of cutlery, a knife pulling down on a wooden board, an onion halved showing rings of pearl; their distinct and separate clarity thrilled me. This was real.

I flew to the phone. My fingers caught in the dial so that twice I made a mistake. *Please be home, please be home!*

He was.

'Furlong. Listen, this is Judith.'

'What on earth's the matter?'

'My novel. *The Magic Rocking Horse.*'

'But Judith, I just got home. I've hardly had more than a few minutes to glance at it. But tonight –'

'The point is, Furlong, I've decided not to go ahead with the novel.'

'What do you mean – not go ahead? Judith, my girl, you've already done it.'

'I mean I want you to dispose of it. Burn it. Tear it up. Now. Immediately.'

'You can't be serious. Not after all your work.'

'I can. I am.' *Christ, he's going to be difficult.*

'Judith, won't you sleep on it. Give it some thought.'

'I really mean this, Furlong. Listen to me. I mean it. I'm a grown-up woman and I know what I'm doing.'

'Judith.'

'Please, Furlong.' I was close to tears. 'Please.'

He agreed.

'But on one condition. That you at least let me finish reading it. You may not have any faith in it, but I think, from the little of it I've seen, that it's not entirely hopeless.'

'I don't care, Furlong, just as long as you keep your promise to get rid of it. And please don't ever discuss it with me. I couldn't bear that.'

'Oh, all right. I promise, of course. But what are you going to do, Judith? Try another novel? Take another tack?'

'I'm going to write a biography.'

'Who this time?'

'I was thinking of Susanna Moodie.'

I had said it almost without thinking, only wanting to reassure Furlong that I wasn't mad. But the moment I uttered the name Susanna Moodie, I knew I was on my way back to sanity, to balance. I was on the way back to being happy.

The very next morning I began.

Sunday afternoon.

We are late, but since it is icy and since Martin is reluctant to go at all, we drive very slowly down the city streets to Furlong's party. I feel under my heavy coat for my wrist watch. We should have been there at one-thirty, and it's almost two now.

I am sitting in the front seat beside Martin, and through my long apricot crepe skirt the vinyl seat covers feel shockingly cold. Because of the snow I have had to wear heavy boots, but my silver sandals are in a zippered bag on the seat.

Meredith is in the back seat and she is leaning forward anxiously, concerned about being late and concerned even more about how she looks. She has been invited at the last minute. Mrs Eberhardt phoned only this morning to suggest that she come along with us. I had hung about near the telephone listening, knowing for certain that she was being invited to replace some guest who was not able to come, knowing she would be filling in as a fourth at one of the inevitable little tables set up in Furlong's dining room. I had been to Furlong's parties before and knew how carefully the glasses of Beaujolais were counted out, how the seating would have been arranged weeks before and how the petit fours, the exact number, would be waiting in their boxes in the pantry. I would have cheered if Meredith had refused, if she had said she had other plans for this afternoon, but of course she didn't, nor would I have done so in her place.

Under her navy school coat she is wearing a dress of brilliant patchwork, made for her by Martin's mother last Christmas and worn only half a dozen times. She has done something marvellous and unexpected with her hair, lifted it up in the back with a tiny piece of chain, her old charm bracelet perhaps, and her neck rises slenderly, almost elegantly, out of the folds of her coat collar. But her nervousness is extreme.

Martin brakes for a red light and comes slowly, creepingly to a halt. I see his jaw firm, a rib of muscle, he wants only for this afternoon to be ended, to be put behind him.

Now is the moment, I think. Right now in the middle of the city, with apartment buildings all around us. I should ask him now about the eight bundles of wool that had been in his drawer. The fact that Meredith is here with us will only make it seem more normal, just a matter-of-fact question between husband and wife.

'Godamn,' he mutters. 'We should have bought those snow tires when they were on sale.'

I sit tight and don't say a word.

Furlong and his mother live in a handsome 1930s building built of beef-red brick encircling a formal, evergreened courtyard. There

84

is a speaking tube in the walnut foyer, rows of brass mail boxes; and today the inner door is slightly ajar, propped open with a spray of Christmas greenery in a pretty Chinese jardinière. We make our way up a flight of carpeted stairs to the panelled door with the brass parrot-headed knocker. Beyond it we can hear a soft rolling ocean of voices. Meredith and I bend together as though at a signal and exchange our boots for shoes, balancing awkwardly on each foot in turn. Only when we are standing in our fragile sandals does Martin lift the knocker.

It seems miraculous in all that noise that we can be heard, but in a moment Furlong throws open the door and stands before us. He is flushed and excited, and only scolds us briefly for being late. 'Of course the roads are deplorable. Meredith, we are delighted, both of us, that you were able to come. You must excuse our phoning you so late, but it just occurred to us that you were a grown-up now and why on earth hadn't we asked you earlier. But give me your coats. I want you to taste my Christmas punch. Martin, you are a man of discernment. Come and see if you can guess what I've concocted this year.'

He leads us into a softly lit living room where small circles of women in fluid Christmas dresses, and men, darkly suited and civilized, stand on the dusty-rose carpet. It is a large pale room, faintly period with its satin-covered sofa, its brocaded matching chairs, a cherry secretary, a Chinese table laid out with a punch bowl and a circle of cut-glass cups.

Furlong pours us ruby-pink cups of punch and watches, delighted, as we sip. 'Well?' he asks Martin.

'Cranberry juice,' Martin says.

'And vodka,' I add.

'And something spicy,' Martin continues. 'Ginger?'

'Eureka!' Furlong says. 'You two are the only ones who guessed. Meredith, I'm sure your parents will allow me to give you a little.'

85

'Of course,' she and I murmur together.

In a moment Mrs Eberhardt is upon us, gracious and dramatic in deep purple velvet gathered between her breasts. 'We were so afraid you had had an accident. This wretched snow. But I told Furlong not to worry. I knew you wouldn't let us down. Judith, you look delightful.' She kisses my cheek. 'I can't tell you how grateful we are that you let us have Meredith this afternoon.'

Across the room Roger salutes us gaily. I am beginning to make out distinct faces in the early-afternoon light. I recognize Valerie Hyde who writes a quirky bittersweet saga of motherhood for a syndicated column in which she describes the hilarity of babyshit on the walls and the riotous time the cat got into the bouillabaisse just before the guests arrived. Her estranged husband Alfred is on the other side of the room with a hard-faced blonde in a sea-green tube of silk. Ruthie in cherry-coloured pants and a silk shirt is standing alone sipping cranberry-vodka punch and looking drunk and not very happy. I am about to speak to her when I see an immense fat man in a coarse, hand-woven suit. 'Who's that?' I ask Mrs Eberhardt.

She whispers enormously, 'That's Hans Kroeger.'

'The movie producer?'

'Yes,' she says, hugging herself. 'Wasn't it lovely he could be here. Furlong is so pleased.'

Somewhere a tiny bell is ringing. I look up to see Furlong, silver bell in hand, calling the room to silence. 'I know you must be ready for something to eat,' he announces with engaging simplicity. 'Lunch is ready in the dining room as soon as you are.'

It is a large room painted a dull French grey. Half a dozen little tables are draped to the floor in shirred green taffeta – in the centre of each a basket of tiny white flowers.

Close behind me I hear Martin sighing heavily, 'Jesus.'

'Shut up,' I say happily in his ear.

On the buffet table is Sunday lunch. There is a large fresh salmon trimmed with lemon slices and watercress, a pink and beautiful roast of beef being carved by a whitesuited man from the caterers; cut-glass bowls of salad, tiny raw vegetables carved into intricate shapes, buttered rolls, crusty to the touch, fine and soft and patrician within; Mrs Eberhardt's homemade mayonnaise in a silver shell-shaped dish, cheeses, fruit, stacks of Spode luncheon plates.

We serve ourselves and look about for our name cards on the little tables. I am by the window. There is heavy silver cutlery from Mrs Eberhardt's side of the family, and a thick, luxurious linen napkin at each place. Furlong circulates between tables with red wine, filling each crystal glass a precise two-thirds full.

Everyone is talking. The room is filled with people eating and talking. Talk drifts from table to table, accumulating, rising, until it reaches the ceiling.

Roger is saying: 'Of course Canadian culture has to be protected. For God's sake, you're dealing with a sensitive plant, almost a nursery plant. And don't tell me I'm being chauvinistic. I had a year at Harvard, remember. I tell you that if we don't give grants to our writers now and if we don't favour our own publishers now, we're lost, man, we're just lost.'

Valerie Hyde is saying: 'Of course women have come a long way, but don't think for a minute that one or two women in Parliament are going to change a damn thing. Sex is built-in like bones and teeth, and, remember this, Barney, there's more to sex than cold semen running down your leg.'

Alfred Hyde is saying: 'Tuesday night we had tickets to *The Messiah*. The tenor was excellent, the baritone was passable, but the contralto was questionable. The staging was commendable, but I seriously question the lighting technique.'

Ruthie is saying: 'There's just no stability to anything. Did you stop to think of just where this salmon comes from? The fisherman who caught this fish is probably sitting down to pork and beans right now. And what happens when all the salmon is gone? And that just might be tomorrow. What do you say to that? There's just no stability.'

Hans Kroeger is saying: 'Twenty per cent return on the investment. And that ain't hay. So don't give me any shit about bonds.'

A woman across the room is saying: 'Take Bath Abbey for instance. Have you been to Bath Abbey? No? Well, take any abbey.'

Furlong is saying: 'In my day we talked about making a contribution. To the country. But that sounds facile, doing something for one's country. Now don't you agree that one's first concern must be to know oneself? Isn't that what counts?'

Meredith says: 'I don't know. I really don't. Like in *Graven Images*, first things come first. I've started in on it for the third time. Empathy. That's what it all comes down to. I mean, doesn't it? Maybe you're right, but making a contribution still counts. I mean, really, in the end, doesn't it? Fulfillment, well, fulfillment is sort of selfish if you know what I mean. I don't know.'

The blonde in green is saying, 'Anyone from that socio-economic background just never dreams of picking up a book. What I'm saying is this, intelligence is shaped in pre-adolescence. Not the scope of intelligence. Anyone can expand, but the direction. The direction is predetermined.'

A man is saying in a very low voice. 'Okay, okay, you've had enough booze. Lay off.'

Barney Beck is saying: 'Class. You're damned right I believe in class. Not because it's good, hell no, but because it's there. Just, for instance, take the way kids cool off in the summer. You've got the little proletarians splashing in the street hydrant, right?

And your middle-class brats running through the lawn sprinklers. Because lawns mean middle class, right? Then your nouveaus. The plastic-lined swimming pool. Cabanas, filter systems, et cetera. Then the aristocrats. You don't see them, not actually, because they're at the shore. Wherever the hell the shore is.'

Mrs. Eberhardt is saying: 'The important thing is to use real lemon and to add the oil one drop at a time, one drop at a time.'

And I, Judith Gill, am spinning: I feel my animal spirit unwind, my party self, that progressive personality that goes from social queries about theatre series to compulsive anecdote swapping. I press for equal time. *Stop*, I tell myself. *Let this topic pass without pulling out your hospital story, your vitamin B complex story, your tennis story, your Lester Pearson snippet. Adjust your eyes. Be tranquil. Stop.* I admonish myself, but it's useless. I feel my next story gathering in my throat, the words pulling together, waiting their chance. Here it is. I'm ready to leap in. 'Speaking of bananas,' I say, and I'm off.

Martin, at the next table, is not talking. What is he doing? He is lifting a forkful of roast beef, and slowly, slowly, he is chewing it. What is he doing now?

He is listening.

January

I t was on the first day of the new year that I discovered the reason for Martin's secret cache of wool; the explanation was delivered so offhandedly and with such an aura of innocence that I furiously cursed my suspicions. What on earth had I expected – that Martin had slipped over the edge into lunacy? That, saddened and trapped at forty-one, he might be having a breakdown? Did I think he nursed a secret vice: knitting instead of tippling? Or perhaps that he had acquired a mistress, a great luscious handicraft addict whose fetish it was to crochet while she was being made love to? Crazy, crazy. I was the one who was crazy.

On New Year's Day Martin sat talking to his mother and father who had come from Montreal for the weekend. His father is a professor too, himself the son of a professor; he teaches history at McGill. Gill of McGill, he likes to introduce himself to strangers. He is a spare, speckled man, happiest wearing the loose oatmeal cardigans his wife knits for him and soft old jackets, frayed at the pockets and elbows. His habitual stance is kindly (a Franciscan kindness) and speculative; he is what is known in the world as a good man, possessing all the qualities of a Christian with the exception of faith.

The relationship between Martin and his father is such as might exist between exceedingly fond colleagues. Like brothers they flank Martin's mother, Lala to us, a small woman who except for an unmanageable nest of sparrow-brown, Gibson-girlish hair is attractive and bright, known to her friends in Montreal as a Doer. Her private and particular species of femininity demands gruff male attendance, and she is sitting now in our family room between 'her two men,' although that is a phrase which she herself would consider too cloying to use.

We have had a late breakfast, coffee and an almond ring brought by Lala from her local ethnic bakery in Montreal. The sun is pouring in through the streaky windows making us all feel drowsy and dull. Richard and Meredith, both of them blotchy with sleep, sprawl in front of the television watching the Rose Bowl Parade. There are newspapers everywhere, on the floor and on the chairs, thick holiday editions. And cups and saucers litter the coffee table. Lala leans back on the sofa, lazily puffing a duMaurier.

Grandpa Gill asks Martin how his course load is going and whether he is doing a paper at the moment. Lala leans bird-like towards them, eager to hear what Martin has to say. I too am roused from torpor. We all wait.

Martin tells his father about the paper that has been turned down. 'I'll show it to you if you like,' he says. 'Apparently it just didn't measure up in terms of originality. One of the referees, anonymous of course, penciled "derivative" all over it.'

'That was bad luck,' Grandpa Gill nods.

'What a shame, Martin,' Lala adds.

I marvel for the thousandth time at the constancy and perfect accord with which they underscore their son's ability.

'To be honest,' Martin continues, 'it was pretty dull. But I'm working on something else now which might be a little different.'

'Yes?' his mother sings through her smoke.

'Well,' Martin says, addressing his father automatically, 'I think I can say that I actually got this idea from you.'

91

'Really?' Grandpa Gill smiles.

'Remember that chart you showed me. In your office last fall? A coloured diagram with the structure of world power charted in different colours?'

'Oh, yes. Of course. The Reynolds Diagram. Very useful.'

'Well, after I saw that I got to thinking that it might be a good idea to use a diagram approach to themes in epic poetry. To *Paradise Lost* specifically.'

'But how would you go about it?' his mother presses him.

'I thought it might be possible to make a graphic of it,' Martin says. 'Like the Reynolds Diagram, only using wool instead of paint since the themes are so mixed. In places it's necessary to interweave the colours. Sometimes, as you can appreciate, there are as many as four or five themes woven together.'

His father nods and asks, 'And how have you gone about it?'

'I thought about it for a long time,' Martin says.

Where was I while he thought so long and hard?

'Finally I decided on a large rectangle of loose burlap for each of the twelve books. That way the final presentation could be hung together. For comparison purposes.'

'I don't get it, Martin,' I say, speaking for the first time.

He looks faintly exasperated. 'All I did was to take a colour for each theme. For instance, red for God's omnipotence, blue for man's disobedience, green for arrogance, and, let's see, yellow for pride and so on. But you can see,' he says, turning again to his father, 'that one theme will predominate for a time. And then subside and merge into one of the others.'

'And how do you know just where in the text you are?' Grandpa Gill asks.

'I wondered about that,' Martin says.

Where was I, his wife, when he wondered about that?

'And I decided to mark off the lines along the side. I've

got them printed in heavy ink. The secretary helped ink them in.'

She did, did she?

'I think that sounds most innovative,' his mother says nodding vigorously and butting out her cigarette.

'Is it nearly finished?' his father asks.

'Almost. I hope to present it in March.'

'Present it where?' I ask, trying to control the quaver in my voice.

'The Renaissance Society. It's meeting in Toronto this year. I've already sent in an abstract.'

'I'm anxious to see it,' Lala says. 'Is it here at home?'

'No. I've been putting it together at the university. But next time you come down I'll show it off to you. It should be all done by then.'

'But Martin,' I say, 'you've never mentioned any of this to me.'

'Didn't I?' He gazes at me. 'I thought I did.'

I give him a very long and level look before replying, 'You never said a single word about it to me.'

'Well, now that I have told you, what do you think?'

'Do you really want to know?'

All three of them turn to me in alarm. 'Of course,' Martin says.

Wildly I reach out for the right word – 'I think it's, well, I think it's absurd.'

'Why?' Martin asks.

'Yes, why, Judith?' his father asks.

I am confused. And unwilling to hurt Martin and certainly not wanting to upset his parents whom I like. But the project seems to me to be spun out of lunacy.

I try to explain. 'Look,' I say, 'I can't exactly put it into

93

words, but it sounds a bit desperate. Do you know what I mean?'

'No,' Martin says, more shortly than usual.

'What I mean is, literature is literature. Poetry is poetry. It's made out of words. You don't work poems in wool.'

'What you're saying is that it's disrespectful to the tradition.'

'No, that's not really it. I don't care about the tradition. It's just that you might look foolish, Martin. And desperate. Don't you see, it's gimmicky, and you've never been one for gimmicks.'

'For Christ's sake, Judith, don't make too much of it. It's just a teaching aid.'

The children have turned from the television now and are watching us. Grandpa Gill and Lala, almost imperceptibly, shrink away from us.

'Martin, you've always been so sensible. Can't you see that this is just, well, just a little undignified. I mean, I just feel it's beneath you somehow.'

'I don't see what's so undignified about trying something new for a change. Christ, Judith. You're the one who thinks the seventeenth century is such a bore. Literature can be damn dull. And especially Milton.'

'I agree. I agree.'

'What I'm doing is making a pictorial presentation of themes which will give a quick comprehensive vision of the total design. It's quite simple and straightforward.'

'Couldn't you just do a paper on it?'

'No. No, I could not.'

'Why not?'

'How can you put a design image into prose?'

'What about that paper they turned down. Couldn't you do that one over for them?'

'No.'

'So instead you've dreamed up this lunatic scheme.'

'Judith, we're talking in circles. I don't think it's all that idiotic. What do you think, Dad?'

Grandpa Gill regards me. Clearly he does not want to join in the foray, but he is being pressed. He speaks cautiously. 'I think I partially understand what Judith is worried about. The publish-or-perish syndrome does occasionally have the effect of forcing academics to make asses of themselves. But, on the other hand, cross-disciplinary approaches seem to be well thought of at the moment. A graphic demonstration of a literary work, with the design features stressed, might make quite an interesting presentation if –'

I interrupt, out of exasperation, for I know he can go on in this vein for hours. 'Look, Martin there's another thing. And I hate to say this because it sounds so narrow-minded and conventional, but I, well, the truth is – I can't bear to think of you sitting there in your office weaving away. I mean – do you know what I mean? – do you – don't you think it's just a little bit – you know – ?'

'Effeminate?' he supplies the word.

'Eccentric. It's the sort of thing Furlong Eberhardt might dream up.'

'And I suppose you think that reference will guarantee instant dismissal of the whole idea.'

'Oh, Martin, for heaven's sake, do what you want. I just hate you to look ridiculous.'

'To whom? To you?'

'Forget it. I don't even know why we're discussing it.' I start picking up newspapers and gathering together the coffee cups. Lala springs to my side, but I tell her not to bother; I can manage.

I feel strange as I carry the cups into the kitchen. A nervy dancing fear is spinning in my stomach, and I lean on the sink for support. A minute ago I had been overjoyed that Martin's wool was to be put to so innocent a purpose. What has happened? What am I afraid of?

Guilt presses; I should have been more consoling when his paper was turned down. I should take greater interest in his work. Year after year he sweats out the required papers and what interest do I show? I proofread them, take out commas, put his footnotes in order. And that's it. No wonder he's developed a soft spot on the brain. To conceive of this bit of madness, actually to carry it through.

And to carry it out furtively, covertly. For I am certain he deliberately withheld the project from me. Perhaps from everyone else as well. He probably even pulls the curtains in his office and locks the door when he weaves. I try to picture it – Martin tugging at the wool, sorting his needles, tightening his frame, and then pluck, pluck, in and out, in and out. My husband, Martin Gill, weaving away his secret afternoons.

It might even be better if he did have a mistress. One could understand that. One could commiserate; one could forgive. But what can be done with a man who makes a fool of himself – what do you do then?

Martin is crazy. He's lost his grip. Or is it me? I try to think logically, but my stomach is seized by pain. I try to construct the past few months, to remember exactly when Martin last mentioned something about his work. I sit down on the kitchen stool and try to concentrate, but my head whirls. When did he last discuss the seventeenth century? *Paradise Lost*? The Milton tradition? Or something temporal such as his lecture schedule. When? I can't remember.

And then I think with a stab of pain, when did we last make love with anything more than cordiality?

My head pounds. I open the cupboard and find a bottle of aspirin. And then, though it is just a little past noon, I creep upstairs and get into bed. The sheets are cool and deliciously flat. Below me in the family room I can hear the Rose Bowl Game beginning.

Hours later I awake in the darkened room. In the upstairs hall the light is burning brutally; long, startling El Greco shadows cut across the bedroom wall. Footsteps, whispers, the rattle of teacups. Someone reaches for my hand, places a cold cloth on my forehead.

'Thank you, thank you,' I want to say, but my voice has disappeared, in its place a dry cracked nut of pain. My lips have split; I can taste blood. The inside of my mouth is unfamiliar, a clutch of cottonwool.

'Drink this,' someone says.

'No, no,' I rasp.

'Please, Judith. Try. It may help.'

Lala was sitting on the edge of my bed, a figurine, a blue-tinted shepherdess. She was pressing a teaspoon toward me. I opened my mouth. Aspirin. Aspirin crushed in strawberry jam; its peculiar bitter, slightly citrus flavour reaches me from the forest of childhood (my father crushing aspirin on the breadboard with the back of a teaspoon when my sister and I had measles, yes).

A drink of water, and I lay back exhausted. Again the cool, wet cloth. Again the mellifluous voice. 'There, there. Now just sleep. Don't worry. Just rest, dear.'

What choice had I but to obey; the lack of choice, the total surrender of will enclosed me like a drug. I slept.

There followed another long blurred space.

Several times I woke up choking on the thick cactus growth in my throat. And to my inexplicable grief, every time I opened my eyes it was still dark. If only it were light, I remember thinking,

I could bear it. If only this long night would end, I would be all right.

But when the light finally did come, milky through the frosted-over windows, I couldn't look at it without pain. It battered my stripped nerve ends, pierced me through with its harsh squares. Anguish. To be so helpless. The wet plush tongue of the facecloth descended again. Coolness. It was Meredith.

In all her sixteen years I had never heard such sadness in her voice. It curled in and out of her breath like a ballad.

'Mother. Oh, Mother. Are you any better?'

Was that my voice that squawked 'yes'? I said it to comfort her, not because it was true.

'The doctor's coming. Dr Barraclough is coming. Any minute, Mother. After his hospital rounds. He said as soon after ten as he could make it.'

I moaned faintly, involuntarily.

'Is there anything you'd like, Mother? A nice cup of tea?'

In my angle of pain I could only think of what a strange phrase that was for Meredith to use – a nice cup of tea. Did I ever say it? My mother certainly did. Lala did too. Even Martin did. But did I? Out of kindness or ritual or sympathy did I ever in all my life offer anyone such a thing as a 'nice cup of tea'? If not, then how did I come to have a daughter who was able to utter, unself-consciously, such a perfect and cottage phrase – *a nice cup of tea*?

Her voice rocked with such mourning that I felt I must accept. From the roof of my mouth a small scream escaped, saying 'Yes please.'

She fled to the kitchen joyfully, only to be replaced by Martin. 'My poor Judith. My poor little Judith.'

Again it was the phrase I perceived, not the situation. 'My poor little Judith,' he had called me. Echoes of courtship, when he had used those exact words often. And I am not little. Tall and lanky then, I am tall and large now, not fat, of course, only what the world calls a fair-sized woman; my size has always defined my sense of myself, made me less serious, freer of vanity, for good or bad.

'My poor little Judith,' he had said. I reached out a hand and felt it taken.

'Poor Judith. My poor sick Judith.'

So that was it: I was sick.

'Just try to rest, love. You've got some kind of flu. And you've had a bugger of a night.'

I strangled with agreement.

'Mother and Dad had to leave. Early this morning. They were awfully worried, especially Mother.'

I thought of Lala sitting on the edge of my bed in some half-blocked fantasy. Aspirin and strawberry jam. We had met at that level. I clutched Martin's hand harder. I wanted him to stay and, miraculous, he didn't hurry away.

Richard poked his head around the doorway. I was shocked at his size, for viewed from this unfamiliar angle, he seemed suddenly much taller. A stranger. And miserably shy.

'Meredith says, do you want some toast?'

'No,' I croaked. Then I added, 'No thank you.' Etiquette. My mother's thin etiquette surfacing.

I fell asleep again, woke momentarily to see the tea, cold and untouched in its pottery cup. Sleep, sleep.

The doctor comes. A provincial tennis champion, now barely thirty-five. Too young to wield such power. Permanently suntanned from all those holidays in the Bahamas, hands lean across the backs, a look of cash to his herringbone jacket. Money rolling in, but who cares, who cares?

'Well, well, what have we here?' he whistles good cheer.

Sullenly I refuse to answer or even listen to such heartiness.

He does the old routine, listens to heart – is my nightgown

clean? – temperature, pulse, blood pressure. A searing little light with a cold metal tip pokes into throat, nostrils, ears. Eyelids rolled back.

'You're sick,' he says leaning back. 'A real sick girl.'

And you're a fatuous ass, I long to say, but how can I, for he and only he can deliver me from my width of wretchedness. Already he is writing something on a pad of paper. I can – I can be restored.

He speaks to Martin; perhaps he considers that I am too ill to comprehend. 'I can only give her something to make her more comfortable. It's a virus, you know, a real tough baby, it looks like, and there's nothing we can give for a virus.'

'Nothing?' Martin asks unbelieving.

'Rest, plenty of liquids, that's about it.'

'But how about an antibiotic or something?'

'Won't work,' he says, brushing Martin off – how dare he! – picking up his overcoat, feeling in his pocket for his car keys.

Meredith sees him to the door, and Martin and I are left in immense quiet. The Baby Ben is ticking on the night table. In spite of my contagious condition, Martin lies down on his side of the rumpled bed. He lies carefully on top of the bedspread and in less than a minute he has fallen asleep. I am obscurely angered that he has violated my bed with his presence. The walls dissolve, the silence is enormous. I think, *I can't bear this*. And then I too fall asleep.

For days the fever laps away at me. My scalp, after a week, feels so tender that I can hardly comb my hair. My arms and legs ache, and my back is so sore that I keep an extra pillow under it.

The efforts of Martin and the children to comfort me are so great and so constant that I wish I could rouse myself to gratitude. But it is too tiring. I can do nothing but lie in bed and accept.

I have never in my adult life been so ill. I can hardly believe

I am suffering from something as ubiquitous as flu, and it seems preposterous that I can be this ill and still not require hospitalization. The doctor comes once again, pats me roughly on the back and says, 'Well, Judith, I think you're going to surprise us and weather this after all.'

My illness shocks me by giving me almost magical powers of perception; the restless, feverish days have sharpened my awareness to the point of pain. Phrases I hear every day acquire new meaning. I find myself analyzing for hours what is casually uttered. The way, for instance, that Dr Barraclough calls me Judith now that I have become an author. All sorts of people, in fact, whom I know in a remote and professional way began using my first name the moment my first book came out, as though I had somehow come into the inheritance of it, as though I had entered into the public domain, had left behind that dumpy housewife, Mrs Gill. *Judith.* I became Judith.

And Meredith who has called me Mother for years is suddenly calling me Mommy again. I lie here in bed, a sick doll, my limbs helpless, living on asparagus soup, and am called Mommy by my sixteen-year-old daughter.

Another observation. Richard doesn't call me anything. He pokes his head in, sometimes even sits for a minute on the edge of the bed. 'Would you like the newspaper?' he will ask. Or 'Do we have any postage stamps? Any air-letters?' But these statements, requests, questions have, I notice, a bald quality. I analyze them. I have time to analyze them. What gives them their flat spare sound is the lack of any salutation. I ponder the reasons. Is he caught in that slot of growth where Mommy is too childish, Mother too severe and foreign? What did he use to call me? When he was little? Now that I think of it, did he ever call me anything? I can't remember. It's curious. And worrying in an obscure way which I am unable, because

of my present weakness or because of a prime failing, to understand.

After ten days I began to stay awake longer. The nights lost their
nightmare quality, and the joints in my body tormented me less.
I was cheered by a letter from my sister and wryly amused by
another from my mother. Martin had phoned to tell her I was
sick; she was not to worry if she didn't get her weekly letter.
Her letter to me was a harping scold from beginning to end. I
did too much, she wrote. I wore myself out, wore my fingers to
the bone. I should get Martin to take over more of the household
chores. Meredith should be washing dishes at her age, and there
was no reason she couldn't take over the ironing. Richard could
be more helpful too. But basically, I was at fault. I had done too
much Christmas entertaining, she accused. Too much shopping,
sent too many cards. I shouldn't have invited Martin's parents
for New Year's; they had a home of their own, didn't they? And
very comfortable too. And why didn't Martin's sister in P.E.I. have
them for a change. I should forget about my biographies until the
children were older and off my hands.

I read it all, shaking my head. It had always been that way.
My sister and I had been scolded for every scraped knee – 'I
told you you weren't watching.' There were no bright badges
of mercurochrome for us – 'Next time you'll be more careful.'
For diarrhea we were rewarded with 'Play with the Maddeson
children and what do you expect?' Even our childhood illnesses
were begrudged us. I thought of Lala spooning aspirin into me
on New Year's night. And I recalled the first time I had met her.
Martin had taken me home for a weekend to Montreal, and he
had mentioned to his mother that he had a slight rash on the
back of his hands. 'Oh dear,' she had cried, 'what a bother! That
can be so irritating. Now let me see. I think I have just the thing.

Just squeeze a little of this on, and if that doesn't work we'll just pop you over to the doctor.'

I had listened amazed; such acceptance, such outpouring concern. Such willingness to proffer cups of tea, cream soups, poached eggs on toast. Imagine!

And so, although I lie suffering in my arms, legs, stomach, sinus, throat, skin, ears, eyes and kidneys, I am, at least, free of guilt. It is incredible, but no one with the exception of my mother – and she is far away in her multihued bungalow in Scarborough – no one blames me for being sick. Indeed, they almost seem to believe that I am entitled to an illness; that I have earned the right to take to my bed.

I heard Meredith talking to Gwendolyn on the telephone, her voice arched with pride, saying that I had never been sick before. And when Roger dropped in one evening to bring me an armful of magazines, Martin told him in a somewhat self-congratulatory tone, 'First time in her life that Judith's been hit like this.'

The children went back to school early in January, and Martin too had to go back to the university. But he left me only for his lectures, spending the rest of the time at home. It was curious, the two of us in the house together day after day, reminiscent almost of our early married years when he had been a graduate student and we had lived a close, intimate and untidy apartment life with no special hours for meals or bedtimes; our rituals were in their infancy then.

He works at the little card table in our bedroom where I usually work. Because he is here so much and because my sinuses hurt too much for me to read, I find myself locked into an absorbing meditation with Martin, my husband Martin, at its centre. Endlessly I think about him and the shape his life has taken and about the curious but not disagreeable distance that has grown between us. My days of fever confer on me a ferocious insight, and I find I can observe Martin with a startling new, almost X-ray vision.

Martin. Martin Gill, I try to define you, and since I've no machinery, no statistical tools, I do it the easy way, by vocation – but you know yourself how little vocation defines anyone. I play categories; I take the number of universities in this province – it's about ten, isn't it? – and divide that number into departments, allowing about one-twelfth of any university involved in the teaching of English language and literature. And then I divide that in six, allowing for Am. Lit., Can. Lit., Anglo-Saxon, Elizabethan, Victorian, Mods – better make that about one-seventh in Renaissance, and there – I have you pinned down, Martin. You see, you are statistically definable, but where do we go from here? Isolate the Renaissance group and ask, how many of them are in their early forties, own a house with a still sizable mortgage, are married to largish wives with intellectual (but not really) leanings. And children. Children with the usual irritations but, thank God, cross yourself unbeliever though you be, no mongoloids, no cleft palates, no leaky hearts, leukemia, no fatal automobile accidents, no shotgun weddings, no drug charges, just two normal children, and we do love them, don't we Martin?

Once, about ten years or so ago, I came across a pile of Martin's lecture notes. And scribbled in the margin were clusters of scribbled notations in his handwriting. 'Explain in depth.' 'Draw parallel with Dante.' 'Explain cosmos – the idea at the time – use diagram.' 'Joke about Adam's rib – ask, is it relevant?' 'Stress!!!' 'Question for understanding of original sin.' 'Don't push this point – alien concept.' 'What would Freud say about this response?' 'Ask for conclusions at this point – sum up.'

They were messages. Messages partly cryptic, partly illuminating, the little knobs upon which he hung his communications, notations to himself. *Did I write messages to myself? What were they?* Martin's fringe of marginal notes and messages reminded me – yes, I admitted it – reminded me that he possessed an existence of his own to which I did not belong, which I did not understand and which – be truthful now, Judith – which I did not really want to understand.

On Martin's side of the family, no one has the slightest degree of mechanical ability. His grandfather never even learned to drive a car, and his father cannot do the simplest household repairs; he is even somewhat vain about his lack of dexterity. A handyman, a Mr Henshawe who is almost a family retainer, comes regularly to change washers, rehang doors, even to install cuphooks.

It is only natural that Martin has inherited the family ineptness – how could it be otherwise? – but unlike his father, it is not a source of pride with him. Handymen are expensive and unreliable nowadays, and professors do not earn large salaries. I suspect he would like to be able to fix the water heater or put up bookshelves himself. When he looks at Richard he must see that his son will be heir to his inabilities and subject to his niggling expenses. What does he think then?

About three years ago Martin came home with a small flat box from the Hudson's Bay Company. I was making a salad in the kitchen, and I glanced at the box hopefully, thinking that he might have bought me a gift as he sometimes does. 'What's that?' I asked, slicing into a tomato.

He folded back a skin of tissue paper and lifted out a small bow tie, a small crimson silky bow-tie, and held it aloft as though it were a model aircraft, rotating it slowly for my inspection.

I was so astonished I could only gasp, 'What is it?'

'A tie.'

'But who is it for?'

'For me,' he said, smiling and holding it under his chin.

'But you've never worn a bow tie.'

'That's where you're wrong. I wore one for years. A red one. Just like this. Every Friday night at the school dance.'

'But Martin, that was back in the days when people wore bow ties.'

'They're making a comeback. The man at the Bay said so.'

'I can't see you in it,' I said. 'I just can't see you actually wearing a thing like that.'

And he never did. When I straighten his top drawer I always see that same flat Hudson's Bay box, and inside is the bow tie still in its tissue paper. When I see it I can't help but speculate about the moment that prompted him to buy it, but the impulses of others are seldom understandable; they seem to spring out of irrational material, out of the dark soil of the subconscious. But I have respect for impulses and for the mystery they suggest. Even the madness they hint at. That's why I have never mentioned the tie to Martin again. I just straighten his drawer and put everything back neatly and then shut it again.

Why then can't I shut out the wool?

Martin Gill, B.A., M.A., Ph.D. (with distinction)

Age – forty-one

Appearance – somewhat boyish. Never handsome but has been described as agreeable looking, pleasant; his greatest physical charm springs from a slow-motion smile (complete with good-looking eye crinkles, dimple on left cheek, decent teeth) and accompanied by rough-tumbling tenor laugh.

Profession – Associate Professor of English. Speciality – Milton.

Politics – Leftish, Fabianish, believes socialism is 'cry of anguish.' Like his father, grandfather, etc. Milton would have been a socialist, he believes, if he were alive now. He has made this remark, at the most, three times. He is not a man who is 'given' to certain expressions.

Likes – simple things (one friend calls him Martin the Spartan). Reads newspapers, a few magazines, anything written before 1830 and a selection of contemporary writings. Also likes family, friends, a good meal, a good beer, a good laugh, a well-told story, a touchdown or a completed pass, Scrabble (if he is winning), sex (especially in the morning and with a minimum of acrobatics), children (his own exclusively), a clean bathroom in which to take a vigorous shower with very hot water.

Prospects – getting older. More of same. One or perhaps two more promotions, continued fidelity.

Susanna Moodie always called her husband Moodie. His name was John Wedderburn Dunbar Moodie, but she called him Moodie, and I frequently wonder how a woman could love a man she called Moodie. But she must have loved him, at least at first. I am reminded of a girl I knew at university, a small, rodent-faced girl, excessively intellectual and rather nasty, named Rosemary, who was majoring in modern poetry and who, when I told her I was going to marry Martin Gill, said, 'How could anyone fuck a Milton specialist?'

Martin has a touching respect for modern technology, regarding it as a cult practised by priests in another dimension of human intelligence.

Once when our car was still new, we were driving in an ice storm, and he turned on the defrost button. Together we watched a semicircle of glass mysteriously clear itself; soft, moist breath came out of nowhere, ready at the touch of a button to lick through the ice. 'Wonderful,' he murmured, smiling his slow smile. He shook his head and said it again, 'Wonderful.'

Another time we phoned to Canada from England. I stood with him in the cramped and freezing corner callbox. The operator said, 'Just a minute, love,' and somehow the wires obeyed. Voices actually filtered through, recognizable voices from across the ocean. He could hardly believe it. He held the receiver a little away from him and regarded it with wonder. 'God,' he said to me, 'can you believe it?'

And flying home to Canada in the gigantic jet he watched out the window as the wing flaps went through their taking off performance. The wheels rushed under the floor, a stewardess passed out chewing gum; everything seemed wonderfully orchestrated; even the no-smoking signs blinked in time and a quartet of lissome stewardess demonstrated an oxygen mask in the aisle, stylized as a ballet. When we were aloft with the green fields curving beneath us, Martin looked out the window, incredulous, almost mad with joy, gripping my hand. 'What do you think of that?' he whispered.

The little battery shaver I gave him for Christmas holds magic for him. He cups it in his hand, loving its compressed and secret energy. The timing mechanism of my oven delights him, and he likes to think of the blue waterfalls performing inside the dishwater. Sometimes I think he has not quite caught up to this age, that he is hanging back a little on purpose out of some mysterious current in his disposition which hungers for miracles.

I am still sick. Not in a state of suffering as I was, but exhausted. The least effort is too much for me. Yesterday I got up to look for a library book, and after a moment's searching I collapsed back into bed. It wasn't worth it; I am too tired to read anyway.

In the mornings I lie in bed listening to the radio. The melange of music, news spots and interviews soothes; it is a monotonous droning, familiar and comforting; it demands nothing of me. I welcome passivity.

One morning Martin climbed back into bed with me. We scanned the newspapers together and then lay back to listen to the radio. We heard some funny tunes from the Forties, an interview with an ecologist whose passion leaked out over the airwaves, a theatre review, another interview, this one quite funny. I noticed that Martin and I, lying on our backs, laughed in exactly the same places. Almost as though we were reading cue cards. We have never done this before, never lain in bed all morning listening to the radio, laughing together. The novelty of it is striking. It comes as a surprise. And it is all the more surprising because I had thought there could be no more surprises.

Martin fell in love with me because of my vivacity, or so he says, which would mean that he at forty-one is sadly swindled. Perhaps he didn't understand that what he took to be vivacity was only a gust of nervous energy which surfaced in my early twenties, a reaction probably to the cartoon tidiness of Scarborough. Whatever it was, it has more or less drained away, appearing only occasionally in lopsided, frenetic moments. But I can still, if I try, conjure it up. I can charm him still, make him look at me with love. But it requires a tremendous effort of the will. Concentration. Energy. And that may eventually go too. People change, and I suppose everyone has to accept that.

I've noticed, for instance, something about my mother, who all her married life busied herself redecorating her six small rooms in Scarborough; plaster, paint, paper, varnish, they were her survival equipment. But when my father died, a quiet death, a heart attack in his sleep, she stopped decorating. The house seemed to fall away from her. She still lives there, of course, but there is no more fresh paint, no newly potted plants; she has not even rearranged the furniture since he died. And though I know this must be significant and that it must in some way say something about their life together, I am reluctant to dwell on the reasons. I want to push it away from me like Martin's plans to reproduce *Paradise Lost* in wool. (He has not mentioned it since New Year's Day; he has, in fact, very carefully avoided it. And so have I.)

I am feeling well enough to have visitors. Nancy Krantz came one day bringing a chicken casserole for the family, and for me, a new Iris Murdoch novel, expensively hard-covered and just exactly what I had yearned for.

Roger Ramsay brought us a bottle of his homemade wine, and he and Martin and I sit one evening in the bedroom sipping it, I in my most attractive dressing gown, propped up by pillows. But to my tender throat the wine is excruciatingly acidic.

Roger is despondent; his blue jean jacket hangs mournfully from his shoulders, and his hair falls in his eyes. It seems he and Ruthie have quarreled and that she has left him. Where has she gone? I ask him. He doesn't know. He phones the library where she works every day, but she refuses to speak to him. What is the problem? I ask. He shrugs. He isn't sure.

I find I cannot join into his depression. Three weeks in bed have made me incapable of sympathy. Besides I cannot believe Ruthie would leave him for good.

We sip wine and talk; it's only nine-thirty and already I'm wearing down. Martin notices, and I see him signal Roger that it's time to go. He stands up awkwardly, buttons his denim jacket, kisses my hand with such gentleness that I feel tears standing in my eyes. Poor Roger.

Ruthie doesn't come to see me, but she sends a basket of fruit and a card saying only: 'Jude, take care. I love you, Ruthie.'

Furlong brings a huge and expensive book of photographs.

$21.50. He has neglected to detach the price. *Canada: Its Future and Its Now*, the sort of book I seldom pick up. But it's somehow perfect for convalescence. And his mother sends along a jar of red currant jelly which is the first good thing I've tasted all month. She made it herself and poured it into this graceful pressed-glass jar. Meredith spreads it on toast every day and brings it with a pot of tea before she leaves for school. She brings bread from our favourite Boston Bakery which means she walks an extra two miles. I could weep.

Richard lends me his portable record player and from his allowance he buys me a new LP. Stravinsky. He has grown shy. He doesn't quite look me in the eye, but he talks about 'when you get better' as though all things of worth hinge on that condition.

Martin is attentive. Unfailing. Why am I so surprised? Is it because he's not been tested before? He sets up my typewriter on the bed one day when I feel that I've neglected Susanna Moodie long enough.

Susanna. I've reached a place in her life where she makes, with a single imaginative stroke, an attempt to rescue herself, an attempt to alter her life. It is the single anomaly of her life, an enormous biographical hiatus, a time-fold, a geological faultline which remains visible for the rest of her life.

Bizarre though it may seem today, her single decisive act proceeded directly out of the skein of her desperation, and it's possible that her intercession wasn't all that remarkable in the context of her time.

The situation couldn't have been worse. John Moodie, Susanna's husband had botched it as a farmer; not his fault perhaps, for the sort of gentlemanly farming he had envisioned was simply not possible in the Canadian bush. But he had gone down with a deplorable lack of style, and comes across as a limping, whining man, a poor loser, dogged by misfortune, the sort of misfortune which is almost invited. He sold his only possession, a military commission, and squandered the money on worthless steamboat stock. Although Susanna tried gamely to lighten his portrait here and there by referring to his flute playing, his literary discourse, his attempts at writing, he is ever sour and irritable and heavy-footed, not a man to grow old and mellow with.

By 1837 he admitted that he had failed as a backwoodsman; he was in debt; his wife was expecting her fifth child, and winter was coming. Their condition was deteriorating rapidly when they received word that a rebellion had broken out in Toronto. Almost all the ablebodied men in the neighbourhood, including John Moodie, were called away to fight, and the prospect of regular pay was greeted with joy. Moodie sent home some of his money to Susanna who used it to pay off debts. Alone all winter with her children and a hired girl, she had a chance to reflect on the family prospects. She too admitted the farm had been a mistake. Worse still, Moodie wrote that the rebellion was over and the regiment was about to be disbanded; he would soon be without pay again.

Driven nearly to madness, Susanna sat down and wrote a long confessional and impassioned letter to Sir George Arthur who was the Lieutenant-Governor of Upper Canada, outlining the series of disasters that had befallen the family and begging him to keep her husband on in the militia. Her efforts were rewarded, for Moodie was soon made Paymaster to the Militia and later appointed Sheriff of the District of Victoria.

The letter is astonishing enough; but even more extraordinary is the fact that John Moodie never knew about it. He speculated that he was probably awarded the paymaster position because of his exemplary sobriety while in the militia. And the office of sheriff because of his honest performance as paymaster.

It seems almost beyond belief that the story of the letter never leaked out, that Susanna herself never once in all those years let slip to her husband the true cause of his sudden elevation in society. Or was John Moodie bluffing? It is a possibility; to save face he may have neglected to mention the enormous step his wife took to save him. But it is just as possible, even probable, that she kept her secret, kept it all her life, either to spare his pride or to avoid seeming too much the schemer.

They were a married couple, shared a bed, faced each other over a supper table well into old age – all this with a secret between them. Secrets. I never did tell Martin that I had read John Spalding's manuscripts. He would not have liked it; he would have looked at me with less than love; it might even have damaged the balance between us. And he, for perhaps the same reason, put off telling me about the woollen tapestries. He must have guessed how I would react. Secrets are possible. And between people who love each other, maybe even necessary.

One night I woke at one o'clock. I had been asleep for two hours; the house was deathly quiet, and beside me, Martin was breathing deeply. I sat up and wondered what had wakened me so suddenly and so completely. A loud noise? a branch breaking? an icicle falling? a burglar? I listened. There was nothing but a faint gnawing of wind. I got out of bed and went over to the window. There everything was serene; the curving road was touched with ice-blue shadows. The street light poured a steady milk-white light on the snow, beautiful.

Then I realized what it was that had wakened me: I was well. I was restored to health. In the complicated sub-knowledge of my body chemistry, health had been reannounced. A click like an electric switch marked the end of illness. I stretched with health, with a feeling almost of being reborn. Strength, joy.

I had been sick almost a whole month, enclosed in the wide,

white parentheses of weakness, part of a tableau of trays and orange juice and aspirin tablets. I had inhabited a loop of time, been assaulted by an uneasy coalition of suffering and perception, and now I was to be released.

Outside the window, possibility sparkled on every bush and tree. My household was asleep; in dark caves my husband and children dreamed. Heat puffed up from the basement furnace and entered every corner of the house. In the kitchen marvellous things lay on shelves, delicate and tempting. The refrigerator held the unspeakable pleasures of bacon and eggs. I was starved.

Downstairs I switched on a light, blinded at first by the brightness. I found a frying pan and butter, lots of butter, and humming I prepared my feast. And ate it all, believing that nothing had ever tasted so good before.

Thoughts stormed through my head, plans, what I would do tomorrow, the next day, the next. I paced. There was no point in going back to bed in this state. I poked in the family room for old magazines, something, anything to read.

Graven Images lay upside down on the arm of the green chair where Meredith had left it. Furlong glinted at me from the back cover. I picked it up thinking, why not see what it's about. This was the perfect time.

I slung myself on the sofa, my feet dragging over one end, my dressing gown pulled around me, for I was beginning to feel chilly. And the greyness of fatigue was making my head ache. But I opened the book and began to read.

I went through the first chapter quickly, irritated by the familiar Eberhardt style. But I went on to the second chapter anyway, proceeding through waves of boredom into shock, incredulity, anger. I finished the last chapter at dawn, at seven o'clock, a thin nervous time, my whole body chilled with disbelief and dull accumulated rage. How could you, Furlong!

My heart was beating wildly; I could feel it through the heavy quilting of my dressing gown. Anger almost choked me, but in spite of it (or maybe even because of it), I fell instantly asleep where I was, cramped on the sofa with *Graven Images* upside down on my chest.

February

'These severe cases of flu are almost always followed by depression,' Dr Barraclough warned me. 'Watch out not to get too tired or emotionally overwrought. Just sit back, Judith. No running around. And above all,' he warned, 'no worrying.'

But the minute I was on my feet, the solicitude around me evaporated. Meredith's morning trays came to a halt and Richard took back his record player. Martin woke me at seven-thirty sharp to make breakfast. If it hadn't been for Frieda who came once a week to clean the house, we would have fallen apart completely. For I *was* tired. I *was* depressed; the world did indeed seem full of obscure threatening dangers, treacheries, mean cuts and thrusts, insults briskly traded, conniving jealousies, nursed grudges, selfish hang-ups, greed, opportunism, ego, desperation and stupidity; in addition, I felt too weary to cope with the overpowering, wounding and private betrayal of *Graven Images*.

I dragged through the first week of February alternating between rage and depression, sore to the bone and overwhelmed by exhaustion. Furlong Eberhardt and his casual treason plucked at me hourly. I could not forget it for a minute. I had been used. Used by a friend. Taken advantage of. Furlong who had been trusted (although not always loved) had stolen something from me, and that act made him both thief and enemy.

So simply, so transparently, and so unapologetically had he stolen the plot for *Graven Images* – stolen it from me who had in turn stolen it from John Spalding who – it occurred to me for the first time – might have stolen it from someone else. The chain of indictment might stretch back infinitely, crime within crime within crime.

But the fact remained that it was Furlong who had actually gone through with it. A nefarious, barefaced theft. I had at least resisted temptation; and although it had not been the thought of plagiarism which had deterred me, but rather the inability to reconcile the real with the unreal – 'that willing suspension of disbelief' when the moment required – still I had resisted, and that resistance bestowed on me a species of innocence. I was no more than a neutral party, a mere agent of transfer. On the other hand, was corruption transferable by simple infection?

I preferred not to think about it; large abstract problems of sin have never been my specialty. It is the casual treason between individuals, the miniature murders of sensibility which chew away at me, and what Furlong had done was to help himself to something that had been mine. That it hadn't been mine in the first place was immaterial, for as far as he knew the plot had been my idea, my conception, my child.

Would it have mattered, I asked myself, if he had told me, or if he had asked permission; if he had perhaps suggested that, since I wasn't interested in developing the idea myself, would I mind terribly if he more or less appropriated it? Would I have smiled, gracious at such a request? Would I have said, of course, help yourself, someone might as well have the use of it, as though it were a pound of hamburger he was borrowing or the use of my typewriter?

I doubt it. I'm too possessive, and besides I would then have had to confess my theft from John Spalding. And the thought of

John Spalding was beginning to weigh on me. Furlong, after all, had done quite well with the sales of *Graven Images*. It was, in fact, selling better than any of his previous books for the simple reason that it was better than any of the others. And there was no doubt about the reason for that: it was the first book he had ever written which contained anything like a structure, a structure which was derived from a plot which he had stolen, which he had acquired (to use horse-breeders' jargon) by me out of John Spalding.

Not only were his royalties promising, but he had sold the film rights for what Martin assured me must be a handsome figure. He was going to benefit enormously, while John Spalding, in contrast, sat tormented and constipated in Birmingham, lusting for recognition and trying to stretch his lecturer's salary, month by meagre month, to cover the cheapest existence he could devise: bacon dripping on his bread, I imagined, and doing his own repairs on the third-hand Morris, tripe and onion instead of Sunday joint, and smoking his Woodbines down to their frazzled ends. It was monumentally unjust.

Of course I realized I would have to confront Furlong; it was unthinkable to let this pass. But for that I needed strength. I would have to wait until I was stronger. The phrase 'girding my loins' occurred to me. I would need to arm myself, for I was still weak, hardly able to cook a meal without flopping exhausted back into bed. And for reasons which Dr Barraclough might recognize, I was continually on the verge of weeping.

Tears stood like pin pricks in the backs of my eyes. I was prepared to cry over anything. Martin called from the university to say he would be staying late to work. He didn't say what he would be working on, but we both knew; and when I thought of him in his cork-walled solitude, selecting and blending his wools, threading his needles and weaving away, woof and warp, in and out, I wanted to sob with anguish.

Meredith encloses herself in her room. She is re-reading all of Furlong's books, and our copy of *Graven Images* has been marked and underlined. Exclamation points stand in the margins, the corners of pages have been turned under to indicate her favourite passages. She listens to music and reads and reads. Her loneliness and the sort of love she is imagining tears at me, but there is nothing I can do but leave her to her disc jockeys and the comfort of printed pages.

And I bleed for Richard. There was no letter for him this week. He could hardly believe it at first. Then we read about the postal strike in Britain, and he breathed with relief. The reason, at least, was known. Circumstances were beyond his immediate control; he would have to wait.

He checks the newspapers daily for news of the strike, mentioning it offhandedly to us so we won't suspect how much he cares or how dependent he has grown on the weekly letters from Anita Spalding. 'When the strike ends, there's going to be a real bonanza,' he says, picturing the accumulated letters pouring in all at once. The thought sustains him for a while, but then he worries because his letters aren't getting through. Will she understand about the strike? he wonders. Of course, we assure him, how could she not understand? He hears somewhere that top priority mail is trickling through, and he feels obscurely that he deserves to be top priority, that his letters matter.

The strike drags on, and Martin and I suggest things he can do to keep busy. Martin takes him skiing, and in spite of my fatigue I help him with a school project on Tanzania. We trace maps; I type an agricultural output chart for him. He has taken to sighing heavily.

Even Susanna Moodie has let me down. I am writing now about her later life when she has moved with her husband and children to the town of Belleville. No longer destitute, she has

119

grown cranky. She says unkind things about the neighbouring women. She minimizes the efforts of the town builders; she has lost the girlish excitement and breathless gaiety which made life in the bush cabin seem an adventure; the glory of fresh raspberries and the thrill of milking a cow are forgotten pleasures. She is a matron now, and she makes hard, grudging judgments. She has lost her vision. She is condescending. The action goes too fast; she telescopes five years into a maddening paragraph. There are no details anymore.

It would help if it snowed. The ground is covered with old crusted snow and pitted with ice. The roads and sidewalks are rutted and hard to walk on, and driving is dangerous. A layer of grime covers everything. One soft and lovely fall of snow might at least keep me from this overwhelming compulsion to put my head down and cry and cry and cry.

I don't really feel like cooking, but I feel so sorry for Roger that one night we invite him for a family dinner. He hasn't heard from Ruthie. He doesn't know where she's living. He would feel better, he tells me, if he knew where she was staying.

'Are you really that worried about her?' I ask, putting a slice of meatloaf on his plate.

'No. I know she's all right because she's at work.'

'What then?'

'I just want to know where she's living.'

'You've tried her girl friends?'

'Yes. And they don't know.'

'What about her family?' I ask. I know she is from a small town in northern Ontario. 'Couldn't you write to them?'

'God, no. They never liked the idea that we were living together. Not married. They're pretty rigid.'

'Why don't you follow her home from work?' Richard asks, taking the words out of my mouth.

'Don't be stupid,' Meredith says sternly. 'This isn't a James Bond movie. That would be just plain sneaky, following her like that.'

I say nothing. Roger shakes his head sadly. 'I couldn't. Believe me, I've thought about it, but it does seem to be an invasion – and, I don't know – I just couldn't.'

Martin interrupts us with, 'Look, if she wants it this way, isn't it better to leave her alone. You've got to get your mind on something else, Roger.'

'God knows I'm busy enough at work,' Roger says. 'It seems I've just got the Christmas exams marked, and now we're onto a new set. I don't even have time to do enough reading to keep up.'

'What did you think of *Graven Images?*' I ask him suddenly.

'Great.' He barks it out. 'Absolutely his best.'

'Why?' I ask, trying not to sound too sly.

'I don't know, Judith. It's got more – more body to it.'

'A better plot?' I suggest.

'That's it. A real brainstorm. No wonder the films snatched it up.'

'I just loved it,' Meredith murmurs.

Martin says nothing; he still hasn't got around to reading it.

'Tell me, Roger,' I ask, 'would you say that Furlong is an original writer?'

'Damn right I would.'

'How is he original?' I ask. 'Tell me, in what way is he original?'

Roger leans back, shaking his thick curls out of his eyes, and for a moment Ruthie is forgotten, for a moment he seems happy. He is recalling phrases from his thesis. 'All right, Judith, take his use of the Canadian experience. Now there's a man who actually comprehends the national theme.'

'Which is what?' Martin asks.

'Which is shelter. Shelter from the storm of life, to use a corny phrase.'

'Corny is right,' Richard says.

'Who asked you, Richard?' Meredith tells him.

In the kitchen I serve ice-cream drizzled with maple syrup; I haven't the energy to think of anything else. Meredith carries in the plates for me. Roger is expanding on the theme of shelter.

'I don't, of course, mean just shelter from those natural storms which occur externally. Although he is tremendous on those. That hail sequence in *Graven Images* – now didn't that grab you? Even you'd like it, Martin. It's got a sort of Miltonic splendour. Like the hail is a symbol. He makes it stand for the general battering of everyday life.'

'So what about the shelter theme?' Martin is smiling broadly, happy tonight.

'Okay, I'm getting to that. Remember the guy out on the prairie, Judith, just standing there. And the hail starts. Golfballs. His dog is killed. Remember that?'

'Christ,' Martin says. 'It sounds like *Lassie Come Home*.'

'It sounds bad, I'll admit. But that's the beautiful thing about Furlong. He can carry it off when no one else can. What someone else makes into a soap opera, he makes part of the national fabric.'

'But Roger,' I plead, 'getting back to originality for a moment, do you really think he comes up with original plots?'

'Well, we don't use that word plot much anymore. Not in modern criticism. But, yes, sure I think he does. You read *Graven Images*. Wasn't that a real heart-stopper?'

'What about the others though?' I ask. 'Where do you think he got the ideas for those early books? Did you go into that when you wrote your thesis?'

'I suppose you want me to admit that his stories are a bit on the formula plan. So, okay, I admit it. But *Graven Images* confirms what I said then – that he's a pretty original guy.'

'He really is,' Meredith says smiling.

'Hmmmm,' Martin says.

I say nothing. I am sitting quiet. Girding my loins. I know that my present weakness is trivial and temporary. Next week, I promise myself, next week I'm going to have it out with Furlong. He's going to have to do some explaining. Or else.

Or else what? Endlessly, silently, I debate the point.

What power do I have over Furlong? Who am I, the far from perfect Judith Gill, to judge him, and how do I hope to chastise him for his dishonesty?

I only want him to know that I know what he did.

Why? What's the point? Why not let it pass?

Because what he's done may be too small a crime to punish, but at the same time it's too large to let go unacknowledged. Talk about scot-free.

Is Furlong a bad man then? A criminal?

No, not bad. Just weak. Complex, intelligent, but weak. I've just discovered how weak. But he has a glaze of arrogance, a coloratura confidence that demands that I respond.

In what way is he weak?

Let me explain. When I was about fifteen years old I read a very long and boring novel called *Middlemarch*. By George Eliot yet. I got it from the public library. (All girls like me who were good at school but suffered from miserable girlhoods were sustained for years on end by the resources of the public libraries of this continent.) Not that *Middlemarch* offered me much in the way of escape. It offered little but a rambling plot and quartets of moist, dreary, introspective characters, one of whom was accused by the heroine of having 'spots of commonness.' I liked that expression, 'spots of commonness,' and even at fifteen I recognized the symptoms, interpreting them as a familiar social variety of measles.

Furlong suffers more than anyone I know from this exact and debilitating malady. Witness the framed motto he once had in his office, and witness also the abrupt banishment of it. Observe the clichés on his book jacket, remember his cranberry-vodka punch, his petty jealousies of other writers, his dependence on nationality which permits him his big-frog-in-little-pond eminence.

His sophistication is problematically wrought; it's uneven and sometimes, when instinct fails, altogether lacking. He can, for instance, be too kind, too lushly, tropically kind, a kindness too rich and ripe for ordinary friendship. And, in addition, he is uncertain about salad forks, brandy snifters, and how to use the subjunctive; he finds those Steuben glass snails charming and he favours Renoir; he sometimes slips and says supper instead of dinner, and, conversely, in another pose, he slips and says dinner instead of supper; he is spotted, oh, he is uncommonly spotted.

But is he less of a thief for all that?

A thief is a thief is a thief.

Very profound. But don't forget, you stole the plot in the first place.

That was different. I didn't actually go through with it. And I didn't profit from it the way Furlong has profited.

So that's what's bothering you. You're jealous.

No, no, no, no. Not for myself. For Martin maybe. Here is Furlong, enjoying an unearned success. And Martin gets nothing but crazy in the head.

Are there no mitigating circumstances in this theft?

Many. Obviously he was desperate. He admitted that much, letting slip the fact that the well had gone dry. He was on the skids, hadn't had a good idea for two years. Poor man, snagged in literary menopause and sticky with hot flushes. And he *is* nice to his mother. And patient with his students. And always touchingly, tenderly gallant with me, actually thinking of me as a fellow writer, and accepting me, great big-boned Judith Gill, as charming, a really quite attractive woman. And what else? Oh, yes. He has a passionate and pitiable desire to be loved, to be celebrated with expletives and nicknames, to be in the club. And then, an alternating compulsion to draw back, to be insular and exclusive and private. Psychologically he's a mess. I suppose he was driven to theft.

But who does it really harm?

I refuse to answer such an academic question.

Don't you like him at all?

Like him? I do. No, I don't, not now. I suppose I'm fond of him. But no matter how charming he will be in the future, no matter how he disclaims his act of plunder and he will, no matter what amends he may make for it, I will not be moved. I don't know why, but he will never, he will never, he will never be someone I love. Only someone I could have loved.

Nancy Krantz and I went out to lunch one day to celebrate my recovery from the flu. We went to the Prince Lodge where Paul Krantz is a member (and has a charge account) and sat at one of the dark oak tables which are moored like ships on the sea of olive carpet. Around us quiet, dark-suited businessmen in twos and threes talked softly; glasses and silver clinked faintly as though at a great distance.

'Two dry sherries,' Nancy told the waiter briskly. I longed to tell her about Furlong's plagiarism, but that was out of the question since it would have necessitated the disclosure of my own theft, not to mention my prying into John Spalding's private manuscripts.

We ordered beef curry, and while we waited we discussed the alternating vibrations which regulate female psychology.

'Up and down,' Nancy complained. 'A perpetual see-saw ride. Pre-menstrual, post-menstrual. Optimism, pessimism.'

I agreed; it did seem that the electricity of life consisted mainly of meaningless fluctuations in mood, so that to enter an era of happiness was to anticipate the next interlude of depression.

'Of course,' Nancy said, 'there are those occasional little surprises which make it all worthwhile.'

'Such as?' I asked.

'The peach,' she said. 'Did I ever tell you the peach story?'

'No,' I said, 'never.'

So she told me how, last summer, she and Paul and their children, all six of them, had been stalled in heavy traffic. It was a Friday evening and they were working their way out of the city to get to the cottage sixty miles away. The children were quarrelsome and the weather was murderously humid. In another car stalled next to them, a fat man sat alone at the steering wheel, and on the back seat, plainly visible, was a bushel of peaches. He smiled at the children, and they must have smiled back, for he turned suddenly and reached a fat hand into his basket, carefully selected a peach, and handed it out the window to Nancy.

She took it, she said, instinctively, uttering a confused mew of thanks. Ahead of them a traffic light turned green, and the fat man's car moved away, leaving Nancy with the large and beautiful peach in her hand. It was, she said the largest peach she had ever seen, almost the size of a grapefruit, and its skin was perfect seamless velvet without a single blemish. Paul shouted at her over the noise of the traffic to look out for razor blades, so she turned it over carefully, inspecting it. But the skin was unbroken. And the exact shade of ripeness for eating.

'What did you do with it?' I asked.

'We ate it,' Nancy said. 'We passed it around. Gently. Like a holy object almost, and we each took big bites of it. Until it was gone. One of the children said something about how strange it was for someone to do that, give us a peach through a car window like that, but the rest of us just sat there thinking about it. All the way to the cottage. A strange sort of peace stuck to us. It was so – so completely unasked for. And so undeserved. And the whole thing had been so quick, just a few seconds really. I was – I don't know why – I was thrilled.'

I nodded. I was remembering something that had happened to us, an incident I had almost forgotten. It was perhaps a shade less joyous a story than Nancy's, but the element of mystery had, at the time, renewed something in me.

It had happened, I told Nancy, on our first day in England. We had taken a train from London to Birmingham. Everything was very new and crowded and confused; the train puffing into Birmingham seemed charmingly miniature; the station was glass-roofed and dirty with Victorian arches and tea trolleys and curious newspapers arrayed in kiosks; odd looking luggage, belted and roped, even suitcases made of wicker, were stacked on carts. Martin, the children and I struggled with our own bags, hurrying down the platform, disoriented by the feel of solid ground underfoot, bumped and jostled at every step by people hurrying to board the train we had just left. Passengers pulled down the train windows, leaned out talking to their friends while paper cups of tea changed hands and kisses flew through the air. Children with startling red cheeks, wearing blue gabardine coats, hung onto their mothers' hands. A cheerful scruffiness hung over the station like whisky breath.

And at that moment a short, dark little man stopped directly in front of me and pushed a small brown paper parcel at me. I must have shaken my head to indicate that it wasn't mine, but he pushed it even harder at me, speaking all the time, very rapidly, in a language I didn't recognize. Certainly no species of

English; nor was it French or German; it might have been Arabic we speculated later.

I pushed the parcel back at him, but he placed it all the more firmly in my hand, speaking faster and more agitatedly than before. 'Come on, Judith,' Martin called to me. So clutching my suitcase again as well as the parcel, I followed Martin and the children out into the thin sunshine where we flagged a taxi and drove the mile or two to the Spaldings' flat.

The parcel was forgotten for an hour or more; then someone remembered it. I opened it slowly while the children watched. Inside was a box of stationery. Letter paper. About twenty sheets of it in a not very fresh shade of pale green. There was some sort of pinkish flower at the top of each sheet, and at the bottom of the box there were piles of slightly faded looking envelopes.

For a day or two we speculated on what it could mean. We examined every sheet of paper and looked the box over carefully for identifying marks; we tried to recall the man's appearance and the sound of his voice. 'He must have thought you'd left it on the seat in the train,' Martin said, and in the end we all agreed that that was the most likely answer, the only sensible conclusion really. But it didn't seem quite enough. The little man had been running on the platform. He had searched the crowd, or so I believed, and for some reason he had selected me. And he had run away again in a state of great excitement. We never thought for a moment that the parcel might have been dangerous since this occurred before the invention of letter bombs, but Richard did suggest we run a hot iron over the sheets of paper in the hope of discovering messages written in invisible ink.

Those first few days in England were so filled with novelty, with odd occurrences and curious sights, that this tiny incident, bizarre as it was, seemed no more than a portion of that larger strangeness, and we soon ceased to talk about it. I even used the writing paper for my first letters home, and when it was all gone I forgot about it. Or almost.

For if it seemed a commonplace enough adventure at the time, it grows more strange, more mysterious as time passes. This afternoon, telling Nancy about it, it seemed really quite wonderful in a way, utterly unique in fact, as though we had accidentally brushed with the supernatural.

And the two of us, stirring sugar into our cups of coffee at the Prince Lodge, smiled. It was after three; the businessmen had crept away without our noticing, back to their conference rooms, to their teak desks and in-trays. Here in the restaurant two waiters fluttered darkly by a sideboard, and in all that space I felt myself lifted to a new perspective: far away it seemed, I could see two women at a table; they are neither happy nor unhappy, but are suspended somewhere in between, caught in a thin, clear, expensive jelly, and they are both smiling, smiling across the table, across the room, smiling past the dark stained panelling, out through the tiny-paned window to the parking lot which is slowly, slowly, filling up with snow, changing all the world to a wide, white void.

'It's over. I just heard it on the news,' Richard yells. 'While I was getting dressed. It's all settled.'

'What's settled?' It's early, eight o'clock, and I'm pouring out glasses of orange juice, not quite awake.

'The postal strike.'

'The postal strike?'

'You know. In the U.K. Don't you remember?'

'Oh, yes, that's right. Heavens, that's been going on a long time.'

'Three weeks.'

'Really? Where does the time go?'

He sits down at the table and cuts the top off his boiled egg.

CAROL SHIELDS

Joy makes him violent, and the slice of egg shell skitters to the floor. He leans over to pick it up. 'Man, it'll be a real pile-up. Three weeks of mail!'

I pour my coffee and sit beside him. 'It'll take a while to sort it all out.'

'I know.'

'I mean, you mustn't expect any mail for a while.'

'I know. I know.'

'It may be several days. A week even.'

'Is there any honey?'

'In the cupboard.'

'Say about six days. Today's Tuesday. I should be getting something by next Monday.'

'Hmmmmm.'

'What do you think? Tuesday at the latest?'

'Maybe, but don't count on it.'

'Don't worry about me.'

He managed to get through the week, casting no more than a casual eye at the hall table under the piece of red granite where I keep the mail. Over the weekend we all went skiing, and time passed quickly.

But when he came home from school at noon on Monday, I could tell how disappointed he was. He spooned his soup around in circles, and picked at his sandwich, and for the first time I noticed how pale he looked. On Tuesday, because again there was no mail for him, I made him waffles for lunch. But even that failed to cheer him.

'Look, Richard,' I told him, 'have you looked in the newspapers? Did you see that picture of all the unsorted mail. A mountain of it. It's going to take longer than we thought.'

'I guess so.'

He kept waiting. Watching him, I observed for the first time the

130

simplicity of his life, the almost utilitarian unrelieved separation of his time: school, home, sleep. Endless repetition. He needed a letter desperately.

On the weekend we skied again, scattering our energies on the snow-covered hills and coming home in the late afternoon. Richard was so weighted with sleep that England must have seemed far away, indistinct and irrelevant, a point on a dream map.

But Monday morning he tells me he feels sick. His throat is sore, he says, and his head aches. I can hear an unfamiliar pitch of pleading in his voice, and know intuitively that he only wants to be here when the mail arrives. Martin is impatient and peers down his throat with a flashlight. 'I can't see a thing,' he says. 'And his temperature is normal.'

'He might as well stay home this morning,' I say, 'just in case he's coming down with something.' (How expertly I carry off these small deceptions. And how instinctively I take the part of the deceiver.) Richard, listening to us debate his hypothetical sickness, looks at me gratefully. And humbly crawls back into bed to wait.

The mail comes at half-past ten. There is quite a lot for a Monday. Bills mostly, a letter from Martin's parents, two or three magazines. And a letter from England. A tissue-thin blue air letter. But it is from a friend of Martin's, not from Anita Spalding.

I go up to Richard's room, a tall glass of orange juice in my hand and an aspirin, for I want to continue the fiction of illness long enough for him to recover with grace. 'Take this, Rich,' I say. 'You may even feel up to going to school this afternoon.'

'Maybe,' he says. 'Any mail?'

'Nothing much,' I say, duplicating his nonchalance.

'Wonder if the mail's getting through from England,' he speculates as though this were no more than an abstract topic.

'I think it is, Richard,' I tell him quietly. 'Dad got one this morning.'

'Oh.'

'But I suppose it will just trickle in at first.'

'Probably.'

'It may take another good week to clear it all.'

'Yeah.'

'How do you feel?'

'A little better,' he says.

'Good,' I say. 'After lunch, how about if I drive you over to school?'

'Okay,' he says.

But there was no mail for him that week or the next. The month was slipping by, and I still had not confronted Furlong. I weighted it in my mind, rehearsed it; I fortified myself, gathered my strength, prepared my grievances. Soon.

But there are other things to think of. Meredith will be seventeen on February twenty-seventh, and Martin suggests we all go to Antonio's for dinner. I fret briefly about the cost, but listening to my own voice and hearing the terse economical echoes of my mother, I stop short.

'A good idea,' I say.

The day before her birthday I take the downtown bus and shop for a birthday present. This is a far different quest than shopping for my mother or for Lala; for them we can never think of anything to buy. But for Meredith, for a girl of seventeen, the shops are groaning with wonderful things. Things. It is the age for things, each of which would, I know, bring tears of delight rushing into her eyes. There are Greek bags woven in a shade of blue so subtle it defies description; chunks of stone, looking as though they were plucked from a strange planet, fastened into chains of palest silver; there are sweaters of unfathomable softness, belts in every colour and width, jeans by the hundreds, by the thousands, by the millions. Things are everywhere. All I have to do is choose.

But I can't. Instead I buy too much. I spend far more money than I'd intended; it is irresistible; it is so easy to bring her happiness – it won't always be this easy – so easy to produce the charge plate, to tuck yet another little bag away. But finally the parcels weight me down; my arms are filled, and I think it must be time for me to catch my bus. But first a cup of coffee.

In the corner of Christy's Coffee Shop I sink into a chair. The tables here are small, and the tile floor is awash with tracked-in snow; there is hardly room for me to stow my parcels under the table. At all the other little tables are shoppers, and like me they are weary. The February sales are on, and many of these women are guarding treasures they have spent the day pursuing. Waitresses bring them solace: cups of coffee, green pots of tea, doughnuts or toasted Danish buns, bran muffins with pats of butter. Outside it's already dark. Only four-thirty and the day is ending for these exhausted, sore-footed women. All of them are women, I notice.

Or almost all. There is one man at a table in the back of the room. Only one. Oddly enough, he looks familiar; the bulk of his body reminds me of someone I know. I do know him. I recognize the tweed overcoat. Of course. It's Furlong Eberhardt. With a cup of tea raised to his lips.

And who's that with him? Two women. Students? Probably. I peer over the sea of teased hairdos and crushed wool hats. Who is it?

One of them looks like Ruthie. What would Ruthie be doing here with Furlong? Impossible. But it is Ruthie. She is pouring herself a cup of tea, tipping the pot almost upside-down to get the last drop. She is lifting a sliver of lemon and squeezing it in. The small dark face, Latin-looking. It is Ruthie.

And who is that other girl? I can't believe it. But the navy blue coat thrown over the back of the chair is familiar. Its plaid lining is conclusive. The slender neck, the lift of dark brown hair. I am certain now. It is – yes – *it's Meredith!*

Every day I work for two or three hours on the Susanna Moodie biography. What I am looking for is the precise event which altered her from a rather priggish, faintly blue-stockinged but ardent young girl into a heavy, conventional, distressed, perpetually disapproving and sorrowing woman. And although I've been over all the resource material thoroughly, I'm unable to find the line of demarcation. It seems to be unrecorded, lodged perhaps in the years between her books, or else – and this seems more likely – wilfully suppressed, deliberately withheld.

There are traumatic events in her life to be sure. Illness. The drowning of a son which she mentions only in passing. Poverty. And the failure of her husband to assume direction. Perhaps that's it – her husband, John W. Dunbar Moodie.

There's a clue in an essay he wrote as an old man. It is a sort of summary of his life in which he lists the primary events as being, one, getting stepped on by an elephant as a young man in South Africa, two, the breaking of a knee in middle life and, three, painful arthritis in old age. He was, it would seem, a man who measured his life by episodes of pain, a negative personality who might easily have extinguished the fire of love in Susanna.

But despite her various calamities she survived, and it seems to have been her sense of irony that kept her afloat when everything else failed. Over the years she had abandoned the sharp divisions between good and evil which had troubled her as a young woman; the two qualities became bridged with a fibrous rib of irony. Sharp on the tongue, it became her trademark.

Irony, it seems to me, is a curious quality, a sour pleasure. Observation which is acid-edged with knowledge. A double vision which allows pain to exist on the reverse side of pleasure. Neither vice nor virtue, it annihilated the dichotomy of her existence. Smoothed out the contradictions. Forstalled ennui and permitted survival. An anesthetic for the frontier, but at the same time a drug to dull exhilaration.

For example, when Susanna was a middle-aged woman and ailing from unmentionable disorders, she took a cruise to see Niagara Falls. It was, she says, what she had dreamed of all her life.

The imagined sight of that mountain of water had sustained her through her tragic years, and now at last the boat carried her closer and closer to the majestic sight.

She can hear the thunder of water before she can see it, and her whole body tenses for pleasure. But when she actually stands in the presence of the torrent, she loses the capacity for rhapsody. She has exhausted it in anticipation.

But irony rescues her from a pitiable vacuum. Turning from the scenery, she observes the human activity around her, and, paragraph by paragraph, she describes the reactions of her fellow tourists. Their multiple presence forms particles through which she can see, as through a prism, the glorious and legendary spectacle of Niagara Falls. Once again she finds her own way out.

I easily recognize the nuances of irony because, lying sleepless in bed on this last night in February, I too am rescued; I too do my balancing act between humour and desperation.

It seems I've always had a knack for it. Perhaps I was born with it; maybe it came sealed in the invisible skin of a chromosome, ready to accompany me for the rest of my life. I can feel it: a tough-as-a-tendon cord which stretches from the top of my head to my toes, a sort of auxiliary brain, ready as a knuckle to carry me through.

All through my endless barren childhood I had my special and privileged observation platform. My parents did not succeed in souring me as they did my sister Charleen who writes and publishes poems of terrifying bitterness. My sad lank father and my sad nervous mother have faded to snapshot proportions. They have not twisted or warped me or shaped me into a mocking image of themselves. There may be warnings in the blood, but, at least, there are no nightmares.

And now, in spite of my insomnia – that too is temporary – I find I'm able to coexist with Richard's agony as, day after day, the mail doesn't come for him. Somewhere in a larger pattern there's an explanation; I am confident of it.

And the complex dark secrecy of the scene in Christy's Coffee Shop – Furlong, Ruthie, Meredith – I can absorb that too, and I can even refrain from quizzing Meredith about it. I can put it aside, tuck it away; I can title it 'An Anomaly.'

Detached and nerved by irony, I can even look squarely at Furlong's devious theft. And at my own role as an agent of theft. I can live outside it. I can outline it with my magic pencil. Put a ring around it.

Martin's madness is more difficult to assimilate, but my vein, my good steady vein of irony, gives me just enough distance to believe he may be only temporarily deranged. And so, although everything seems to be falling apart and though I'm assailed by an unidentifiable sadness and though it has snowed solidly for eight days – there is one thing I am certain of: that, like Mrs. Moodie of Belleville, I will, in the end, be able to trick myself; I can will myself into happiness. No matter what happens I will be able to get through.

If only I can get through tonight.

March

'You swine, Furlong. You swine.'

    'Judith! Are you talking to me?'

    'You thieving swine!'

'Judith, what is this? Some kind of joke?'

It is not a joke, not even a nightmare; this is real. At last I am confronting Furlong.

'Swine.'

'Judith.'

This isn't the way I'd planned it. But here we are, the two of us in the hall of Professor Stanley's country house with its pegged oak floors and its original pre-Confederation pine furniture and the acre of land which he and his wife Polly always refer to as 'the grounds.' We are face to face in front of the cherrywood armoire, and now that I have begun, I can't stop.

'Swine.'

'Judith, are you serious? Are you calling me a swine?'

'That's exactly what I said. An evil swine.'

'Come on, Judith.' He steps back, half-shocked. And then enrages me further by allowing a curl of a smile to appear behind his beard.

Where had I got that word – swine? It is a word I haven't used since – since when? Since 1943 at least, since those fanatical early Forties, the war years, when the villains in our violent-hued comic books were resoundingly labelled swine by the hero, Captain Marvel, Superman, Captain Midnight, whoever it might be.

Swine meant the ultimate in the sinister, a being who was evil, whose skin was tinged with green and whose eyes were slits of gleaming, poisonous, rancid, incomprehensible Nazism. Japanese and Germans were swines (we didn't know how to pluralize it, of course), Hitler being the epitome of swinehood. It was a word we spit out between clenched teeth, saying it with a fiendish east European accent – 'You feelthy schwine.' When we jumped on tin cans at the school scrap drive we shouted, 'Kill the swine.'

I remember, years later, taking part in a school play called 'The Princess and the Swineherd,' and the term swine was explained to me for the first time. How disappointing to find that it meant no more than pig, for though I associated pigs with filth and gluttony, that animal didn't begin to approach the wickedness of swine.

'You heard me, Furlong. I said swine. And I meant swine.'

'My dear girl, what on earth is the matter?'

'I am not your dear girl.'

We are at a party, an annual get-together for the English Department, traditionally hosted by the department chairman and his wife, Ben and Polly Stanley.

I am fond of them both. Ben is reserved but charming, a specialist in Elizabethan literature, a man who at fifty seems perpetually surprised by his own dimensions. One hand is constantly rummaging through his coarse, silver-grey hair as though it cannot believe that such beautiful hair exists on so common a head. The other hand, nervously, mechanically, pats and circles the sloping paunch which bulges under his suede jacket, as if he is questioning its clandestine and demeaning swell.

His wife Polly is about fifty too, a woman both stout and shy. Sadly she is the victim of academic fiction, for she is never free of her role as faculty wife; she plays bridge with the wives, bowls with them, discusses Great Books with them, laments pollution, listens to string quartets, attends convocations, all with an air of brooding and bewilderment. Despite her girth, her charm is wispy, a fragile growth which advances and contracts in spasms. I would not want to embarrass her.

'I don't care if they hear us,' I hiss.

'Well, damn it, I do.'

As it happens, no one hears us. Everyone has gone into the wainscoted dining room for a buffet of clam chowder and the Stanley speciality, chunks of beef afloat in red wine, which they will carry on plates into the living room, the den, the solarium, anywhere they can find a perch. We are alone in the hall, Furlong and I, but nevertheless I lower my voice.

'Furlong, I want you to know that I know everything.'

'You know everything,' he repeats numbly. He is not smiling now.

'Everything.'

'Everything,' he echoes.

'You might have known I'd find out.'

'I didn't. No, I didn't.'

'How could you be so devious, Furlong?' I ask. Already I have passed from the peak of rage into vicious scolding.

He has the grace to cover his face with both hands, and I notice with satisfaction that he is swaying slightly.

'How could you be so deceitful?' I say again.

'Ah Judith.' His hands extend in a gesture of helplessness. 'This is all much more complicated than you seem to think.'

'Complicated? Devious is more like it.'

'Believe me, Judith, I never meant to hurt anyone.'

'All you wanted was to watch out for yourself and your precious reputation.'

'You're wrong. There were other considerations. Really Judith, you're being unbelievably narrow-minded. And it's not like you.'

'Please, please, please spare me any semblance of flattery, Furlong. I'm not in the mood.'

'All I'm saying is, and for God's sake, lower your voice won't you, try to think of this in a broader perspective.'

'Deception is deception,' I say lamely but loudly.

'Believe me, Judith, I never meant for this to get out of hand.'

'You admit then that it did get out of hand?'

'Of course I do. My God, do you think I've got no conscience at all?'

'I wonder about that.'

'If you only knew. I've felt the most terrible remorse, believe me. I've been tormented day and night by all this. There were times when I thought I should go on television, on national television, and make a public confession.'

'Well? Are you going to?'

He winces. Takes a step backwards. Raises his hand as though to ward me off. Sinks down on one of Polly's ladder-back chairs.

'Sit down. Please, Judith, we have got to talk this over sensibly.'

I sit facing him. My knees buckle with faintness. 'We *are* talking this over, Furlong.'

'Now listen closely, Judith. I am not defending what I did.'

'I hope not.'

'I am not bereft of honour, whatever you may choose to think.'

'I wonder if you know what I really do think.'

'I can guess. You are utterly disgusted. You trusted me, and now you find out what a sham I really am.'

'You're getting close,' I say cruelly.

'Do you know something, Judith. I even hate myself. When I look in the mirror I cringe. I actually cringe.'

'You'd never guess it from the pitch on your book jackets.'

'I don't write those, as you perfectly well know. The publishers look after that.'

'I see.'

'You don't see. You're being deliberately rigid, Judith, and I'm doing my best to explain to you the full circumstances.'

'Go ahead. Try. I want to hear how you're going to explain this away.'

'All right then.' He takes a deep breath. 'It seemed a harmless enough thing to do at the time. That's all. What more can I say. Perhaps I lacked perspective at the time. Yes, I definitely lacked a sense of balance. And then I just got trapped into it. Everything happened too fast. It just got away from me, that's all.'

'And that's what you call an explanation?'

'It's not much. It's not much, I'll admit, but it's all I have. My God, Judith, you love to twist the knife when you get hold of it, don't you?'

'Well, I *am* the injured party.'

'The injured party?'

'I'm the one you took advantage of.'

'Why you?'

'For heaven's sake, Furlong, don't be obtuse. I can't stand that on top of all this rotten deception.'

'I'm afraid I must be obtuse. I just fail to see why you are more injured than anyone else.'

'You really can't?'

'No. I'm afraid not. I mean, all right, you're a member of the public. Maybe a little more astute than some, but you're just one member of a large public, and I can't see what gives you the right to be personally aggrieved.'

I can't believe what I'm hearing. 'Think, Furlong,' I say, 'think hard.'

'I am. But I can't for the life of me think why you should feel persecuted.'

'I can't stand this.'

'You think I'm enjoying it. I came here tonight expecting to enjoy myself, and I hardly get in the door and you leap on me.'

'Believe me, I would have leapt a lot sooner than this, but I took a few weeks to cool off.'

'And you call this being cool? If you don't mind my saying so, Judith, this really isn't your style, not at all. Pouncing on an old friend in public and yelling "swine" at him.'

'Well, you behaved like a swine, Furlong, and I don't see that you deserve any special consideration now.'

'Didn't I tell you I was guilty. Do you want me to go down on my knees. And I really am sorry about it, Judith.' His voice cracks, dangerously close to tears. 'If you only knew what I go through. Do you know that I have to take sleeping pills almost every night. Not to mention my preculcer condition.'

'If that's the case, what in heaven's name made you do it?'

'I told you. I got trapped. It didn't seem so dreadful at the time. But listen, Judith. You're an old friend. I know I acted like a bloody fool and that I've no right to ask this of you, but do you think we could – you know – do you think we could more or less keep this between ourselves? I mean, now that the damage is done, do we have to spread it around?'

'What you're really asking is, can we sweep it neatly under the rug.'

'Of course I don't mean that. I just mean, couldn't we confine this thing?'

'I don't know. I'll have to think.'

'Judith. Please.' His eyes fill with real tears and his nose reddens, making him look piercingly elderly. 'Please.'

I can't bear it; he is going to cry. 'All right,' I say grudgingly. 'I

143

suppose nothing would be served by a public disclosure.'

'Oh, Judith, you are kind.' He reaches blindly for my hand. 'You've always been so kind, so good.'

'But,' I say firmly, drawing my hand away, 'I do think you owe me, at the very least, an apology.'

His face straightens; his eyes cloud with opaque bafflement. 'Tell me, why do I owe you a *personal* apology?'

'It was, after all, my plot that you stole.'

'Your plot. I stole your plot?'

'For *Graven Images*. As you perfectly well know.'

'You think I stole a plot from you for *Graven Images*?'

'You certainly did. From my novel. The one I wrote for your class. And you promised me you'd destroyed it. And then you went and took it. Maybe not incident by incident, but the main idea. You took the main idea. And made a killing.'

'Come, come, Judith. Writers don't steal ideas. They abstract them from wherever they can. I never stole your idea.'

'You must be joking, Furlong. Do you mean to sit there and tell me your novel bears no resemblance to the one I wrote?'

He answers with an airy wave of his hand, an affectionate pull at his beard. 'Possibly, possibly. But, my good Lord, writers can't stake out territories. It's open season. A free range. One uses what one can find. One takes an idea and brings to it his own individual touch. His own quality. Enhances it. Develops it. Do you know there are only seven distinct plots in all of literature?'

'So you told us in creative writing class.'

'Well, can't you see?' He is smiling now, suddenly sunny. 'This is no more than a variation on one of those great primordial plots.'

I am hopelessly confused. It is unbelievable that he should be sitting here beside me smiling. That he has shaken off every particle

144

of guilt like an animal shaking water from his coat. My mouth is open; I am literally gasping for air; I cannot believe this.

'I'm sure you'll understand, Judith, when you take time to think about it.'

My hands are shaking, and my mouth has gone slack and shapeless like a flap of canvas! I am unable to speak for a moment. Finally I sputter something, but even to me it is unintelligible.

'Ah, Judith, just think for a minute, where did Shakespeare – not that I am placing myself in that orbit for a second – but where did Shakespeare get his plots? Not from his own experience, you can be sure of that. I mean, who was he but another young lad from the provinces? He stole his plots, you would say, Judith. Borrowed them from the literature of the past, and no one damn well calls it theft. He took those old tried and true stories and hammered them into something that was his own.'

'It's not the same,' I manage to gasp.

'Judith, Judith, it is. Surely you can see that this is all a terrible misunderstanding.'

I am numb. Is it all a misunderstanding? I try to think. But at that moment Polly Stanley, doing her hostess rounds, discovers us. 'Oh, dear. I've been neglecting you two,' she frets. 'Here I am, about to serve dessert, and I don't believe you two have had a thing to eat.'

'We were having a chat.' Furlong beams. 'Judith and I were discussing some old established literary traditions.'

'Oh, dear, shop talk.' She giggles faintly, but she is clearly annoyed that we have confused the progression of her dinner, and she takes Furlong firmly by the arm and leads him into the dining room. He goes off gratefully, and I follow behind them, mechanically filling a plate with food. The beef is rather cold; there is a dull skin of grease floating on top, but I load my plate anyway.

Furlong hurries away to join a cheerful group in the solarium, and I am left.

Something is wrong. There is something I have not quite managed to assimilate. Furlong has declared his innocence. He has refused to accept a grain of guilt. He is emphatic; he is all sweet reason.

But then what in heaven's name have he and I been talking about?

'Judith.'

'Yes.' I am almost asleep. I had thought that Martin was asleep too.

'Why don't you come with me?'

'To Toronto?' I ask. Martin is leaving on the morning train for the Renaissance Society meeting.

'Why not come, Judith? Meredith could look after things here, and it would do you good to get away.'

'I could never never be ready in time.'

'We could take a later train.'

'I don't know, Martin. Richard is so sort of depressed that I hate to leave him.'

'Richard?'

'He still hasn't got a letter from England. What do you suppose has happened?'

'Oh, I wouldn't worry, Judith. Everything comes to an end eventually.'

'I suppose so,' I say.

I lie very still on my side of the bed. I am waiting for Martin to encourage me, to list the reasons why I should go to Toronto with him, and to brush aside my petty objections. I wait, believing that he will succeed in persuading me. I could wear my green skirt on the train; my long dress is back from the cleaners; I could have my hair done in Toronto; leave the rest of the ham for the children; phone them in the evening.

A street light shines into our bedroom from the place where the curtains don't quite meet, making a white streak down the bed. About two inches wide I estimate. It is very quiet. I can hear the Baby Ben ticking. Martin has set the alarm for six so he can make the early train.

Under the electric blanket I lie at attention. In a moment he will speak again, pressing me to go. But five minutes pass. I check the luminous dial of the clock. Ten minutes. I lift myself on one elbow to look at Martin.

He is very relaxed. His eyes are shut and he is breathing regularly, very deeply with a low diesel hum, and I notice that he is definitely asleep.

'Teenagers are often sulky, resentful and hostile,' writes Dr Whittier Whitehorn in the second of a series of articles on adolescent behaviour. 'And because they revolve so continuously around their own tempestuous emotions, they tend to interpret even the most general remarks as applying to themselves.'

I read these newspaper articles less for their factual information than for the comfort of their familiar, kindly rhetoric. I know that Dr Whitehorn can do no more in the end than counsel patience for 'this difficult and trying emotional time,' and I skip through the paragraphs to the closing line, noting with cheerful satisfaction that 'in the battle to win a teenager's confidence, sensitivity and patience are the only weapons a wise parent can wield.'

I let the newspaper fall to the floor, switch off the bedside lamp and try to sleep. When Martin is away the bed feels irrationally flat; I kick a leg out sideways, testing the space.

Dr Whitehorn's advice glows in front of me as I review in my mind the strange, almost surreal discussion I had with Meredith this morning.

She had slept late, and at eight-twenty on a Monday morning she was still tearing through the house looking for her books.

'Do you have your bus tokens?' I asked her.

She answered with a short and heavy, 'Yes, Mother.'

'Your books?'

'No. I can't find *Graven Images*.'

'What do you want with that?'

'I'm doing a report on it. For English.'

'A report on *Graven Images*?'

'Why not?' she asked sharply. 'Most people consider that it's quite good.'

'It's in my room,' I confessed.

'Do you mind if I take it?' she asked, elaborately polite now.

I replied with a tart, heavy-on-every-syllable voice, 'Not in the least.'

She whirled around, studied my face closely, and pronounced, 'You really do have something against Furlong.'

'I suppose.'

'What?'

I shrug. 'I just don't trust him.'

'Why not?'

'I used to,' I said, 'but not anymore.'

She was plainly alarmed at this. And hastened to his defence. 'Look, Mother, I think I know what you're saying. About not trusting him. I mean, I know what you think.'

'What?'

'I – I can't say anything. But just take my word for it that it's not true. It may look true at this moment but it isn't.'

'What isn't?' I asked.

'That's all I can say. Just that it isn't true.' And then with a touch of melodrama she added, 'You'll just have to trust me.'

'You'll miss your bus, Meredith,' I said suddenly.

Why had I said that? Because it was all I could think of to say.

Now, Dr Whitehorn, what do you make of that? Is that enigmatic enough for you? Perhaps I have remembered the conversation imperfectly. Or perhaps I have missed some of the underlying nuances, failed to exercise that sensitivity you're so big on. But why is my daughter talking in these tense, circular riddles? And why is it that I, her mother, can't understand her?

Nancy Krantz is a practising Roman Catholic, but she is also a believer in signs. Nothing so simple as horoscopes or palm reading; the signs she watches for and obeys are subtle and, to the casual eye, minuscule. She has come to rely on these small portents (a postage stamp upside-down, an icicle falling on the stroke of midnight, a name misspelled in the telephone book) but she is uneasy about admitting her faith in them. 'If I confessed to sign-watching,' she says, 'I would be asked to name a Regulating Agent who sets up the signs and points the way.' She prefers to see her omens as part of a system of electrical impulses which relate unlike objects, suggesting mysterious connections in another dimension of time. But admitting to such a belief, she says, leaves her open to charges of superstition or worse, marks her as a follower of the cult of intuition. Yet, she believes in signs and, furthermore, she believes that most other people do too.

Susanna Moodie, in one of her splendidly irrelevant asides, says much the same thing. 'All who have ever trodden this earth, possessed of the powers of thought and reflection, have listened to voices of the soul and secretly acknowledged their power; but few, very few, have had the courage boldly to declare their belief in them.'

And today I too have received a sign. Nothing flimsy like a dream, or mysterious like the surfacing of a familiar face: just a word, a single word, that started a chain reaction.

It began with a book by Kipling which Richard is reading for school. He hates it; it's dull, and he doesn't like the stylized way in which the characters speak. It is also rather long. Every night he brings it home from school, puts it on the front hall table, and in the morning he carries it back again, unopened. It is an old book from the school library. The binding is an alarming tatter of cloth and glue, and the dull-red cover is frayed around the edges. Its position on our hall table is becoming familiar, part of the landscape now; we expect it to be there. The lettering on the cover is shiny gold, and the title is curved along a golden hoop. Underneath it, curled the other way, is the name Rudyard Kipling.

Rudyard. Poor man to have such a strange name. Cruel Victorians to name their children so badly. I am struck by something half-remembered. Of course! Furlong's real name is Rudyard. His mother let it slip out once by mistake when she was talking to me. He never uses it, of course, and as far as I know no one else knows it. Rudyard. A secret name.

Secret. It hints at other secrets. Why is it I have kept this particular secret to myself? Why not? – it is a trifling fact – but it seems strange I've never mentioned it to Martin or to Roger.

Roger. Does Roger know about the name Rudyard? He did his Ph.D. thesis on Furlong. He is the authority on Furlong Eberhardt in this country; he cornered that little market about six years ago and stuffed it all into a thesis.

Thesis. Where is Roger's thesis? It is, without a doubt, where all doctoral theses are – on microfilm in the university library.

Library. What time does the library close? It's open all evening, of course. Until eleven o'clock. Martin is still in Toronto and I have the car.

The car. It is sitting outside on the snowy drive. The tank is full of gas and the keys are on the hall table. I can go. I can go this very minute.

Roger's thesis proved to be disappointing.

I had no trouble finding it. The librarian was helpful and polite: 'Of course, Mrs Gill. I'm sure we have Dr Ramsay's thesis here.' With her bracelet of keys she opened cupboards and pulled out metal drawers which were solidly filled with rows of neatly boxed microfilm. Hundreds of them. Each loaded with information which had been laboriously accumulated and assembled and then methodically stuffed away in these drawers where they were wonderfully, freely – almost, in fact, recklessly – available.

The films were arranged alphabetically, and it took only a few minutes before I found what I wanted: Ramsay, Roger R. – *Furlong Eberhardt and the Canadian Consciousness*. I yanked it out, electrified with happiness; it was so easy.

It took something like two hours to read it on the microfilm machine, but after the first hour I contented myself with skimming. For there was almost nothing of interest. And it was hard to believe that Roger with his fat yellow curls and Rabelaisian yelp of laughter could have produced this river of creamy musings. He had actually got past the examining committee with these long, elaborate, clustered generalizations, all artificially squeezed between Roman numerals and subdivided and re-subdivided until they reached the tiny fur of footnotes, appendices and, at last, something called the Author's Afterword? Hadn't someone along the line demanded something solid in the way of facts?

And the timidity, the equivocation – the use of hesitant pleading words like conjecture, hypothesis, probability – alternating with the brisk, combative, masculine 'however' which introduced every second paragraph, as though Roger had been locked into debate with himself and losing badly.

His design, as outlined in the Preface, was to survey the texts of Furlong's first four novels, collate those themes and images which were specifically related to the national consciousness – which were, in short, definitively Canadian – all this in order to prove that Furlong Eberhardt more or less represented the 'most nearly complete flowering of the national ethos in the middle decades of this century.'

I had to remind myself that I hadn't come to carp at Roger's prose or even to question his ultimate purpose; I had come to unseal some of the mystery surrounding the person of Furlong Eberhardt. I had come for biographical material, and in that respect Roger's thesis was useless.

The explanation for the omission of personal data came in the Afterword in which Roger explained at length that in his study of Eberhardt he had attempted to follow the dictates of the New Criticism, a critical method which, he explained, eschewed the personality and beliefs of the author and concentrated instead on close textual analysis.

It was a disappointment. And it came as a surprise to me after spending a year and a half painfully abstracting the personality of Susanna Moodie from the rambling, discursive body of her writing, that anyone would deliberately set out to purify prose by obliterating the personality that had shaped it.

A paradox. I saw that I would have to find another way.

Thursday. I wake up early remembering that this is the day Martin is to make his presentation to the Renaissance Society.

When I drove him to the train on Monday I noticed that, in addition to his battered canvas weekender, he was carrying a heavy cardboard carton to which he had attached a rough rope handle. His woven tapestries must be packed inside, although he didn't mention them to me. Were they finished. I wondered. How had they turned out? How would he display them? But because they seemed to represent something obscurely humiliating, I kept silent. The subject of the *Paradise Lost* weavings had been so assiduously avoided by both of us, that I felt a last-minute plea on my part to abandon the presentation would be ridiculous.

So I said nothing; only kissed him and told him I would meet his train on Friday night, and watched him walk toward the train in a wet sludgy snow, carrying the shameful suitcase, a ludicrous umbrella from Birmingham days, and the damning cardboard box that banged against his leg as he climbed aboard, set on his lunatic journey. Oh, Martin!

This morning at ten o'clock he is scheduled to give his talk and presentation. I have seen the conference program which says 'Dr Martin Gill – *Paradise Lost* in a Pictorial Presentation.' I will have to keep busy; I will have to make this day disappear.

It strikes me that I might as well continue my pursuit of information regarding Furlong. So after lunch I go to the big downtown library.

Granite pillars, crouched lions, the majestic stone entrance stairs covered with sisal matting and boards for five months of the year (what a strange country we live in!), a foyer imperial with vaulting, echoes, brass plaques, oil portraits, uniformed guards, a ponderous check-out desk and on it, purring and whirring, the latest in photostatic machines. Two librarians, tightly permed, one fat, one thin, stand behind the desk. The card catalogue snakes back and forth in a room of its own; surely I will find something here.

I carry books to a table, check indexes, cross-check references, try various biographical dictionaries and local histories, and conclude after several hours that Furlong had done a remarkable job of obscuring his past. He seems hardly to have existed before 1952 when his first book was published. I do find two passing references to a Rudyard Eberhart in the forties; the surname is misspelled and the geographical location is wrong; they are cryptic notations which I don't really understand but which I nevertheless make note of. I will have to go to the Archives if I am to discover anything more. Another day.

This is the library where Ruthie St Pierre works, and as I put on my coat and scarf, I think that it would be nice to stop and have a chat with her.

Her office is on the top floor, a tiny glassed-in cubicle in the Translation Department. I climb the stairs and go past a maze of other tiny offices.

And then I glimpse her through the wall of glass. She is bending over a filing cabinet in the corner and she is wearing a pantsuit of daffodil yellow and platform shoes of prodigious thickness. She finds what she wants, straightens up and turns back to her desk.

And I would have knocked on the glass, I would have gone in and embraced her and told her how much I had missed her all winter (for I *had* missed her) and told her how morose and sullen and seedy Roger is looking and how he doesn't even know where she is living or how she is getting along – but I don't go in because I can see plainly that she is in the seventh, perhaps eighth, and who knows – she is such a tiny girl – maybe even the ninth month of blooming, swelling, flowering pregnancy.

I watch her for a moment to be sure, to be absolutely certain, and then, quickly and quietly, I make my retreat.

Afterwards, driving home, I can't understand why I had left her like that. It was a shock, of course, and then too I hadn't wanted to create what for Ruthie might be a painful and embarrassing meeting. Certainly she had gone out of her way to avoid friends all winter.

When I was sick with the flu she had sent a basket of fruit – not ordinary apples and oranges, but wonderful and exotic mangoes, kiwifruit, red bananas, passion fruit, figs and pomegranates, and I had written her a thank-you note, mailing it to the library where she works. Once in the following weeks she had phoned to see if I was better. 'I'm fine now, Ruthie,' I had said, 'but how are you?'

'Fine, Jude, fine.' (She is the only person in the world who consistently calls me Jude.) 'I guess you know that Roger and I have called it quits.'

'Well,' I said uneasily, 'yes, and I'm sorry.'

'It's all for the best. Roger's not one for settling down, you know. Look, Jude, I've got to go. The big boss is prowling today. Bye for now. Keep the faith.'

'You too,' I said, not knowing which faith she referred to, but sensing that she had meant: respect my privacy, leave me alone for a while, ask me no questions, hold off, give me time, keep faith in me.

So I hadn't phoned her again, and today I hadn't rushed into the little office. But later I wished I had. She had looked both brave and fragile in her yellow suit, and I had been moved by the gallantry with which she concentrated on her filing cabinet, pencil in hand, and that enormous abdomen bunching up in front of her.

I am late getting home from the library. It is dinner time, and Richard suggests we send out for a pizza.

When it arrives Meredith and Richard and I eat it in the family room, along with glasses of ginger ale. The curtains are pulled and the television is on. It gets late and I should send the children to bed; I should remind them that this is a school night, but I am reluctant to break up our warm, shared drowsiness. Ruthie is far away now, as far away as a character in a story – did I really see her? Furlong Eberhardt seems foreign and trifling – what matters is our essential clutter of warmth and food and noise.

Eleven o'clock. The news comes on. More Watergate, more Belfast, another provincial land scandal, and then, to wind up the news, a lighter item. Dr Martin Gill is introduced. Unbelievably his face spreads across the screen.

There is not a sound from us. The three of us, Meredith and Richard and I, do not speak; we do not even move; we are frozen into place.

The interviewer explains that Dr Gill has startled both the art and the literary world by creating – he consults his notes – a graphic presentation of *Paradise Lost* (a famous seventeenth century poem, he explains to all of us out in TV land). Presented today at a national symposium on literature, it was a tremendous sensation. Two art galleries have already made impressive bids for the tapestries. 'Is that true, Professor Gill?' the interviewer asks.

The camera goes back to Martin. 'Yes, it does appear to be true,' he says with engaging modesty.

The interviewer continues with a long information-packed question, 'In that case, it would seem that this work of yours, quite apart from the interest in connection with the poem, has an intrinsic, that is, a beauty of its own.'

'I am really quite overwhelmed by the response,' Martin says, his slow, slow smile beaming out across the country. Beautiful. It is a highly individual smile, both provocative and sensual – I've never noticed that before.

The two faces fade, giving way to sports and weather, and the children and I slowly turn to look at each other. Richard and Meredith are staring at me and their mouths hang open with awe. And so, I perceive, does mine.

And then we leap and dance around the room; singing, shouting, laughing, hugging each other. We order another pizza, a

large special combination. Friends phone to ask if we've seen
Martin, and we phone Martin several times at his hotel and
finally, at two o'clock in the morning, we reach him and talk
and talk and then dizzy, crazy, mad with happiness we go
stunned to bed.

In the morning there are three things for me to read. First the
Toronto newspaper – a write-up on Martin and a picture of him
posing in front of the weavings. I peer intently at the tapestry
but, as in most newsphotos, it is smeary and porous and not
very effective. Martin though, with his nice white teeth open in
a smile, comes out very well.

PROFESSOR WEDS ART TO LITERATURE

English professor Martin Gill delighted his colleagues at the
Renaissance Society yesterday with a change from the usual
staid academic papers. His presentation was a pictorial
representation of *Paradise Lost*, Milton's famous epic master-
piece. Using the techniques of tapestry making, Dr Gill, a
distinguished scholar, used different colours to represent
the themes in the poem, and produced not only a visual
commentary on the piece, but a stunning work of abstract
art. Three art galleries, including the National Gallery, have
placed bids for the work.

The idea was intended as a teaching aid, Dr Gill explained.
'The poem is so complex and so enormous that often the
student of Literature loses the total Miltonic pattern.'

Dr Gill is the son of Professor Enos Gill of McGill
University, author of *Two Times a Nation*. His wife is Judith
Gill, the biographer. About the future Dr Gill denies that
he will divorce literature for art. 'It's only been a temporary

romance,' he said to reporters with a chuckle. 'I wouldn't trust my luck twice.'

Next I read a note from Furlong. I had been expecting this, knowing that once he realized he had tipped his hand, he would make haste to smooth over the traces.

My dear Judith,

I'm sure you regret as much as I our little misunderstanding the other night. I must say I was more than usually rattled by your startling lunge at my throat, and I'm afraid I lost what the youth of today would call my cool. No doubt I babbled like a complete looney. As soon as I realized what it was that concerned you – I refer to your mistaken impression that I had appropriated your plot for *Graven Images* – I came to my senses, and can only hope that you came to yours as well. Judith, my pet, we have been good friends for too long to allow this misunderstanding to come between us. The truth is, I value your friendship and, yes, I admit it, perhaps I did get a new slant from your aborted novel, but as I explained to you, writers are no more than scavengers and assemblers of lies. You have done me a good turn; perhaps I may be able to do the same for you one day.

Fondly,

FURLONG

Last of all I read an air-letter from England. At first, seeing the bright blue paper and feeling the familiar feather-weight paper, I thought that Anita Spalding had finally come through. But no, it is addressed to us, to Dr and Mrs Martin Gill.

Dear Dr and Mrs Gill,

First of all let me thank you for your very kind Christmas card. I apologize for the silence from this end. I will be passing quite near you in a month's time, and if it is not too terribly inconvenient, might I call on you? I will be in New York for a few days conferring with my publisher (I am about to have a novel published) and there is an item of some urgency which I am anxious to discuss with you. In addition, I am most desirous of making your acquaintance. Please do not go to any trouble for me. I shall be in the city only two nights (I have already secured hotel accommodation) and I should be distraught if my sudden appearance were in any way to inconvenience you.

I remain,

Your obedient servant,

JOHN SPALDING

P.S. We have had a nasty winter compounded by strikes and fuel shortages, not to mention my own distressing personal affairs. I trust all is well with you and your family.

Js

April

I wake early one morning. Something is amiss. A wet smell. What is it? I sniff, and instead of the usual hot metal smell of the furnace, I smell something different.

And I hear something. Water running. Someone has left a tap on all night. 'Martin,' I say. 'Are you awake?'

'No,' he says crossly. 'It's only six-thirty.'

'What's that sound, Martin?'

'I can't hear anything.'

'Listen. It's water dripping. Can you hear it?'

He listens for a minute. 'I think it's just the snow melting,' he says. 'It's the snow on the roof.'

I listen again. It *is* the snow; it's running off the roof in rivulets. It's pouring through the downspout.

And that explains the funny smell. It's the grey-scented, rare and delicate-as-a-thread smell of the melt. Spring.

At last.

Hurriedly I write a letter to John Spalding.

Dear John, (*I use his first name, availing myself of the North American right to be familiar.*)

We were delighted to get your letter and look forward to seeing you at the end of the month. Are you sure you wouldn't like to change your plans and stay with us? We

160

have plenty of room and would enjoy having you. Martin and I are anxious to know if you are bringing your wife and daughter. All of us, and especially Richard, of course, would love to meet them. If this note reaches you before you leave England, do drop us a line and let us know.

Our congratulations to you on the publication of your novel. We look forward to hearing more about it.

Sincerely,

JUDITH GILL

(*And then because no letter to or from Britain seems complete without a reference to the weather, I add –*) P.S. We have had a long winter and lots of snow, but spring is on the way now, and by the time you arrive the last of the snow will be gone.

JUDITH

In a week I had a reply.

Dear Judith, (*Aha, familiarity is contagious.*)

Thank you for your kind offer of a bed which I accept with gratitude. As for my wife, she and I have recently separated. Isabel has returned to Cyprus and has taken Anita with her. I supposed – wrongly I see – that Anita had written to your son about the chain of events. But then she has not even written to me very regularly. All this is rather upsetting to her, no doubt. Her mother has attached herself to a rogue of a gigolo, a cretinous beach ornament, and Anita has no doubt seen more of the unsavoury world in the last month than is good for her. The whole subject is exceedingly painful to me at the moment; thus, perhaps it is for the best that you know before I come.

161

There are daffodils blooming all over Birmingham. Truly glorious.

Best wishes,

JOHN SPALDING

Isabel Spalding gone off with gigolo! I picture him, heavy with grease, cunningly light-fingered and handsome. And her, pale and sluttish in a bikini. Poor Anita.

I hasten to tell Richard about what has happened in far-off Cyprus. For although the correspondence may be ended, it is better for him to know that there is, at least, an explanation; he has not been rejected; he has not accidentally written something offensive, he has not been the victim of a love that was unrequited.

I explained to him how traumatic a sudden shift in geography can be to a child, not to mention the catastrophic splintering of a family. He nods; he can understand that. Later she may feel like writing, I tell him. Yes, he says, perhaps. I gaze at him, trying to think of something further to comfort him, but he dashes away saying, it doesn't matter, it doesn't matter. Does he mean it? He has survived this long.

BUFFET SUPPER
WHERE – *62 Beaver Place*
WHEN – *April 30th, 8:00*
Judith and Martin Gill

We are going to have a party. Or, as my mother would say, we are going to entertain. Not that entertaining was something she ever did. Only something she would like to have done. She would love to entertain, she always said, if only the slipcovers were finished, if only the lampshade was replaced, if only Bert –

162

our father and her husband – would fix the cracked piece of tiling in the bathroom. She would entertain if she had more room, if the children were older and off her hands, if chicken weren't so expensive, if her nerves didn't act up when she got over-tired.

But she never did. Only her sister and a few close relatives and neighbours ever sipped coffee at our kitchen table. Mrs Christianson, Loretta Bruce who lived across the street in a bungalow identical to ours, which my mother always said needed some imagination as well as some spit and polish, a Mrs McAbee; timid women, all of them, who flattered our mother on her 'taste,' who asked, when they had finished their Nescafé, well, what have you been doing to the house lately? Then she would lead them into the living room, or bedroom or whatever, and point out the new needlepoint cushion or the magazine rack with its felt appliqué, and they would chorus again how clever she was. Poor swindled souls, believing that women expressed their personalities through their houses. A waste. But maybe they really thought differently.

The buffet supper was Martin's idea. 'We have to do something with him,' he said when he read John Spalding's letter. 'Besides we haven't had a party since December.'

I make up a list of people. About thirty seems right. Nancy and Paul Krantz, the Parks and the Beerbalms from the neighbourhood. And some university people. Furlong? I can't decide what to do with him, first thinking that nothing could persuade me to have him, the traitor, the thief, the liar. But it is unthinkable, on the other hand, to exclude him. Besides, I might have a chance to ask him a few searching questions. But then, I argue, why should I invite him, especially after that self-serving note he sent me in which he cast me in the role of a crazy woman who lunged and who took easy neurotic offence, and himself as the worldly artist, just self-depreciating enough to admit to minor dishonesties. Swine. But I had to invite him. For one thing, Mrs Eberhardt must be invited, for I could depend on her to draw out John Spalding, should he turn out to be someone who needed drawing out.

And what about Ruthie? Should I invite her? She would probably refuse, but just what if she didn't? I decided to consult Roger, so I phoned him at his office.

'Roger,' I said, 'we're having a party. Martin and I. In a couple of weeks.'

'Terrific.'

'John Spalding is coming from England. Remember hearing about him?'

'Sure. Your old landlord.'

'Right. Well, I'm writing invitations and I wonder if – well – I'd like to invite Ruthie, of course, but I don't want to put either of you on the spot.'

'Ruthie,' he mused.

'Just tell me what you think, Roger. Shall I ask her or not?'

A pause. And then he said, 'Sure. I suppose we can't avoid each other forever. Not in a city this size.'

'Okay then,' I said. 'Ruthie's on the list. I'll have to send this to her at the library I suppose. Or have you discovered where she's living?'

Another pause. Longer this time. 'Well, yes. I guess I do know where she's living.'

'Really? Where?'

'This may sound odd, Judith, but it seems she is staying at the Eberhardts' apartment.'

I am surprised. Very surprised. 'At Furlong's? Ruthie is staying at Furlong's?'

'Yeah.'

'Are you sure?'

'Sure I'm sure.'

'How'd you find out?'

'Well,' he paused again, 'the truth is – I guess I should come right out with it – the truth is I followed her home one night. From the library.'

'And she went to Furlong's?'

'Yes. Amazing isn't it. I couldn't believe it at first, so the next night I followed her again. Same time. Same place.'

Cunningly I asked, 'How did she look, Roger? I mean – is she okay?'

'Fine, as far as I could tell, fine. It was fairly dark, of course. I'd love to say she was thin and pinched and lonely looking, but actually she looked quite okay. I think she's even put on some weight.'

'Really?'

'Yes. And, of course, when I thought it over, it isn't all that extraordinary you know. Her staying there. They were always good to both of us, both Furlong and his mother. Sort of adopted us. And God knows she's safe enough with Furlong. As you well know.'

'Roger. This is sort of a personal question and you don't have to answer if you don't want to.'

'What is it, Judith?'

'Why is it you and Ruthie never got married?'

'I had a feeling you were going to ask that. Well, the answer is that Ruthie never wanted to get tied down.'

'That's funny.'

'Why?'

'Because she once said the same thing about you. That you didn't want to get tied down.'

'I suppose we both spouted a lot of nonsense.'

'Do you suppose things would have worked out if you had been married?'

'I suppose. I mean, it makes it a little more difficult to split if you've got all that legal mess.'

'Is it really over then, Roger? With you and Ruthie? Not that it's any of my business.'

'I'd hate to think so. I think she just needs time on her own. To sort things out. Get her head together.'

I had been sympathetic to this point, but suddenly I was enraged. 'Damn it, Roger. Damn it, damn it.'

He sounded alarmed. 'Judith, what have I said?'

'All that blather about getting heads together.'

'It's just an expression. It means –'

'I know what it means. But it's so – so impossibly puerile. Do you think anyone ever gets it all sorted out? Gets it all tidied up, purged out, all the odds and ends stowed away on the right shelves? Do you really believe that, Roger?'

'Sometimes you need time. How can you think in a thicket?'

'That thicket happens to be a form of protection. It's thinking in a vacuum that's unreal.'

'Judith, I just don't know,' he sighed. 'I just don't know anymore.'

'Look, Roger, I think I'll just send this invitation to Ruthie's office. I don't want her to know that I know where she's staying if it's such a big mystery.'

'Good idea.'

'She probably won't come anyway.'

'Probably not,' he said dolefully.

I am putting the finishing touches on Susanna Moodie. In the mornings I go over the chapters one by one, trying to look at her objectively. Does she live, breathe, take definite shape? Is the vein of personality strong enough to bridge the episodes? The disturbing change in personality: it bothers me. Dare I suggest hormone imbalance? Psychological scarring? It's unwise to do more than suggest. I'm not a psychologist or a doctor, as the critics will be quick to point out. But I do have a feeling about her. I wonder though, have I conveyed that feeling?

Aside from her two books about life in Canada, Susanna Moodie wrote a string of trashy novels, potboilers really, limp wristed romances containing such melodramatics as last minute rescues at the gallows and death-bed conversions and always, unfailingly, oceans and oceans of tears. She was desperate for money, of course, so she wrote quickly and she wrote for a popular audience, the Harlequin nurse stories of her day.

But one of the books she wrote has been invaluable to me. It is a novel entitled *Flora Lindsay* or *Episodes in an Eventful Life*. Astonishingly, it is Susanna's own story, or at least an idealized picture of it, an autobiography in fictional form. The heroine, Flora, is like Susanna married to a veteran of the Napoleonic Wars. Like Susanna, Flora and her husband (also named John) emigrate to Canada. Even the ship they sail on bears the same name, the *Anne*. Like Susanna, Flora has a baby daughter and, like her again, she has employed an unwed mother as a nurse for her child.

Thus, by watching Flora, I am able to see Susanna as a young woman. But, of course, it isn't really Susanna; it's only a projection, a view of herself. Flora is refined, virtuous, bright, lively, humorous; her only fault is an occasional pout when her husband places some sort of restraint on her. Did Susanna really see herself that way?

How do I view myself? – large, loose, baroque. Compulsively garrulous, hugely tactless, given to blurts, heavy foot in heavy mouth. Fearsome with energy, Brobdingnagian voice, everything of such vastness that my photographs always surprise me by their relatively normal proportions – ah, but that's only my public self. And Martin, does he view himself – now flushed with victory from the Renaissance Society – as a cocky counterculture academic? Does he carry a newsreel in his head

167

with himself as maverick star, a composed and witty generalist who nimbly leaps from discipline to discipline, who proved his wife wrong about the whole concept of poetry portrayed in wool, but resists saying I told you so? Just smiles at her his slow and knowing smile and thinks his secret thoughts, maybe wondering how he would look with long hair and that ultimate obscenity on middle-aged men, beads?

Susanna wrote *Flora Lindsay* when she was a middle-aged woman, and she had by that time suffered repeated trials, many births, several deaths, unbearable homesickness and alienation, not to mention a searing lack of intellectual nourishment. Looking back, she may have viewed that early life, that time of high expectations and simple married love as a period of comfort and happiness, seeing herself as the nimble and graceful heroine, not the prudish, rather shallow and condescending woman she more than likely was. She was so shrewd about her fellow Canadians that she enraged them, but nevertheless seemed to have had little real understanding of herself. Is it any wonder then, I ask myself as I send the manuscript off to a typist – is it any wonder that I don't understand her?

'Why hello, Mrs Gill.'

'Judith! Long time no see.'

'What can we do for you today, Mrs Gill?'

They know me at the Public Archives. I've spent hours and hours in these shiny corridors working on my biographical research, exploring filing cabinets, pulling out envelopes, and going through the contents, sometimes finding what I need, but just as often not. And always I am astonished at the sheer volume of trivia which is being watched over.

The librarians guard their treasures diligently, and they are unfailingly kind in their willingness to spend an hour, sometimes two or three, finding the origin of a single fact. But today

I don't need any help. I am quite sure I can find what I want.

Name and year: Furlong Eberhardt (possibly Rudyard Eberhart). As for dates, I work backwards from the present.

It takes longer than I think. A clue, tantalizing, leads nowhere, and I spend an hour in a cul-de-sac; just when I think I'm finding my way out, the reference turns out to apply to someone else. I press my hands to my head. Exhaustion. What am I doing here?

In the cafeteria I have a bowl of soup and a sandwich, and later in the afternoon I get lucky. One reference leads to another; I skip from drawer to drawer, putting the pieces together. And they fit, they fit! I have it. Or almost. I'll have to check at the Immigration Department, but I know what they'll say. I am already positive.

It's this: Furlong Eberhardt, Canadian prairie novelist, the man who is said to embody the ethos of the nation, is an American!

I want to hug the fact, to chew on it, to pull it out when I choose so I can admire its shiny ironic contours and ponder the wonderful, dark, moist, hilarious secrecy of it.

Rudyard Eberhart, born Maple Bluffs, Iowa, only son of Elizabeth Eberhart, widow.

Eligible for draft in 1949 (Korean War), left Maple Bluffs the day notice was delivered.

Landed immigrant status (with mother) in Saskatchewan.

Attended U. of Sask., was once written up in local paper as grand loser (shortest fish) in a fishing competition.

Began writing short stories under the name of Red Eberhart. Gradual shift to Eberhardt spelling, finalized with publication of first novel, 1952.

Christened Furlong by a kindly critic, after which he travelled from strength to strength until arrival at present eminence.

Ah, Furlong, you crafty devil.

I could not remember being so wonderfully amused by anything in all my life. My throat pricked continuously with wanting to laugh, and for the first few days it was all I could do to keep the corners of my mouth from turning up at inappropriate moments, so amused was I by the spectacle of Furlong Eberhardt who, with scarcely a break in stride, traded Maple Bluffs for the Maple Leaf; marvellous!

But in my delight I recognized something which was faintly hysterical, something suspiciously akin to relief. What had I expected to find? That Furlong had his novels written for him by a West Coast syndicate? That he might be guilty of a crime more heinous (murder? blackmail?) than mere trifling with the facts of his private life? That something unbearably sordid had poisoned his previous existence? Yes, I had been badly frightened; I admitted it to myself.

Poor Furlong. I could see it all: how he had – I recalled his own words – got into it innocently enough and then was unable to extricate himself, taking a free ride on the band wagon of nationalism and unable to jump off. Well, don't worry, Furlong, I won't betray you now.

Poor Furlong, so eager to be accepted, to be loved.

Poor Furlong, suffering in miserable and ageing secrecy.

Poor Furlong. Dear Furlong.

'Martin,' I whisper after the lights are out, 'what do you think of John Spalding?'

Pause. 'He seems okay,' Martin says. 'Not quite the nut I expected.'

'Me either. Where did I get the idea he was going to be short?'

'And fat! Christ, he's actually obese. Cheerful guy though.'

170

'Shhhhh. He's only one thin wall away.'

'Never mind. He should be dead to the world after those three brandies he tucked away.'

'Did you ask him about his wife? While I was making coffee?'

'Good God, no. What would you have me say, Judith? "Sorry to hear you've been made a cuckold, old man."'

'Did you at least mention that we were having a party tomorrow night?'

'Yes.'

'What did he say?'

'Just sort of rumbled on about how he hoped we weren't going to any trouble for him.'

'He certainly is different than what I expected. It's a good thing we had him paged at the airport or we'd never have found him.'

'Funny, but he said the same thing about us.'

'What?'

'That he wouldn't have recognized us in a thousand years. He had us pictured differently.'

'Really? I wonder what he thought we were like.'

'I didn't ask him.'

'I would have.'

'You would have, Judith, yes.'

'It might have been interesting. Don't you ever wonder, Martin, how you look to other people? The general impression, I mean.'

'No,' he said. 'To be truthful, I don't think I ever do.'

'That's abnormal.'

'Are you sure?'

'No. Maybe it's abnormal the other way. But still I would have asked him.'

I turn to look at Martin. The street light shining into our room and neatly bisecting our bed, permits me to study him. He is lying on his back, relaxed with his hands locked behind his head. And on his face I see a lazy, enigmatic smile. I peer at him intently.

'Why are you smiling, Martin?'

'Me? Am I smiling?'

'You know you are.'

'I suppose I was just thinking foul and filthy midnight thoughts.'

'About?'

He runs a hand under my nightgown. Stops in the slope between my thighs.

'Sshhhhhh,' I say. 'He'll hear us.'

'Fuck him.'

'Well, that's a switch.'

'Shhhhhhhh.'

Nancy Krantz came a little early to give me a hand with the party.

Martin and Paul Krantz and John Spalding drank gin tonics in the living room, and she and I flicked dust bits out of wine glasses with paper towels, heated pots of lasagna and cut up onions for the salad. My party menus (like my décor, my hair style, my legally married status) are ten years out of date; I know that elsewhere women, prettier than I and wearing gowns of enormous haute daring, are serving tiny Viennese pancakes stuffed with herring, or scampi à la Shanghai, but I willingly, wilfully, shut my eyes to all of that.

Nancy, larky and ironic, takes note of our female busy work; contrasts us to the booze swillers in the next room, lolling in chairs, dense in discussion. She is in violent good cheer, dextrous with the stacks of plates and cutlery, ingenious with the table napkins, setting out candles in startling asymmetrical arrangements, never for an instant leaving off her social commentary. 'Parties are irrational but necessary. Where are the extra ashtrays, Judith? If you set aside those parties which are merely chic, which exist just for the sake of existence, then there is something biblical and compelling about raining down a lot of food and drink on a lot of people gathered under a single roof at an appointed hour. Almost the fulfilment of a rite. And it brings on a sort of catharsis if it really works. And why not? You've got an artificial selection of people. The personalities and the conditions are imposed. A sort of preordered confrontation. I thought you had one of those hot tray things, Judith.'

'I do. Now where did I put it last time I used it?'

She finds it on the top shelf above the refrigerator, polishes it briefly, plugs it in. Ready to go.

Roger is the first to arrive. 'I know I'm early,' he apologizes, 'but I wonder if – you know – is Ruthie coming? Or not?'

'Not,' I tell him. 'She phoned to say she'd like to come but couldn't make it.'

'Why not?' he says, flinching visibly.

'She didn't say.'

'Oh, Jesus,' he says. 'I knew it.'

'Come on, Roger. I want you to meet John Spalding. He's in the living room.'

'Oh yeah,' he says. And whispers, 'What's he like?'

'I don't know. I've hardly seen him. He slept until noon and had an appointment this afternoon. We haven't had too much time to talk to him.'

'Nice guy?'

'Nice enough,' I say. 'But I'd stay off the topic of faithless women. He's in the midst, so to speak.'

'Righto,' he says, disappearing into the living room.

After that things get busy. The doorbell rings continuously it seems, and since it is raining heavily outside, I am occupied with

CAROL SHIELDS

finding places for boots while Richard ferries dripping umbrellas to the basement and Meredith hangs raincoats upstairs on the shower rail.

From the living room, the family room and even the kitchen there is a rising tide of noise, stemming at first from polite muted corners, erupting then into explosive contagious laughter, passing through furniture, through walls, melding with the mingled reverberations of wood, china, cutlery, a woman's shrill scream of surprise.

Bodies are everywhere, slung on couches, chair arms, kitchen coutners; I have to move two people aside to find room to set the casseroles down.

Our parties are always like this, a blur from the first doorbell to the last nightcap – fetching, carrying, greeting, serving, clearing, scraping, rinsing, smiling hard through it all, wondering why I ever thought it was going to be a good idea, and yet exhilarated to fever pitch and this on barely half a glass of wine.

I am at the centre of a hurricane, the eye of calm in the middle of ferocious whirling circles. Between the kitchen and hall I pause, trying to sense the pattern. What has become of John Spalding, guest of honour whom I have introduced to absolutely no one? Ah, but Martin has looked after him. There he is in the exact centre of the beige sofa, plumply settled with a brimming glass, a woman on either side of him and Polly Stanley, awkward but surprisingly girlish, on the floor at his feet. All are laughing; I can't actually hear them laughing, not over all this noise, but they are locked into laughing position, heads back, teeth bared.

Mrs Eberhardt is sitting in our most comfortable chair doing what she was invited to do, drawing out quieter guests and being charming and kindly and solid; she is the oldest person in the room. By far the oldest. Does she mind? Does she even notice?

Ben Stanley and Roger have their heads very close together

174

near the fireplace; they look vaguely theatrical as though they had selected this location to accent the seriousness of their discussion. I can tell from the confidential tilt of their heads that they are on the subject of departmental politics. Roger is mainly listening and nodding as befits his junior status. Beside he is apolitical; power doesn't interest him yet.

From far away I hear the telephone briefly pierce the hubbub. Two rings and someone answers it. Someone's baby sitter probably. No, it's for Furlong. Meredith goes to find him. She discovers him refilling a plate with salad, and she whispers lengthily into his ear. I can see them talking. Meredith is distraught; her hands are waving a little wildly. Furlong puts down his plate and hurries off to the phone where he talks for some time, cupping his hand to shut out the noise. After that I am too busy to watch.

Someone knocks over a glass of wine. I wipe it up. I set out cream and sugar on the table. Check the coffee. Someone arrives late and I find him some scrapings of lasagna and a heap of wilted salad. But later, serving plates of chocolate torte, I see that Meredith and Furlong are again conferring earnestly in a corner. After a moment they motion to Roger to join them, and the three of them huddle together. Furlong is explaining something to Roger who is leaning backwards, stunned, shaking his head, I don't believe it, I don't believe it.

'How about some dessert?' I break in on them.

There is a sudden catch of silence. Embarrassment. Uncertainty. A fraction of a second only. Then Furlong takes my hand gently, 'Judith, you must forgive me, but I'm afraid I'll have to leave early. Something unexpected has come up.'

'Nothing serious?' I ask, for I'm suddenly alarmed by their shared gravity.

'No. Not exactly.'

'You'd better tell her,' Meredith directs.

'Perhaps I'd better.'

'I wish to Jesus someone had told me,' Roger says, half-sullen, half-violent.

'What's happened?' I demand.

'It's Ruthie.' Furlong says her name with surprising tenderness.

'Ruthie?'

'I don't suppose you know, but she is – well – expecting a baby.'

'Yes, I did know, as a matter of fact.'

'I *knew* you suspected something,' Meredith says ringingly.

'Why didn't you tell me, Judith?' Roger charges. 'You never said a word to me about it.'

'I've only known for a few weeks. I saw her. At the library. She didn't see me, but I saw her. I haven't told anyone. Except Martin, of course.'

'You could have phoned me. One lousy phone call.'

'Look, Roger,' Furlong says, 'Ruthie didn't want you to know. That was the point.'

'I have a right to know. Who has a better right?'

'Well now you know.'

'How did *you* find out, Meredith?' I ask.

'I met her one day. A couple months ago. Downtown after school. Furlong had just taken her to the doctor. They sort of had to tell me. I mean, it was pretty obvious.

'Anyway, Judith,' Furlong breaks in, 'that was Ruthie on the phone a few minutes ago.'

'Don't tell me –'

'Yes. At least she thinks so. She's had a few twinges.'

'But it's not supposed to be for another two weeks,' Meredith says.

'What kind of twinges?' I ask Furlong.

'I don't know. That is, I didn't ask her what sort. Baby twinges, I presume.'

'How far apart?'

'I didn't ask her that either.'

'I'm surprised,' I can't resist chiding him. 'All those women in your books who die of childbirth. I would think you'd at least ask how far apart the pains are.'

'Twenty minutes,' Meredith interrupts. 'I asked her.'

'Christ. Twenty minutes.' Roger moans.

'I think I'd better be going,' Furlong says. 'She's all by herself. She's been staying with Mother and me for the last little while.'

'Yes. I think you'd better go too,' I say. 'And you'd better hurry. It could be quick.'

'Jesus.' Roger yells.

'Why don't you go too, Roger?' I say.

Furlong nods. 'Maybe he should.'

'What about me?' Meredith pleads. 'Can't I come too?'

Furlong glances at me. I nod.

'The three of us then,' Furlong says. 'Mother can get a taxi later. I'll just have a word with her on the way out.'

In a moment they are gone, and no one has even noticed their leaving. The wall of noise encloses me again; the volume after midnight doubles, trebles. In the living room I hear singing: 'There's a bright golden haze on the meadow.' Someone is rolling up the rug; someone else has found Meredith's rock records.

Unexpectedly I come across Richard who is carrying towers of coffee cups into the kitchen. As he passes I reach out automatically to pat the top of his head. The springy spaniel hair is familiar enough, but there is something different. My hand angles oddly; can it be that he's grown this much?

He shouts something into my ear. What is it? 'Great party, Mother,' he seems to be saying. Or something like that.

Finally they go home, the last guest disappears into the rain-creased darkness, the last car swerves around the corner of Beaver Place where all the other houses are dark. It's after three.

Martin carries a pot of tea into the wreckage of the living room, three cups on a tray, milk and sugar, a fan of spoons. 'Sit down, Judith,' he commands.

John Spalding, boulder-like, is still occupying the middle of the sofa. Has he moved all evening, I wonder?

At this hour we abandon the last remnant of formality. I kick off my silver shoes, note where the straps have bitten into the instep, and put my stockinged feet on the coffee table. Martin pours tea and hands me a cup.

'John,' he says, 'surely you'd like some too.'

'Please,' he booms from the cushions.

We sip in silence, letting the quiet wash over us.

Martin inquires about John's plane. It leaves at ten-thirty, a mere seven hours away. Martin has an early appointment, so it is decided that I will drive John to the airport.

'I hope the noise wasn't too much for you tonight,' I say.

'Not in the least. I enjoyed it all. My first glimpse of North American informality. Spontaneous and delightful.'

'I'm sorry your visit has been so short,' I tell him. 'We've hardly had a chance to get acquainted.' He waves aside my remarks with a plump hand. 'I feel I've got to know you well just by staying with you.'

'Perhaps you'll be back this way before long,' Martin says politely. 'Seeing publishers and so forth.'

'When exactly is your novel coming out?' I ask.

'In about a month's time,' he says. 'And that reminds me, there was a little something I wanted to mention to you both.' He looks around the room, glances at his watch and says, 'That is, if it's not too late for you?'

'Oh, no,' I say. 'It's not too late for us. Is it, Martin?'

'No, of course not,' Martin says wearily.

'Well, the fact is,' John Spalding says, making an effort to sit up straight, 'the fact is that this isn't the first novel I've written.'

'Really?' I say brightly. Too brightly?

'The truth is I've written several. But none of them was ever published. I never seemed to hit on an idea worth developing. Until a year or so ago.'

'Yes?' Martin and I chorus.

'Finally I struck on something workable. And I owe the idea for my novel to you. To your family that is.'

'To us.'

'You see, I have, in a matter of speaking, borrowed the situation of your family. A Canadian family who spend a year in England.'

'Your novel is about us?' Martin asks incredulously.

'Oh, no no no no. Not really about you, not exactly about you. Just the situation. A professor on sabbatical leave comes to an English university in an English city.'

'Birmingham?'

'Well, yes. But I'm calling it Flyxton-on-Stoke. They have two children –'

'A boy and a girl?'

'Right. You've got the picture.'

'But,' Martin says, setting down his cup, 'I suppose the resemblance ends there.'

'Almost,' John Spalding says, smiling a little nervously. 'You may find a few other trifling similarities. That was why I wanted to mention this to you. So that when you read it, if you read it, you won't think I've – well – plagiarized from real life. If such a thing is possible.'

'But how did you know anything about us?' I ask.

He laces his fingers across his broad stomach and, settling back, says, 'Firstly, one can tell something about people simply by the fact that they have occupied the same quarters.'

I nod, thinking of the bag of lightbulbs in the Birmingham bathroom, the sex manual under the mattress. Not to mention the shelf of manuscripts.

'Then there were the letters,' he continues.

'But we never wrote you any,' Martin says. 'The university arranged the letting of the flat.'

'No no no no no. I mean Anita's letters. The letters which your son Richard, a fine boy by the way, wrote to our daughter.'

'You read the letters?'

'Good Lord yes. We all quite looked forward to them. Anita used to read them aloud to us after tea. Ah, those were happier days. He writes a fine letter, your lad.'

Martin and I exchange looks of amazement. 'And your novel is based on Richard's letters?'

'Oh, no no no no.' Again he fills the air with a spray of little no's like the exhaust from a car. 'I didn't exactly *base* the novel on it. Just got a general idea of the sort of people you were, how you responded to things. That sort of thing.'

'And you just took off from there?'

He beamed. 'Exactly, exactly. But I did want you to know. I mean, in case you had any objections.'

'It seems it's too late for objections even if we did have some,' Martin says dryly.

'Well, yes, that is more or less the case. But you see, a writer must –'

'Get his material where he can find it,' I finish for him.

'Quite. Quite. Exactly. And, of course, I have changed all the names entirely.'

'What are we called?' I asked eagerly.

'You, I have called Gillian. Martin is simply inverted to Gilbert Martin.'

'Very clever,' Martin says, tight-lipped.

'We'll look forward to reading it,' I say 'Will you send us a copy?'

'You may be sure of that. And I'm more than pleased that you seem to understand the situation.'

'What I can't understand,' Martin says, 'is how you could find material for a novel out of our rather ordinary domestic situation. I mean, what in Christ did Richard write you about?'

'Yes what?' I ask.

John Spalding opens his mouth to speak, but we are interrupted by someone banging on the back door.

Martin rises muttering, 'Who on earth?'

'Oh,' I suddenly remember. 'It's Meredith. I completely forgot about her.'

'Meredith! I thought she was in bed hours ago. What's she doing out at three in the morning?'

She's standing before us, a raincoat over her long patchwork dress, her hair clinging siren-like to her slender neck. Her face is shiny with rain, but more than that, it is irridescent with happiness, and she says over and over again as though she can't quite believe it, 'It's a boy. It's a boy, seven pounds, ten ounces, a beautiful, beautiful baby boy.'

May

I t is the morning after our party, the first morning in May.

'I know what you think,' Meredith charges, 'and it isn't true.'

'What isn't true?' I ask. I am cleaning up after the party, putting away glasses, trays, and casseroles that won't be needed again. Until the next time.

'About Ruthie's baby.'

'What about Ruthie's baby?'

'I'm just saying that I know it looks suspicious. With Ruthie living at the Eberhardts' and all that. But it really isn't the way it looks.'

'Meredith!' I face her. 'You've got to make yourself clear. What is the awful thing that you suspect me of suspecting?'

'I know you've had doubts. I can tell by the way you talked about Furlong.'

'And how exactly did I talk about Furlong?'

'You said you didn't trust him. Remember? You didn't trust him anymore.'

'Well, that may be true.'

'But if you'd only listen to me for a minute, I'm trying to tell you that it wasn't Furlong at all.'

'What wasn't Furlong?'

Meredith sighs and with enormous deliberation pronounces, 'Furlong is not the father of Ruthie's baby.'

182

'But, Meredith, I never thought he was.'

'You didn't?' she says, her voice draining away.

'No, not for a minute.'

'But –'

'Whatever gave you that idea?'

She flounders. 'I just thought – well here was Ruthie, big as a barn – and living with Furlong – what else could you possibly think?'

'Well, I never once thought of Furlong. You can be sure of that.'

'But why not?'

Can it be that she doesn't realize about Furlong? Must I tell her? 'Meredith,' I say, 'don't you know that Furlong – well – surely you must have noticed – I mean, I just wouldn't ever suspect Furlong of anything like that. It's just not the sort of thing he would do. At all.'

For some reason she has started to cry a little, and, sniffing, she says, 'I thought for sure you thought it was Furlong.'

'No, Meredith, no,' I tell her. 'Never for a moment. Truly.'

She reaches blindly for a Kleenex, blows her nose and looks at me wetly, smiling somewhat foolishly, and I am struck, not for the first time, by her unique blend of innocence and knowledge; a curious imbalance which may never be perfectly corrected; out of stubborn perversity she wills it not to be, conjuring a guilelessness which is deliberate and which perhaps propitiates life's darker offerings. Always at such moments she reminds me of someone, someone half-recalled but never quite brought into focus. I can never think who it is. But today I see for the first time who it is she reminds me of: it's me.

Now that the warmer weather is here to stay, Richard and his friends are outside most of the time. Baseball has taken possession of him, but not only baseball. His disappearances are often long and unexplained, and his comings and goings marked only by the banging of the back door.

Lately the phone rings for him often, school friends, kids in the neighbourhood, and one day there is someone who sounds almost girl-like.

It is a girl. His startled blush confirms it. She begins to phone fairly often – her name is Maureen – and sometimes he talks to her for an hour or more. About what? I don't know because he speaks in his brand-new low-register voice and cups his hand carefully over the receiver. And says nothing to us.

But he is suddenly happy again. I knew, of course, that it would come, knew that he was too young and resilient to be slain by the death of a single love. Martin told me he would get over it. And I knew all along that he would.

But I never dreamed it would be this; something so simple, something so natural.

And so soon.

'Living meanly is the greatest sin,' Nancy Krantz tells me. 'Needless economy. It thins the blood. Cuts out the heart.'

It is so warm this morning that we have carried our coffee cups out on the back porch. 'What about thrift?' I ask her.

'A vice,' she says, 'but an okay vice. Thrift, after all, implies its own raison d'être. But cheapness for its own sake is destructive.'

We swap frugality stories.

She tells me about a man, a lawyer, well-to-do, with a beautiful house in Montreal, a summer place in the Rideau, annual excursions to London, the whole picture. And whenever he wanted to buy any new clothes, where do you think he went? You'll never guess. Down to the Salvation Army outlet. He'd pick through piles of old clothes until he'd find a forty-four medium. And that's what he wore. Pinstripe suits with shiny elbows. Navy blue blazers faded across the shoulders. Pants that bagged at the knees. Fuzzy along the pockets. He just didn't care. He'd take them home with him in a shopping bag and then he'd put them on and look at himself in the mirror. And he'd say, 'Well, I'm no fashion plate but it only cost me three and a half bucks.'

'Terrible, terrible,' I breathe.

And I tell her about a widow, not wealthy, not even well-to-do, but not poverty-stricken either. She owns her own house, has an adequate pension and so on. But she had to have a breast removed, a terrible operation, she suffered terribly, cancer, and after she was discharged from the hospital she took the subway home. The subway! With a great white bandage where her left breast had been. On the subway.

'That's awful,' Nancy says in a shocked whisper.

'But,' I tell her, 'that's not the worst part.'

'What could be worse than that?' she asks.

I hesitate. For Nancy who is my good, my best friend, has never been an intimate. But I tell her anyway. The really awful thing was that the woman with the sheared-off breast riding home on the subway was my own mother.

'Oh, Judith, oh, Judith,' she says. 'Why didn't I tell you?'

'Tell me what?'

She gives a short harsh laugh. 'That the man with the second-hand suits – was my father.'

After that we sit quietly, finishing our coffee not talking much.

What have we said? Nothing much. But we have, for a minute, transcended abstractions. Have made a sort of pledge, a grim refusal to be stunned by the accidents of genes or the stopped-up world of others. We can outdistance any sorrow; what is it anyway but another abstraction, a stirring of air.

*　　　*　　　*

Although Ruthie no longer believes in the Catholic Church, or in marriage for that matter, she and Roger have asked a priest to officiate at their wedding. Not a priestly priest, Roger tells us. Father Claude is young and liberal-leaning, attached in some nebulous way to the university; his theology is aligned with scholarship rather than myth; he is a good guy.

Both Roger and Ruthie want to have the ceremony out-of-doors, but this proves difficult to arrange. A hitherto unknown bylaw prohibits weddings in city parks. And going outside the city involves a procession of cars, which is aesthetically unacceptable to them. And, besides, what if it rains?

They ask us if they can have the wedding in our back yard. At first I protest that our yard is too ordinary for a wedding, having nothing to offer but a stretch of brownish grass, a strip of tulips by the garage, a few bushes, and a fence.

'Please,' they say, 'it will be fine.'

And it is fine. The sunshine is a little thin, but there's no wind to speak of; for the middle of May it's a chilly but reasonable afternoon. The boys next door agree to carry on their ball game at the far end of the street, so it's fairly quiet except for an occasional thrust of birdsong. Best of all, the shrubs are in their first, pale-green budding.

Ruthie wears a long, wide-yoked dress printed with a million yellow flowers, and Roger arrives in that comic costume of formality, a borrowed navy blue suit.

There are no more than fifteen guests, a few friends of Ruthie's from the library, Furlong and his mother (in purple crimplene and mink stole), a friend of Roger's who makes guitars, a gentle couple (he batiks, she crochets) who live in the flat beneath them. Ruthie has not invited her parents; they would not feel comfortable at this type of wedding, she thinks.

She and Roger and Father Claude stand near the forsythia, and

186

the rest of us wait, shivering slightly, in a circle around them. Ruthie, who has been taking a night course in jewelry making, has made the rings herself out of twisted strands of silver. Roger has written the wedding service which, surprisingly, is composed in blank verse. 'For you, Martin,' he says. 'I want you to be able to speak your part to a familiar rhythm.'

We all have parts which we read from the Xeroxed scripts Roger has prepared; even Richard and Meredith have a few lines. I read:

> Let peace descend upon this happy day
> That Man and Woman may with conscience clear
> Respect each other yet remain themselves
> Their first commitment to the inner voice.

(A dog barks somewhere, a delivery van whines around the bend in the road; a few neighbourhood children peer hypnotized through the fence.)

After the exchange of rings, Meredith fetches the baby from the pram (our wedding gift) which has been parked in a spray of sun near the garage. Bundled in a blanket, he is brought forward and christened Roger St Pierre Martin Ramsay, a name lushly weighted with establishment echoes. Roger loves it: 'Listen to that roll of r's,' he says. 'Pure poetry.'

A friend of Ruthie's sits cross-legged on the grass and plays something mournful on an alto recorder, and then we go into the house to drink Roger's homemade wine and eat the plates of exotic fruit which Ruthie has brought. And a surprise: Meredith has made a beautiful multilayered cake topped with flowers, beads and sea shells. Why sea shells? 'For fertility,' she deadpans.

The afternoon drains away, leaving us steeped in a pale, translucent peace, relaxed, very much at our ease, talking quietly, content, but it occurs to me finally that there is a distinct lack of festivity. Something is missing from this gathering. It's joyous enough, but it's contained and diminished in some way. At first – out there in the garden – I had felt something more, something trying to come into being. Perhaps it was those heavy iambic lines we uttered or the sombreness of the recorder music, but there is no fine edge of nerve in this marriage rite, no undercurrent, no sense of beginning or expectation. Why?

I look at the bridal pair. Ruthie rocks little Roger St Pierre while big Roger leans over them, bottle in hand, anxiously testing it against his wrist. Ruthie looks up at him, and what passes between them is a look of resignation, a little tired already, an arc of strain so subtle I think afterwards that I may have imagined it.

At five the baby begins to cry, and Roger and Ruthie go home. Everything has been fine, just as they said it would be. Just fine. I want to rush after them and tell them: everything will be just fine.

Near the end of the term the English Department has a dinner. As always it is held at the Faculty Club, and as always we eat thinly sliced roast beef, mashed potatoes, peas, and, for dessert, molded ice cream.

Whoever arranges these things, Polly Stanley probably, has placed me next to Furlong. (I have only this morning received a communication from the Citizenship Branch informing me that one Rudyard Eberhart was made a Canadian citizen in a private ceremony two years ago.)

'Well, well, Judith,' he says. 'How is Susanna Moodie these days?'

'About to got to the publishers,' I tell him. 'The typist has it now.'

'And did you do it this time, Judith? Did you really wrap it up?'

I sense his genuine interest. And am oddly grateful for it. 'No,

188

not really,' I admit. 'I have a few hunches. About the real Susanna. But I can't quite pin it all down.'

'You mean she never came right out and admitted much that was personal?'

'Hardly ever. I had to look at her through layers and layers of affectation.'

'Such as?'

'Oh, the gentle lady pose. The Wordsworthian nature lover. And the good Christian mother. She's in there somewhere, lost under all the gauze.'

'Perhaps,' he suggests, 'all those layers act as a magnifying glass.'

'How do you mean, Furlong?'

'Simply that instead of obscuring her personality, they may pinpoint her true self. Those particles of light which are allowed to escape, and I assume she occasionally emitted a few, can be interpreted in a wider sense. In a way it's easier than sorting through buckets and buckets of personal revelations.'

'If I'd only been allowed five minutes with her,' I tell him. 'Five minutes, and I could have wrapped it up.'

'I don't know, Judith. Perhaps you're expecting too much. People must be preserved with their mysteries intact. Otherwise, it's not real.'

'Do you really believe that?'

'From my soul.'

'Can I take that as a particle of light?'

'You may.'

'Well, next time I'm going to write about someone still living. So I can get those five minutes.'

'Who is it to be?'

'I'm not sure,' I tell him. Then I smile and say, 'Maybe I'll do you, Furlong.'

I have startled him; he isn't sure whether or not I'm serious. 'Surely you're joking?' he asks.

'Why not, Furlong? You're an established writer. Your life story might make fascinating reading.'

'It wouldn't, it wouldn't, I assure you. And besides I'm not nearly old enough to have a biography written about me.'

'Lots of younger people have been done. We could title it *A Biography Thus Far*. That sort of thing.'

'Judith, you're not serious about this?' He is genuinely alarmed now.

'Wouldn't you like it?' I ask teasingly.

'Absolutely not. I prohibit it. I'm sure I have that right. I refuse permission, Judith.'

'But I never asked.'

'Judith, you know perfectly well you can't write about a living subject if he objects.'

'But you're famous. You're in the public domain.'

'It doesn't matter. Now Judith, tell me you're not serious.'

I tell him. 'I'm not serious, Furlong. I was only joking.'

'Fine, fine.' He relaxes, goes back to his ice cream. 'And now let's talk about something interesting. Tell me what Martin has up his sleeve for the next Renaissance Society meeting. Tell me what you're planning for the summer. Tell me about the children. That's a lovely dress you're wearing. And isn't your hair different? Tell me, Judith. Tell me anything.'

Any day now John Spalding's book will be out. *Alien Interlude* it's called, and when I think about it, my breath hardens in my chest. We are about to be revealed to ourselves. It's a little frightening.

Martin and I have decided not to tell Richard about the book and the fact that he was unwittingly the provider of material. For one thing it would make a mockery of his own jealous secrecy, and he might, with reason, look upon it as an act of treachery.

Martin and I, a little nervously, await our promised autographed copy. 'Chances are,' Martin tells me, 'we won't even recognize ourselves. Remember what he told me when we met him at the airport? That we didn't remotely fulfil his image of us.'

'And he didn't look the way we had pictured him either,' I add. 'Which proves something.'

'Besides, writers use material selectively.'

'Right.'

'And another thing, Judith, I have a feeling that John Spalding is given to wild hyperbole.'

'What do you mean?'

'Remember the famous Cyprus beachboy who carried his Jezebel-Isabel away?'

'Yes?'

'Just before the party, when he and I and Paul were talking about Cyprus, he happened to mention that when they were there his wife had been rushed into hospital one night for an emergency appendectomy. And while she was there she fell in love with her doctor. It turns out the gigolo he wrote us about, is also chief surgeon in a Nicosia hospital.'

'I see,' I say slowly.

'Not quite the penniless, suntanned seducer we were led to believe.'

'Interesting,' I say.

And though I don't tell Martin, I too have reasons to believe we may not recognize ourselves in *Alien Interlude*. I have seen how facts are transmuted as they travel through a series of hands; our family situation seen through the eyes of pre-adolescent Richard and translated into his awkward letter-writing prose, then crossing cultures and read by a child we have never seen, to a family we have never met, then mixed with the neurotic creative juices of John Spalding and filtered through a publisher – surely by the time it reaches print, the least dram of truth will be drained away.

And there is something more. When I drove John Spalding to the airport, I brought up the subject of Furlong Eberhardt and his book *Graven Images*. 'Have you read it, by any chance?' I asked him.

'Curiously enough,' he answered, 'I did read it. Stuffy prose. But a ripping good yarn I thought.'

Astonishing. He hadn't recognized his own plot which had passed first through my hands and then into Furlong's. More fuel for the comforting fire.

Martin says we'll probably get a good laugh out of the whole thing. Maybe. Maybe not.

Anyway, we're waiting.

With true capitalistic finesse, Martin has sold his tapestries of *Paradise Lost* to the highest bidder, an anonymous private collector; for us it is a sizable sum.

And with true middle-class flair, we have used the sum to lighten our mortgage, a fact that depresses us somewhat. Have we no imagination?

'Let's at least go out to a good dinner,' Martin says. 'Let's go to the revolving restaurant.'

It has another name – something French and chic, but in this city it is always known as the revolving restaurant. We've not been there before, although it was constructed more than two years ago. It is expensive, we've been told, and quiet with subdued lighting and intimate tables; the food is rumoured to be good but routinely international, running from shrimp Newburg to steak Diane. Nothing unexpected. Just a nice evening out.

When we arrive at eight o'clock for dinner, having carefully made reservations, the restaurant is almost deserted. 'That seems odd,' I say to Martin. 'Hardly anyone here.'

'It's Monday night,' he reminds me. 'Probably pretty slow early in the week.'

'Why are we whispering?' I say over the tiny table.

'I don't know,' he whispers back.

There is another whispering couple next to us, and a short distance away is a party of eight. But, strangely enough, they aren't talking at all. I don't understand it.

But when the waiter comes to light our little claret-tinted hurricane lamp and my eyes become focused, I see what it is that is so puzzling about the group of eight: they are a party of deaf-mutes.

Their hands wave madly in the half-dark, making shadows on the walls, and their heads bob and dip over their shrimp cocktails.

The unreality of the scene enthralls me. I order mechanically – mushrooms à la grecque and pepper steak. Salad? Yes, Thousand Island please. Martin orders a bottle of wine, but I hardly notice what he's asked for. I am watching the delicate opening and closing of those sixteen hands.

Their animation is apparent, and that is what is so startling, for it is an animation which is associated with voices, with sounds, with noise. And from this circle of people, this circle of delicately gesturing hands, fringed and anxious as the petals of an exotic flower, comes a cloud of perfect, shapely silence.

They are eating their salad now. They indicate to the waiter the type of dressing they prefer, and something amuses them. Their faces break, not into laughter, but into the positions of laughter, the shapes, curves and angles of mirth. It is not quite real.

One of them has chosen filet of sole which the waiter expertly bones at a side table. This leads to a mad flurry of wrists and flying fingers, takes the shapes of birds, flowers, butterflies, the rapid opening and closing of space, shaping a private alphabet of air.

They are drinking wine, several bottles and, though it does not loosen their tongues, they grow garrulous; their hands fly so fast that they have hardly a moment to take up their knives and forks and, by the time they eat their desert, Martin and I have caught up with them.

There are three women and five men, all about the same age, in their late thirties probably. It must be a club, and this, perhaps, is their end-of-season wind-up.

What does the waiter think as he hands them their Black Forest cake and fresh strawberries? Will he knock off work tonight happier than usual? Sail home in the knowledge that he has shared in a unique festival of silence? Will he climb into bed with his wife and tell her how they pointed out their choices on the menu, how they were never still for a moment, how they, with consummate skill and, yes, grace, communicated even over the final coffee and liqueurs?

Martin watches them too. But for him it is no more than picturesque. A charming scene. He will remember it, but not for long.

For me it's different. I am expanded by the surreal and passionate language of their speechlessness. Their gathered presence enlarges me; we revolve together through the lit-up night. I can imagine them parting from each other after this evening is over, boarding their buses or taxis and branching out to their separate destinations, trailing their silence behind them like caterpillar silk. I can see them producing keys from pockets, opening doors, and entering the larger stories of their separate lives.

I am watching. My own life will never be enough for me. It is a congenital condition, my only, only disease in an otherwise lucky life. I am a watcher, an outsider whether I like it or not,

194

and I'm stuck with the dangers that go along with it. And the rewards.

They are rising from the table now. Shaking hands. Exchanging through their fluttering fingers a few final remarks. A benediction. I am watching them, and out of the corner of my eye I see Martin watching – not them – but me. He has no need of the bizarre. What he needs is something infinitely more complex: what he needs is my possession of that need. I am translator to him, reporter of visions he can't see for himself.

Though I can't be sure even of that. Furlong may be right about embracing others along with their mysteries. Distance. Otherness. Martin's wrist on the table: it hums with a separate and private energy.

But I note, at least, the certainties, the framework, the fact that he will shortly add up the bill, overtip about 5 per cent, smile at me from across the table and say, 'Ready, Judith?'

And I, of course, will smile back and say: 'Yes.'

Charleen

For my son John

Chapter 1

What was it that Brother Adam wrote me last week? That there are no certainties in life. That we change hourly or even from one minute to the next, our entire cycle of being altered, our whole selves shaken with the violence of change.

Ah, but Brother Adam has never actually laid eyes on me. And could never guess at the single certainty which swamps my life and which can be summed up in the simplest of phrases: I will never be brave. Never. I don't know what it was – something in my childhood probably – but I was robbed of my courage.

Even dealing with the post-adolescent teller in my branch bank is too much for me some days. She punches in my credits, my tiny salary from the *Journal*, the monthly child support money (I receive no alimony), and the occasional small, minuscule really, cheque from some magazine or other which has agreed to publish one of my poems.

And the debits. I see her faint frown. Perhaps she thinks that's too much rent for a woman in my circumstances. So do I, but I do have a child and can't, for his sake, live in a slum. Though the street is beginning to look like one. Almost every house on the block is subdivided now, cut up into two or three apartments; sometimes even a half-finished basement room with plywood walls and a concrete floor rented out for a few extra dollars a month.

Oh, yes, and a cheque for thirty dollars written out to Woodwards. A new dress for me. On sale. I have to have something to wear on the train. If I turn up in Toronto in one of my old falling-apart skirts, my sister Judith will shrink away in pity, try to press money into my hands, force me with terrible, strenuous gaiety on a girlish shopping trip insisting she missed my birthday last year. Or the year before that.

Food. I am frugal. Seth at fifteen undoubtedly knows about the other families, those laughing, coke-swilling, boat-tripping families in bright sports clothes who buy large pieces of beef which they grill to pink tenderness on flagged patios, always plenty for everyone. Second helpings, third helpings. We have day-old bread sometimes. Bruised peaches, dented cans on special. Only the two of us, but food still costs. It's a good thing Watson insisted we have only one child.

And what's this? A cheque made out to the Book Nook. I had forgotten that. A hardcover book, bought on impulse, a rare layout. Snapped up in a moment of overwhelming self-pity. *I'm thirty-eight, don't I have the right to a little luxury now and then? They never have anything new at the library – you have to sign up for requests and then wait half the year to get your hands on it and this way it comes all swaddled in plastic, you just can't get into a library book the same way, why is that?* I'll have to be more careful. But I'll have it to read on the train.

It's not only bank tellers. Landladies wither me with snappish requests for references.

'And why did you move from the west side, Mrs Forrest? You say you're divorced; well, just so you pay regular.'

And I do. I am my mother's daughter; cash on the line and cash on time. Her saying. She had hundreds like it, and although it's been twenty years since I left home, her sayings form a perpetual long-playing record on my inner-ear turntable.

The squeaky wheel gets the grease. No need to chew your cabbage twice. A penny saved – this last saying never fully quoted, merely suggested. A penny saved: we knew what that meant.

By luck Watson came from a family with a similar respect for cash; thus he has never once defaulted on the small allowance for Seth. The cheque is mailed from The Whole World Retreat in Weedham, Ontario where he lives now. On the fifteenth of every month; no note, nothing to indicate that we once were husband and wife, just the cheque for one hundred and fifty dollars made out to me, Charleen Forrest.

My name, the name Forrest, is the best thing Watson ever gave me. After being Charleen McNinn for eighteen years it seemed a near miracle to be attached to such a name. Forrest. Woodsy, dark, secret, green with pine needles, exotic, far removed from the grim square blocks of Scarborough, the weedy shrubs and the tough brick bungalows. Forrest. After the divorce friends here in Vancouver suggested that I announce my singlehood by reverting to my old name. Give up Forrest? Never. It's mine now. And Seth's of course. I may not be brave but I recognize luck when I see it, and I will not return to the clan McNinn.

McNinn: the first syllable sour, familial; the second half a diminishing clout, a bundle of negative echoes – minimum, minimal, nincompoop, ninny, nothing, nonentity, nobody. Charleen McNinn. No, no, bury her. Deliver her from family, banktellers, ex-husbands, landladies, from bus drivers who tell her to move along, men on the make who want her to lie back and accept (this is what you need, baby), friends who feel sorry for her. Deliver me, deliver me from whatever it was that did this thing to me, robbed me of my courage and brought me here to this point of time, this mark on a nowhere map, this narrow bed.

You made your bed, you can lie in it, my mother always said.

*　　*　　*

'You really ought to get into meditation,' the Savages urge me as we wait for the waiter to bring us our food.

'Why?' I ask.

They exchange quick, practised looks of communion. Doug receives from Greta the miniature nod to proceed.

'For true peace of mind, Char,' he says. 'For release.'

'Look,' I say in what I think of as my Tillie the Toiler voice, flip bravery mingled with touchiness, 'who says I need peace of mind? Or release. I'm not ready to die yet.'

'We're talking about serenity,' Greta leans over the hurricane lamp so that her tiny, earnest creases are transformed by shadow into grey, lapped folds; a seared, oddly attractive gargoyle of a face. Her pouched eyes plead with me.

'It's really far more than serenity,' she urges softly. 'It's an answer, a partial answer anyway, to – you know – fragmentation. Isn't it, Doug? I mean, it gives you a sense of your own personhood.'

'What Greta means is that it frees you from trivia,' Doug explains. 'And who, I ask you, needs trivia? You want to trim it off. Like fat off a chop. Cut it out.' He sits back, pleased with himself.

Doug and Greta Savage are in their mid-forties. Where do butterflies go when it rains? Where do hippies go when they get old? They get frowsier, coarser, more earnest or more ridiculous like the Savages; they look funnier in their beads and long hair, they become desperately reverent about their causes, they become almost stridently tolerant and fair-minded, but they do, at least, become more well-meaning. And more possessive of friends.

The Savages, of course, were never more than weekend hippies. Doug is a scientist, a botanist; in fact, he is a scientist with an enviable reputation, employed by a reputable university. They live comfortably, if a trifle unconventionally, on two acres of woodland at the edge of the city. Their kindness is exquisite, a work of art.

In fact, they fuss in an almost parental way about their younger friends, of whom I am one. Childless (who would bring children into a world like this?) they adopt their friends. I am perhaps their favourite child. They take me out to the Swiss Chalet for dinner – very campy, Doug says, but at least it's pure camp – and they invite me around to their house on Friday nights for red wine and crêpes; they confer enthusiastically about my mental outlook, and lately they have been hinting hugely that Eugene is not nearly good enough for me.

They have even offered to look after Seth while I am in Toronto next week. They are unbelievably fond of him and worry about the lack of a male influence in his life. (Eugene doesn't count; they see him as a negative influence.) Greta is concerned about Seth's natural ease with people and his ability to form indiscriminate friendships, and even Doug maintains that there's such a thing as being too well-adjusted.

'You don't want him falling into the middle-class-mentality trap with nothing but straight teeth to recommend him. Some of these high school teachers have never been out of British Columbia and the only reason they're teaching school anyway is for the tenure.'

'Well, you have tenure too,' I remind him cheerfully.

'Ah, but university tenure has a place,' he cries. 'It exists for a reason.'

'That's right,' Greta says.

'Why is it different?' I ask. They are buying me this meal, this succulent chicken. They are paying for the bottle of good French wine. I shouldn't argue with them, but watching Doug squirm out of his bourgeois lapses is one of the few entertainments I can afford. 'What's different about university tenure?'

'Simply that at university level it's necessary to project views which are independent, which are not a part of the university philosophy, the provincial philosophy, or any other damn philosophy. Tenure guarantees livelihood while permitting positive deviation in thought.'

'Hear, hear,' Greta says, and Doug scowls in her direction. (What would Brother Adam think of that speech? What would he think of that scowl?)

Slyly I ask, 'Don't school teachers need protection too?'

Doug spreads his hands. Charmingly. Paternally. 'Perhaps,' he admits. 'In the abstract. But look at the reality. All they really want is money enough to hustle themselves into split levels with their bowling, curling wives and Pablum-dribbling babies . . .'

'Pablum,' Greta murmurs. 'What was that we were reading about Pablum, Doug? Just the other day? In Adelle Davis.' Greta tends to forget exact references. Information sleeps beneath her pores, for she is an intelligent woman, but it is always disjointed, disassociated; she's never been the same since she underwent shock therapy. 'Remember, Doug, Pablum is a really remarkable food. Or something like that.'

'Vitamin B,' he pronounces, nodding in her direction. 'But getting back to meditation, Char; it's not a gimmick. It's a positive power. By forcing the brain to concentrate on an absurdity . . .'

Greta's tiny mouth puffs into a circle of protest, but he hurries on.

'. . . by forcing the brain to concentrate on an absurdity, you let the mind go free.'

'What exactly do you mean by "free"?' I ask. My question is not frivolous, nor am I stalling for time. Free might apply, for instance, to any of Greta's passions over the years – free love, free bird houses to the citizens of New Westminster, free thought, free food stamps, free university, free rest cures for the mothers of battered babies, free toilets in airports (she picketed outside one for two weeks in support of that cause), free lunch-time concerts for office workers, free tickets home for runaway teenagers. The word 'free' ranges wildly and giddily in Greta's consciousness, and often – a special irony – it means something like its opposite since she will go to extraordinary lengths to enforce her concept of freedom.

'Into peace,' Greta says, leaning toward me again. 'Into a larger peace than I ever knew. And I should know – if anyone does.' She is referring, Doug and I know, to the breakdown she suffered in her middle thirties and which she mentions at least once on every occasion we are together.

'But you've only been in the meditation thing for a month,' I remind her, playing my role of visiting sceptic.

'You're right,' she whispers, and the bones of her small face gleam with alabaster zeal through her unbelievably fragile skin. Such a tiny woman, she is far too small to hold all that latent forcefulness. But her voice is full, chalky with mysticism, rich with caring. 'I thought I knew myself before, but I was wrong. I didn't know what real peace was.'

'Really?' I ask.

'Charleen, Charleen,' Doug says fondly but disapprovingly. 'You are the ultimate disbeliever.'

'Me? A disbeliever?'

'You. Don't you believe in anything?'

I chew my chicken and think hard. They watch me and wait patiently for an answer. Their concern touches me; I want to please them.

'Friends,' I say. 'People. I believe in people.'

They relax. Smile. Sit back. We sip the last of the wine slowly and fold our red linen napkins with bemused inattention. Doug pays the bill and we rise together.

Arms linked, the three of us stroll down Granby. I walk in the middle as befits my position of erstwhile child. The street is full of people leaving restaurants, buying newspapers, walking dogs. Drunks and lovers lounge in the greyed shadows of buildings, and, though it is eleven o'clock at night, there is a Chinese family, a father, mother and a string of smiling children strolling along ahead of us. We are all melting together in this soft and buzzing electric blaze.

Greta and Doug walk me all the way home. I know they would like me to invite them up for coffee. They are pleased with me tonight, cheered by my declaration of faith and by the warmth of our friendship. They don't want to let me go. I sense their yearning for my straw-matted living room and my blue and white striped coffee mugs, my steaming Nescafé. Their faces turn to me.

But I shake my head. Hold out my hand. 'Thank you both for a good evening,' I stretch out that little word *good* to make it mean more than it does. 'I'll see you when I get back from Toronto.'

Doug embraces me; Greta kisses my cheek, a crêpe paper grazing. I get out my key and don't turn around again.

My apartment consists of three rooms on the second floor of a narrow, old house. I don't count the kitchen which is no more than a strip of cupboards and a miniature stove in a shuttered off end of the green and white living room. The living room has a serenity which does not in any way reflect my personality; perhaps I am attempting, with these white walls and this cheap, chaste furniture, to impose order and bravery on my life; it takes courage to live with wicker; it takes purity, a false purity in my case, to resist posters, beaded curtains and one more piece of handthrown pottery. There is a small, blue Indian rug on the wall which Watson and I bought for our first apartment. There is a painted plywood cube for a coffee table; Seth made it in grade eight woodworking class. A few books, some greenery on the window sill, a glowing jewel of a cushion which Greta Savage made for me years ago. My friends believe this to be a totally unremarkable room. This is not a room for a poet, they perhaps think, for it lacks even a suggestion of eccentricity or excitement; instead of verve there is a deep-breathing dreaminess, especially in the evening when the one good lamp throws soft-edged shadows halfway up the wall.

There are two bedrooms, a room for Seth and a room for me. That's all we need. His door is closed, but I push it open and in the rippled dark see his humped form under a light blanket. I listen, just as I listened when he was a baby, for the sound of his breathing. He has probably been asleep for hours. His tuba sits on the floor on the tiny hooked rug I made for him years ago. (A blue swan swimming on a pale yellow sea.) I move the tuba beside his dresser, tiptoeing, but there is no need to worry about waking him up. He sleeps deeply, easily, and his ability to sleep is one more point of separation between us, another notch for evolutionary progress. I almost always sleep poorly, jerkily, my nights filled either with hollowed-out insomnia or strings of short, ragged kite-tail dreams that flap and jump in the dark and leave me sad-eyed in the morning, like the worndown women in coffee commercials. Seth's nervous system seems to have been put together by agents other than Watson or me; Watson with his combination of creative energy and lack of talent was predestined to fall apart. And I, suffering from a lack of bravery, must expend all my energies preparing for the next test. And the next. And the next.

Seth. I adore his blunt normalcy and good health. His unspectacular brain. His average height and weight. His willing-ness to please. His ability to go along with things, not objecting for instance, to staying with Greta and Doug for a week, even though he knows they will stuff him with peanut and raisin casseroles and counsel him endlessly on attaining personal peace. He just smiled when I told him. Smiled and nodded. Sure, sure, he said. And when I told him that Eugene might be going along with me to Toronto, all he said was, great, great. Ah Seth, I do love you. Sleeping there, breathing. Keep puffing your tuba, keep smiling, keep on, and, who knows, you might get out of this unscathed.

There's a whole list of things to be done before I leave for Toronto. First, I must pick up my pay cheque at the university, and this means seeing Doug Savage again after having bid him a final goodbye in front of my apartment last night. Something inside me cringes at the carelessness of this oversight; it is the sort of messy misarrangement I create instinctively. Tag-ends. Clutter. A lack of cleanliness. An inability to end things neatly. What Brother Adam would classify as non-discipline. But there is no question of my not going to pick up the cheque; I need the money.

Why in the seven years on the *Journal* have I never thought of having the cheque mailed to me at home or, better yet, sent directly to the bank? Other people make such easy and sensible arrangements without thinking. But from my first month on the *Journal*, Doug has handed me my cheque personally, more often than not with his inked signature still wet on the paper. He pushes it my way off-handedly, avoiding my eyes; sometimes it comes floating loosely on top of a pile of proofs. It is as though a more formal payment might rupture our relationship, might make of my job on the *Journal* something serious and official instead of a part-time piece of noblesse oblige, a pittance for an abandoned woman, a soupçon for the bereft wife of his former friend. Nevertheless the cheque is never late, an acknowledgement that though my position might be undefined, my need for cash is absolute and recurring.

Not that I don't work hard. The *National Botanical Journal* comes out quarterly, and except for selecting the articles which are to appear, I do everything. The *Journal* is a generally dull and uninspired affair with its buff-and-brown cover and the names of the main articles listed on the front. Our next issue is devoted almost entirely to new disease-proof grains with a short piece on 'Unusual Alberta Wildflowers' tacked on as a sort of dessert. It is a periodical (it would be too much to call it a magazine) by academics and for academics.

Doug is the nominal editor and I am the only employee. First I edit the manuscripts which is a long, picky, and sensitive tightrope of a job; it is essential not to under-edit since clarity and a moderate level of elegance are desirable, but I must not over-edit and thereby obliterate personal style and perhaps injure the feelings of the submitting authors. (Will he object if I pencil out his 'however'? Will he fly into a tantrum when I chop his sentences in two or sometimes three or even four? Will he mind if I switch the spellings to Canadian standard or rearrange the tangle of his footnotes?) Sometimes I consult Doug.

'You worry too much, Char,' is what he usually says, or 'Screw the bastard, he's lucky we're going to run his lousy article at all.' Doug inherited the editorship of the *Journal* from Watson who abandoned it along with his other responsibilities, and not surprisingly he regards it as a time-consuming stepchild. He is entirely unwilling to worry about the theoretical sensitivities of contributing botanists. But I do; I rarely make a change in an article without anticipating a blast of indignation. In actuality it hardly ever happens, because, for some reason, these unseen scientists are astonishingly submissive to the slash of my red pencil; they quite willingly accept mutilations to their work, the dictates of Charleen Forrest, a thirty-eight-year-old divorcée who knows nothing about botany and who has no training beyond high school unless you count a six-week typing course. Amazing.

After the galley proofs and the layout dummy come the vandykes, these blueprints of the final round, and then another issue is on its way. Time to begin the next. It is relentless but sustaining. Maybe rhythm is all I need to keep me going.

I only work in the mornings since there isn't enough money to pay a full-time employee, and theoretically my afternoons are saved for the writing of poetry, what Doug Savage calls the practice of my craft. Craft. Craft. As though one put poetry together from a boxed kit. Not that it matters much what you call it, for it is a fact that in the last two years I've hardly written a line. What once consumed the best of my energies now seems a dull indulgence.

My afternoons just melt away. Sometimes I meet Eugene if he isn't too busy at the office. I shop for groceries, read, worry. I write letters to anyone I can think of, for chief among my diseases is an unwillingness to let friendships die a natural death. I cling, pursuing old friends, dredging up school mates from Scarborough like Sally Cork and Mary Lou Lester. I write to Mary Lou's mother, too, and to her sister in Winnipeg whom I scarcely know. I badger the friends Watson and I once had with my insistent, pressing six pages of hectic persevering scrawl. I even write regularly to a woman named Fay Cousins in northern California who once shared a hundred-mile bus ride with me. And for the last fifteen months I've been writing to Brother Adam, the only correspondent I've ever had who approaches me in scope and endurance.

I cannot let go. It is a kind of game I play in which I pretend, to myself at least, that I, with my paper and envelopes, my pen and my stamps, that I am one of those nice people who care about people. A lovely person. A loving person, a giving person. I dream for myself visions of generosity and kindness. I *care* about Fay Cousins' drinking problem, about Mrs Lester's ulcerated colon, about Sally's home freezing and Mary Lou's fat braggart of a husband. I *care* about them. At least I want to care.

To my mother I write once a month. And that's hard enough.

CHARLEEN

To my sister Judith perhaps three or four times a year; I would write to Judith more often if I were not so baffled by her lack of neuroses; we had the same childhood, but she somehow survived, and the margin of her survival widens every year so that, though I can talk easily enough to her when I see her, I cannot bear the thought of her reading my letters in the incandescent light of her balanced serenity. Does she understand? Probably not.

And Watson. I never write to Watson. Nor does he write to me; no one hears from him anymore except Greta who, by trading on a belief that she and Watson are partners in emotional calamity, manages to elicit an occasional note from him. Watson is not cruel; it is only that he is missing one or two of the vital components which happy and normal people possess. Nevertheless, I ache to write to him; just thinking about it makes my fingers want to curl around the words, to smooth the paper. I *long* to write to him. He lives in a commune in Weedham, Ontario, with God only knows who, and all he sends me is child support money. Every month when it comes I examine the handwriting on the cheque, hoping it will contain some kind of declaration, but it is always the same; one hundred and fifty dollars and no cents. Signed, Watson Forrest. That's all.

Sometimes I go for walks in the afternoons and quite often I go all the way to Walkley Street, past the house where Watson and I used to live. We paid exactly $17,900 for that house, and all but one thousand dollars was mortgaged. It is in much better condition than it used to be. The hedges are shaped into startled spheres, and pink and white petunias tumble out of nicely-painted window boxes. There is a new stone patio by the roses, my roses, where I used to park Seth's pram. The curtains are generally drawn in the afternoons as though the owners, an English couple in their fifties I'm told, are anxious about their polished antiques and Chinese carpets. A ginger dachshund yelps from a split cedar

213

pen. An electric lawnmower gleams by the garage. I am unfailingly reassured by these improvements – I rejoice in them, in fact – for I can foresee a time when this house will pass out of our possession altogether, piece by piece replaced so that nothing of the original is left.

At the university, which I reach by a twenty-minute bus ride, I work in a cubicle of the Natural Science Building. On my door there is a sign which says: 304 Botanical Journal. I have one desk equipped with a manual typewriter, a gunmetal table and matching wastebasket, a peach-coloured filing cabinet with three drawers, two moulded plastic chairs and one comfortable, worn, plushy typing chair in bitter green. There are Swedish-type curtains in a subtle bone stripe, by far the best feature of the room, and the walls are painted a glossy café au lait. From the ceiling a fluorescent tube pours faltering institutional light onto my desk. Oddly enough there is no lock on my door. All the other offices on the third floor have locks, but not mine; the lack of a lock and key seems to underscore the valuelessness of what I do. This might be a broom cupboard. Nothing worth guarding here.

This morning when I arrive, Doug is already in the office, bending over the pile of manuscripts on my desk. 'Hiya, Char,' he says, not bothering to turn around. 'I'm just seeing what we should stick in the fall issue.'

Though it is only May, we are already beginning to think about the autumn number; we are perpetually leaping across the calendar in six-month strides, so that this job, besides paying only enough to keep me from starving, simultaneously deprives me of a sense of accomplishment. Completion, realization, fulfilment are always half a year away, a point in time which, when finally reached, melts into so much vapour. Now the fall issue is being conceived before

214

the summer has taken shape and before the spring is even back from the printers.

Clearly Doug has been expecting me. Without taking his eyes off the pile of manuscripts, he slides my pay cheque across the desk. I accept it wordlessly, fold it in two lengthwise (I can never remember if it is all right to fold a cheque) and put it in my wallet. The awkward moment passes, and now Doug turns and smiles at me. 'Well, are you all set for tomorrow?'

'Almost,' I tell him. 'Just a few odds and ends to clear up.'

'Greta and I thought we'd pick up Seth right from school tomorrow. That okay with you?'

'Oh, no, Doug. Really, that's not necessary at all. He can get a bus.'

'No trouble, Char. We'd like to.'

'No, that's just too much bother. It's enough that you've offered to have him.' I'm playing my game again, protesting, modest, conciliatory, anxious to please.

'For Christ's sake, Charleen, the poor kid will have his suitcase and tuba and everything. We'll pick him up.'

'But he's already planned to come out to your place by bus. He mentioned it this morning.'

'Look, Char,' he sighs, 'Greta wants it this way. She wants to pick him up. You know how she gets. I promised her we could do it this way.'

I nod. When Doug and I are alone together without Greta, our relationship undergoes a radical reshaping. We drop all pretense of Greta's being our friend and equal; instead we conspire to protect her, to smooth her path, to bolster her up, knowing full well that her present tranquillity is a fragile growth. If she has made up her mind to pick up Seth from school, it must be done.

'Sure,' I tell Doug, 'I'll tell him. I'll make sure he understands that you'll be along.'

CAROL SHIELDS

'Ah, Char,' he says fondly, 'you're an angel.'

Endearments. That's another of the ways in which we change when we're alone. Doug calls me angel, sweetheart, love, baby – words he would never use if Greta were with us, words which are really quite meaningless but which allow him to toy with certain possibilities of freedom. For he is just slightly in love with me, so slightly that I would never have recognized it, were it not that I find myself responding with sprightly manifestations of girlishness. I grin at him wickedly across the desk. I say 'shit' when the printer is late with the proofs. Sometimes I poke a pencil in my hair, give a little catstretch at eleven-thirty, put my stockinged feet on the chair, call him 'Bossman' in a throaty, southland drawl, and grumble about the work he loads on me.

'I need a week away from here,' I tell him. 'I've had it with tubers and pollen. And mangled prose structure.'

'I hope you get a chance to relax when you're away, Char,' he says searchingly. 'You need a chance to get away from here and think.'

'Now what exactly do you mean by that?' I demand.

'Nothing, nothing. Just that we all need a break now and then.'

'Now don't go backing down, Doug. I want to know why you think I need to get away and think. Just exactly what do you believe I should be thinking about?'

'Well,' he hesitates a small, slightly theatrical instant, 'to be honest, you might think about where you're headed. Greta and I have been wondering if you weren't, you know, on the wrong track as it were.'

'I suppose you must be talking about Eugene?'

'Not just about Eugene, not only that. But, well, what he represents. The whole bag you might say.'

'You've only met him once,' I say waspishly. 'And that was just for a few minutes.'

216

'Now, now, Char, don't go getting defensive.'

'What am I supposed to do? I happen to be very fond of Eugene. *Very* fond.'

He waves aside my words. 'I can tell you aren't all that sure of yourself about where you're going with Eugene.'

'How can you be so sure?'

'Do you really want to know?'

'I asked you.'

'Because you never talk about his job.'

'Aha,' I say triumphantly, 'I knew that's what was bothering you.'

'Be honest, Charleen baby. Doesn't it bother you a bit?'

'It's an honest profession,' I declare piously. 'My mother, for one, would think it was the height of success.'

'But what do you think?'

'What's wrong with it?'

'An orthodontist. Think about it! A guy who stands around all day putting little wires on little kids' teeth . . .'

'Somebody has to do it,' I say. My head aches and I feel a desire to squeeze my eyes shut and weep, but I can't betray Eugene so easily. 'It's a service,' I sum up.

'Some service. Milking the middle class. God! Dispensing ersatz happiness through the pursuit of perfect middle-class teeth.'

'Well, he did a good job on Seth.'

'Seth! The poor kid. Thrown to the vanity peddlers before he's old enough to protest.'

'Look, Doug,' I say, shaping the words into hard little rectangles, 'it was the bite. Get it? It wasn't to make him beautiful, it was to correct his bite.'

'And on your salary?' Doug mutters softly in his puzzled surrogate-father voice. 'How any guy could take fifty bucks a month out of your salary and not be second cousin to a crook –'

Should I tell him that Eugene would not take any money after the first twenty-five dollar consultation? That he steadfastly refused, once even tearing my cheque into little pieces? Better not risk the suggestion that I was a woman willing to sell her body for dental care, that a pathetically self-sacrificing compulsion had driven me to an absurd martyrdom; it wouldn't take Doug more than a minute to reach that kind of interpretation. 'Let's just drop the whole subject of Eugene,' I say.

'All I'm saying is that it's probably a good thing you're getting away with him for a few days. To sort of see things *in context*.' His voice softens. 'I'm only thinking of what's best for you, Char.'

'Okay, okay,' I say, stuffing the manuscripts in a drawer and slamming it shut.

Why is it I inspire such storms of preaching? It's not only Doug Savage; my most casual acquaintances press me with advice. Doug, though, has become a full-time catechizer; great gushes of his energy are channelled into the sorting out of my life. In an obscure way he seems to feel responsible for Watson's defection, as do all the friends Watson and I once had, as if they shared a guilty belief that their presence in our lives may have proved the fatal splinter. Which is nonsense, of course. But Doug seems to feel he must look after me. He invented this job for me as a therapeutic and practical rescue mission, and at the time I was grateful. I still am. But isn't it time he got back to his plants, I want to tell him. Or concentrated a little more on Greta who rocks continuously between birdlike vagary and thorny obsession, between her wish to reconcile and her appetite for separation. Does Doug realize that Greta, after all these years, still smothers Watson with letters? That she is perhaps outdoing herself as Seth's fairy godmother, wishing him well but not knowing how to make an acceptable present of her particular caring magic? She is – why doesn't Doug see it? – she is possibly slipping into darker and wilder delusions than he realizes.

But since kindness is a sort of hobby with me, a skill which I feel compelled to perfect, I try to look at Doug kindly. It is not really his fault, I tell myself, that Doug judges Eugene harshly. It is part of his generation, this bias, my generation too, to see people in terms of their professions. It is, after all, a logical outgrowth of the work ethic; vocation forms the spiritual skin by which we are recognized and rewarded. Doug Savage is a botanist, a specialist in certain forms of short ferns. He is defined by his speciality just as his ferns are defined by their physical properties. His wife Greta is saved from genuine ordinariness by the fact that she is a professional weaver. Doug's curriculum vitae for her would run: Greta Savage, weaver, wife. Her actual weaving is immaterial; it is *being* a weaver which endows her with worth. In the same way he thinks of me pre-eminently as a poet, a kindly classification, since I am more clerk than poet these days. He is able to ignore the lapse of my talent just as he has been able to ignore the presence of Eugene Redding for the last two years.

The Savages' objection to Eugene is, I sometimes suspect, rather lumpily conceived and certainly it is seldom mentioned: silence says it all. For the most part they have chosen to ignore Eugene just as they have ignored my other, briefer liaisons: with Bob the insurance adjuster, with Maynard the dry-cleaning executive, Thomas Brown-Davis the tax lawyer (lawyers are okay but only if they practise labour law or take on prickly civil liberties cases – even then their value may be marked down by a hyphenated name or a preference for handmade shirts).

At parties Doug Savage always introduces me by saying, this is Charleen Forrest, you know, the poet. Then he disappears leaving me to explain with enormous awkwardness that my last book came out more than three years ago and that, though I still dabble a little, poetry is part of my past now. What I don't bother to explain is that having written away the well of myself, there is nowhere to go. The only other alternative would be to join that corps of half-poets, those woozy would-bes who burble away in private obscurities, the band of poets I've come to think of, in my private lexicon, as 'the pome people'. They are the ones for whom no experience is too small: brushing their teeth in the morning brings them frothing to epiphany. Sex is their private invention, and they fornicate with a purity which cries out for crystallization. They can be charming; they can be seductive, but long ago I decided to stop writing if I found myself becoming one of them.

Both Doug and Greta fear for the future of Seth, that his straight, white teeth and middle-class amiability may propel him toward the untouchable ranks: public relations, stock brokerage, advertising, or even, given the situation, orthodontics.

And if Doug Savage had been acquainted with Eugene for twenty-five years instead of twenty-five minutes, he would still think of him as Eugene the Orthodontist. Pseudo-scientific, or so Doug believes, cosmetic-oriented, a man who tinkers with the design of nature. A shill for pearly teeth. A charlatan with carpeted waiting room, expensive machinery and golf-club manners. Doug sees the already-suspect profession of orthodontia as being coupled with a lack of creativity or discovery; if only he were a real dentist who dealt with the reality of pain and suffering. Eugene, sadly, is in one of the repair professions, a fact which for Doug places the seal on his insignificance. And worse, as far as the Savages are concerned, Eugene is abundantly rewarded for what he does.

I sigh heavily, suddenly weary, and Doug says, 'Don't give a thought to the manuscripts, Char.' He nods in the direction of my desk. 'They can wait.'

'Fine, fine,' I say absently. I am thinking of all the things I have to do before leaving. Laundry, packing, phone Eugene, make sure Seth has bus fare for school. And there must be something else. Something I've forgotten. Laundry, packing, phone, bus fare? Something is missing.

The wedding present!

'I never bought a wedding present,' I cry out. 'I completely forgot about it.'

Doug says nothing.

'How could I forget!' I marvel. And then I add, 'Do you think there's something Freudian about that? Forgetting to buy my own mother a wedding present?'

He shrugs. Drums his fingers on my desk. He is determinedly nonchalant about my oversight, but I can see by the faint, grey frown on his face that he has stored it carefully away. Something Freudian. Hmmm. Yes.

When my mother wrote from Toronto early in April to tell me that she was planning to remarry, the first thing I thought of was her left breast. No, not her left breast but the place where her left breast had been before the cancer.

What I pictured was a petal of torn flesh, something unimaginably vulnerable like the unspeakable place behind a glass eye or the acutely sensitive and secret skin beneath a fingernail. A pin-point of concentrated shrinking pain. A wound almost metaphysical, pink edged, so tender that a breath or even a thought could break it open.

I haven't seen her since her operation which was two years ago. In fact, I have not seen her for five years. She lives alone in the Scarborough bungalow where my sister and I grew up. What fills her life I cannot imagine; I have never been able to imagine. Plants. Pots of tea. Her pension cheque. The daily paper with the advertised specials. Taking the subway to Eaton's. Her appliquéd shopping bag, maroon and moss green, the wooden handles faintly soiled. Her housecoat (a floral cotton, washable), her reading glasses, and toast cut into triangles. Her kitchen curtains, her waxed linoleum. The decaffeinated coffee which she drinks from thick, chipped cups – the rows and rows of bone china cups and saucers, stamped with violets and bordered with gilt, are preserved in the glass-fronted china cabinet for the by-now entirely hypothetical day when guests of inexpressible elegance arrive unexpectedly to sip coffee and sit in judgement on my mother.

My mother is getting married. I have known for a month now – since her short, awkwardly-phrased letter with its curiously bald declaration, *Mr Berceau has asked me to marry him* – but the thought still sucks the breath from the floor of my chest. I cannot believe it. I cannot believe it.

And why not? Why this perplexity? Certainly there is nothing improper about it; she has, after all, been a widow for eleven years, since our father, to whom she was married for thirty years, died in his sleep, a heart attack in his sixtieth year. A massive heart attack, the doctor had called it. Massive. I pictured a tidal wave of pressure, a blind wall – darkness crushing him as he lay sleeping beside my mother in the walnut veneer bed. He never woke up. My mother, always a light nervous sleeper, heard only a small sound like someone suppressing a cough and that was all. By the time she had switched on the pink glass bedside lamp with its pleated paper shade, he was gone.

And next week she is getting married again. To someone called Louis Berceau, someone I have never seen or even heard of. On a Friday afternoon at the end of May, she is getting married. And why shouldn't she, a healthy woman of seventy? Why not? Only someone bitterly perverse would object to what the whole world celebrates as a joyous event. But easy abstractions are one thing. It is something else to absorb an event like this into the hurting holes and sockets of real life. I should rejoice. Instead a sucking swamp

222

tugs at me, a hint of Greek tragedy, dark-blooded and massive like the violent seizure of my father's heart. My timid, nervous, implacable mother with her left breast sheared off and her terrible indifference intact, is getting married. It can't be happening, it can't be coming true.

When I leave the office I run for the bus, waving like a crazy woman at the driver, 'Wait, wait!' The sun is blinding and I stumble aboard fumbling for a five dollar bill and handing it to him.

'That all you got? Nothing smaller?'

'No,' breathlessly, 'I'm just going to the bank now.' *Never apologize, never explain*, Brother Adam wrote.

'Okay, okay.'

I sink into a seat only to be struck anew by panic: did I drop my pay cheque in my frantic search for change? I grope; there it is, folded in my wallet.

I am perspiring heavily. The weather is more like mid-summer than spring, and the air is weighed down with dampness. My blouse clings to me across the back. It is an old blouse, six years old at least, with a collar that sags. There is too much material under the arms suggesting rolls of mottled matronly flesh; I should have thrown it out long ago.

What I should do, I think, is go and get my hair cut. But that would cost at least fifteen dollars, even if I could get an appointment and there isn't much hope of that. Like my sister Judith I have heavy, wiry, wavy hair. Crow black hair. Irish hair, my mother always called it with a hint of contempt. Wild. I've never been able to formulate a plan for it. I'm tall, too, like Judith, but rangier, craggier, more angled than contoured; she is older by three years and beginning to widen slightly. I probably will too.

Yes, I decide, I must get my hair cut. Definitely. Right after I finish at the bank. I pat my purse with the cheque folded inside.

In addition to the cheque I have something else in my purse; a three-by-five card with Brother Adam's address written on it. It is really less a piece of information than a personal note to myself, for Brother Adam's address is firmly engraved on my brain: The Priory, 615 Beachwood, Toronto. Nevertheless, leaving the office, I scribbled it down on impulse and tucked it in the zippered middle section of my purse. Impulse? Of course not, I admit to the leafing-out trees; and hedges outside the bus window. I shake my head, a smile fanning out across my face; I have planned this from the very day I decided to go to Toronto for my mother's wedding. Not actually planned it; no, nothing so definite as that. The idea formed itself like a clot in the back of my head, gradually knitting itself into a possibility: I could, if I had time, that is, visit Brother Adam.

Perhaps not an actual visit. Just a phone call, just to say hello. This is Charleen Forrest. Remember? From the *Botany Journal*. Yes, it *is* a surprise, well, I just happened to be in Toronto for a few days, sort of a family reunion, and well, I just couldn't come this close and not give you a call when your letters have meant such a lot to me and, and, then what?

Maybe I could drop in. Why not? That would be better, nothing like a direct face-to-face after all. Then I could see just what sort of place the Priory is. I'd wear something decorous, my new dress probably, pants wouldn't do, and I could wear a little kerchief on my head; no, that would be ridiculous. I would ring the bell. Or lift the knocker. A heavy old knocker, probably wrought iron, rusted slightly, ornately carved with religious symbols. A tiny, frocked figure would eventually appear at the door, and I would state my purpose. My name is Charleen Forrest and I am anxious to see Brother Adam for a few minutes. If he can be spared, that is. No, I'm not actually a friend of his, but we correspond. Through letters, you know. For over a year now.

And I thought since I was in Toronto anyway on family business that . . .

Perhaps I should send a little note first. Plain white note paper. Nice small envelope, very maidenly, expressly plain. If I mailed it today it would be there in a day or two. Then I wouldn't have to worry about taking him by surprise. Really much more polite and, well, thoughtful. The sort of thing that lovely, caring people do, the sort of thing *he* might do: Dear Brother Adam, I know how busy you are with your grass research and spiritual studies and so on, but I wondered if you could spare a few minutes to see me. I'm going to be in Toronto for a few days visiting my family, and there are so many things I'd like to talk to you about, and some things are hard for me to write about. Your letters have meant so much to me – much more than I can tell you – as I have no one I can really talk to, Brother Adam, no one in the world.

At Mr Mario's Beauty Box the eyes of the receptionist transfix me. Green-hooded, beetle bright, too close together, riding above a sharp little nose like glued-on ornaments from a souvenir shop.

'I don't know if we can fit you in today,' her voice clinks away uncaringly. 'What about tomorrow at three?'

'I have to go out of town,' I stutter. Am I pleading? Am I giving way to my tendency to be obsequious? I firm up my voice, 'It has to be today.'

'Well,' she says tapping a pencil on the appointment book – and already I can see she is going to work me in – 'Mr Mario himself is free in twenty minutes. If you only need a cut, that is.'

'That's all I need,' I chant gratefully, 'just a cut, just a simple cut.'

She stands up suddenly, reaches across the kidney-shaped desk and tugs a hank of my hair. 'About three inches?' she demands.

Three inches off? Three inches left on? What?

CAROL SHIELDS

'Three inches?' she asks again, more sharply this time.

'Yes, yes, three inches, that would be fine.'

I have never been to Mr Mario's before. In fact, I avoid beauty salons almost entirely except for the occasional cut and one or two disastrous hair-straightening sessions in the days when Watson was trying to transform me into a flower child. Mr Mario's place shimmers with pinkish light. Light spills in through the shirred Austrian curtains and twinkles off the plastic chandeliers. Little bulbs blaze around the mirrors reminding me of movie stars' dressing rooms. Pink hair dryers buzz and the air conditioners churn. The wet, white sunlight of the street is miles away. I wait for Mr Mario in a slippery vinyl chair, suddenly struck with the fear that this rosy elegance might hint at undreamt of prices. Much more than fifteen dollars, maybe even eighteen. Or as much as twenty. Twenty dollars for a haircut, am I crazy? I turn to the kidney desk in panic, but the receptionist eyes me coldly, leanly. 'Now,' she says.

Mr Mario marches me to a basin, thoroughly, roughly, drenches my hair and neck, and then he seats me in front of his mirror. For a moment I am reassured by his relative maturity; he has a mid-life shadow of fat under his chin, and his fingers are competently plump and strong. Taking hold of my hair at both sides he pulls it straight out and regards my image in the mirror. Together we stare in disbelief: such Irish coarseness, such obscene length, such unspeakable heaviness.

'What did you have in mind?' he inquires sleepily.

'I don't know,' I gasp. 'Something different. Just go ahead and cut.'

'Okay,' he yawns and stepping back he examines me from another angle. 'Okay.'

The sight of the razor raises new fears – where did I hear that razor cuts are more haute than scissor cuts? This might even cost

226

– I feel faint at the thought – as much as twenty-three dollars. And then I'll have to tip him. Another dollar. God, god.

My hair begins to fall to the floor, and without a hint of delicacy he kicks it to one side where it is almost immediately swept up by a girl in a green uniform. Too late now.

He combs, sections, and clips silently and steadily, his lips curled inward with concentration. 'Coarse,' he says finally, breaking the silence.

'Yes,' I confess, 'it runs in the family.'

'Italian?' he asks with a flicker of interest.

'No. Half Irish, half Scottish.'

'Yeah?' His interest evaporates.

To my right a small shrunken woman of enormous old age sits swathed in a plastic cape; her wisps of hair are briskly sectioned for a permanent, and the pink scalp shows through like intersecting streets. One by one I watch the tight plastic rollers being wound and pinned to the bony scalp. I imagine the ammonia burning through her thin, pink skin, aching. Why does she do this to herself? Her chin wobbles like a walnut as though a scream is gathering there. Her lips move, but she says nothing.

On the other side of me a vigorous woman of about fifty bends forward and lights a cigarette while her rollers are removed by the slimmest of boys in striped purple jeans. 'Yesterday,' she says, blowing out puffed clouds of smoke, 'I went all the way to the fish market for some red snapper.'

'For what?' the boy asks, leaning toward her.

'Red snapper. It's a fish. And ex-pen-sive! But I was in the mood for a splurge. Well, I cooked it in a little butter. Then you cover it, you know, and leave it just on simmer. Not too long, say about ten minutes.'

'Ten minutes,' he murmurs back-combing her gunmetal shrub.

'Ten minutes. Then just a little lemon, you know, cut in a wedge

227

to squeeze. And my husband said to me, you know, you could serve this to the P.M. if he happened to drop by.'

'He liked it, eh?'

'So he said, so he said, and he's a hard man to please. Tonight I'm going to do lamb chops. You like lamb?'

'Not too much.'

'It's all in how you do it. Most people don't get all the fat out, and with lamb you've got to get all the fat out. But do you know what really makes it?'

'What?' he listens. I listen. Even Mr Mario seems to listen.

'After you brown it really well, you add just a sniff of white wine.'

'White wine?' The striped-pants boy seems a little disappointed.

'You don't have to use the expensive stuff. Why waste good booze in cooking. Just the ordinary poison will do you.'

'Do you want to have a little hairspray?'

'Just a little. My husband says it's bad for the lungs. Did you know that?'

'Maybe.'

'No, it's true. The whole atmosphere's being destroyed by spray cans. But just a little. It's awfully humid out. And I've got to pick up the lamb chops. That husband of mine.'

Husband. Strange word. Medieval. Husbandry, husband your flocks; keep, guard, preserve, watch over.

'Bitch,' Mr Mario whispers lazily in my ear as she leaves.

I say nothing, only smile, obscurely gratified that I have some-how gained his favour. He cups my head with his hands, turning it slightly, then begins cutting again, slowly, slowly, alternating between razor, scissors, clippers; razor, scissors, clippers. Cautious as a surgeon.

'Hold still now,' he hisses. 'The back of the neck is the most important.'

I begin to feel sick. Could this possibly cost as much as twenty-five dollars? In New York haircuts cost up to forty dollars – where did I read that? Mr Kenneth or something. But this is Vancouver. Still with inflation and everything, twenty-five dollars is not impossible. Twenty-five dollars! Stop cutting, I want to cry out. That's enough. Stop.

Then he is going all over my head with an electric blower and a little round brush, catching my hair from underneath and drawing it out into rounds of dark fur. Turning, rolling, curving. Stop, stop.

At last. Flick, flick with the brush. Off with the towel. A puff of spray. I stagger to the kidney desk.

He follows me, drowsy-eyed.

Now.

'How much?' my mouth moves.

'Fifteen dollars,' he drawls.

I pull out the bills. Blindly stuff an extra dollar in the pocket of his smock. Run for the door. And in the dancing, white heat I see myself blurred across the window. Or is it me?

Oh, Mr Mario, Mr Mario. Always, always, always I've wanted to look like this. Soft, shaped, feathered into a new existence. Me.

My lips perform the smallest of smiles. My neck turns a fraction of an inch. My legs stretch long and cool and slow. What's the hurry. Slowly, slowly, I walk home.

Greta telephones to say good-bye. 'Is it true,' she asks, 'is it true what Doug says? That Eugene What's-his-name is going with you?'

I picture her holding the phone in an attitude of anxious, frowning disbelief, her crow's-feet deepening. (Greta's crow's-feet reach all the way to her soul.)

'Yes,' I tell her briskly. 'Yes, Eugene happened to have a convention in Toronto at the same time. Wasn't that lucky?'

'A dentists' convention,' Greta says sadly, dully.

I want to comfort her. Poor Greta with her Gestalt therapy, her psychodrama, her awareness clinic, her encounter group, her trauma team, her megavitamin treatment and now her obsession with meditation. All she needs is just enough psychic epoxy to keep her from slipping apart. Can't I summon a few words to reassure her? Is my heart so hard that I can't give her those few words?

'Look Greta,' I say, 'thanks for phoning, but I've got to run. Seth just got in from band practice and I've got a million things to do.'

'Seth,' I turn to him.

'Yes.'

'You have the phone number in Toronto? If anything goes wrong?'

'It's on top of the list you gave me.'

'Well, look, Seth, if you lose it, just on the wild chance that you might lose it, you can ask the Savages. I gave it to Doug too. You never know.'

'Okay.'

'And you've got enough money?'

'Sure.'

'Positive?'

'All I need is bus fare and milk money.'

'You might have an emergency.'

'I've got plenty.'

'Just to make sure, you'd better take this extra five.'

'You keep it, you'll need it.'

'I've got lots. Your father's cheque came yesterday. And I got paid today. I'm rich for once. You take it.'

He pokes it in his back pocket. 'I'll take it but I won't need it.'

'I wish you were coming. I hate leaving you here like this.'

'It's okay,' he smiles across at me. 'Anyway, there's band practice every day this week.'

'At least we'll be back for the concert. Did you get the tickets?'

'Yeah.'

'For Fugene too? And his kids?'

'Yeah. In my wallet. Want me to hang on to them till Saturday night?'

'Maybe you'd better, the way I lose things. Anyway, I hope everything goes O.K. here.'

'Why wouldn't it?'

'It's just that Doug and Greta can be a little . . . well . . . you know.'

'Uhuh.'

'A little too much.'

'I know.'

'Just tune them out, Seth. If they start getting to you.'

'Okay.'

'You'll be ready after school? When they pick you up?'

'I'll be ready.'

'And you won't forget your suitcase?'

'No.'

'There are clean socks for every day. And I put in your Lions T-shirt in case it stays hot like this.'

'Thanks.'

'And your retainer is in a plastic bag under your pyjamas.'

'Okay.'

'Your toothbrush. What about your toothbrush?'

'I'll put it in tomorrow morning.'

'Don't forget.'

'I won't.'

'I sound like a clucking hen. I know I sound like an old hen.'

231

'No, you don't.'

'It's just that I'm sort of nervous, I guess. All the rushing around and the whole idea of Grandma,' – I say the word Grandma with a sliding self-consciousness since Seth cannot even remember seeing his grandmother – 'getting married and everything. It's just got me a little more rattled than usual.'

'That's okay.'

'That's why I'm clucking away at you like this.'

'I don't mind,' he says smiling.

'You've got a nice smile, you know that?'

'I ought to for eight hundred bucks.'

'I don't mean your teeth. I mean you *have* really got a nice smile.'

'Thanks. So do you.'

'Really?'

'Yeah, sort of.'

'I wish you were coming.'

'I'll be okay,' he says. And then he adds, 'And you'll be okay too.'

Chapter 2

'There's nothing about myself that I like,' I say to Eugene as we lie side by side in our lower berth. Contentment, momentary contentment, has lulled me into confession. 'The bottoms of my feet are scaly,' I tell him, 'and have you ever noticed what big ugly feet I've got? Slabs. And two huge corns. One on each foot. I've had those same corns since I was thirteen.'

'Luckily no one dies of corns.'

'My big toes are crooked,' I continue. 'I'd go to see a chiropodist if I weren't so ashamed of my feet. And they're the kind of feet that are always clammy, summer and winter. At least in the winter I can cover them up with shoes. But then as soon as it's warm enough for sandals, hot like it was today, that's when I remember how much I hate my feet.'

'Try to sleep, Charleen.'

'It's too lurchy on this train to sleep.'

There is a pause, and for a moment or two I think Eugene may remind me that it had been my idea to take the train. But he doesn't. His divorce has made him cautious, fearful of anything resembling marital bickering. Instinctively he shuns that almost unconscious coinage that passes between husbands and wives: *I told you it wouldn't work. Remember, this was your big idea. What will you think of next? Didn't I tell you? Not again! Are you going to start in on that? Don't you ever listen*

233

when I'm talking to you? Don't you care anymore? Don't you love me?

'Try to sleep anyway,' Eugene says gently.

'I keep meaning to buy a pumice stone for my feet,' I tell him. 'Do you know something, Eugene – I've been meaning to buy a pumice stone since I was fifteen and read in *Seventeen* that there was such a thing. And now, here I am, thirty-eight. What's the matter with me, I can't even organize my life enough to buy a pumice stone.'

'We'll buy you one in Toronto.' He is only faintly mocking.

'I would love to have beautiful feet.'

'Great.'

'It would be a start.'

Eugene says nothing but yawns hugely.

'It would be a start,' I say again, drifting off. I am wearying of my self-hatred. It's only a tactical diversion anyway, a pale cousin to the ferocious self-inquiry which ransacks me on nights less peaceful than this. This is more reflex than ritual, stuffing for my poor brain, packing for the wound I prefer not to leave open.

But it opens anyway, freshly perceived, when I'm wakened at three A.M. by the long, pliant, complaining train whistle. Somewhere in all that darkness we are bending around an unseen curve. It's cold in the Pullman, and my nightgown is wound across my stomach. Reaching over Eugene and jerking the blind up an inch or two, I admit a bar of blue light into our dim shelf. Moonlight.

Sharp as biblical revelation it informs me of the total unreality of this instant: that I am lying in bed with a man who is not my husband, rolling through mountains of darkness to my mother's marriage. This is not melodrama (though the vocabulary it requires is); this is madness, lunacy, calling into doubt all the surfaces and shadows of my thirty-eight years.

Berth. Birth. My yearning to see things in symbolic form is powerful; it always has been; it is the affliction of the hopelessly, cheerlessly optimistic, this pinning together of facts to find patterns. And it is a compulsion I resist, having long ago discovered it to be a grandiose cheat. The rhythms of life are random and irreducible.

Suddenly I am shivering from head to foot. I would like to wake Eugene for the warmth of his body, but at this moment I can't bear to include him. And besides, his green-pyjamaed back slopes away from me at an angle that suggests an exhaustion even greater than my fear.

Both of us, Eugene and I, are secondary victims of separate modern diseases, mid-century maladies hatched by the heartless new social order: Eugene because his wife abandoned him for the Women's Movement and I, because I married a man who couldn't bear to leave his youth behind.

We are the losers. (Misery loves company, my mother always said.) The hapless rejectees, the jilted partners of people stronger than ourselves. Social residue. Silt. Whatever exists between Eugene and me – and Doug Savage is at least partly accurate when he accuses me of bewilderment – is diminished by the fact that each of us has been cast aside, tossed out like some curious archeological implement whose usefulness is no longer understood. Even our lovemaking is lit with doubt: are we anything more than two cripples holding each other up? Can our passion be more than second-rate? Can anything come from nothing?

'She was always something of a bitch,' Eugene said about his wife, Jeri, shortly after I met him, 'but at least in the early days she confined her bitchiness to outsiders. Like waiters in restaurants. The first time I took her out to dinner – I'd only known her a week or so then and I wanted to take her somewhere, you know, impressive. To show her that country boys don't necessarily dribble soup out of the corners of their mouths. We went to the Top of the Captain and she sent the rolls back because they were cold.'

'No!' I gasped delightedly. 'Really?'

'Really. She said that she thought more people should take that kind of responsibility when the service wasn't up to standard. Sort of a battlecry with her.'

'And you married her after that! Oh, Eugene, how could you?'

'There's one born every minute, you know.'

'What else did she do?' I asked greedily.

'Well, then she got into the consumer thing. That must have started after we'd been married a year or so. She started out by returning groceries.'

'Like what?'

'You name it. Once she had a jar of apricot jam with a wasp in it. That was the worst, I guess. She mailed that to Ottawa.'

'And what happened?'

'All she got, I think, was a form letter. It was being looked into or something She took back all kinds of things to the store. Lettuce that was brown in the middle. Coffee if it tasted a bit off. Fungussy oranges from the bottom of the bag. Smashed eggs, bony meat. Once, as a joke, I accused her of deliberately buying rotten stuff so she'd have something to return.'

'And . . . ?'

'Jeri never did have much sense of humour.'

'Why did she do it anyway? Did she really care all that much?'

Eugene shrugged. 'I could never figure it out. I mean, even then we weren't all that hard up for cash. She always said it was the principle of the thing. She seemed to be mad at the whole world. And consumerism kind of opened a somewhat legitimate channel to her. God, she could work up a rage. Nothing timid and retiring about Jeri. Funny, at first she had seemed, I don't know, just discerning. Knowledgeable. Discriminating. How the hell was I supposed to know if rolls should be served warm. I'd never even thought about it. We never had rolls at home. Bread maybe, or biscuits, but never rolls. And here was this dish with long, blonde hair knowing all about rolls.'

'You're too trusting, Eugene.'

'Later it got so every supermarket manager in the greater Vancouver area knew her. Once she tried to get me to return something for her. A box of broken cookies. Gingersnaps. It was raining like a bastard and she was about eight months pregnant with Donny and she wanted me to get the car out of the garage and go give the store manager hell.'

'And did you?'

'No. Absolutely not. I told her I just couldn't get that worked up about a few broken cookies. I've never seen anyone cry the way she did that Saturday afternoon. She cried so hard she was sick. And she couldn't stop being sick. She was kind of half kneeling on the bathroom floor with her head on the edge of the toilet. I finally phoned a drugstore for a tranquillizer, and when she heard about that she started all over again. Hadn't I ever heard of thalidomide? Was I trying to mutilate the baby and maybe kill her?'

'Maybe she really was crazy.'

He paused, thinking. 'Sometimes I used to think so. Now I think she was just plain angry. An angry, angry woman. And probably still is. The only decent thing she's ever done is let me have the two boys for weekends. How they've survived I don't know. You know, sometimes when she was at her worst I would lie awake for hours and make up dialogue. Daydreams, only mine were at night. Just lay there and dreamed up things for her to say, the things I wanted her to say. I'd invent whole scenes just like movies. I'd have her running in the front door all smiling and her hair falling all around her and she would be saying something like, "look at these beautiful apples," and then she'd bite into one of them. Or she might be bending over me in bed, smiling and telling me how she was the most –' he stopped, smiling, 'the most *satisfied* woman on the Pacific coast and that for once she was contented.'

'She must have been satisfied once in a while,' I said knowingly to Eugene.

'I don't know. I can't ever remember her looking really happy until she joined the West Van Consumer Action Group. The night she got elected secretary-treasurer was the horniest night we ever had in eight years of marriage. Of course I was more or less incidental to the whole scene.' He drew a breath. 'God, I still think of that night with a kind of glow.'

'Why did you have to say that?'

'What? About feeling a glow?'

'Yes,' I said, for I liked to think Eugene had nothing but the most wretched memories of Jeri. Eugene is the same: he prefers to think of Watson as a pure, black-hearted villain.

'Actually Watson was a psychic disaster,' I volunteered helpfully.

'Like Jeri,' Eugene said. 'Selfish, immature.'

'Never should have married anyone.'

'She couldn't see past her own dumb self-satisfaction.'

'He could be utterly, utterly unfeeling.'

'Blind. And biting. Even with the kids.'

Thus we reassure ourselves, Eugene and I, by contesting the unworthiness of our former partners. Sometimes we grow shrill in our denunciations; they were shallow, insensitive, childish, pathetic. I match Eugene, horror story for horror story, as we conspire to reduce our two partners to ranting maniacs; if they hadn't walked out on us when they did, they would most assuredly have been committed to an institution, no doubt about it.

In this way we contrive our innocence. We reshape our histories; we have not been abandoned, only misled, and we insist that we now are liberated from the impossible, the unbearable, that we are free. I am happy now, I tell Eugene. He is happy too, he says, happier than he ever was with Jeri.

We cling together. Legs entwined, playing at love, we wake early in the morning (who could sleep with all this racket?) and we lie in our lower berth clinging together like children.

In the dining car we are served breakfast by a serious young man with a raw, new haircut and a glistening red neck. A university student, probably, hired for the summer. Under the eyes of anxious authority his hands tremble slightly as he puts down our glasses of chilled grapefruit juice. His eyes never leave the rims of the glasses and his mouth sags open slightly in concentration. It's only May; by August he'll be performing with the gliding familiar detachment of a professional.

Who dreams up breakfast menus on trains? Someone splendidly elevated and detached from the rushed, sour determinate of instant coffee sloshed onto saucers, the whole crumbly-cupboard, soggy cornflake world. Here fresh haddock is offered, haddock in cream, imagine. With a tiny branch of parsley. Poached eggs exquisitely shivering on circles of toast. Or a bacon omelet. Nested in homefries. Marvellous. Served with a broiled tomato half. The pictorial effect alone is dazzling. English muffins on warmed plates. Yes, please. Honey or raspberry jam? Ahh, both please. Butter, carved into chilly balls on a green glass dish. Coffee brewed to dense perfection and poured from a graceful silvery pot. Well, just one more cup. Eugene smiles across at me.

A tenderness seizes us for a middle-aged man sitting all alone at the next table and, half turning, Eugene and I exchange pleasantries with him. Over third and fourth cups of coffee he talks about how he found happiness by selling his car.

'Suddenly it came to me,' he tells us. 'I had an ulcer. You know? I'm a worrier, and you know what they say. Finally I said to myself, look, what are you always worrying about? And do you know what it was?'

'What?' I ask. I am always polite, and besides it is part of the burden of my life to pretend that I am a benevolent and caring person. 'What were you worrying about?'

'Well,' he continues, 'I didn't realize it then – it was like a kind of subconscious thing with me – but what I was always thinking about was my car. Like any minute the brake linings were going to need replacing. So I'd be driving along and all the time I'd be listening to some little noise in the engine. My wife used to say I'd get a crick in my neck from bending over listening like that. Every time I heard any knocking in there I'd always automatically think the worst. Like the motor was stripped for sure. Or the carburetor was giving out. I used to have nightmares, honest to God nightmares, about needing four new tyres all at once.'

'And did it ever happen?' I ask.

'No. That's the thing, it never happened like that. Maybe there would be a dirty sparkplug or some two-bit wiring job, and when they told me at the garage that was all it was, I'd break into a sweat. A cold sweat. Well, finally I couldn't take it anymore. Landed in hospital and I was only forty-three years old. An ulcer. I bled twenty-four hours, they couldn't stop it. I'm telling you, that makes you think, when something like that happens.'

'I'll bet,' I agree emphatically.

'So to hell with this, I said. I want to live my life, not worry it away.'

'So you sold your car?'

'That's exactly what I did. Just called over a second-hand dealer and said, "Take it away, I never want to set eyes on it again." And the day I sold it was like a stone was rolled off my shoulders. You know what?' He paused. 'I was happier that day than the day when I got my first car.'

'And you're really happier now?' I ask earnestly. I'm not feigning kindness anymore, for I collect, among other things, recipes for happiness. 'You really are?'

'You're darned right,' he said, draining his coffee cup and setting it thoughtfully on the saucer. 'So I spend a buck or two on a taxi now and then. And train fares and all the rest. But I've got my health, and what's more important than that? I'm telling you, I didn't know what happiness was.'

A prescription for contentment. I think of Greta Savage in Vancouver who, for the moment at least, has found a quiet place to store all her missionary longings. And Brother Adam – what did he write me? The only way to be happy is to have no expectations. How fortunate they are to have found their perfect, definable, tailored-to-fit solutions.

And my mother. My mother who achieved, if not happiness, at least a sort of jealous, truncated satisfaction in perpetually revising and reordering her immediate surroundings. All the time my sister and I were growing up, for at least twenty-five years, the main focus of her life was an eccentric passion for home decoration, an enslavement all the more bizarre because of the humbleness of our suburban bungalow, a brick box on a narrow, sandy lot with a concrete stoop, a green awning, and a clothes line at the back.

Always one of the six small rooms was in the process of being 'done over', so that we never at any one time in all those years lived in a state of completion. Decorating magazines formed almost the only reading matter in our house, and from those pages, which my mother turned with anxious, hungering fingers, she fanned her fanatical energy. She could do anything. Velvet curtains, swagged and bordered by hand for the living room, were cut up a year later to make throw cushions. She was nothing if not resourceful, for the throw cushions were later picked apart and upholstered onto the dining-room chairs. End tables were cut down and patiently refinished. Often wallpaper samples were propped up along the mantel of the imitation fireplace for months at a time before a decision was reached. Her options were limited, of course, by our father's modest income (he was a clerk in a screw factory). She saved quarters in a pickle jar for two years in order to buy a fake-crystal ceiling fixture for the hall.

She learned to make the most complicated and sheerest of curtains complete with miles of ruffling. She learned to paint, solder, wallpaper, stain and upholster. Several times she rewebbed and covered the armchairs in the living room. Mother. A tall woman with a caved-in, shallow chest; she went about the house wearing an old shirt of my father's over her print house-dresses and on her feet, socks and running shoes; her legs, I remember, were a mottled white with clustered purplish, grape-jelly veins at the backs of the knees. Sometimes we would wake up in the morning to find that she was already at work, the dining-room floor covered with drop-cloths, the step ladder set up, and there she tottered, her bush of hair snugged in an 'invisible' net, her Scottish jaw set, painting a stencilled cornice around the ceiling. A sea-shell motif in antique ivory.

Her decorating effects were invariably too heavily baroque. Not that I realized this at the time; what I felt in that house was a curious choking pressure as though the walls were being slowly strangled; we were all smothering in layers and layers of airless drapery and plaster. Over the years she showed a tendency toward progressively darker, richer textures. The pine buffet was transformed to walnut, an effect laboriously achieved with the aid of stain and graining tools. In the tiny front hall under the chandelier hung a great, gilded imitation-Italian mirror bought at an auction. Under it was a 'gossip bench' painted gold. She ran to luxurious ornamental fabrics, velvets and brocades bought as remnants, and the sumptuous effects of tassles and draping. 'You don't need money,' she used to say, 'if you have taste.'

Taste. Taste was what the neighbours didn't have. Taste and imagination. All they ever did, she scoffed, was open the Eaton's catalogue and order rooms full of mail-order furniture. And if they were short of cash they put up with faded curtains when all they had to do was buy a packet of dye from the chain store. (She herself frequently went on the rampage with dying. Perhaps my great insecurity springs from nothing more serious than the fear that my pink cotton scatter rug might be snatched from me at any minute to reappear later in vivid, startling, foreign purple.) The neighbours didn't know what taste meant, she said, or were too lazy to make any improvements. All they needed was to get busy and roll up their shirt sleeves. 'Just look,' she often sighed, 'look what I've managed to make of this house.'

Our bedroom, Judith's and mine, was a vision of contorted femininity. For us she favoured shirred taffeta or dotted swiss, pale chintz or nylon net. I remember one summer morning, perspiration streaming down her face, dark circles staining the arms of her housedress as she knelt on the floor of our stifling bedroom off the kitchen, her lips grim with zeal and full of pins, attaching an intricately ruffled skirt to our dressing table. Once, for wall hangings, she framed squares of black velvet to which she appliquéd (the discovery of appliqué opened a whole new chapter in her life) stylized ballet figures. A McCall's pattern, twenty-five cents plus postage. She made us a bedroom lamp from an old, pink perfume bottle from Woolworth's and covered the shade with white tulle; this was one of her least successful ideas, for the tulle began to smoke one evening while Judith was studying, and our father had to carry it outside to the backyard and spray it with the garden hose. Our mother watched its destruction with a minimum of sorrow, for any sign of wear or tear or obsolescence immediately opened a hole in the house which her furious energies conspired to fill.

Our father: what did he think of it all? He was so silent and laconic a man, so shy, so nervously inarticulate that it was impossible to tell, but he seemed to sense that the compulsive forces of her personality were cosmic manifestations which must not be interfered with; to stop her was to invite danger or disaster. All I can remember is his occasional resigned sigh: 'You know your mother and her house,' as once again we were plunged into chaos.

While she was working on a room she was in a state of violent unrest, plagued by insomnia and shocking fits of indigestion. She planned her rooms as carefully as any set designer, bringing into life whole new environments. Finally, as the metamorphosis was nearing completion, she would become almost electrically excited, impatiently dabbing on the last bit of paint, taking the last stitch, and, with breath suspended, unveiling her creation.

Later she would suffer agonies of doubt. Was it in good taste or was there something maybe just a little bit tacky or gawdy about it? That pink vase, was it a little too much accent? Too bright? Too garish a shade? Maybe if she spray-painted it dusty rose, yes. Yes.

No one except a few out-of-town relatives and the occasional neighbour ever witnessed her decorating marvels although she always talked of having something, a tea perhaps – the exact type of entertainment was never decided upon – when she got the whole house organized. Organized! And the telephone on the gilded gossip bench seldom rang; she never used it herself except to phone our father at the screw company to ask him to bring home another half quart of enamel for the kitchen cupboards or to tell him she had a headache from the varnish fumes and could he come straight home after work and get the girls some scrambled eggs for supper, she would just slip off to bed if he didn't mind.

I never doubted that she loved the house more than she loved us. Our father and Judith and I only impeded her progress as she plunged from one room to the next. Our very presence made the rooms untidy; sitting on the new chintz slipcover we pulled the pattern off-centre, and our school books on the sideboard disturbed the balance of her ornaments. Once I chipped the Chinese blue kitchen cupboards with the broom handle, thus necessitating a frantic search through all the hardware stores in Scarborough for patch-up paint, a search she suddenly abandoned when it was decided that the cupboards should be painted a pale pumpkin to match the striped café curtains which she planned to 'run up' as soon as she finished gluing on the moulding in the front bedroom.

Suddenly it stopped. Overnight her obsession became a memory, the way she was before she got old. Judith says it was about the time our father died. I think it was a little earlier. It's been years now since she has made even the slightest alteration to the house. All the upholstery is faded, slightly soiled on the arms, and when I was last there five years ago I actually saw a patch of the old Chinese blue paint in the kitchen showing through the pumpkin. And under that? A scratch of pink? Perhaps.

I don't know why she stopped. I must ask her when I see her. Casually mention something like, 'Remember how interested you used to be in decorating – why is it you don't do it anymore?'

But of course I won't actually say anything of the kind. These offhand conversations which I always rehearse in my mind before seeing my mother never materialize because, once in her presence, I freeze back to sullen childhood when all such phenomena were

245

accepted without comment. To question would be to injure the delicate springs of impulse and emotion. For an obsession such as the one that ruled my mother's life could only have existed to fill a terrible hurting void; it is the void we must not mention, for, who knows, it may still exist just below the uneasy quaking surface. Quicksand. So easy to get sucked under. Better to walk carefully, to say nothing.

She may have lost her nerve and become, in the end, finally doubtful about what she had once taken to be taste. Perhaps she simply became exhausted. Or the cost of paint and paper may have strained her small pension. It may be that she suddenly realized one day that all her energy was being poured into an unworthy vessel. Or perhaps she was struck with the heart-racking futility of altering mere surfaces and never reaching the heart: her world was immutable, she may have decided. What was the point of trying to change it?

Because the Vistadome is packed with people, Eugene and I sit side by side in the day coach, I by the window and he in the aisle seat. We are leaving the mountains behind and for an hour we've watched their angles collapse; they are softening and melting into green, elongated hills which, with their hint of cultivation, are mannerly and almost English. Eugene tells me he has never crossed the Rockies by train before.

'Why not?' I ask.

He shrugs; he is a man much given to shrugging, resignation being the principal inheritance of his forty years. 'I don't really know.'

'How did you get out of Estevan in the first place?' I demand.

'Bus,' he says. 'I left on a Thursday afternoon and got into Vancouver late on a Friday night. September. It was the first Friday in September, I remember exactly. I'd just turned eighteen.'

'Why didn't you take the train?' I ask, wanting details.

'The bus was cheaper,' he explains carefully as though I were exceedingly simple. 'Probably only a buck or two, but to my folks –' he stops, shrugging again.

'How did you get home for holidays,' I ask, 'when you were at university?' These questions are necessary, for though Eugene and I have known each other for two years now, there are miles of unknown territory to recover. Thirty-eight years of his life, thirty-six of mine.

'Hitchhiked,' he says. 'Then in my third year I bought that old, tan Chevvy. I told you about that.'

I nod. Eugene's life is chronicled by the different cars he has owned, separated into periods as distinct as the phases of civilization; his stone-age, bronze-age, iron-age. First the Chevvy, a fourth-hand, first love which he restored to humming perfection on lonely, broke, womanless weekends on the street outside his boarding house on west 19th. Then the Volkswagen beetle with only one previous owner; by graduation he had discovered the benefits of good mileage and reliable repair service. With the navy blue Ford Jeri entered his life. The Rambler: Sandy was born and Donny on the way and what with diaper bags, carbeds, safety seats and economy . . . the Plymouth wagon, good for groceries. Then the Chrysler; orthodontics was beginning to be rewarding, and though Jeri didn't believe in luxury transport (she had a small Sunbeam of her own anyway), the dealer had offered a package Eugene couldn't turn down. 'We used it on weekends,' he says, 'but I never really knew it inside out. Not like with the Chevvy.' The Chevvy. He speaks of it tenderly. 'She took me back and forth from Estevan to university three times a year and never once let me down.' He smiles, stretched with nostalgia. 'She was a good girl. A great old girl.'

'And you never once flew.'

'Christ, no. It was all I could do to buy gas. I never even set foot in a plane until I was twenty-six and Jeri wanted to go to Hawaii for our honeymoon.'

Now, years later, he flies routinely as though no other form of transportation exists. When he decided to come with me to Toronto he tried for days to persuade me that we should fly. 'It would save time,' he pressed, 'and you'd have longer with your mother and sister.' (An argument which demonstrates how shallowly he knows me after two years, for what matters to me is to shorten the time in Toronto, not lengthen it.) Besides I went by train the other three times – when I brought Seth as a baby to show him off to his grandparents, then when my father died, and five years ago, when I came home to tell my mother, very belatedly, about my divorce. I had always taken the train; the pattern had been set; and besides, I told Eugene, the train was cheaper.

At the mention of expense, Eugene hesitated, and I knew what he was thinking: that he could easily afford the plane fares for both of us, and since he was planning to attend a dental convention in Toronto, he could write off the whole thing as a business expense. How simple life is for those with professions, savings accounts and good tax lawyers. It was, in fact, this very simplicity that I refused; I'm not ready yet to lay myself open to such soft and easy alternatives.

For days we discussed the matter of plane-versus-train, trading small gently reasoned arguments, each of us having lost the taste for full-scale battle, and, at last, Eugene relented, 'But,' he said, 'if we go by train let's at least come home by air. And let's get ourselves a compartment.'

'I sat up the other three times,' I said, 'and it was fine.' Actually it hadn't been fine, but I had, on those three previous trips, accepted discomfort as a kind of welcome detached suffering.

'A roomette?' he bargained. 'At least a roomette.'

In the end we found we had left it too late; by the time we came to an agreement on the roomette, there was nothing left but one Pullman and at that we were lucky to get a lower. I wanted to pay for half the Pullman but backed down when Eugene began to show signs of genuine impatience. But if he had been even a trifle reasonable I would have preferred to pay my way. Just as I'm not ready for comfort (since I've done nothing to deserve it), neither am I ready to give up what remains of my shattered independence. First it was dinners Eugene paid for; then Seth's dental care; last spring a holiday for the two of us in San Francisco; now my Pullman. And when I went shopping for a new dress for Toronto, he had wanted to pay for that too.

Now, sitting here, I look down at the dress which is really quite comfortable for the train, but like most of my purchases it is proving to be something of a disappointment; a shirt-dress in tangerine knit which, even though it is supposed to be permapress, creases across the lap. It is slightly baggy in the hips and a little snug across the top so that the spaces between the shiny white buttons gap slightly like little orange mouths. And beneath my soft, glossy new hair style of forty-eight hours ago the natural, black, Irish-witch contours are beginning to reassert themselves.

Still the two of us sitting here could pass for any happily married couple. Eugene, prosperous and healthy in his chocolate, doubleknit one hundred-dollar pants and light-weight, brown, ribbed pullover, and I, his wife ('the little wife' you could almost say if I weren't so tall) going along for the ride, a little shopping, a little holiday from the kids. That is to say, there is nothing grotesque about us. We are not perhaps a stunning couple; Eugene has a loose fabric-like face and thin, beige, woolly hair cut too short. Without being actually overweight, there is a somewhat loose look around his stomach and hips. And I have my usual rangy, unconfined awkwardness. Nevertheless we are not in any way identifiable as the victims of failed marriages. Nothing gives us away, a fact which seems remarkable to me. Nothing betrays us, nothing sets us apart. And because I never let go of anything if I can help it, I am still wearing the wedding ring, a band of Mexican worked silver, which Watson gave me when I was eighteen.

Eugene, I'm a little relieved to see, seems to be enjoying the train trip after all. Soon we'll be getting into the prairies, Saskatchewan, the real prairies where he grew up, and he's looking exceptionally thoughtful. It may be that he's thinking about his father again.

By habit he sees almost everything he does through the double lens of his dead father's limitations, and these reflections are necessarily rimmed with regret, for his father, a hard-working farmer on a piece of worthless land, lived a life of unrelieved narrowness. 'My father never slept in a Pullman,' Eugene may be thinking. 'He never made love behind a hairy green curtain going seventy miles an hour through the mountains.' 'My father never slept in a tent,' he had thought when he went camping for the first time at the age of twenty-five. 'My father never rode in a Citroen, never had a glass of wine with his dinner, never went to a concert, never rode in a subway, never ate a black olive, never skied down a hill, never read Hemingway. My father never had a hundred-dollar bill in his pocket. He never wore a ring on his finger in all his life. He never sat in a sauna and watched the steam rising off his chest. He never tipped a bellhop or smoked a cigar. Or watched a tennis match or slept in a waterbed in a hundred-dollar a day room with colour television. For that matter, he died while people were still wondering if there would ever be such a thing as colour television.'

I am right; Eugene *is* thinking about his father. After a minute he begins to tell me how his father introduced him to the mystery of sex. Of course, Eugene explains, it was already too late. He was a boy of thirteen at the time, and on a farm there are no such mysteries. 'But someone must have told my father that he owed me something more. It might even have been my mother. No, on second thought, I don't think so. I think he just made up his mind that he should explain everything about sex to his only son.'

'So he had a long chat with you out in the barn?' I suggest.

'Oh, no. Better than that. Or worse than that, it depends on how you look at it. I mean, he was a man who didn't really know how to have a long talk. They didn't talk much at home, neither of them, and I was the only kid and fairly quiet too. But he must have figured out in his head that the time had come for sex. It was when we were at the fair. The same fair we had every year in town. More of a carnival really, pretty junky, but there were some farm animals and home preserving and all that too. We always went, it was the big deal, the three of us. There wasn't all that much else to do.'

'Go on about the sex.'

'Well, this particular day when we were standing in the fairgrounds, he turned to my mother and said that he was going off with me for a while and we would meet her later by the cattle judging yard. So off we went.'

'Where?'

'To a girlie show.'

'No! Really?'

'Really. It was in one of the tents way, way at the end of the grounds. There was a big sign – "See The Prairie Lovelies – Only Twenty-five Cents."'

'The Prairie Lovelies?'

'And under that was another sign. "Twenty-five cents extra for the Whole Show". Only there was a circle around the W. The Hole Show.'

'And did you know what that meant?'

'Christ, yes, I was thirteen. But I didn't want to go in, at least not

251

with my old man. And I don't think he really wanted to either. He just wasn't that kind of guy. I think he figured he owed it to me or something. God only knows.'

'And how were the Prairie Lovelies?'

'Well, we went in and stood around this platform and out came these three girls in kind of Arabian Nights costumes. And they started dancing around. Over at one side some guy was playing the accordian.'

'Were they any good?'

'Terrible. Not that I'd ever seen any dancing girls before, but even I could tell they were no good. The audience, of course, was all men, farmers mostly, standing around in their overalls. One of the girls was so fat we could hear her huffing and puffing the whole time she was dancing.'

'Wasn't it erotic at all?'

'I suppose, in a way, it was. First the veils came off. Then whatever they were wearing on top. Only this was a few years back and they had flower petals on their nipples. And G-strings under their skirts.'

'What about the Hole Show?'

'That came after. That was when the accordian player stopped and announced that we'd have to pay an extra quarter for the Hole Show. The Hole Show. I can remember how he smacked his lips when he said it. He passed a plate around, and I guess pretty well everyone stayed for that.'

'And . . . ?'

'Then two of the girls kind of faded away, and the other one, the fat one, started in with the bumps and grinds and the accordion going faster and faster all the time while she untied the sides of her G-string. It seemed like forever before she got it off. It was so hot in there you wouldn't believe it, and my father and I standing right in the front. Finally, there she was, peeled right down and sort of squatting and turning so everyone could have a chance to see. There sure wasn't much to see, just a blur really. Then she started dancing again, grinding away, and suddenly she leaned over and grabbed my father's hat off his head.'

'His hat?'

'A work hat. A blue cloth hat he had with a peak in front. He never went anywhere without that hat, not that I can remember anyway. You just didn't see farmers bareheaded in those days.'

'And what did she do with it?'

'First she sort of bent over and started rubbing it up and down her thighs, wiggling away all the while. Everyone was clapping and yelling like mad by then and banging my father on the back. And then she got wilder and wilder and starting rubbing the hat up against her crotch.'

'No!'

'Then everyone went crazy and so did she, just rubbing it and rubbing it.'

'What did your father do?'

'Just stood there. Paralysed. Stunned. Remember he was over fifty then. He just stood there with his mouth open. And his hands reaching out for his hat. Finally she took it and kind of swept it under his nose – that was the worst part – and then she banged it on top of his head.'

'Oh, Eugene.'

'He grabbed hold of it and ripped it off his head. And threw it on the ground and stomped on it. Then he took hold of my arm, hard, and pushed me on out through the whole damned bunch of them. Right out the doorway. Past the next bunch of suckers lining up outside for the next show. God.'

'And what did he say? Afterwards?'

'Nothing. Not one damn thing. I didn't either. We just walked fast all the way to the other end of the fairground where my mother was waiting. He walked so fast I had to run to keep up. I wanted to say something, to tell him it was okay, that I didn't mind all that much about the hat thing, but we never said anything, either of us. Not then or ever.'

'Ah, Eugene. And that was your sex education.'

'I'm almost sure that's what he intended it to be. Because he sure as hell would never have blown two bits just for the fun of it. He never wasted money. There was never any to waste. I think it was all for me. And she blew it for him, the poor old guy, by grabbing his hat. And so did I by not saying anything.'

Eugene shakes his head and, looking out the window, remarks flatly, 'It seems a long time ago.'

We sit quietly. When Eugene talks about his life, it is always with a sorrowing regretful futility as though the thin distances of his childhood could produce nothing better. But for me there is something compelling about his family, a sort of decency that surfaces unconsciously. I see them in prairie gothic terms, stern but devoted, humble but softened by an unquestioned tradition of love. Nevertheless, at the same time, I find myself listening for something more robust and redeeming, a note of valour perhaps; in Eugene's stories he seems deliberately to choose for himself a lesser role. I yearn for him to demonstrate an aptitude for heroism, and I don't know why. I must ask Brother Adam about that – why do I require bravery from Eugene when I don't possess it myself?

I rest my hand in his lap. We are racing past tiny towns raised to significance by brightly painted grain elevators. Beyond them, fields, a sullen sky, a pulsing lip of brightness behind the clouds. Our train, shooting through air, is the slenderest of arrows, a hairline, a jet trail; it cares nothing for the space it splits apart and nothing for us; all we are required to do is sit still and watch it happen.

*   *   *

254

From Winnipeg I phone Seth. There is only twenty minutes, but luckily the call goes right through. And it's a good connection.

'Hello. Is that you, Doug?'

'Yes. Charleen! Where are you?'

'Winnipeg. We've just got a few minutes, but I thought I'd phone and see how everything was.'

'Everything's fine here. We're all getting along fine.'

'Is Seth there?' I ask, and suddenly realize that it is two hours earlier on the coast; Seth might be asleep.

But surprisingly Doug says, 'Sure he's here. Hang on a minute, Char, and I'll get him.'

I hang on for more than a minute, two minutes, unbelievable! Here I am calling long distance. Long distance – I remember how my mother used to say those two words, her voice stricken, worried and worshipful at the same time.

'Hello.'

'Seth,' I say, 'where were you just now?'

'I was just here,' he says maddeningly.

'Well, how are you getting along?'

'Fine.'

'How come you're up so early on a Saturday?'

'I just woke up now.'

'And you're getting along fine?' I ask again.

'Yeah, just fine.'

'You sound all out of breath.'

'Oh? I guess I'm just surprised to hear from you.'

'I had a few minutes in Winnipeg and I thought I'd just make sure everything was okay.'

'How are you?'

'Oh, fine. We get in tomorrow night. Aunt Judith will already be there. She'll probably meet us. At least I think so.'

Silence from Vancouver.

'Hello, Seth. Can you hear me? Are you there?'

'I'm still here. I can hear fine.'

'Good. Well, I'd better go. Just phone me if you need anything, okay?'

'Okay.'

'You've got the number?'

'Yeah.'

'Well, I guess I'd better say good-bye.'

'Good-bye.'

Two years ago when Seth started the orthodonture treatment he was advised to give up his tuba temporarily; for the year and a half while the bands were on his teeth he played the double bass. He was good at it; everyone remarked about how quickly he picked it up.

We bought the double bass third-hand through the want ads; we got it cheap because there was no case. It's a big, waxy, humming buzzard of an instrument, and because its bulk so nearly approximates that of a human being, I soon began to think of it as a sort of half-person, a rather chuckly, middle-aged woman, rather like me in fact.

One day Seth forgot to take it to school and he phoned me between classes asking if I could drop it off. I took it on the bus, feeling enormously proud of her polished, nut-brown hippiness, her deep-throated good nature, the way the sun struck off gleaming streaks on her lovely sides. Seth waited for me on the steps outside the school, frowning and a little anxious that I might be late. When he saw me getting off the bus he jumped up and ran to meet me, taking the instrument out of my arms, whirling about with it and kissing the air about its bridge. I can never get that picture out of my mind, how extraordinarily and purely happy he looked at that instant.

But the minute he had the bands off his teeth he went back to playing the tuba. I can't understand it. A tuba is such an awkward machine with its valves and convolutions; it's such an ugly brassy armload, and I don't understand what Seth likes in the choking, grunting noise that comes out of it.

There seems something rather perverse about his preference. He explains that he likes the tuba better because it's his voice that makes the sounds; the double bass has a voice of its own – it's just a question of letting it out, something anyone can do. I don't think he's touched the bass since. It stands, serene as ever, in a corner of his bedroom. He keeps a beach towel draped over it to keep off the dust, but no one loves it anymore.

Sometimes I think there's something symbolic about it, but symbolism is such an impertinence, the sort of thing the 'pome people' might contrive. (God knows how easily it's manufactured by those who turn themselves into continuously operating sensitivity machines.) Of course, symbols have their uses. But something – my cramped Scarborough girlhood no doubt – ties me to the heaviness of facts. Tubas and double basses are not symbols but facts, facts which can be – which must be – assimilated like any of the other mysterious facts of existence.

As the train moves closer to Toronto I decide I must warn Eugene a little about my mother. 'She's always been a difficult person,' I say.

'How do you mean, difficult?'

'Well, to begin with – you'll notice this right away – she's never been what you'd call demonstrative.'

'But she must have loved you. You and your sister?'

'It's hard to explain,' I say. Hard because she *had* loved us but with an angry, depriving love which, even after all these years, I don't understand. The lye-bite of her private rancour, her bitter shrivelling scoldings. When she scrubbed our faces it was with a single, hurting swipe. When we fell down and scraped our knees and elbows she said, 'that will teach you to watch where you're going.' Her love, if that's what you call it, was primitive, scalding, shorn of kindness. I can't explain it to Eugene; instead, I give him an example.

'When she brushed our hair in the morning, Judith's and mine, when she brushed our hair . . .'

'Yes?'

'She yanked it. Hard. It really hurt. She'd catch us in our bedroom, just before we left for school. She'd be holding the brush in her hand. When I think about it I can still feel her yanking my head back.'

Eugene listens without comment.

I shrug, afraid I've betrayed a streak of self-pity. 'That's just the way she is, and don't ask me why. I don't understand it. So how could you.'

I had forgotten about the thousand miles of bush between Winnipeg and Toronto. But here it is. Eugene and I are sitting high up in the Vistadome with nothing but curved glass separating us from turquoise lakes, whorled trees, the torn, reddened sky and, here and there, clumps of Indian cabins. We're sitting close to the front and so high up that we can overlook our whole train from end to end. We seem to vibrate to a different rhythm up here; the side-to-side swaying is gone; from this position we glide on cables of pure ozone. And music pours sweetly out of the chromium walls: Some Enchanted Evening. The hills are alive with the Sound of Music. Dancing in the Dark. Temptation – a tango – *You came, I was alone, I should have known you were temptation*. Eugene reaches over and takes my hand.

We met two years ago through mutual friends, the Freehorns, at a small dinner party in late May. It had been an utterly respectable occasion, in every way the reverse of my meeting with Watson which had occurred in a run-down neighbourhood drugstore, a meeting which was described in those days as a pick-up. *Watson was someone who picked up people. I was someone who had allowed myself to be picked up; was that what doomed us?*

But the meeting between Eugene and me was impeccably prearranged, although Bea Freehorn assured me before the party that even though she was inviting a single man, I was not to suspect her of matchmaking. 'There's nothing that burns me up more than being accused of fixing someone up,' she told me over the phone. 'But Eugene's a pet, you'll like him. Merv thinks he's terrific.'

Merv and Bea are old friends, so old that they date from the days when I was still married to Watson; the four of us, in times which now seem impossibly idyllic, used to take Sunday picnics up to the mountain; I would bring potato salad and a cake and Bea always brought salami and corned beef and sometimes cold chicken. Now they give dinner parties; I've tried to fix the year when they stopped inviting me to dinner and started inviting me to dinner parties. Sometime when Merv was between assistant and associate in the Law School. Or maybe after they moved into the new house, yes, I think that was it. They have a patio overlooking the ocean where Bea likes to serve dinner on tiny lantern-lit tables. She is an accomplished cook, and I would never turn down one of her dinner invitations with or without a suspicion of matchmaking.

'Actually,' Bea had confided, 'you and Eugene have something in common.'

'What?' I asked cautiously.

'You were both married for exactly eight years.'

It's hard sometimes to tell when Bea is being serious. I waited for the rough curl of her laughter but heard only earnest confidence. 'He's really had a rough time of it. His wife got screwed up with Women's Lib and just took the two kids one day and moved out. He has the boys on weekends, nice kids, but she won't take a penny from him, so in a way he's lucky. Anyway, he's a nice guy.'

Nice. Yes, I could see that right away when I met him. Nice, meaning polite, presentable, moderate, inquiring and almost sloshily good-natured. He arrived a little late with his right hand freshly bandaged and was apologetically unable to shake hands with the Freehorns, the Stevens, the Folkstones, or with me.

'I was cutting off a piece of beef at noon today,' he told us sadly. 'The whole plate slipped suddenly and there I was with a bloody gash.'

'Oh, Eugene,' Bea crooned kindly, 'did you need stitches?'

'A few,' he said bravely. 'The whole thing's been so damned stupid.'

I was prepared to dislike him. First for so perfectly fulfilling the role of the inept and picturesque bachelor who couldn't make a sandwich without sawing through his hand. And second for being a self-pitying poseur, and now monopolizing the conversation with his idiotic stitches.

'How are you going to be able to work?' Merv asked him conversationally, and, turning to me, he explained that Eugene was an orthodontist and thus required the use of his hands.

Eugene shrugged and smiled somewhat goofily, 'I'll take a week off. There's nothing else to do really.'

'What about all your appointments?' Gordon Stevens asked.

'I'll have to get Mrs Ingalls to cancel everything Monday morning.'

'What a shame,' Bea mourned, 'what a rotten shame. But look, Eugene, let Merv get you something to drink. That hand must be painful.'

'It *is* a bit,' he admitted.

Did I detect a hint of a whine? Was this ridiculous tooth straightener trying to solicit sympathy? If so, I was not prepared to give it. No wonder his wife ditched him, the big baby. I sipped my gin and tonic sullenly.

'Merv says you're a poet,' he said to me later, sitting beside me at one of the little tables along with Gord Stevens and Clara Folkstone. I gave him a long look; with enormous difficulty he was eating his stuffed artichoke with his left hand.

'Yes,' I said knowing that he was about to tell me he never read poetry.

'I can't pretend to know much about poetry,' he said. 'Except the usual stuff we had at school.'

'That's all right,' I said socially. 'It's a sort of minority interest. Like lacrosse.'

I had dressed for this evening with deliberate declassé nonchalance, aware that Bea expects me to contribute a faint whiff of bohemia to her parties; I wore a badly cut gypsy skirt and black satin peasant blouse, both bought at an Anglican Church rummage sale. Fortunately Bea's expectations conform to what I can afford. I had also brought my special party personality, the rough-ribbed humorous persona which I had devised for myself after Watson left me. I earn my invitations and even for an old friend like Bea Freehorn I knew better than to sulk all evening. So I smiled hard at Eugene as Bea brought round the veal fillets.

Encouraged he asked, 'What sort of poet are you? I mean, what kind of things do you write about?'

'About the minutiae of existence,' I said with mock solemnity. He looked baffled and, putting down his fork, he leaned over to whisper in my ear. Now, I thought, now he is going to ask me why poetry doesn't rhyme anymore.

But I was wrong; in a very low murmur, so low that I could hardly hear him, he asked if I would mind cutting up his meat for him.

I almost laughed aloud. But something stopped me; perhaps it was the extraordinary humility of the request or the reserve with which he made it. I leaned over, my elbows grazing his chest and, picking up his knife and fork, I began sawing through the pale, pink veal. My arm sliding back and forth touched the top of his wrist. Clara and Gordon smiled and watched at what seemed a great distance. Three, four, five pieces. I kept cutting, my eyes on Eugene's plate, until I had finished. Then I sat back breathless.

For while I was cutting Eugene's meat, a sudden blood-rush of tenderness had swept over me. A maternal echo? I had once cut Seth's meat in just this way. Perhaps someone had once cut up mine – I half remembered. Eugene's helpless right hand wound in beautiful gauze lay on the edge of the table, and it was all I could do to keep from seizing it and holding it to my lips. I wanted to put my arms around him, to cover him with kisses. The brutal knife, the surgical stitches, the vicious wife who had left him and exposed him to all the hurts of the world – I wanted to stroke them away; I wanted to comfort, to sooth, to minister. I wanted – was I crazy? – I wanted to love him.

We're not far from Toronto now. Another hour and we'll be there. It's getting darker; the towns are closer together now and the farmland is falling into round derby-shaped hills. Eugene is holding my hand and with his middle finger he is tracing slow circles on the palm of my hand. Around and around. The Vistadome where we sit is a tube of darkness. Now he is moving his thumb back and forth across the inside of my wrist. Slowly, slowly. I relax, put back my head, half-shut my eyes. The soundtrack of

Zorba the Greek is washing over us. Lighted towns, squared and tidy, flash by. Eugene has slipped a finger between the buttons of my dress and I can feel it sliding on my nylon slip. Then it retreats; he is carefully, quietly undoing one of the buttons. Now his hand is inside. It is spelling out something on my stomach, a sort of code. I smile to myself.

We flash by Weedham, Ontario. Watson. I had forgotten he was so close to Toronto. No more than thirty miles. Not much of a place; the train doesn't even stop.

Eugene's hand is slowly, slowly inching up my slip, gathering the folds of material. It slides easily. There. He's reached the lace hem. Now I can feel his hand on my bare thighs, the inside of my thighs. The music swamps us. I want to say something but nothing comes; my lips move in miniature as though they were preparing tiny, perfect chapel prayers.

He has reached the edge of my nylon elastic and for an instant we seem balanced on the brink – I think for sure he is stopped. We sit so still.

Then I feel his fingers slip quickly under the elastic and move toward darkness, moisture, secrecy. We are covered with darkness, but on the horizon the sky is soft with reflections. I sit still, half-drowning in a stirring helium happiness. The music rises like moisture and presses on the dark windows, and in this way we ride into the city.

Chapter 3

'Well,' I whisper to Judith when we are finally alone.

'Well,' she answers back, smiling.

It's midnight and we're standing in our slips in our mother's bedroom at the front of the old house in Scarborough. White nylon slips; Judith's is whiter than mine and fits better. Is there something symbolic about that? No, I reject the possibility.

I love Judith. I had forgotten how much I loved her until I saw her standing with her husband Martin and our mother behind the chaste iron gate at Union Station. She and Martin had come from Kingston on the morning train; we would have a few days together before the wedding.

Judith looked larger than I had remembered, or perhaps it was the colour and cut of her floppy, red denim dress. She has even less fashion sense than I, but unlike me she's able to translate her nonchalance into a well-meaning, soft-edged eccentricity which is curiously touching and even rather charming. She's aged a little. I haven't seen her since she and Martin were in Vancouver for a conference three years ago, and since then she's had her fortieth birthday. And her forty-first. Her daughter is eighteen now and her son is almost as old as Seth. I find myself involuntarily listing the areas of erosion: a small but generalized collapse of skin between her nose and mouth, the forked lines like fingers of an upturned hand between her eyes which make her look not querulous, but

264

worried and kindly, a detached dry point madonna. Her eyes are dreamier than I remembered. Our mother used to fret that Judith would ruin her eyes from so much reading as a girl, swallowing Lawrence and Conrad and Dreiser on summer afternoons stretched on a bath towel in our tiny backyard. Her eyes were sharper then, darting and energetic, the sort of eyes you would expect to harden with age, but they now show such softness. Of course, Judith's life has been embalmed in a stately, enviable, suburban calm. She has a husband who loves her, healthy children, a large, airy house in Kingston, not to mention a respectable reputation as a biographer. And most important, she has a seeming immunity to the shared, sour river of our girlhood.

The house is quiet. Our mother with a long, shrunken, remembered sigh has surrendered to us her bedroom. Green moire curtains discoloured in the folds, a forty-watt bulb in the ceiling fixture. And on the walnut veneer bed, a candlewick bedspread, here and there missing some of its fringe. There is a waterfall bureau, circa 1928, on which rests a precisely-angled amber brush and mirror set which has never, as far as I know, been used. This was our father's bedroom too; how completely we have put away that silent, hard-working husband and father. His wages met the payments on this bungalow; his bony frame rested for thirty years on half of this bed, and yet it seems he never existed.

Since there are only three bedrooms in the house, there was really no other way to arrange the sleeping. No one, of course, had counted on Eugene, least of all Eugene himself who would have preferred a downtown hotel room. It is at my perverse last minute insistence that he is staying here in Scarborough.

Why do I need him here? Perhaps because playing the role of pathetic younger-sister-from-the-west places too great a strain on me. Maybe I am anxious to make a final defiant gesture and give rein to my self-destructive urge which relishes awkward situations

– such as how to introduce Eugene to my mother. 'This is a friend of mine. Eugene Redding.'

Friend? But in my mother's narrow lexicon women don't have male friends. They have fathers, husbands and brothers. Her face, meeting Eugene at the station, had dissolved into a splash of open pain. Had I intended to cause such pain? Why hadn't I written ahead to explain about Eugene? But no one voiced these questions. Nevertheless she shook Eugene's hand slowly as if trying to extract some sort of explanation through his finger tips.

'I really don't want to put you out, Mrs McNinn,' Eugene had insisted. 'I told Charleen I would be perfectly happy in a hotel.'

There followed a small silence which could be measured not by seconds or minutes but by the cold, linear dimension of my mother's hurt feelings.

'I'm sure we can find room for everyone,' she said at last, sounding half paralysed, like someone who had recently suffered a stroke. 'Of course,' she trailed off defensively, 'it's only a small house.'

There was, naturally, no possibility of Eugene and me sharing a room. Anxious to please, I suggested sleeping with my mother and putting Eugene in the spare room, but she shuddered visibly at this idea. 'I'd never sleep a wink,' she said, plainly vexed. 'I'm used to sleeping alone.'

Another silence as we absorbed the irony of this statement; in less than a week she would be sleeping with a stranger called Louis Berceau.

Finally it was agreed that Martin and Eugene should take the twin beds in our old bedroom off the kitchen. Judith and I would occupy our mother's double bed, and our mother, perhaps for the first time in her life, would sleep in the old three-quarters bed in the spare room.

'Couldn't I sleep on the chesterfield?' Eugene suggested desperately.

We waited, breathless, for what seemed like the perfect solution. 'No,' our mother said with finality. 'No one on the chesterfield. That won't be necessary.'

What Eugene didn't know, what he couldn't possibly guess, was that no one had ever slept on our chesterfield. Never. Years ago our father, exhausted after a day at work, would occasionally stretch out for a minute and close his eyes. She would poke him, gently but relentlessly. 'Not here, Bert. Not on the chesterfield.' It was as though she saw something threatening in the way he spread himself, something disturbing and vulgar about the posture of ordinary relaxation.

'Not on the chesterfield,' she had said, giving us her final terms, and, like children, we accepted her decree. But inwardly I bled for Martin and Eugene in their forced awkward fraternity. I could imagine their inevitable stiff conversation – *All right with you to open the window? Whichever you prefer. Maybe you'd rather have the bed by the closet? You don't mind if I read for a while? Not at all, not at all.* – Strangers, two men in their early forties, shut up from their women in a tiny back bedroom with no more than a foot or two between their beds, and nothing in common in all this world but a bizarre attachment to the McNinn sisters, Charleen and Judith; they might, for that matter and with good reason, be silently questioning that attachment at this very moment. Martin, an easy man, though somewhat remote, would accept the situation, but he could not help minding the separation from Judith. He had even pleaded for the spare room himself. He and Judith wouldn't object to the three-quarters bed, he had said. But our mother, who seemed to feel that her hospitality was being challenged, had insisted on taking the spare room herself.

'Well?' Judith says again from across the room.

'How do you think she looks?' I ask.

That is always our first question when we're together, how is she, how does she look. Our voices dip and swim with the novel rhythm of concern, children's concern for a parent.

'Better than I expected,' Judith says.

'When did you see her last?'

'A couple of months ago. I came down on the train with the kids for the weekend.'

'She's still getting treatment?'

'She goes every month now. But next year it will probably be less. Down to every three months.'

'You talked to the doctor?'

'Yes. A couple of times. He thinks she's made a fantastic recovery.'

'What about a recurrence?'

'It could happen. That's why they want her to keep coming to the clinic.'

'She looks so thin.'

'She was always thin, Charleen. You've forgotten.'

'Well, then, she looks old.'

'She is old. She's seventy.'

'She's so pale though.'

'Not compared to what she was after the operation.'

'How soon after did you see her?'

'A month. She never told me she was even having an operation. Which was odd when you think how she always used to complain about her aches and pains. She never told anyone. She just went.'

'I didn't know until you wrote.'

'When I heard – the doctor finally phoned and told me – I came down and spent a week with her. She was feeling fairly strong by then and there was a nurse who came round every day to check up. She never talked about it. It. The breast. Just about the hospital and how rude the nurses had been and how thin the blankets were and how they hadn't given her tea with her breakfast. You know how she goes on. But the breast – she never mentioned it.'

'Does it hurt do you think?'

'I don't know. She never says.'

'What does she wear? I mean, does she have one of those false things?'

'It looks like it to me. What do you think?'

'She looks just the same there. With her dress on anyway.'

'Did you ever see her breasts, Charleen? I mean when we were little.'

'Never. You remember how she used to dress in the closet all the time. That was why it was so odd when you wrote me about the operation.'

'How do you mean, odd?'

'That she had a breast removed. It never seemed real to me. I just never thought of her as someone who had breasts.'

'What did she call them?'

'Breasts? I don't know. She must have called them something.'

'Not that I can remember.'

We sit on the bed thinking. The house is still and through the window screen we can hear a warm wind lapping at the edge of the awning.

'Developed,' Judith says at last, 'I think she just used the verb form. Like how so-and-so was developing. Or someone else was very, very developed or maybe not developed.'

Remembering, I smile. 'She always thought Aunt Liddy was too developed. Poor Liddy, she used to say, she's too developed to buy ready-made.'

Judith and I laugh together, quietly so no one will hear. This is the way it used to be. Lying in bed at night, laughing.

'Can't you just hear her telling the doctor that she has a lump in one of her developments,' I say.

'And he says, sorry to hear that, Mrs McNinn, but we'll just have to remove half your development.'

We laugh again, harder this time, so hard that the bed rocks. Crazy Judith. I put my hand over my mouth but Judith lets out a yelp of the old girlish cackle. Now we are both shaking with laughter, but there is something manic about all this mirth; it occurs to me that we are perilously close to weeping, and for that reason I reach over and switch off the light.

In the dark Judith asks, 'Were you absolutely stunned to hear about Louis?'

'Stunned!' I say. 'I'm still trying to get used to it. Is that the way you pronounce his name? Looey?'

'Yes. Like Louis the fourteenth, fifteenth, and sixteenth.'

'Have you met him?'

'Last time I was down. But just for a minute. He's coming over tomorrow though. To get acquainted with all of us.'

'Where on earth did she meet him? I mean, she never goes anywhere.'

'At the cancer clinic,' Judith says.

'Really?'

'Yes.'

'You mean . . .'

'Yes.'

'What exactly?'

'You mean what kind of cancer?'

'Yes.'

'I'm not sure. That is, she didn't go into details. But he's had three operations.'

'Three operations?'

'Amazing, isn't it?'

'Judith. Do you realize – that means he's missing three parts.'

'Possibly.'

270

'What,' I speak slowly, 'do you think they could be?'

'I don't know. But he doesn't look all that sick. At least not the quick look I had at him.'

'What *does* he look like, Judith?'

'Thin. Naturally. And I'm not sure but I think he may be a couple of inches shorter than she is.'

'Three operations! I can't get over it. What I mean is . . . don't you think . . . I mean, imagine embarking on marriage when you're in that state.'

'Maybe they were only minor operations.'

'Is he the same age she is?'

'Two years older. He's seventy-two.'

'But he was married before. She wrote that – that he had been married before.'

'Yes, but I don't know anything about his first wife, when she died or what.'

'Where does he live?'

'He has a furnished room. Not so far from here, just a few minutes. But he's giving it up and moving in here. After the wedding.'

'After the wedding,' I repeat the words.

'Doesn't it sound crazy? *The Wedding*.'

'And he's retired. What did he do before he was retired?' I reflect suddenly that I'm not so different after all from Doug Savage; what did he do – that was what I had to find out.

'He taught manual training. In a junior high school.'

'Manual training?'

'You know, like woodworking. And metalwork. Like when the girls went for cooking and sewing. Remember?'

'And that was his job? That's what he did?'

'Apparently.'

'And he lived in Toronto?'

271

'I think so. He doesn't speak a word of French, in spite of the French name; I asked him. But he used to be a Catholic.'

'A Catholic?'

'Uhuh.'

'How do you know?'

'She told me. When she told me about the manual training and all that.'

'She would never have told me that. She never tells me anything.'

'She doesn't tell me much, either,' Judith says. 'She writes every week, but it's always about the same old thing: the weather and her aches and pains or how much everything costs these days. I had to pump her about Louis.'

'I don't think she's ever forgiven me for running away with Watson.'

'Oh, Charleen, that was ages ago. I'm sure she never thinks about it anymore.'

'The scandal of it all,' I say bitterly. 'Having all the neighbours think I might be pregnant.'

'Charleen, you exaggerate.'

'Well, she never tells me anything.'

'Actually, there's something she hasn't told me. And I'm dying to know.'

I can't see Judith's face in the dark. 'What?' I ask.

'If she loves him. If he loves her.'

'I suppose they must. At least a little.' But I say this doubtfully.

'I'd give anything to know.'

'It's your biographical urge coming through.'

'It could be. What I want to know is, do they say romantic things like . . . well, like, "I love you" and all that.'

'I can't imagine *her* saying it.'

'I can't either. But maybe he does. Anyway, I wish I knew.'

'I don't suppose you could ask her?'

'God, no!' Judith says. 'She'd have a fit.'

'What I'd like to know is *why*.'

'Why what?'

'Why she's getting married. It just doesn't make sense. She's comfortable enough. Why on earth does she want to go and get married?'

There is a long pause. Perhaps Judith has fallen asleep, I think. Then I hear her short sigh, and what she says is: 'Well, why does anyone get married?'

'What I'd really like,' I say into the darkness, 'is some coffee.'

'So would I,' Judith says. 'I wonder if she's got any. She mostly drinks tea now.'

'Let's look,' I say, slipping out of bed.

'We'll wake everyone up.'

'Not if we're quiet.'

We move down the darkened hall. Judith walks ahead of me in an exaggerated clownish prowl, her knees pulling up through her yellow cotton nightgown in a burlesque mime of caution. The door to the kitchen is shut; she turns the knob slowly so that there is no sound, and we close it behind us with the smallest of clicks, snap on the overhead light and breathe with relief. Judith faces me, her upper teeth pulled down over her lower lip, girlish and conspiratorial.

Here in the kitchen there is a faint smell of roasted meat. Lamb? A fresh breeze blows through the window screen and the mixed scent of dampness and scouring powder rises from the sink. A newspaper, yesterday's, is folded neatly under the step-on garbage can beside the back door so that there will be no rust marks left on the squared linoleum; it has always been like this.

Our room, the bedroom that Judith and I shared as girls, leads off the kitchen; it is the sort of back bedroom that was commonplace in depression bungalows. Eugene and Martin – it excites me a little to think of it – are sleeping there now. Their door, which stands between the refrigerator (a model from the early fifties) and the old cupboard, is shut; Judith and I freeze for a moment in front of it, listening, straining to hear their fused breathing, but all we hear is the stirring of the wind outside the kitchen window. The trees in the backyard are swaying hugely, and I picture their new green buds, not yet fully opened, turning hard and black in the darkness. 'It looks like rain,' Judith remarks.

I find the jar of instant coffee at once; without thinking my hand finds the right shelf, reaches for the place beside the tea canister where I know it must be. A very small jar, the lid screwed tightly on. Judith boils water in the green enamel kettle and finds the everyday cups, and then we sit facing each other across the little brown formica table.

Suddenly there is nothing to say. We are uneasy; we are guilty invaders in our mother's clean-mopped kitchen; we have disturbed the symmetry of her lightly stocked shelves, have helped ourselves to sugar from her blue earthenware sugar bowl with its two flat-ear handles and its little flowered lid. 'Never leave a sugar bowl uncovered,' she always said. 'You never know when a fly might get in.' It is as though she is sitting here with us now, measuring, observing, censoring, as though she is holding us forcibly inside the sudden, unwilled silence we seem to have entered. I try to drink my coffee, but it's too hot.

Judith says at last, a little warily, 'Eugene seems nice.' It is not a statement; Judith would never make a statement as banal as that; it is a question.

And I answer conversationally. 'I wrote you about him, didn't I?'

As always there is a kind of ritual to our dialogue, for of course I know that I have written to Judith about Eugene and she knows it too. I wrote to her long ago telling her I had met Eugene, that he was working on Seth's teeth, that we had taken a holiday together in San Francisco. I can even recall some of the careful phrases I used in my letters to her. She has not suddenly forgotten, not Judith. It is only that she and I see each other so rarely that we are afraid we might misjudge the permitted area of intimacy. It is necessary to prepare the ground a little before we can speak. There is on Judith's side a wish not to weigh too heavily what I might have written off-handedly and perhaps now regret. On my side there is a wish to project nonchalance and laxity, to preserve at least a shadow of that fiction she half-believes me to be, a runaway younger sister, a casual libertine who has the edge on her, but only superficially, as far as worldliness goes. West-coast divorcée, free-wheeling poet, and now a sort of semi-mistress. We talk in careful, mutually drawn circles.

'When exactly did you meet him, Charleen?'

'Two years ago,' I tell her, 'two years now.'

'And?' Judith asks.

'Just that. Two years.'

'What about marriage?' she asks suddenly, recklessly, apparently tiring of fencing with me.

'I don't know,' I tell her.

'He's divorced too?'

'Yes.'

'It's all final and everything?'

'Yes. It's not that. Actually he'd like to get married again. I like his two boys and they like me. There's nothing to stop us really.'

'But you're not quite sure of him? Is that it?'

'I just can't seem to think straight these days.'

'What about Seth? What does he think of Eugene?'

'That's no problem. He likes Eugene. And he gets on great with the two kids. Seth likes everyone.'

It's so quiet in the kitchen. The red and white wall clock over the stove says five minutes past two. The refrigerator whines from its muffled electric heart and a very fine rain blows against the screen over the sink. Judith gets up and shuts the window.

'Seth likes everyone,' I say again. To understate is to risk banality, and these words echoing in the silent kitchen sound both trite and untrue. But they are true; he *does* like everyone, a fact which makes me feel – and not for the first time – a little frightened at my own child's open, unquestioning acceptance. Is it natural? Is it perhaps dangerous?

Judith doesn't notice. 'That's good,' she says. And waits for me to go on.

'I'm just waiting until I'm sure,' I tell her. 'I'm not rushing this time. I'm going to wait.'

How can I tell her what it is I'm waiting for; I hardly know myself. But I feel with the force of absolute, brimming certainty that there is something bulky and positive in the future for me, a thing, an event perhaps, that is connected with me in some way, with me, Charleen Forrest. If I were superstitious I might say it was written in the stars, and if I were half as bitter as Judith believes me to be, I might say it is because I deserve something at last. I know it's there. The numbers tell me: I lived in this brick bungalow for eighteen years. Then I was married to Watson Forrest for eight years. Now I have been divorced for twelve. The shapes, the pattern, the order of those random numbers spell out a kind of logic in my brain; they suggest the approach of another era, another way of being. I'm not a mystic but I know it's there, whatever it is.

*   *   *

I tell Judith about Brother Adam.

She is, as I might have expected, sceptical. Though she prizes her tolerance, in actual fact the edges of her life are sealed to exclude the sort of human flotsam which I have always been able to embrace. The title Brother is not definitive enough for Judith; it is loosely and embarrassingly sentimental, hinting at imposed familiarity and chummy handshakes.

'What's it supposed to mean exactly?' she questions. 'Is he a priest? Or what?'

'I think so. I'm not sure.'

'You mean in all these letters you've written, you've never asked him?'

I pause; it's hard to explain; some things do not yield to simplicity. 'That's the sort of question he might consider trivial. Too particularized, if you see what I mean.'

'But you think he *might* be a priest?'

'Well, he lives in a place called the Priory.'

'Which priory.'

'Just "The Priory".'

'And it's in Toronto?'

'Yes. In the Beaches area.'

'Are you going to see him?'

Another pause. 'Maybe,' I mumble this 'maybe', chewing the side of my cup, trying to conceal the leap of sensation this 'maybe' excites in me.

'But he *is* a botanist?' Judith asks.

'Yes. In a way. Actually, it's hard to tell.'

'What do you mean?'

'He seems to know all about plants. And he sent an article to the *Journal*. I more or less assumed that only a botanist would submit an article to a botanical journal.'

'What was it about?'

'Grass.'

'Grass? Was it any good?'

'Yes. And no. I liked it. But Doug – you remember Doug Savage, you met him in Vancouver when you were there – he thought it was hilarious.'

'You mean actually funny?'

'It wasn't funny. He wasn't trying to be funny at all. It was a serious article, passionately serious, in fact. And scientific in a way. It was a sort of sociology of grass, you might say. He has this theory about the importance of grass to human happiness.'

'Maybe he's talking about marijuana.'

'No. Just ordinary grass. Garden grass. He's trying to prove that where people don't have any grass, just concrete and asphalt and so on, then the whole human condition begins to deteriorate.'

'It sounds a little fanciful,' Judith's old scepticism again.

'In a way. I don't understand it all, to tell you the truth. But he writes with the most pressing sort of intensity, something much larger than mere eloquence. Anguished. But reflective too. Not like a scientist at all. More like a poet. Or like a philosopher.'

'But nevertheless the *Journal* turned it down?'

'Naturally. Doug thought it was just plain crazy.'

'And he gave you the job of returning it.'

'Yes. I send back all manuscripts we can't use. And usually I do it fairly heartlessly. But with Brother Adam it was different. I couldn't bear to have him think we utterly rejected what he'd written, that we sneered at what he believed in. I mean, that would be like saying no to something that was beautiful. And humiliating someone who was, well, beautiful too. Don't look so exasperated, Judith. I know I sound fatuous.'

'Go on. You sent the manuscript back to the Priory?'

'Yes. But instead of the usual rejection card, I enclosed a little note.'

'Saying . . . ?'

'Oh, just that I'd enjoyed reading the article, at least the parts I understood. I thought I'd better be honest about it. And I said I thought it was a shame we couldn't use an article like that now and then to break the monotony. Everything we print is so detached. You wouldn't believe it, Judith. I should send you an issue. It's inhuman. The prose style sounds factory-made, all glued together with qualifying phrases. And here at last was an article spurting with passion. From someone who really loved grass. To lie on, to walk on, to sit on. Or to smell. Just to touch grass, he feels, has restorative powers.'

'Why grass? I mean, why not flowers or fruit or something? Or trees, even? Isn't grass just a little, you know, ordinary? After all, there's a lot of it around. Even these days.'

'That's partly why he loves it, I think. The fact that grass is so humble. And no one's ever celebrated grass before.'

'Walt Whitman?'

'That was different. That was more of a symbolic passion.'

'What happened after you wrote to him?'

'Nothing at first. A month at least, maybe even longer. Then I got a parcel. Delivered to the *Journal* office.'

'From Brother Adam.'

'Yes. But you'd never guess what was in it.'

'Grass.'

'Yes.'

We both laugh. 'It wasn't really grass, of course.' I explain. 'It was only the stuff to grow it with. There was a sprouting tray. And some earth in a little cloth bag. Lovely earth really, very fine, a kind of sandy-brown colour. It was clean, clean earth. As though he'd dug it up especially and sieved it and prayed over it. And then

279

there was the packet of seeds. Not the commercial kind. His own. He does his own seed culture.'

'And a letter?'

'No. No letter. Not even instructions for planting the seeds. Just the return address. Brother Adam, The Priory, 256 Beachview, Toronto.'

'How odd not to send a note.'

'That's what made it perfect. A gift without words. As though the grass *was* the letter. As though it had a power purer than words.'

Judith laughs. 'You always were a bit of a mystic, Charleen.'

'But what really touched me, I think, was the parcel itself. The way it was wrapped.'

'How was it wrapped?'

'Beautifully. I don't mean aesthetically. After all, there's a limit to the power of brown paper and string. But it was so neatly, so handsomely done up.'

With such touching precision. The paper, two layers, that crisp, waxy paper, every corner perfect, and the knots were tight and trimmed and symmetrical like the knots in diagrams. And the address was printed in black ink in lovely blocky letters. 'I hated to open it, in a way,' I risk telling her.

Opening it I had had the sensation of being touched by another human being; I had felt the impulse behind the wrapping – and the strength of his wish, his inexplicable wish to please me. Me!

Judith smiles and says nothing, but from her amused gaze I see she thinks I am absurd. Nevertheless she's waiting to hear more. My account of Brother Adam cannot really interest her much – though she is currently writing a biography of a nineteenth-century naturalist and is somewhat curious about the scientific impulse – but she listens to me with the alert probing attention that she has perfected.

'At first I thought of planting the grass at the office, but I was worried it would go dry over the weekend. Besides I didn't want to answer any questions about it. Doug Savage has a way of taking things over.' *And besides it would have given his imagination something to feed on; he and Greta cherish my eccentricities as though they were rare collectables.*

'Go on.'

'So I took the whole thing home on the bus. Seth thought it was a wonderful present, not at all peculiar, just wonderful. And we put in the seeds that same day. There's quite a lot of sun in the living room. At least for Vancouver. Anyway you don't need strong sunlight for grass. One of the things Brother Adam likes about grass is the way it adapts to any condition. It has an almost human resilience. He hates anything rigid and temperamental like those awful rubber plants everyone sticks in corners these days.'

'I like rubber plants.'

'Anyway, grass can put up with almost anything. I have it in a box by the window and it does well there.'

I have to hold my tongue to keep from telling Judith more: the way, for instance, I felt about those first little seeds. That they might be supernatural, seeds sprouted from a fairy tale, empowered with magical properties, that they might produce overnight or even within an hour a species of life-giving, life-preserving grass. How that night I fell asleep thinking of the tiny, brown seeds lying sideways against the clean, pressing earth, swelling from the force of moisture, obeying the intricate commands of their locked-in chromosomes. Better not tell Judith too much; she might, and with reason, accuse me of overreacting to a trifling gift. She, who has never doubted herself, couldn't possibly understand how I could attach such importance to a gift of grass seed or the fact that it placed a burden on me, a responsibility to make the seeds sprout; their failure to germinate would spell betrayal or, worse, it would summarize my fatal inability to sustain any sort of action.

'Was it any good?' Judith asks. 'The grass seed, I mean?'

'Within three days,' I tell her, making an effort to speak with detachment, 'the first, pale green, threadlike points of grass had appeared. I watered them with a sprinkling bottle, the kind Mother used to dampen clothes on the kitchen table. Every morning and again at night. Sometimes Seth took a turn too.'

'And then you wrote to thank Brother Adam for the grass and that was the start of your friendship?'

'Actually I made myself wait two weeks before I wrote. I wanted to make sure the grass was going to survive. By the time I wrote, all of it was up. Some of it was over an inch high. And I cut two or three shoots with my manicure scissors and Scotch-taped them to the letter.'

Judith smiles dreamily; I have managed, I can see, to delight her. 'But what,' she asks, 'does one do with a box of grass?'

'It's strange, but I've become very fond of it. It's divinely soft, like human hair almost. And brilliant green from all that water. I have to trim it about once a week with sewing shears. Sometimes I sprinkle on a little fertilizer although Brother Adam says it's not really necessary.' *I also like to run my hand over its springy tightly-shaved surface, loving its tufted healthy carpet-thick threads, the way it struggles against the sides of the box, the industry with which it mends itself.*

'And you've been writing to each other ever since?'

'Yes, more or less.'

'Often?'

'Every three or four weeks. I'd write more often but I don't want to wear him down.' There is also of course, the fact that an instant reply would place Brother Adam in the position of a debtor – and to be in debt to a correspondent is to hold power over a creditor, a power I sensed he would not welcome.

'What do you write about, Charleen?'

I have to think. 'It's funny, but we don't write much about ourselves. He's never asked me anything about myself – I like that. And I don't pester him either. He usually writes about what he's feeling at the moment or what he's seeing. Like once he saw a terrible traffic accident from his window. Once he wrote a whole letter about a wren sitting outside on his fire escape.'

'A whole letter about a wren on a fire escape!'

'Well, yes, it was more on the metaphysical side.'

'And you do the same?'

'Sort of. I don't so much write as compose. It takes me days. I've hardly written any poetry lately. All of it seems to go into those letters, all that old energy. Writing to him is – I don't know how to explain it – but writing those letters has become a new way of seeing.'

'Therapeutic,' Judith comments shortly, almost dismissively.

'I suppose you could call it that.'

'I wish you wrote to me more often.'

'I wish you wrote to me too.'

'We always say this, don't we?'

'Yes.'

'Charleen?'

'What?'

'What does Eugene think of your . . . your relationship with Brother Adam?'

Judith has always been clever. A bright girl in school, a prizewinner at university; now she is referred to in book reviews as a clever writer. But her real cleverness lies not in her insights, but in her uncanny ability to see the missing links, the ellipses, the silences. Like the perfect interviewer she asks the perfect question. 'What does Eugene think?' she asks.

Eugene doesn't know, I tell her. He doesn't know Brother Adam even exists.

*   *   *

After a while Judith asks me if I'm feeling hungry. 'We could make some toast,' she suggests.

I nod, although I'm not so much hungry as emptied out; a late night hollowness gnaws at me, the grey, uneasy anxiety I always feel in this house. The rain is coming down hard now, leaving angry little check marks on the black window, and the house has grown chilly.

In the breadbox we find exactly one-third of a loaf of white, sliced bread. The top of the bag has been folded down carefully in little pleats to preserve freshness. 'A penny saved . . .' our mother had always said. Meagreness.

A memory springs into focus: how I once asked for a piece of bread to put out for the birds. 'They can look after their own the same as we have to,' she replied. Ours, then, had been a house without a birdfeeder, a house where saucers of milk were not provided for stray cats. This was a house where implements were neither loaned nor borrowed, where the man who came to clean the furnace was not offered a cheering cup of coffee, where the postman was not presented with a box of fudge at Christmas. (Such generosities belonged only to fairy tales or soap operas.) In this house there was no contribution to the Red Cross nor (what irony) to the Cancer Fund. Meagreness. I had almost forgotten until I saw the bread in the bread-box.

'Maybe we'd better not have any toast after all,' Judith says, tight-lipped. 'She'll be short for breakfast.'

Instead we make more coffee, stirring in extra milk and sugar. I turn to Judith and ask if she has bought a wedding gift for our mother.

'Not yet,' she says clutching her hair in a gesture of frenzy. 'And it isn't because I haven't thought and thought about it.'

'I haven't bought anything either,' I admit. 'Not yet anyway.'

'Do you have any idea what she'd like?'

'Not one.'

'Why is it,' Judith demands, 'that it's so hard to buy our own mother a present? It isn't just this damned wedding present either. Every Christmas and birthday I go through the same thing. Ask Martin. Why is it?'

I'm ready with an answer, for this is something about which I've thought long and hard. 'Because no matter what we give her, it will be wrong. No matter how much we spend it will be either too much or too little.'

'You're right,' Judith muses. (I marvel at her serene musing, at her willingness to accept the way our mother is.)

'She's never satisfied,' I storm. 'Remember when we were in high school and put our money together one Christmas and bought her that manicure kit. In the pink leather case? It cost six dollars.'

'Vaguely,' Judith nods. (Fortunate, fortunate Judith; her memories are soft-edged and have no power over her.)

'I'll never, never forget it,' I tell her. 'We thought it was beautiful with the little orange stick and the little wool buffer and scissors and everything all fitted in. It was lovely. And she was furious with us.'

'Why was that?' Judith wonders.

'Don't you remember? She thought we were criticizing her, that we were hinting she needed a manicure. She told us that if we worked as hard as she did we would have ragged finger-nails too.'

'Really? I'd forgotten that.'

'And the things we made at school. For Mother's Day. I made a woven bookmark once. She said it was nice but the colours clashed. It was yellow and purple.'

'Well,' Judith shrugs, 'gratitude was never one of her talents.'

'Eugene suggested I give her an Eaton's gift certificate. But

285

CAROL SHIELDS

you know just what she'd say – people who give money can't be bothered to put any *thought* into a gift.'

'That's right,' Judith nods. 'Remember how Aunt Liddy used to send us a dollar bill for our birthdays, and Mother always said, "Wouldn't you think with all the time Liddy has that she could go out and buy a proper birthday present."'

'Poor Aunt Liddy.'

'I thought of a new bedspread,' Judith says, 'but she might think I was hinting that her old one is looking pretty beat up. Which it is.'

'And *I* thought of ordering a flowering shrub for the yard, but she would be sure to say that was too impersonal.'

'On the other hand,' Judith says, 'if we were to get her a new dressing gown that would be *too* personal.'

'There's no pleasing her.'

'Why do we even try?' Judith asks lightly, philosophically. 'Why in heaven's name don't we give up trying to please her?'

This is a question for which I have no answer, and so I say nothing. I drink my coffee which is already cold. We're on a psychic treadmill, Judith and I; we can't stop trying to please her. There's no logic to it, only compulsion; even knowing it's impossible to please her, we can't stop ourselves from trying.

I hadn't intended to talk about Watson; my divorce is a subject I've never really discussed with Judith. It should be easy these free-wheeling days to discuss ex-husbands, but it is never easy for me. In spite of the statistics, in spite of the social tolerance, there is nothing in the world so heavy, so leaden, so painfully pressing as love that has failed. I rarely talk about it – I make a point not to talk about it – but somehow Judith and I have got on to the subject.

We've crept back into bed, and, shivering under a light blanket, I ask Judith if she minded turning forty.

286

'Yes,' she answers thoughtfully, 'but only a little.'

'You didn't feel threatened or anything?'

'Not really. Of course, it helps that Martin gets to all the terrible birthdays first.'

'But what about Martin? Didn't he mind?'

'I don't know,' Judith says, sounding surprised. And then she adds, 'But he doesn't *seem* to mind.'

'Eugene is forty,' I burst out.

There is a pause; Judith doesn't know what to do with this information.

'Is he?' she says politely.

'And he doesn't mind a bit. He insisted we go out and celebrate it. Cake, candles, the works.'

'Well, why not?'

'He likes being forty. I think he'd even like to be older. Forty-five, fifty maybe.'

'That's nice for him,' Judith comments.

'It's a little worrying, don't you think, rushing into old age like that?'

'Maybe his youth wasn't all that marvellous,' she suggests.

I think of Jeri and agree.

'Anyway,' Judith says, 'the saving grace of reaching forty is that most of your friends get there about the same time.'

'I suppose that's a comfort.'

'It helps.'

'Watson is forty-two,' I say. 'Imagine!'

'That's right,' Judith says, 'he was about the same age as me.'

'It must have killed him turning forty.'

'Why do you say that?'

'Remember how he went berserk at thirty? Forty must have been a funeral for him.'

'Of course,' Judith says slowly, 'I never knew Watson very well, but it's hard to believe that a mere birthday could hit anyone so violently.'

'It did though. I saw it coming, of course. Even when he was twenty-seven he was starting to get a bit shaky. Once I even heard him lie about his age. He told some people we met, for no reason at all, that he was only twenty-five.'

'Strange.'

'He seemed to take it into his head that he could go backwards in time if he put enough energy into it. And that was the same year he started hanging around with his students all the time, especially the undergraduates. And talking about the university as "they". He even had me go and get my hair straightened so I'd look like one of his students.'

'Poor Char,' Judith says softly.

Her sympathy is all I need. Now I can't stop myself. 'Then he really began to get desperate. The first time I saw him wearing a head band I was actually sick. Literally. I went into the bathroom and was sick. I wouldn't have minded if someone had given him the head band, one of his students maybe, but what killed me was the deliberation of it all, that he woke up one day and decided to go to a store – it was Woolworth's – and buy himself an Indian head band. And then picking it out and paying for it and then slipping it on his head. And looking at himself in the mirror. That's the moment I couldn't live with, the moment he looked in the mirror at his new head band.'

Judith sounds puzzled. 'Lots of people wore head bands at one time.'

'But don't you see, other people sort of drift into it. They don't suddenly make a conscious decision to hold on to their youth by running out and buying some costume accessories.'

'And then what happened?' She is right when she says she scarcely knew Watson. She met him only twice and all she knows about the divorce is that Watson suffered a breakdown. A breakdown?

Perhaps not really a breakdown, although that was the term we used at the time, since it was, at least, medically definable. It was Watson's breakdown that made him a saint to Greta Savage: she saw it as a powerful link between them, as though their mutual lapse from the coherent world spelled mystical union, impenetrable by those of us coarsened by robust mental health.

But what Watson suffered was something infinitely more shattering than poor Greta: more of a break up than a break down. He broke apart. At the age of thirty he fell apart. Watson broke into a thousand pieces, and not one of those pieces had any connection with past or future.

'When he was twenty-nine,' I tell Judith, 'he decided we should sell the house so he and Seth and I could walk across Europe.'

'*Walk* across Europe.'

'With backpacks and sandals, a sort of gypsy thing. He had this crazy idea that he could earn enough money by playing the recorder, you know, in the streets of Europe.'

'Did Watson play the recorder? I didn't realize he was musical.'

'He wasn't. It was another of his delusions. Oh, he could play all right, about three tunes, and one of them was "Merrily We Roll Along". It was awful. I don't know where Seth got his musical ability but it wasn't from Watson.'

'How odd.'

'Doug Savage says he became totally detached from reality. In fact everyone we knew told him he was crazy, but he wouldn't listen. He actually had this image of himself tootling away in cute Greek villages with all the fat, red-faced fishermen loving him. I was supposed to write poems, Joan Baez style, and he would set them to music. And if this scheme fell through, he wasn't worried.

He was into brotherly love – remember love-ins? – and he was convinced that love was a commodity, like cash, that could take us anywhere. All we had to do was project it.'

'What do you suppose would have happened if you'd actually gone?' Judith asks.

'I've asked myself that a hundred times. What if I'd said okay, I'll come. What if I'd taken him at his word, bought myself an Indian skirt and a guitar and followed him. At one point, you know, I had almost decided to go.'

'Why didn't you then?'

'Two reasons. First, he stopped wanting me to come. By that time he'd already quit the university. Just walked in one day and told Doug Savage he was finished with Establishment values. He used the word "establishment" all the time as if it was a hairy, yellow dog nipping at his heels. And then, overnight, it seemed I was part of the Establishment too. Wife. Kid. House. We were all part of it. He stopped talking about walking across Europe with us. We just weren't in the picture any longer. For that last year, in fact, I was his wife on sufferance.'

'So he left alone?'

'The day after his thirtieth birthday. Which we did not celebrate, needless to say. He must have got up at dawn. Later I reconstructed the whole thing – I used to torture myself with it. He probably wanted to see the sun rise on the first day of his new life. He was like that you know, very big on symbols. I could just picture how he must have stood in the doorway of our house, very theatrical, with the sun coming up over the hedge. And the note he left! It was like the head band, very studied, very deliberate. A big, fat gesture. I tore it up. Oh, Judith, it was so terribly dumb. I've never told anyone about the note. It was just page after page of youth cult hash. Abstractions like freedom and selfhood, you know the thing. I've never had any stomach for words like "challenge" and "fulfilment" anyway, but from Watson . . . I could have died. I was so embarrassed for him.'

'Oh, Char.'

'I tore it up. And I wanted to burn it but of course we didn't have a fireplace in that house. And bonfires are illegal in Vancouver, so I burned all the little pieces in the habachi out in the yard. And all the time I was burning them I thought how he would have relished the symbolism. He hated barbecues. He always thought they were the altars of North America where people gathered to worship big pieces of meat. He was already into vegetarianism, of course. In fact – and that was what I hated most – he was into everything. Name any branch of the counter-culture and Watson had swallowed it whole. Oh, it was all so desperate. And so badly done. Do you know what I mean? If only he had done it . . . gracefully.'

For a minute Judith says nothing. Then she says, 'You said there were two reasons.'

'What do you mean?'

'You said there were two reasons you didn't go with him to Europe. What was the other one?'

'Because,' I say with a short, harsh laugh, 'because I was afraid of what Mother might think.'

'What about Seth?' Judith asks after a long pause.

'What about him?'

'I don't suppose he remembers Watson. He was only three, wasn't he?'

'No, he doesn't remember anything. Not even the house we lived in.'

'He must be curious about him. His own father. You'd think he'd want to meet him.'

'No, it's funny but he's never mentioned wanting to meet him. But once he told me he was going to write him a letter. He was about ten then, I think, and it was just after the monthly cheque

291

came. Just before he went to sleep he told me he had decided to write a letter.'

'And did he?'

'Yes, he did, and he spent a long time on it. I helped him a little. And it really was a nice kid-like letter all about school and sports and hobbies and his favourite TV programs, sort of a pen pal thing.'

'And did Watson ever write back?'

'No. Months and months went by and I kept thinking any day it'll come. I figured Watson couldn't be so cruel as not to write to his own son – after all, he *does* drop Greta a line now and then. Finally I said to Seth how strange it was his father hadn't answered his letter. And do you know what he said?'

'What?'

'He just laughed and said, "I never mailed that letter." '

'Why not?'

'I asked him why. I asked him two or three times why he hadn't mailed it. But he would never tell me.'

Three-fifteen. The luminous dial of Judith's travel clock announces the hour. She is asleep, lying on her side facing the wall with one arm slung awkwardly, almost grotesquely, over her shoulder. I'm jealous of her ability to sleep, but I am also irrationally pained that she has been able to fall asleep just minutes after I have recounted the miserable story of Watson's breakdown.

My breakdown too; that's the part I didn't confess, the part I conceal even from myself except when I am absolutely alone in the middle of the night as I am now. The day Watson left, everything more or less fell apart for me too. The world, which I was just beginning to perceive, was spoiled. Everything ruined, everything scattered.

Scattered like me, the way I'm scattered through this house:

292

in the spare room where my aggrieved mother sleeps her thin, complaining sleep. And here where Judith lies drugged on my wretchedness. And in the silent back bedroom where Eugene dreams of us riding into Toronto on the Vistadome. In Weedham, Ontario, where Watson Forrest lies amidst the welter of his strange compulsions. And in Vancouver where my son Seth – think of it – I have a fifteen-year-old son who is sleeping safely in a strange glass and cedar bedroom in the corner of the Savages' house.

But it is not three-fifteen in Vancouver. A rib of joy nudges me. No, it is not three-fifteen. In Vancouver it is late evening. There is probably a soft grey rain falling. It is not even midnight yet. The TV stations are going strong; the late show hasn't even begun. Doug and Greta almost certainly are still awake; they never go to bed until one or two in the morning. Greta likes to read in bed – she is addicted to crime thrillers – and Doug likes to smoke his pipe and listen to Bartok on the record player. True, Seth may be asleep; he is usually in bed fairly early, but it isn't as though this were the middle of the night.

I'll telephone. I can dial direct; I know the number by heart. It's long distance, but I can keep track of the time and leave money to cover the call. My mother will object – the thought of the charge on her monthly bill will be grievous to her – but it will be too late then. I should have thought of phoning earlier, but there's no harm in calling now, not if I go about it quietly. In fact, this is a good time to phone because the Savages are sure to be at home.

The telephone is in the hallway, a black model sitting on my mother's gossip bench, a spindly piece of furniture from the twenties, half way to being a real antique. I need only the light of the tiny table lamp, and I dial as quietly as I can, marvelling at the technology that permits me, by dialing only eleven numbers, to sift through the millions of darkened households across the country and reach, through tiny electronic connections, the only person in the world who is really and truly connected with me.

But in Vancouver no one answers. I hang up, wait five minutes and try again. The phone rings and rings. I can picture it, a bright red wall model in the Savages' birch and copper kitchen. It rings twelve times, twenty times. No one is home. Can they possibly sleep through all this wild ringing? Impossible. No one is home.

Why can't I sleep? Why can't I be calm like Judith, why can't I learn to be brave? Why is my heart thudding like this, why can't I sleep?

Chapter 4

I n the morning my mother's bedroom is filled with sunlight.
Someone has opened the curtains, and high above the asphalt-
shingled roof of the house next door floats an amiable, blue,
suburban sky terraced with flat-bottomed clouds, lovely. Shutting
my eyes again I tense, waiting for fear to reassume its grip on me,
but it doesn't come.

The sun has brought with it a calm perspective, and suddenly
I can think of dozens of reasons why Doug and Greta might not
have been at home last night. They might, for instance, have had
concert tickets; Doug is a music lover and never, if he can help
it, misses the symphony. They might have gone to an exhibition
at the university and taken Seth along; hadn't I seen a notice
about the opening of a pottery show or something like that in
the Fine Arts Building? Or they might have gone out for a late
dinner. (Greta frequently has days when, maddened by the world's
unhappiness, she cannot summon the strength to cook a meal.)
Or taken in a movie. Or gone for a stroll on the beach. There
were countless possibilities, none of which had occurred to me
the night before.

And this morning, waking up, I yawn, stretch, smile to myself.
Nine o'clock. There is no reason to hurry. This evening I can
phone Vancouver again; if I phone about ten o'clock I will be
sure to catch them at home.

I dress lazily, savouring the rumpled feel of the unmade bed, the open suitcases on the floor, the faintly stale bedroomy air. Through the shut door a burr of lowered voices reaches me, my mother's, Martin's, and whose is that other voice? Of course, Eugene's.

A determined indifference is the perfect cure for anxiety. That's what Brother Adam wrote me. I take my time. I unpack and hang up my clothes in my mother's closet, arranging them next to her half dozen dresses – such dresses: limp, round-shouldered, jersey-knit prints, all of them, in off-colours like maroon and avocado, grey and taupe. They give off a sweetish-sourish smell, very faint, a little musty. Beside them my new orange dress appears sharply synthetic and aggressively youthful. I am sorry now I bought it. For today, I decide, I will put on my old beige skirt instead. And a blouse, a dotted brown cotton which is only slightly creased across the yoke.

In the living room I find Martin, hunched on the slipcovered chesterfield with several sections of the *Globe and Mail* scattered around him. After all these years I scarcely know him. He is an English professor, Renaissance, and as is the case with a good many academics, his essential kindness is somewhat damaged by wit. And a finished reserve. As though he had spent years and years simmering to his present rich sanity, his pot-au-feu pungency. He is a little uneasy with me – I am so brash, so non-Judith – but his uneasiness has never worried me; our present non-relationship has a temporary, transitional quality; at any moment, it seems to me, we will find our way to being friends. For Martin is a man with a talent for friendship, and in this respect I once believed that Watson resembled him, Watson who knew hundreds and hundreds of people, whole colonies of them secreted away in the cities and towns between Toronto and Vancouver. The difference, I later observed, was that for Watson friendship was not a pleasing dispensation of existence but a means, the only means he knew, by which he could be certain of his existence.

'Well,' Martin greets me, 'I hear you and Judith made a night of it last night.'

'We had a lot of catching up to do,' I say. 'I hope I didn't wear out her ear drums.' I add this apologetically, feeling that Martin might begrudge me a night of Judith's companionship while he himself has been relegated to the back bedroom.

But he smiles quite warmly and says, 'Why don't you come and spend a week with us after the wedding and really get caught up?'

'I wish I could,' I tell him, 'but Seth's staying with friends. And there's my job.'

'Surely you could take a few days?' he urges.

Does Martin think I have no responsibilities, nothing to nail me down? No life of my own? And what about Eugene? But I sense that his invitation is no more than a rhetorical exercise; cordial, yes, but mechanically issued. Martin grew up in a hospitable, generous Montreal household where the giving and receiving of invitations was routine, as simple as eating, as simple as breathing.

'Where's Judith now?' I ask, looking around.

'She went out for a few groceries.'

I nod, remembering the few slices of bread and the half quart of milk in the refrigerator. 'Has everyone had breakfast?'

'Everyone but you. Judith thought you'd prefer to get some sleep. Afraid we didn't leave you anything though. She's gone for some more coffee and bread,' he looks at his watch, 'but she should be back in a few minutes.'

In the kitchen my mother stands washing dishes in the sink; Eugene in a well-pressed spring suit stands next to her, drying teacups and valiantly trying to make conversation. Seeing me in the doorway he almost gasps with relief. 'Charleen!'

'Well, you had yourself a good sleep,' my mother says, not turning around. (Couldn't she even turn around? Does Eugene notice this greeting, this lack of greeting?)

'Yes,' I say, determined to remain unruffled. 'I thought I'd be lazy today.'

She turns around then, carefully assessing me from top to toe, hair, blouse (creased), skirt, stockings, shoes, and says tartly, 'Mr Berceau – Louis I should say – is dropping by this morning to meet you.'

'Good,' I answer, rather too lightly, 'I'm looking forward to meeting him.'

'In that case it's too bad you picked this morning to sleep in. Because you haven't had your breakfast and he's coming at ten o'clock. He's always right on time, right on the dot. We all had breakfast at eight o'clock. Toast and coffee. I told Dr Redding,' she nods sharply at Eugene, 'that I hoped he wasn't expecting a big breakfast. We never were a bacon and egg house here. I can't eat all that fried food for breakfast anyway. We just have toast and coffee and always have, guests or no guests. But there's no toast for you. We just completely ran out of bread. That's something I never do normally, run out of things. I plan carefully. You remember, Charleen, how I always planned carefully. There's no excuse for waste, I always say. Of course, I didn't know Dr Redding would be here, you didn't write about him staying here, or I would have bought an extra loaf. Martin always eats at least three pieces of toast. Not that he needs it. I told Judith this morning he should watch his starches. I never have more than one. I've never been a heavy eater, and a good thing with the price of food. Well, we're right out of bread. Martin even ate the heel, not that there's anything wrong with that. Waste not. Then Judith said, never mind, she'd go down to the Red and White. You'd never know the Red and White now. The floor, it's filthy, just filthy, they used

298

to keep it so clean in there; you remember, Charleen, it used to be spotless when the old man was alive. Spotless. And they let people bring their dogs in, and I don't know what. I thought Judith would be back by the time you woke up but she isn't. I don't know what in the world's keeping her. She always was a dawdler, it's only a block away and it shouldn't be crowded at this time of the morning. And here you are up already. Judith thought you'd sleep in until she got back and here you are and there's nothing for breakfast. You should have got up with the rest of us. And here's Dr Redding wiping dishes, he insisted, and he's in a rush to get downtown. But Judith said the two of you were up half the night talking away. I thought I heard someone up banging around in the kitchen. You and Judith need your sleep, you don't need me to remind you about that, and here you are up to all hours. How do you expect to get your rest when you sit up all night? You've got all day to talk away. The rest of us need our sleep too.'

Eugene, rose-stamped teacup in hand, listens stunned. I have to remember that he has come unprepared, that he has never met anyone like my mother, that she has always been like this. Nevertheless I feel an uncontrollable tremor of pity seeing her this morning in her exhausted, chenille dressing gown, white-faced, despairing and horribly aged, her wrists angry red under the lacy suds.

I watch Eugene standing by the sink, slightly stooped, tea towel in hand, looking at once humble and affluent with his well-trimmed, woolly hair and faintly anxious and uncomfortable expression. It isn't difficult for me to imagine the questions taking shape in Eugene's head, questions he would never voice or perhaps even acknowledge as his own. Questions like: Why is Mrs McNinn angry with Charleen? What has Charleen done? Why don't these two women, mother and daughter, embrace? Why don't they smile at each other? Why doesn't Charleen ask

299

CAROL SHIELDS

her mother how she's feeling? Why doesn't Mrs McNinn ask if
Charleen slept well?

As I imagine the questions, the answers too spring into being,
the answers which Eugene would almost certainly formulate:
Mrs McNinn is angry because she is not in good health; she
is possessed of a rather nervous disposition; it is probable that
she slept poorly last night. She is, in addition, confused about
who I, Eugene Redding, am, and she is somewhat bothered by
the fact that she hadn't been expecting an extra guest. She is
unused to house guests and is now embarrassed because she has
run short of food. But it is nothing serious; it will pass.

I am able to frame these answers because I know Eugene
and trust him to find, as he always does, the most charitable
explanation, the most kindly interpretation. Kindness, after all,
comes to him naturally; he was hatched in its lucky genre and
embraces its attributes effortlessly. Gentleness, generosity and
compromise are not for him learned skills; they have always been
with him, wound up with the invisible genes which determine the
woolliness of his hair and the slightly vacant look in his grey eyes.
It may, for all I know, have existed in his family for generations.
He is not at the frontier as I am.

For me kindness is an alien quality; and like a difficult French verb
I must learn it slowly, painfully, and probably imperfectly. It does *not*
swim freely in my bloodstream – I have to inject it artificially at the
risk of all sorts of unknown factors. It does *not* wake with me in the
mornings; every day I have to coax it anew into existence, breathe
on it to keep it alive, practise it to keep it in good working order.
And most difficult of all, I have to exercise it in such a way that it
looks spontaneous and genuine; I have to see that it flows without
hesitation as it does from its true practitioners, its lucky heirs who
acquire it without laborious seeking, the lucky ones like Eugene.

*   *   *

300

Louis Berceau arrives precisely at ten o'clock in a small, dark-green Fiat which he parks at the curb in front of the house. When he knocks at the back door, Judith is making fresh coffee, and Eugene has just left by taxi for the dental convention downtown, an extravagance which both shocked and impressed my mother. ('Doesn't he know we have a subway? Well, I know it's pokey, but it's good enough for most people.')

Judith has been mistaken about Louis's height; he is considerably shorter than our mother, perhaps as much as six inches. And he is thin – certainly I had not expected that he would be robust – with enormously wrinkled, whitish-yellow skin; his gnarled peanut face – how humble he looks! – and his thickish, wall-like eyelids make him look like a dwarfed, jaundiced Jesus. This man has had three operations, I chant to myself. Three operations.

Judith puts down the coffee pot, and he takes both her hands in his and presses her warmly, a warmth which takes Judith by surprise; they have met only once before. Then he turns to me and I see him hesitate an instant before speaking. He has a choked and gummy voice – did tumours nest in that plugged up throat? – but friendliness leaks through. 'So this is Charleen.'

For a man, he has a tiny hand, harshly formed, dry and papery as though the flesh were about to fall away from the gathered bones. His clothes, too, seem curiously dry, an old, blue suit, far too hot for today, with faintly dusty seams and buttonholes.

Martin comes into the kitchen to be introduced, and with his hearty 'How do you do, Mr Berceau,' we all breathe more easily. My mother, like a minor character in a play, has frozen during these introductions, literally flattening herself against the refrigerator

301

door, nervously observing Louis's presentation of himself to the 'family'.

'I've just made some coffee,' Judith announces.

'Exactly what I need,' Louis replies from the top of his strangled, phlegm-plugged throat. 'I've been up for hours.' And with a rattling sigh he sinks down at the kitchen table.

'We could go into the living room,' my mother says with the pinched voice she uses when she wants to be genteel.

'The kitchen is fine, Florence,' Louis says, breathing rapidly. Florence! Well, what had I expected?

We sit down at the table while my mother finds cups and saucers in the cupboard. There is a moment's silence which I rush to fill; it seems so extraordinarily painful for Louis Berceau to speak that all I can think of is the necessity of sparing him the effort.

'I'm really very happy to meet you,' I rattle away inanely. 'At first I thought I wasn't going to be able to come. But I managed to get a week off work, and some friends offered to keep an eye on Seth – my son – and I thought, why not?'

Louis stirs his coffee and lifts his eyes in a disarming, skin-pleated smile. Gasping between spaced phrases he manages, 'We are so grateful – both of us – your mother and I – that you could come all these – thousands of miles – to be with us – on Friday. We are – we are –' he searches for a word, then with a final burst says, 'we are honoured.'

Honoured! Honoured? I glance at my mother, take in her tightly shut lips, and look away. Louis is honoured – how touching – but only Louis.

'It was Mr Berceau's idea,' my mother explains sharply, 'to have a proper wedding. And invite,' she pauses, 'the family.'

'Well, you see,' Louis chokes, 'I never . . . never had a family.'

'Well, now you do,' Judith says with firm cheerfulness. (How easily I can picture her performing at faculty receptions.) 'The

302

children, my two kids that is, have exams this week, but they'll be coming on the train Friday in time for the wedding.'

'I hope,' Louis says, his thick lips cracking puckishly, 'that I'll get to know them well in time.'

He drinks his coffee with a long, pleasurable slurp, leans back in his chair – such tiny shoulders – quite amazingly relaxed. Again he strains to speak, and we lean forward, Martin, Judith and I, to catch what he says. 'Do you mind . . .' he whispers raspily, 'if I smoke?'

He puffs contentedly on a Capstan, using, to my astonishment and horror, the rim of my mother's saucer for an ashtray. The smoke curling from his lips and rather oily nostrils makes him look exceptionally ugly. He has always – I feel certain of this – been ugly; he wears his ugliness with such becoming ease, as though it were a creased oilskin, utilitarian and not at all despised. And as he smokes, he talks, a light and general conversation, faintly paternal with a scattering of questions, the sort of conversation that has rarely filled these rooms. I feel myself grow tense at the obvious exertion of his voice, its separate sounds eased out of the creaking wooden machinery of his throat, dry, high-pitched, harshly monotone, a voice pitted with gasped air as though his windpipe is in some dreadful way shredded and out of his control.

Judith and Martin and I attend scrupulously to his questions, making our replies as lengthy as possible in order to relieve him of the torment of speaking. Turning deferentially to Martin, he inquires about his position at the university, and Martin, not quite blushing but almost, tells Louis that he has recently been appointed chairman of his department.

I am startled. Judith has never mentioned Martin's promotion to me; indeed, at that moment, listening to her husband describe the duties of his new office, Judith fidgets, rises, reheats the coffee, even yawns behind a politely raised hand. She has never pretended to be a standard, right-hand wife, but her nonchalance about Martin's success seems excessive, almost indifferent.

Is Martin himself pleased about his promotion? I wonder. It is difficult to tell because, with his academic compulsion toward truth, he outlines for Louis the enormous liabilities of the position, the toll it takes in terms of time, patience and friendship. Never have I heard Martin so expansive, never so carefully expository, and it occurs to me that he is deliberately prolonging his explanation out of an inclination to break through the aura of surrealism that possesses us, to flatten with his burly, workaday facts the sheer unreality of our being gathered here around this particular kitchen table on this particular late May morning.

Louis turns next to Judith – I am becoming accustomed to his dry-roofed rasp – and asks her whether she has read the biography of Lawrence Welk, a question that disappoints me somewhat by its banality. (Already I am investing Louis with wizened, cerebral kindliness.)

No, Judith answers, she hasn't read it but she respects those who discover ways, whatever they may be, of uncovering currents of the extraordinary in even the most ordinary personalities. Actually, Judith protests, she doesn't believe there is such a thing as an ordinary person, at least not when examined from the privileged perspective of the biographer. What consumes her now, she tells Louis, is her investigation into the scientific impulse – no, not impulse, she corrects herself; in the case of scientists, impulse becomes compulsion. Louis nods; his twisted muzzle face registers agreement. Judith continues: science, she says, often drowns men with its overwhelming abstractions, snuffing out human variability and hatching the partly true myth of the cold, clinical man of science. Human whim, human dream if you like, become obscured, and for the biographer, Judith admits, not unhappily, the scientific life is the most complex of all to write.

Louis questions me next – I wonder if he has rehearsed the pattern of our discussion – asking me if dreams inspire the poems I write. (It is a morning for speeches, each of us taking a turn, except, that is, our mother who sits in one corner of the table, peevishly sipping her coffee and filling the dips and hollows of our phrases with nervous, trailing 'yes's' and 'well's'.) No, I tell Louis, I never write poems inspired by dreams.

'Why not?' he creaks.

I shrug, thinking of the Pome People who treasure their dreams as though they were rare oriental currency blazoned with symbolic stamping. For me dreams are no more than rag-ends caught in a sort of human lint-trap, psychic fluff, the negligible dust of that more precious material, thought. To value one's dreams is to encourage the most debilitating of diseases, subjectivity. (Watson nearly died of that disease; our marriage almost certainly did.) To pretend that dreams are generated whole out of some vast, informing unconsciousness is to imagine a comic-strip beast (alligator, dragon?) slumbering in one's blood. The inner life? I shrug again. The poet has to report on surfaces, on the flower in the crannied wall, on coffee spoons and peaches, a rusted key discovered in the grass. Dreams are like – I think a moment – dreams are like mashed potatoes.

Martin awards me a yelp of laughter. Louis smiles a yellow, fish-gleam smile, and Judith, smiling approval, refills my cup. She is flushed with her own impromptu eloquence and proud of mine. And puzzled too. Is it Louis's questions that have stirred us? Or our desire to make him understand exactly how far we have travelled from this cramped kitchen?

After this it is Louis's turn to speak.

'With your permission,' he begins hoarsely, 'I would like to invite each of you – you, Judith and you, Charleen – to have lunch with me.' He stops; a coughing fit seizes him, shaking his thin shoulders with wrenching violence. We watch helplessly, tensely, listening to the dry, squeezed convulsions of his heaving chest.

'It's just the asthma,' our mother tells us calmly, almost flatly, sipping again at her coffee. 'It happens all the time.'

Three operations *and* asthma!

At last Louis's coughing stops and he pulls out a handkerchief and blows his nose noisily. Half choking, he begins again, explaining how he hopes to get better acquainted with us by taking us in turn, Judith today and me tomorrow, out for a nice, long lunch. (The order, I can only think, is dictated by our relative ages; Judith being older has priority, and I cannot help smiling at the thoroughness of his planning.) When he has finished his arduous invitation, he sits back again, smashes his cigarette in my mother's saucer, and asks 'Well?'

Judith – brave, kind, curious Judith – leaning over the table and placing her hand on Louis's amber-stained fingertips, repeats the word Louis used earlier, a word that has never before, as far as I know, been used in this house and which is now being spoken for the second time in a single morning. 'I would be honoured,' she pronounces.

'In that case,' Louis says rising, 'I think we should be on our way.'

'You mean right now?' Judith stammers.

'I know a nice quiet place,' he rasps, 'in the country. It'll be after twelve o'clock before we get there.'

Turning to me he says, 'Tomorrow then, Charleen? We can . . .' he coughs his parched, tenor cough, 'we can talk some more about poetry.'

Judith, a little bewildered, picks up a sweater and her handbag and they leave by the back door, walking together around the lilac tree at the side of the house. My mother rises at once to place the cups in the sink. Martin returns to his newspaper and I, following him into the living room, watch the two of them move toward the car; Judith is a full head taller than Louis; she seems to lope by his side.

It is very strange watching Louis walk to his car. Louis, sitting in the kitchen and puffing his cigarette, seemed dwarfed and bleached and freakish, like an aged yellowed monkey, but Louis walking to the car is close to nimbleness; with his lightsome step, his short, little arms swinging cheerfully, and his head tossing as though he were searching out the best possible breath of air, he appears, from the back and from a distance, like a man in his prime.

We have scrambled eggs on toast for lunch, Martin, my mother and I.

In this household, guests have never been frequent: occasionally when we were children my Aunt Liddy, my mother's older sister who lived in the country, would come to spend a day with us. And there was a second cousin of our father, Cousin Hugo, who owned a hardware store, a large, fat man with wiry black hair and curving crusts of dirt beneath his fingernails. And once a neighbour whose wife was in the hospital with pneumonia had been invited for Sunday lunch, an extraordinary gesture that remained for years in my mother's mind as the 'time we put ourselves out to help Mr Eggleston'. Always on these occasions when guests were present she would serve scrambled eggs on toast.

Doubtless she considered it a dish both light and elegant. She may have read somewhere that it was the Queen Mother's favourite luncheon dish (she is always reading about the Royal Family). Certainly she is convinced of the superiority of her own scrambled eggs and the manner in which she arranges the triangles of toast (side by side like the sails of a tiny boat), for she always compares, at length, the correctness of her method w.:h the slipshod scrambled eggs she has encountered elsewhere.

'Liddy doesn't put enough milk in hers and I always tell her that makes them rubbery. If you want nice, soft scrambled eggs you have to add a tablespoon of milk for every egg, just a tablespoon, no more, no less. And use an egg beater, not a fork the way most people do. Most people just don't want to bother getting out an egg beater, they're too lazy to wash something extra. They think, who'll notice anyway, what's the difference, but an egg beater makes all the difference, all the difference in the world. Otherwise the yolk and white don't mix the way they should. Liddy always leaves big hunks of white in her scrambled eggs. And she doesn't cut the crusts off her toast. She thinks it's hoity-toity and a waste of bread, but I always save the crusts and dry them in the oven to make bread crumbs out of them afterwards so there's no waste, not a bit; you know I never waste good food; you'll have to admit I never waste anything. Most people won't bother, they won't go to the trouble; they're too lazy; they don't know any better. And I always add the salt before cooking, that makes them hold their shape, not get hard like Liddy's but just, you know, firm. But not pepper, never pepper, never add pepper when you're cooking, let people add their own pepper at the table if that's what they want. Me, I never liked spicy food like what the Italians and French like. And Greeks. Garlic and onions and grease, and I don't know what, just reeking of it on the subway these days, reeking of it; I don't dare turn my head sideways when I go downtown. Toronto isn't the same; not the way it used to be, not the way it was way back.'

We eat lunch in the kitchen. Martin is quiet. So am I. Our forks clicking on the plates chill me into a further silence.

'Hmm, delicious,' Martin says politely.

'Yes.' I agree, forcing my voice into short plumes of enthusiasm, 'Really good. So tender.'

Afterwards she washes the dishes and I dry. *Always take a clean tea towel for each meal. It may be a little bit extra in the wash but when you think of the filthy tea towels some people use . . .*

I yearn desperately to talk to her; to say that, despite my foreboding, I have been rather taken with Louis Berceau, that I am immeasurably pleased that he and she have found each other and she will no longer have to endure the loneliness of the ticking clock, the sound of the furnace switching on and off, the daily paper thudding against the door, the calendar weeks wasting, the reminders of time slipping by which must be unbearable for those who are alone. But the words dry in my throat; if only I knew how to begin, if only I could speak to her without shyness, without fear of hurting her. Instead I poke with my tea towel into the spokes of the egg beater.

'Don't bother drying that,' she turns to me, taking it out of my hands. 'Here,' she says, 'I always put it in the oven for a little, the pilot light dries it out; the gears are so old, I've had it since just after the war, it was hard to get egg beaters then. Cousin Hugo got it for me from the store. I don't want the gears to rust, they would if I didn't get it good and dry. I've had it so long and it will have to last me until –'

Until what? Until death? Until the end? That is what she means; the words she couldn't say but which she must have recognized or why did she stop so suddenly? I have never thought of the way in which my mother thinks of her own death. No doubt, though, she has a plan; she will do it more neatly, more thoroughly than her sister Liddy, better than the neighbours, more genteely than Cousin Hugo, more timely than our father; no one will laugh at her, no one will look down on her.

Still, it may be that she is a little uncertain: the way she plunges into vigorous silence over the scoured sink hints at uneasiness, an acknowledgement at least of life's thinned reversal, of the finite nature of husbands and egg beaters and even of one's self.

After lunch Martin carries a kitchen chair out into the backyard (my mother has never owned a piece of lawn furniture) and there in the sunshine he reads a book of critical essays, a recent paperback edition which he opens with a sigh. He is, I suspect, a somewhat reluctant academic, preferring perhaps to while away his time with the small change of newspapers and magazines. Nevertheless he enjoys the warmth and the serious Sisley sky, finely marbled, gilt-veined, surprisingly large even when viewed from the postage stamp of our tiny, fenced yard.

One-thirty. My mother goes about the house closing the curtains, first the living room and then the three bedrooms. (Much of her life has gone into a struggle against the fading of furniture and curtains and rugs.) Then she goes into the spare bedroom where she slept last night and closes the door. She is going to lie down, she is going to have her rest. She has always, since Judith and I were babies, had a 'rest' after lunch. Never a nap, never a sleep, never, oh never, a doze, but a rest. She will remove her laced shoes and her dress, she will button a loosely knit grey and blue cardigan over her slip and she will turn back the bedspread into a neat fan; then she will get into bed, and there she will remain for between an hour and an hour and a half. Sometimes she falls asleep, sometimes she just 'rests'. 'A rest is as good as a sleep,' she has said at least a hundred times. A thousand times?

Quietly I carry the *Metropolitan Toronto and Vicinity* telephone book from the hall into the kitchen and settle myself down at the table. I turn to the P's, running my finger down a column, looking for The Priory, Priory, the. For some reason my heart is beating wildly. But there is nothing listed. I look under the The's where I find quite a few listings: The Boutique, The Factory, The Place,

The Shop, The Wiggery. But not The Priory. I even look under the B's for Brother Adam. There is no Brother Adam, (nor any other Brothers) then I try Adam, Brother. Nothing.

Perhaps the Priory is listed under Religious Houses or under Churches, but my mother has no Yellow Pages. I decide to phone Information.

It is necessary to whisper into the phone because my mother is resting a few yards away behind a closed door; she may even be sleeping. The operator is enraged by my muffled voice and my lack of specificity – 'Did you say it was a church?'

'No.'

'Well, is it or isn't it?'

'I'm not sure. I think it is but I'm not –'

'Is Adam the first name or last name?'

'His first. I think.'

'I have to have a last name.'

'I've got the address. It's on Beachview.'

'Sorry. I need the last name.'

'But I don't have it.'

Actually, I reflect hanging up, it was absurd of me to think that a contemplative man like Brother Adam would have a telephone. Hadn't he implied in his many letters his ascetic obsession, his distrust of cramped, urban industrial society? A man like Brother Adam would never put himself in bondage to Bell Telephone; a man like Brother Adam would no sooner have a telephone than he would own a car. (He does, however, have a typewriter – all his letters are typewritten – but it is undoubtedly a manual model.)

I carry the phone book back to its place. I am not going to be able to phone Brother Adam after all. And it's too late now to drop him a note. I should have written from Vancouver as I had planned. What's the matter with me that I can't even make the simplest of social arrangements? I'll have to go to The Priory, there's no other solution. If I want to see him at all I will have to turn up at his door unannounced.

But I can't go today; my mother wouldn't like it if I disappeared on an unexplained errand, and besides Eugene is going to phone me from downtown at three o'clock. And tomorrow? Wednesday? Tomorrow is my day to have lunch with Louis Berceau. Friday? – the wedding is on Friday, and Friday night we're flying back to Vancouver.

Thursday – if I go at all I'll have to go on Thursday. Yes, I will definitely go to see Brother Adam on Thursday. He is in the city, he is within a few miles of me, looking out of his window perhaps, sitting in the sun on his fire escape perhaps, and who knows, maybe he is writing a letter, perhaps even a letter to me, a letter beginning Dear Charleen, the sky is benignly blue today, the sun falls like a blessing across this page . . .

Martin is restless. He has brought his chair inside; the sky has clouded over with alarming suddenness, and a few drops of heavy rain have already fallen onto the pages of his book. He is brooding mysteriously by the living room window.

I can never quite believe in the otherness of people's lives. That is, I cannot conceive of their functioning out of my sight. A psychologist friend once told me this attitude was symptomatic of a raging ego, but perhaps it is only a perceptual failure. My mother: every day she lives in this house; it is not all magically whisked away when I leave; the walls and furniture persist and so do the hours which she somehow fills. When Seth was five and started school I came home the first day after taking him and grieved, not out of nostalgia for his infancy or anxiety for his future, but for the newly revealed fact that he had entered into that otherness, that unseeable space which he must occupy forever and where not even my imagination could follow. It is the same with Martin who, year after unseen year, pursues objectives, lives through unaccountable weeks and months. Martin by the window, shut up in his thoughts, might be standing on the tip of the moon.

When my mother wakes up she goes into the kitchen and begins browning a small pot roast on the back of the stove. 'Nothing fancy,' she explains. 'I'm not going to fuss even for company, not at today's prices, not that there's anything wrong with a good honest pot roast and they don't give those away nowadays. Maybe it takes a few hours, you have to brown it really well, each side and the ends too, most people don't want to bother, they'd just as soon take a steak out of the freezer, never mind the cost, and call that a meal.'

Because I make my mother nervous in the kitchen I go into the living room and stand beside Martin. He glances at his watch and says, 'They should be home soon.'

Is it a question or a statement? 'You mean Judith?' I ask.

He nods.

'It's quite a distance,' I remind him. 'Remember? Out in the country somewhere.'

'He's over seventy,' Martin says grimly.

'Seventy-two,' I nod.

'These old coots really shouldn't be on the road,' Martin says with surprising ferocity.

The word 'coots' shocks me; it seems a remarkably uncivilized word for Martin to use. What is the matter with him?

I spring to Louis's defence. 'He seems alert enough for a man of his age. I'm sure he wouldn't drive if he felt he wasn't capable.'

Martin looks again at his watch, and I can see by the involuntary snap of his wrist that he's seriously worried.

'I'm sure he's a careful driver,' I insist again.

'But how do you *know*?'

I shrug. 'He certainly didn't strike me as the reckless type.'

'Didn't strike you,' he says sourly, mockingly. But then he asks seriously, 'How *did* he strike you, Charleen?'

'Why are you so worried, Martin?'

'Because,' Martin says, 'have you considered that we don't know a damn thing about this man? Absolutely nothing.'

'He used to be a Catholic,' I say, as though that fact were exceptionally revealing, 'and he used to teach carpentry or something like that. In a junior high. In the east end I think.'

'Yes, yes,' Martin says wearily, 'but what do we *really* know about him?'

'His health, you mean?'

He sighs, faintly exasperated. 'No, not his health. What I mean is, we don't know anything. Christ, maybe he's queer. Or maybe he molests children. Or sets fire to buildings or passes bum cheques. How would we know?'

I feel my mouth pulling into the shape of protest.

Martin continues, 'He's an odd enough looking bird, you can see that. For your mother's sake we should have looked into him a bit more. And now here he goes off with Judith to God only knows where. We never even asked exactly where they were headed. And now a storm's coming up.' He sighs again. 'I don't know.'

How odd Martin is becoming. I point out to him the obvious facts: that it is not even quite three o'clock yet, that it was after eleven when Judith and Louis left the house; that Louis distinctly said it was an hour's drive. True, we know next to nothing about him, but we couldn't very well call in a detective three days before the wedding; we would have to go by instinct, and my instinct – but would Martin believe it? – my instinct is to trust him. An odd-looking man, yes, and a strange marriage, perhaps

314

– I nod in the direction of the kitchen – but I feel certain, a certainty which I can in no way justify, that there is nothing to be afraid of.

Martin shakes his head, not entirely convinced but obviously wishing to be. He regards the empty street and the pulsing sky; the rain is holding back, squeezing laboured tears out of the scrambled grey clouds. Clearly Martin will not be happy until Judith is safely home; his devotion touches me, especially when I think of Judith's careless departure, how she went off without a thought about how Martin would pass the day, making a swift grab for her bag, yanking a cardigan over her shoulders; she took Louis's arm with huge, loping cheerfulness and sailed past the lilac tree; she drove away in his little Fiat without so much as a good-bye wave. And what else? Oh, yes, she hadn't told me about Martin's promotion; she hadn't, in fact, mentioned Martin at all; it is rather as though he were no more than a distant acquaintance.

I want to reassure Martin about Louis's reliability. 'I don't know how to explain it,' I tell him, 'but I know Louis's okay. And I'm usually right about things like this.' (Am I?)

He smiles a twisted, academic smile. 'Intuition, I suppose.'

I smile back. We will be friends. 'Look,' I say, 'it's a rather odd marriage, but they may surprise us by being happy.'

'Happy?' He looks amused at the idea.

'Well, a kind of happiness.'

Happiness. Such a word, such a crude balloon of a word, such a flapping, stretched, unsightly female bladder of a word, how worn, how slack, how almost empty.

'Happiness,' Martin repeats dully.

And before I can say anything more, the telephone rings. It's Eugene.

'Charleen.'

'Yes. Eugene? How's it going? The conference?'

'Not bad. A bit draggy.' (I rejoice at his detachment. If he had greeted me with ecstasy my heart would have sickened; I am queasy about misplaced enthusiasm.)

'What time are you coming?' I ask him.

'That's why I'm phoning. What I'd really like is if you could come downtown.'

'Tonight?'

'We could have dinner.' His voice slants with pleading. 'Just the two of us.'

'I don't know, Eugene. My mother. She's already making dinner. I don't know what she'd say.'

'Couldn't you say I had to stay downtown later than I'd thought? Because of the conference?'

'I don't know, Eugene,' I say doubtfully, thinking, poor Eugene, this morning must have been too much for him, and last night too, stuck in the back bedroom. Then I think of the pot roast my mother is cooking, reflecting that it is really rather small to feed all of us; wouldn't it, in fact, be a kindness to go out for dinner?

'Okay, Eugene. What time?'

'Any time. We're through for the day.'

'I don't think I can make it before five,' I tell him.

'Five then. Get a taxi and I'll wait for you at Bloor and Avenue Road.'

'I'll come by subway. No need to take a taxi all the way from here.'

'Charleen. Please.'

'Eugene. I can't,' I hiss into the phone. 'My mother.'

'It'll take you hours.'

'No, it won't. Remember, I used to live here. I know the subway.'

316

'You're crazy, you know. I'll be waiting. Bloor and Avenue Road, all right? By the museum.'

'Okay,' I promise. I think of my mother fretfully turning her pot roast in the kitchen, of Martin sighing by the window, suddenly I can't wait to get out of this house. 'See you soon,' I tell Eugene.

Of course my mother minds. Or, perhaps more accurately, she goes through the motions of minding; the pot roast has shrunk alarmingly.

'You might have said something about it this morning,' she says with a short, injured sniff. 'I could have done chops if I'd known there would be only three of us. I'm surprised your Dr Redding, him a doctor and all, didn't have the courtesy to tell me this morning. It isn't like this was a hotel, whatever you may think. But go ahead, go ahead if you've made up your mind. All I say is it's a waste of money eating in fancy restaurants and you never know what you're getting, food poisoning, germs and I don't know what. I'd just as soon have a good honest pot roast if you asked me, not all that foreign food. You don't know what it is. I wouldn't have gone to the trouble of a pot roast if I thought you were going to take it into your head to go eat in a restaurant. I suppose you won't be too late?'

I listen; I bear with it; in a few minutes, I tell myself, she will have exhausted herself and I will be free to go. No, I tell her, we won't be too late. I speak calmly, lightly, remembering to be kind, reminding myself that her nerves are poor, that her health is shaky, that she has never, no never, eaten in a downtown restaurant, that she has been little rewarded in her life for her efforts: her scrambled eggs and careful housekeeping have not won her the regard she might have liked. I remind myself, above all, that she is weak.

And from her weakness flows not gentleness but a tidal wave of judgement. No wonder she has no friends. Over the years those few people who have approached her in friendship have been swept aside as prying and nosy, their gestures of help construed as malicious arrogance. Underpinning all her beliefs is the idea that people 'should keep to themselves'. They should stand on their own feet, they should mind their own business, they should look after their own, they should steer their own ship, they should tend their own gardens. Judgement colours her every encounter: 'Mrs Mallory said she admired my new slipcovers. Imagine that, she *admired* them. She couldn't just say she *liked* them, no, she *admired* them. I don't know what gives her the right to be so high and mighty. I've seen *her* slipcovers.'

The world which she has constructed for herself is fiercely, cruelly, minutely competitive, a world in which each minimal victory requires careful registration. 'Well,' she would say, 'I had my washing out first again today; first in the neighbourhood.' Or, 'At least we don't eat our dinner at five o'clock like the Hannas, only country people eat at five o'clock. I told Mrs Hanna how we always sat down at six o'clock when my husband got home from the office, from the office I said, and that ended that.'

My poor, self-tormented mother with her meaningless rage, her hollow vindictiveness, her shrinking fear – how had it happened? Heredity suggested a partial answer. My mother's mother, Elsie Gordon, had been one of two sisters born in a village in the Scottish lowlands; she had married a farmer named Angus Dunn, and the two of them had immigrated to Ontario where they rented and finally bought a thirty-acre farm and produced two daughters, Liddy (poor witless Aunt Liddy) and, three years later, Florence, our mother. And Florence, as though responding to a cry for symmetry, had also produced two daughters, Judith and me. So here we are, three generations of paired sisters; had we been shaped by a tradition of kindness and had our sensibility been monitored by learning, we might even have resembled Jane

Austen's loving, clinging, nuance-addicted chains of sisters with their epistles and their fainting spells and their nervous agitation and their endless, garrulous, wonderful concern for one another. As it was, we were stamped out of rougher materials: dullness and drudgery, ignorance and self-preservation. Our father too had been a man without ancestors: to go back three generations was to find nothing but darkness; as the 'Pome People' might say, our family tree was no more than a blackened stump. I don't even know the name of the Scottish village my grandparents came from. There have been no pilgrimages, there are no family legends, no family Bible with records of births and deaths, no brown-edged letters, no pressed flowers, few photographs and even those few stiffly obligatory; there are no family heirlooms and, of course, no family pride. Each generation has, it seems, effectively sealed itself off from its lowly forebears. My mother had not wanted to remember the muddy thirty acres where she grew up, the roofless barn, the doorless outhouse, the greasy kitchen table where the family took meals, the chickens that wandered in and out the back door, the thick-ankled mother who could neither read nor write and who had little capacity for affection or cleanliness. Hadn't my mother, in spite of all this, finished grade nine and hadn't she gone to Toronto to work in a hat factory? (Ah, but that was another sealed-off area.) Hadn't she married a city boy, someone who worked in an office, and hadn't they, after a few years, bought a house of their own, paid for it too, a real house in Scarborough with a backyard and plumbing, hadn't she kept it spotless and proved to everyone that she was just as good as the next person, hadn't she shown them? Yes.

Yes, yes, I understand it; why can't I put that understanding into motion? Why am I running down the sidewalk like this? The rain is pouring in sheets off the sides of my borrowed umbrella. My feet in my only good shoes are soaked already.

I'm on my way downtown, running to the subway station. How unfair to blame my mother for the fact that I am taking the subway – I clutch my scratched vinyl purse and admit the truth – I am the one who lacks the largesse to phone a taxi. Meagreness. I am Florence McNinn's daughter, the genes are there, nothing I've done has scratched them out.

My ankles are wet and rimmed with mud. Oh, God, one more block and at least I'll be out of the rain.

As I run splashing along, a sort of song thrums in my crazy head: Seth, Seth, where are you? Oh, Watson, why did you leave me? Brother Adam, why can't you save me? Eugene, Eugene, Eugene.

Actually I love the subway. Not its denatured surfaces, not its weatherless tunnels, but its mad, anonymous, hyperactive, scrambling and sorting: the doors sliding open in the station, the rush of people, their faces declaring serious and purposeful journeys they are undertaking. Then another stop – they push their way out and are instantly replaced with equally serious, equally intent others. Their namelessness pleases me, their contained and dignified singularity comforts me. And it amazes me to think of the intricate, possibly secret connections between them, perhaps even connections of love. I like to think that at the end of each of these rushed, wordless, singular journeys, there is someone waiting, someone who is loved. How extraordinary – of course there are all sorts of chemical explanations – but still, how extraordinary is the chancy cement of love; a special dispensation that no one ever really deserves but which almost everyone gets a little of. Even my unloving mother has found someone finally to love. Even Louis Berceau with his scraped-out lungs and his screwed-up, druid face has found someone to love.

Joy seizes me fiercely, sweetly. I am one of the lucky ones

after all with my hard-as-a-kernel nut of indestructibility. My hereditary disease, the McNinn syndrome, has riddled me with cowardice, no question about it, but happiness will always return from time to time – as on this train blindly tunnelling beneath Bay and Bloor.

At the end of the trip, above ground, Eugene is waiting, his gull-grey raincoat flapping in the wind and his face fixed with its own peculiar flat uncertainty. I am ridiculously happy to see him.

He steers me into a taxi and down the street toward a big, new hotel, through the chrome-framed doors into a warm, bronze-sheeted lobby, strenuously contemporary with revolving lucite chandeliers and motorized waterfalls. The elevator is a cube of perfect creature comfort: softly lit and carpeted, ventilated, soundless and swift.

In a darkened cocktail lounge high over the city, Eugene and I sit on strangely shaped, grotesquely padded chairs and sip long, cold drinks and nibble on tiny smoked, salty, crackling things. And we talk in the strange, curiously shy fashion of reunited lovers. I tell Eugene about Louis Berceau, and he tells me about an old dental school friend he ran into today who asked him how 'his charming wife was'. When Eugene told him he was now divorced, the friend backed off and, in a blind flurry of honesty, said, 'Actually I never could stand Jeri.' Or was it honesty, Eugene wonders now, drumming his fingers on the table. Maybe the friend was, belatedly and pointlessly, scrambling for sides. Maybe he was trying in an unfocused way to comfort Eugene or to congratulate him for having rid himself of an unpleasant wife. 'Strange,' Eugene murmurs, looking into his gin and tonic. 'Strange how people react to divorce. Not knowing whether sympathy is in order or not.'

I agree with him. Death is so much simpler; the rituals are

firmer, shapelier; social custom will never be able to alter or diminish the effect of death; one need never be confused about the proper response.

Later, in the restaurant, we eat marvellous little things from a wagon of hors d'oeuvres. Tiny fishes, oily and frilled with lemon; sculptured vegetables lapped with mayonnaise, glazed and healthy under parsley coverlets, sharp little sausages and miniature onions, gherkins and lovely, lovely olives, black, green, some of them an astonishing pink. After that we have tornedos in cream (the speciality of the house, the beaming, gleaming waiter tells us). I eat less guiltily knowing Eugene will be able to write off almost every penny this meal is costing; at the same time I feel our feast is meanly diminished by that very fact. A paradox. Eugene says he feels the same way. Why?

He says it is a question of puritan ethic: you can only enjoy what you have laboriously worked for. Pleasure must be paid for by sacrifice, at least for those like us. It must not come too easily or too soon. He shakes his head sadly over the fact, but accepts it, admitting that most middle-class rewards will no doubt continue to elude him.

'It might be better for the kids though,' he says, speaking of his two boys, Sandy and Donny, who live with Jeri and stay with him in his apartment most weekends. He is always impressed with their unalloyed enjoyment of the presents he gives them. 'They don't think they have to do a damn thing in return,' he says. 'I mean, God, they're little primitives. They just open their arms to whatever rains down on them. Damned ungrateful too, but maybe that's better than being screwed up with the debt-to-the-devil complex.'

'Maybe,' I say. And yet I'm glad Eugene is not entirely guilt-free about tax deductions; I'm grateful for his company here on the ethical edge, in the no-man's-land between youth and age, between puritan guilt and affluent hedonism; what a pair we are, half-educated, half-old, half-married, half-happy. I should marry him and relieve a little of the guilt he suffers. He would like that: living alone in an apartment is frightening for a man like Eugene; he feels his ordinariness more than ever. Maybe I will marry him. What a nice man he is. I don't even mind his being an orthodontist. What if his proportions are less than heroic? Isn't goodwill a kind of prehensile heroism in this century? Does it really matter that Doug Savage thinks he is miserably average, even slightly substandard, and that Greta fears his mediocrity will place a ruinous stain on Seth's character? I cannot, after all, choose a husband just to please my friends.

Nothing is simple. After dinner we take a taxi back to Scarborough, sitting in the back seat with our arms around each other. The sky has cleared; there's a rounded, whited, theatrical moon cleanly cruising along behind us. Eugene's raincoat is still damp and rather cold against my thighs but I like the feel of his lips on my face, unhurried, soft.

Coming into my mother's dimly lit living room with its flickering television screen and its cleanly shabby furniture, my senses play a perceptual trick on me: I see, it seems, not those who are actually there – my mother with her mending, Judith with her book, and Martin with his newspaper – but the ghostly shadowed presence of those who are missing. My father – shy, secretive, stoic, perpetually embarrassed – reading his paper much as Martin does, with hunched concentration as though he were perched temporarily in a doctor's waiting room. And Judith's children, Richard and Meredith: their absence is marked by her weary inattentiveness to the novel she's reading, the way she jerks the pages over; her real life belongs to another place now. And Seth, the grandson my mother has not even inquired about, the grandson for whom she does not knit mittens or mufflers and whose birthdays she does not remember (he is, after all, the extension of a daughter who has twice disgraced her family, first by running away and then by getting divorced); Seth who is the most important person in my world is suddenly briefly visible, filling this little room with his absence.

'Seth!' I suddenly exclaim.

'What's the matter?' Judith says, looking up.

'I've forgotten to phone Seth.'

'It's not too late, is it?' Eugene asks, hanging up his raincoat.

'Do you mean long distance?' my mother asks.

'I just want to see if he's all right.'

'But it's long distance.'

'It's after eleven,' Judith says helpfully. 'Don't the rates go down after eleven?'

'After twelve, I think,' Martin says.

'It's all right,' I tell my mother. 'I'll leave the money for the call.'

'A waste of money,' she shrugs. 'And when you've been out to a restaurant and everything.'

'I really must see how he is.'

'But you're going home Friday night. Why would you want to go and run up the phone bill for nothing?'

'But I have to. I really must,' I insist, knowing I sound unreasonable and shrill. 'I simply couldn't sleep a wink tonight unless I know everything is all right.'

'But what could go wrong?' my mother says giving one last dying protest.

'There's the phone ringing *now*,' Eugene says. 'Maybe it's Seth calling *you*.'

But it isn't Seth. It's Doug Savage and he's phoning from Calgary.

'Hiya, Char,' he says as breezily as though he were phoning from next door.

'Doug!' I stumble, a little confused. 'Well, hello.'

There is a short pause – perhaps we have a poor connection – and then I hear Doug saying, 'Just wanted to tell you not to worry.'

'Worry?'

'Just wanted to let you know everything's fine.'

'But . . . but what are you doing in Calgary?'

'Oh, you know me, just a little trip. Always here, there, or somewhere.'

'And Greta?'

Another pause. 'Has Greta phoned you at all?'

'No. Was she going to?'

He hesitates. 'Just thought she might give you a buzz.'

'Well, no she hasn't, but as a matter of fact I thought I'd phone her tonight. Have a word or two with Seth.'

'Oh, God, Char, save your shekels. As a matter of fact, I don't think they're home tonight anyway.'

'Are you sure?'

'Yes. Yes, I'm sure. Something about the band. A rehearsal, I think.'

'Oh,' I say, feeling suddenly let down and disappointed. 'I forgot about that.'

'Well, don't let it worry you. Everything's fine. Fine.' His voice trails off.

'Maybe I'll try tomorrow night.'

'Great idea. You do that. Having a good time?'

'What? Oh, yes, uhuh, a good time.'

'Take care then. Bye for now.'

'Bye, Doug. And Doug . . . ?'

'Yeah?'

'Thanks for calling. That was really nice of you to think of phoning. But why . . . I mean why exactly *did* you phone me?'

'Didn't want you worrying, that's all. Just thought I'd let you know everything's fine. Good night then, baby.'

'Good night,' I say. And stupidly, cheerfully, add, 'Sleep tight.'

Chapter 5

'She never talks to me anymore,' Judith is saying of her daughter Meredith. 'Not the way she used to when she was a little girl.'

Children. Judith and I lie in bed listening to our mother in the kitchen making breakfast and we talk about our children.

'I'm always reading those articles about how parents are supposed to keep the lines of communication open,' Judith says. 'And now and then out of duty I make a stab at it.'

'And what happens?'

'Nothing. Absolutely nothing. She – Meredith – just smiles. Mona Lisa. At least *sometimes* she smiles. Other times she cringes. As though the thought that we might have something in common was unspeakable. Everyone's always telling me how charming she is, and it's true she's got this non-McNinn effervescence. And a kind of wild originality too, but to me she doesn't say one word.'

'You don't sound as though you mind all that much,' I say.

'Mind? Oh, I suppose I should. After all, I'm her mother, she's my only daughter, why shouldn't she be able to pour out her heart now and then. But the truth is, Charleen, I couldn't bear it if she did. All that anguish.'

'You must be curious though.'

'In a way. I'm always wondering what she's thinking about. Or what she does when she's not home. After all, she's eighteen. But eighteen is such a . . . well . . . such a suffering age. Remember? Sometimes I feel I've only just recovered from it myself. To listen to her ups and downs would kill me, and I think she knows it too. She senses it. She's got a kind of rare psychic radar – she always had but now and then she looks so bedevilled that I'm afraid she's going to break down and take me into her confidence. She's come close a couple of times. But then she stops herself. I can almost see her mumbling her vows of silence. And, strangely enough, I'm rather proud of her for it, for going it alone. I admire her for it. And I'm grateful, even though I know I'm failing her somehow, I'm grateful to be left alone.'

'What about Richard?' I ask her.

'Richard,' she shrugs. 'He's always kept things to himself. Of course he's a boy. They're always more secretive. I suppose that's what you call a sexist judgement. Does Seth confide in you?'

I pause for a moment, not really wanting to admit that he doesn't. 'No,' I say slowly, 'but I don't think it means anything.'

It's true that most of the time these days Seth and I speak to each other in monosyllables – sure, yeah, okay – but these words are our accepted coinage of familiarity, the sort of shorthand that forms unconsciously between people who are naturally in harmony. It has never occurred to me to think that his lack of explicit communication might be an attempt to hide something from me; his nature has always been exceedingly open, and, if anything, it is this openness that worries me, openness with a suggestion of vacuum, a curious, perhaps dangerous acquiescence.

'I used to think it was strange,' Judith is saying, 'that we never told Mother anything when we were girls. All my friends used to rush home and tell their mothers everything. But we never did. At least I never did.'

'Neither did I,' I say firmly. 'Never once.'

'You know,' Judith says thoughtfully, 'looking back, I don't think it's all that strange. I think she must have sent out a kind of warning signal, a thought wave, saying "Don't tell me anything because I've got enough to cope with as it is."'

'Perhaps,' I nod.

'Anyway,' Judith continues, 'I've come to the place now where I know she and I will never be able to talk. I'm absolutely sure of it.'

Her certainty surprises me; it seems rather shocking to be so final, and I am forced to admit to myself that I have by no means surrendered. Somehow – it is only a question of finding the point of entry – I will break through our terrible familial silence. I came close, very close, yesterday drying the egg beater.

Judith springs out of bed and begins to get dressed, but I lie under the blanket a few minutes longer; I am still sleepy, my mind begins to wander, but I am not thinking about Meredith or Judith or about my mother or even about the girl I once was. For some reason I am thinking about Seth. And the small string of worry that plucks away at me.

After breakfast – toast and coffee in the kitchen – we take up yesterday's small routines. Eugene goes downtown for his conference, and Martin carries his newspaper into the backyard. It is rather cool outside; a woolly sun struggling through massed clouds, the grass still wet from yesterday's rain. My mother sets up the ironing board in the kitchen (the smell and sight of its scorched cover pierces me with nostalgia) and she presses, through a clean, damp tea towel, the dress she will wear for her wedding. Cocoa-brown crimpeline with raised ribs, a row of dull, wood-looking buttons down the front, long sleeves and no collar.

'It came with a scarf,' she says, frowning narrowly, 'as if a scarf made up for no collar.' Her lips turn inward thinly, visible, measurable emblem of her complaint. 'But I'm certainly not going to wear it, all those bright colours, cheap, of course it was in the March sales; nothing is well made anymore, imagine not even a collar. But it will have to do, that's all there is to it.'

I am thinking: the wedding is Friday, tomorrow is Thursday and with luck I'll be seeing Brother Adam at last. Today is Wednesday; today I am having lunch with Louis. He is coming for me at eleven. When I asked Judith if she enjoyed her lunch yesterday, she smiled somewhat mysteriously. 'It was interesting,' she said.

'Did you find out anything about Louis?' I asked.

'A little,' she smiled, 'and so will you.'

For a moment I pondered this, and then I asked, 'Where did you go?'

'A little place in the country.'

'Where exactly?' I pressed her.

'West of Toronto. Weedham. Just a little spot.'

'Weedham? Weedham, Ontario? Are you sure?'

'Yes,' she had answered, puzzled. 'Weedham. Spelled W-e-e-d-h-a-m. Being literal-minded, I naturally expected it to be full of weeds but it turned out to be a pretty little place. You'll like it.'

Weedham. Weedham, Ontario. Watson. I am going to Weedham, Ontario. I am going there today. An arc of anticipation, not unlike sexual desire, brightens inside me. I look at the kitchen clock. Nine-thirty. In an hour and a half I will be sitting in Louis Berceau's little green Fiat bouncing along the road to Weedham, Ontario.

I am sick, oh, I am sick with shame, I am in hell. I want to die of it, oh God, such pain, such humiliation, to be so humiliated. Stupid, stupid, I am sick with shame, it won't go away, it's done, nothing will take it away, dear God.

I am lying on my mother's bed in the middle of the morning, I am rocking from side to side, my fists in my eyes. I want to moan out loud, I want to weep, but no one must hear me, no one must know, oh, the shame of it.

Martin. Martin knows. Will he tell Judith? I cannot bear the thought of Judith knowing. She would think it was – what? – she would think it was *amusing*, too amusing for words. It would be awful to hear her laughing over it; I couldn't stand that.

Yet, isn't it her fault, isn't she the cause of its happening? If I hadn't been thinking about her and her peculiar baffling indifference to Martin, it would never have happened.

She had been so busily occupied after breakfast. She had settled down at the dining-room table with her portable typewriter and her reference books and her lovely calf-hide attaché case which she snapped open on her lap; inside were bundles of five-by-seven cards, each bundle bound with a rubber band; I thought of the way Mafia men carry their wads of money. Her notes, she explained, and with an air of enormous concentration she had selected one bundle, had whipped off the rubber band with a clean snap, and, one by one, she arranged the cards around her in a large semi-circle, a zombie playing at solitaire. I watched admiringly, such concentration, such independence. Judith explained that she had set herself a deadline for her next book. 'It's odd,' she said to me, 'I seem to be getting compulsive in my old age. Writing used to be just a kind of hobby. Now if a single day goes by without working, I feel as though the day's been lost.' Martin, on his way in from the backyard to get his book, had paused and regarded her affectionately. Judith gave him a level look over her circle of cards; she looked at him, but I could tell she didn't really see him; what she gave him was a wide spatial stare, an empty optic greeting as though he were a smallish portion of the wallpaper; then she broke her gaze abruptly, scratched her head with vigour and, slowly, thoughtfully, inserted a sheet of paper into her typewriter.

331

CAROL SHIELDS

Martin picked up his book and went outside, and out of a kind of pity – I think that's what it was – I followed him.

For a few minutes we sat together on the back steps, letting the frail, glassy sunlight fall on our backs. The little lawn looked exceptionally fine. Louis had put some fertilizer on it, my mother had explained with her mixture of shyness and sarcasm, and two pounds of grass seed. Martin seemed rather lonely, rather bored, a little restless, he seemed glad enough of my company. I even dared to tease him a little about how he'd worried about Judith's outing with Louis; he had laughed at himself in an altogether pleasant way, and then we talked for a few minutes about modern criticism. Yes, we were starting to be friends. We were comfortable sitting there together; the sun was growing stronger; it might be a nice day after all, and I was just about to say so when Martin leaned over and whispered into my ear.

'Look, Charleen, just between us, what do you think of the archaic sleeping arrangements here?'

'Pardon?' I said. Our mother had always taught us to say pardon.

'The sleeping arrangements,' he repeated. 'You know, the boys' dorm and the girls' dorm.'

'Well –' I started to say.

He leaned closer, he put his arm around my shoulder, he whispered in my ear, 'How about switching around tonight?'

'Martin!' I breathed, completely shaken.

'We could switch back later,' he leered. 'No one would ever know.'

'Martin,' I said again in a dazed whisper, 'I couldn't. I couldn't possibly.'

There was a short chilly silence. A dead hole of a silence.

Then Martin asked, 'Why not?'

I stood up abruptly, choking back rage, 'Because Judith happens

332

to be my sister. My own sister. What kind of person do you think I am?'

'My good Christ, Charleen, don't go all moral on me.'

'And what makes you think I would want to sleep with you anyway?'

Then, then Martin's expression underwent a profound shocking, nightmarish change. Then suddenly he began to laugh, very softly so that my mother, still ironing in the kitchen, wouldn't hear. Manic tears squeezed out of the corners of his eyes, he rocked back and forth on the step hugging himself, 'Oh, Charleen, oh, my God, I can't stand it, it's so funny. I didn't mean you and me. Oh, God.' He broke into another obscene spasm of laughter.

I stared. What was he laughing about? Had he gone crazy?

Then quite suddenly I understood. Then I knew.

'I meant you and Eugene,' Martin gasped. 'And Judith and me. After all,' he continued, making an effort at control, 'we are joined in holy wedlock and all that.'

I hardly heard him. I dashed away, up the steps and through the back door. I ran past my mother and here I am in the bedroom, rocking and moaning in a suffering parody of Martin rocking and moaning on the back steps. How he laughed. I could die, I could die, I wish I could die.

Louis will be here any minute. I roll over in bed and look at the clock. I must get changed. I must try to look cheerful and eager and grateful to be taken on an outing.

I put on my stockings and slip into my new orange dress. Then I brush my hair, trying to turn it under smoothly the way Mr Mario had done. It doesn't look too bad. And the dress looks surprisingly becoming. I even hum to myself a jerky little comforting tune while I clean my shoes with a Kleenex. They're still a little damp from yesterday.

Too bad about Martin, I say to myself in mock dismissal, peering into the mirror. Just when we were starting to be friends. If only I'd laughed I might have carried it off. Ah well, with my typical faulty reflex I blow it every time, a fatal quarter-step behind the rest of the world. Martin, without a doubt, will have been repelled by my embarrassment; not only that, but I with my gross misinterpretation have left myself vulnerable to a host of other questions: exactly what kind of a woman was I anyway? Just answer that.

Then I hear the little car pulling up in front, I hear Louis and Martin in the backyard talking about lawn care. One last reassuring grimace in the mirror and I emerge.

Louis does not embrace me, but he gives me a smile and a cherishing handshake over the kitchen table. My mother, sighing as she puts away the ironing board, says sharply, 'Don't be too late. I'm making my tunafish bake for supper.'

We walk to the car; Louis is cheerful and nimble and I shorten my steps to match his. The sun is blazing merrily overhead, and Martin and Judith walk with us to the street; Judith's writing is going well this morning and she seems immoderately happy. 'Have a good afternoon,' she sings.

I don't dare look at Martin. But after Louis has turned the ignition and we start to slide away from the curb, I turn back and find my eyes looking directly into his. His eyes look funny as though he is squinting into the sun. No, he isn't, no he isn't. He is – yes – he is winking at me.

Without thinking, without reflecting, I wink back, and then we move down the street, Louis and I, slowly, almost elegantly.

Louis's car is a Fiat 600, a 1968 model, recently repainted, the interior worn but exceedingly clean. This is the car that takes my mother back and forth to the cancer clinic, this is the car that carries her out for Sunday drives, this is the car that in two days will become their car, used for their minor errands, for their weekly trips to the Dominion Store, for their little jaunts into the country.

Louis, as I had predicted, is a cautious driver. He sits tightly in the driver's seat, moving the steering wheel and gearshift with intense little jerks, with careful, choppy, concentrated deliberation. The car moves down the suburban streets, delicately shuddering, and Louis, leaning forward, appears rather gnomelike with his wreaths of wrinkles, his puckered, colourless mouth, his contained and benign ugliness. Taking the 401 he heads west across the city.

On the way to Weedham Louis talks about the wedding. And I think how strange that it is so easy for people to talk in cars. It must have something to do with the enforced temporary proximity or with the proportion of space or perhaps the sealed, cushioned interior silence which must resemble, in some way, the insulated room where Greta Savage meets each week with her encounter group. It is as though the automobile were a specially designed glass talking-machine engineered for human intimacy. Furthermore, in a car the need to watch the road diverts and relieves the passengers, giving to their conversation an unexpected flowing disinterestedness.

Louis clears his throat and explains that both he and my mother were anxious to avoid fuss and expense; that was why they decided to be married in my mother's living room in the middle of the afternoon. Afterwards there would be tea in the dining room. And a small cake which Louis has ordered from a bakery; a United Church minister, a local man, has been asked to perform the ceremony.

This last piece of information surprises me. The McNinns have always been vaguely Protestant; at least Protestant is the word Judith and I supplied when we were asked our religious denomination. But we had never been a church-going family. The reason: I am not entirely sure, but it stemmed, I think, from my mother's belief that people only go to church in order to show off their hats and fur coats and to sneer at those less elegantly dressed. Certainly it had nothing to do with those larger issues such as the existence of God or the requirement of worship.

'Is anyone else going to be at the wedding?' I ask Louis. No, he answers, only the family. He himself has no family, none at all anymore.

The neighbours. I wonder if the neighbours have any inkling that my mother is to be remarried on Friday. Has she told anyone or has she kept her secret? The leitmotif of her anxiety, for as long as I can remember, has been her fear of being judged by the neighbours; what would the neighbours think? When twenty years ago I ran away with Watson to Vancouver, she had been struck almost incoherent with shame: what would the neighbours think? All the other girls in the neighbourhood were going on to secretarial school or studying to be hair-dressers, but her daughter – the shame of it – had eloped with a student, had left a note on her pillow and ridden off to Vancouver on the back of a motorcycle.

Later I learned from Judith exactly how shattered she had been, how for months she'd hardly left the house, how for years she'd been unable to look the neighbours in the face. The fact that I had not been pregnant as she had supposed, the fact that Watson and I had been quite legally if rather sloppily married before we set off for the west, and the fact that Watson, three years later, received his Ph.D. (with honours) -- none of these things seemed to ease the terrible shame of my extraordinary departure. And then the divorce, the embarrassing blow of the divorce which for years I tried to conceal from her. No one else in the neighbourhood had a daughter who was divorced. The neighbours had daughters who were buying property in Don Mills and producing families of children who came visiting on Sundays. Our mother alone had been cursed by strange daughters: Judith with her boisterous disturbing honesty, bookish and careless, and I with my now fatherless child, my unprecedented divorce, my books of poetry. The neighbours' children hadn't dismayed and defeated and failed their mothers.

And now my mother is getting married and she doesn't, it seems, worry at all about what the neighbours will think. She doesn't care a fig; she doesn't care a straw. For after all these years she has, in a sense, triumphed over the neighbours. Or, more accurately, the neighbours no longer exist. Both Mr and Mrs Maddison with their wailing cats and shredded curtains have died. The MacArthurs – lazy Mrs MacArthur, always hanging out the clothes in her dressing gown, and Mr MacArthur with his gravel truck sitting by the side of the house – have moved to a duplex in Riverdale to be near their married daughter. The Whiteheads – he drank, she used filthy language – have gone to California. Mrs Lilly and her crippled sister, so sinfully proud of their dahlias, have disappeared without a trace, and the Jacksons, whom my mother believed to be very common, have become rich and live in south Rosedale. All the houses in our neighbourhood are filled with Jamaicans now, with Pakistanis, with multi-generation, unidentifiable southern Europeans who grow cabbages and kohlrabi in their backyards and rent out their basements. My mother is not in the least afraid of their judgement on her. She has, after all, lived for forty years in her little house, she has lived on the block longer than anyone else, she is widowed old Mrs McNinn, the woman who keeps a clean house, the woman who minds her own business; she is respectable old Mrs McNinn.

*　　*　　*

'We're almost there,' Louis says, steering carefully. 'Another mile or so.'

'What a pretty little town,' I exclaim. For Weedham, Ontario, in the blond, spring sunlight has a tidy green rural face. A sign announces its population: 2,500. Another sign welcomes visiting Rotarians. Still another, a billboard of restrained proportions, urges visitors to stop at the Wayfarers' Inn.

'That's where we're going,' Louis says.

The Wayfarers' Inn at the edge of town is relatively new, built in the last thirty years or so, but in the style of more ancient inns it has a stone courtyard, a raftered ceiling, here and there curls of wrought iron, and rows of polished wooden tables ranged round the walls. Light filters glowingly through stained glass windows which, Louis explains, are the real thing; they were taken from an old house in the area which was being demolished.

'It's charming,' I say politely.

Shyly he tells me, 'I brought your mother here for lunch. When I asked her to marry me.'

I am taken by surprise. In fact, I am dumbfounded, for I cannot imagine my mother submitting to the luxury of lunch at the Wayfarers' Inn. And it is even more difficult to imagine her absorbing – in this room at one of these little tables peopled with local businessmen and white-gloved club women – a declaration of love.

'Was it . . . sudden?' I dare to ask.

His face crinkles over his mushroom soup, engulfed in pleasant nostalgia. 'Yes,' he nods, choking a little. 'Only three months after we'd met at the clinic.'

His openness touches me, but at the same time I am unbelievably embarrassed. Much as I would like to pursue it, to ask him, 'and do you really love each other?' I cannot; Judith might have, in fact she probably did. I am certain he told her too, just as I am certain he would tell me if I asked; why else has he brought me out for lunch if not to make me feel easy about him. But I draw back, I can't ask, not now at least. To pursue the subject beyond Louis's first eager revelation might diminish it, might bury it. Why shouldn't he love my mother? If there *is* such a thing as justice, then surely even the unloving deserve love. She's like everyone else, I suddenly see; inside her head are the same turning, gathering spindles of necessity; why shouldn't he love her?

Louis smiles at me with almost boyish gaiety, his teeth, dark ivory with flashes of gold at the sides, his wrinkles breaking like waves around the hub of his happiness – a happiness so accidental, so improbable and so finely suspended – hadn't Brother Adam written that happiness arrives when least expected and that it tends to dissolve under scrutiny. Better to change the subject.

I glance around the room, taking in the polished wood and coloured glass; a square of ruby-red light falls on Louis's soft old hair. 'How did you find this place?' I ask him. 'Had you been here before . . . before the day . . . you brought her out here?'

'Oh, yes, yes, yes,' he is pleased with my question. 'When I was teaching school – I used to be the woodwork teacher, your mother must have told you. Always was good with my hands.' He spreads them for my inspection.

'Simple carpentry, nothing complicated, knife racks and wall shelves mostly. At the end of the school year, round about the middle of June, I'd say, we used to come out here, all the teachers, and have lunch.' He coughs, a sudden attacking hack of a cough. 'Sort of, you know, a celebration.'

'Which school was it?' I ask politely.

'St Vincent.' He chokes again. 'Not so far from where you went to school.'

'St Vincent,' I say, remembering. 'That's a Catholic school, isn't it?'

He nods, watching me closely.

'Some of the kids in our neighbourhood used to go there,' I tell Louis. 'The MacArthurs. Billy MacArthur? Red hair, fat, always in trouble?'

'I don't think I remember him,' Louis says regretfully.

'Judith and I always kind of envied the Catholic kids. It seemed – I don't know – sort of exotic going to a school like that. Like a pageant. First communion and all those white dresses. And veils even. And catechism. And always calling their teachers Sister this and Father that.'

Louis nods and smiles.

'But,' I say thoughtfully, 'I always thought that the teachers in those days had to be nuns and priests.'

Louis nods again.

'But you . . .'

'Yes,' Louis says.

Silence. 'A priest?' I whisper.

'Yes,' he says in a level voice, 'a priest.'

'I can't believe it.'

'I wanted you to know.'

'Does Judith . . .'

'I told her yesterday.'

'And my mother. Of course she . . .'

'Of course.'

'But –' I try to gather in my words, I struggle for the right words but there don't seem to be any for this moment, 'but weren't you . . . I thought . . . weren't you married before?'

'Only to the Church,' he says with a faint, modest rhetorical edge.

'But now . . .'

'I made the decision to leave,' he says, 'three years ago.'

My mother is marrying a sick, seventy-two-year-old ex-priest, I can hardly breathe, I cannot believe this.

'But Louis,' I stumble on, 'why did you . . . I mean, it's none of my business . . . but why did you leave?'

He is ready to tell me; he has, I can see, brought me here to make me understand. 'It was when I first started to . . . get sick. I know it seems strange. You'd think sickness would make me cling to my vocation. But it wasn't like that.'

'What was it like then?'

'I started to feel afraid.'

'Of death?'

'I could never be frightened of death. I'm still a Catholic.'

'What were you afraid of then?' I ask, but already I know. Oh, Louis, I know what it is to be afraid.

'I wasn't sure. I'm still not sure now. But I think I was afraid I'd missed half my life.'

For a sickening half-instant I think he is referring to celibacy, surely he doesn't mean that.

'I'd never lived alone,' Louis explains carefully. 'I'd never had the strength. But then, when I got sick, it seemed possible. Anything seemed possible. It doesn't make sense, I know.'

But to me it does make sense, for why had I married Watson? Because his sudden arrival into my life had said one thing: anything was possible. Possibility rimmed those first days like a purplish light; love was possible; flight was possible; my whole life was going to be possible.

'So you decided to leave?' I say to Louis.

He nods. His face has become alarmingly flushed. How difficult this must be for him. I want to reach out and pat his arm, but I'm too awestruck to move.

'I've been quite happy,' he says, 'surprisingly so. Of course, being alone has its problems too.'

I know. I know.

'Then I met your mother.'

341

I smile uncertainly.

He makes a little laced basket of his hands and says, 'I hope you don't think . . . you don't think we're just old and foolish.'

'Of course not,' I gasp truthfully.

'Because we don't have . . .' he pauses, 'surely you realize . . . we don't have all that . . . much time.' He says this lightly, he even gives a faint, ghoulish, baffling sort of chuckle which I find both shocking and admirable.

Now I *do* reach out and pat his hand, his chamois-coloured, brown-spotted, hairless little hand. We sit in the red and yellow and blue pooled light without saying a word. A young waitress takes our plates away and brings us ice cream in tiny imitation pewter bowls.

Louis sighs at last and says thickly, 'It would have been nice . . . nice . . . to have a priest at the wedding, that's all. It doesn't matter though. Not really.'

'You mean to perform the ceremony?' I ask him.

'Oh no. That would be a little . . . uncomfortable for your mother, I think. But it would have been nice to have a priest, just to, you know, be there.'

'Couldn't you invite one?' I ask him earnestly.

'It's awkward,' he says. 'I'm a little . . . out of touch.'

I tease the bitter chocolate ice cream with the tip of my spoon. I can't stop myself: I say, 'Look, Louis, I know a priest. As a matter of fact I'm going to see him tomorrow. Why don't I ask him to come? I don't have to tell him anything about your being a priest. I could just invite him – you know – to my mother's wedding.'

He tips his head to one side and smiles a startled amber-toothed asymmetrical smile; pleasure drains into his grouted eyes and, nodding his head, he surprises me by saying, 'Why, that would be very kind of you.'

*   *   *

342

Louis's confession has refreshed him; he looks rather tired but he orders coffee with the happy air of a man who has discharged his purpose.

For me the revelation is not so speedily digested; it hangs overhead like a bank of fresh steam, and my imagination struggles to picture Louis of the clerical collar; Louis of the ivory Sunday vestments, wafer in mouth, cup upraised; Louis as devout young novice; Louis as frightened lonely child – somewhere under the old, soft, yellowed skin that boy must still exist. It is too much for me – the idea of Louis as priest resists belief, but it must, it will be, assimilated.

And what, I ask myself, is so strange about my mother meeting a defrocked priest – an ex-priest, I should say, it is somehow kinder to think of him that way – certainly a lot of them are floating around these days. And how did I imagine they would look if not like Louis? Did I expect them to be exhausted and spiritual, hollow-eyed, pitted with recognizable piety, baroque in manner, fatherly and frightened with damaged holiness sewn into their fingertips? They were men, only men, assorted, various and unmarked. Was Eugene with his moist normalcy and gentle hands identifiable as an orthodontist? And Martin: to see him turning over the pages of the *Globe and Mail* in my mother's backyard, who would suspect the Miltonic peaks and canyons that furnished his intelligence: the very idea was ridiculous.

Meeting Watson Forrest when I was eighteen – there he was drinking orange soda in a run-down, soon-to-be-bankrupt drug-store – a short, frowsy boy of twenty-two with wrinkled corduroy pants, acne scars and tufted crown of reddish hair – I had not believed him at first when he told me he had graduated in botany from the University of Toronto, that he had already written his Master's thesis (what was a Master's thesis? I had asked) on rare Ontario orchids. Later, made restless by the romance of the

North, Watson had turned to Arctic lichens; later still, drawn into the back-to-nature movement, he had focused on the common pigweed and had theorized, often tiresomely, on the pigweed's ability to draw nutrients to the surface of the earth. Orchids to pigweed: Watson had continually evolved toward the more popular, more democratic, more ubiquitous forms of plant life. Specialty was for those who were content to stand still. Watson had resisted, more than most, the stamp of profession.

And as for me, Charleen Forrest, who, seeing me buying oranges in the Safeway or mailing letters on rainy Vancouver corners, who would guess that I am a poet? My bone structure is wrong; all those elongations; all those undisciplined edges, the ridged thighs, the wire-brush hair, the corns on my feet, the impurities in my heart – how could I possibly be a poet, how could I, as some might say, sing in a finer key?

The truth is, I am a sort of phony poet; poetry was grafted artificially onto my lazy unconnectedness, and it was Watson – yes, Watson – who did the grafting. Watson made me a poet – at least he pushed me in that direction – by his frenzied, almost hysterical efforts to educate me. What a shock it must have been, when he recovered from the first sexual ecstasies, to find himself married to an eighteen-year-old girl of crushing ignorance. Our first apartment in Vancouver was crammed with the books he brought me from the library, books I read doggedly, despairingly, in an attempt to conceal from him the shallowness of my learning. I seemed always to be working against time; the bright lights of possibility he had lighted in my head were already flickering out one by one.

I took a short typing course in Vancouver and for three years I supported both of us by typing term papers for graduate students in the cluttered, dusty nest of our one-room apartment. And in between, in order to forestall Watson's ultimate disenchantment,

I sweated through books of history, biography, science; in fact, whatever Watson selected for me. How he had loved the role of tutor, one of his many incarnations: he became a kind of magician and I the raw material to be transformed. His devotion to my education was, to be sure, less than altruistic: his first appointment was in sight; another incarnation, another role – that of brilliant young lecturer – awaited him, and he became, not without reason, worried about the handicap of a stupid wife.

Somewhere along the line my self-education ceased to be a wifely duty. Watson began edging into student politics and laying the groundwork for the *Journal*, and for me, sitting alone in the apartment, literature became a friend and ally. Surrounded by frayed basket chairs, brick-and-board book shelves, a card table desk, studio couch and bamboo blinds – the furniture, in fact, of the newly married – literature became the real world. And poetry, modern poetry, unlocked in me not so much a talent, but a strange narrow aptitude, a knack, at first, and nothing more.

My first poems were experiments; I built them on borrowed rhythms; I was a dedicated tinkerer, putting together the shapes and ideas which I shoplifted. And images. Like people who excel at crossword puzzles, I found that I could, with a little jiggling, produce images of quite startling vividness. My first poems (pomes) were lit with a whistling blue clarity (emptiness) and they were accepted by the first magazine I sent them to. Only I knew what paste-up jobs they were, only I silently acknowledged my debt to a good thesaurus, a stimulating dictionary and a daily injection, administered like Vitamin B, of early Eliot. I, who manufactured the giddy dark-edged metaphors, knew the facile secret of their creation. Like piecework I rolled them off. Never, never, never did I soar on the wings of inspiration; the lines I wrote, hunched over the card table in that grubby, poorly ventilated apartment, were painstakingly assembled, an artificial montage of poetic parts. I was a literary conman, a quack, and the size of my early success was amazing, thrilling and frightening.

But after Watson left us, after he walked out on Seth and me, poetry became the means by which I saved my life. I stopped assembling; I discovered that I could bury in my writing the greater part of my pain and humiliation. The usefulness of poetry was revealed to me; all those poets had been telling the truth after all; anguish could be scooped up and dealt with. My loneliness could, by my secret gift of alchemy, be shaped into a less frightening form. I was going to survive – I soon saw that – and my survival was hooked into my quirky, accidental ability to put words into agreeable arrangements. I could even remake my childhood, that great void in which nothing had happened but years and years of shrivelling dependence. I wrote constantly and I wrote, as one critic said, 'from the floor of a bitter heart.'

And the irony, the treachery really, was that those who wrote critical articles on my books of poetry never – not one of them – distinguished between those poems I had written earlier and those that came later. (What grist for the Philistines who scoff at literary criticism.) To these critics my work was one arresting – 'the arresting Charleen Forrest' – seamless whole. Which goes to show . . .

Louis Berceau takes an enormous amount of sugar in his coffee. Four heaped teaspoons. I watch him – his hands are remarkably steady for a man of his age – dipping into the sugarbowl. The smiling girl of a waitress refills our cups several times, and Louis almost succeeds in emptying the bowl of sugar.

The mind is easily persuaded, a fact which Brother Adam mentioned in a recent letter, and Louis suddenly appears to me to be an altogether holy man sitting here stirring his sticky coffee. A monk. He inspires, in fact, a torrent of confession. In half an hour I have told him rather a lot about my marriage with Watson. He is an excellent listener, something I noticed yesterday in my mother's kitchen; he simply nods from time to time and fixes me with his opaque gaze. And out it all spills.

Watson, I tell him, was a man without a centre; he took on the colour of whichever landscape he happened to stumble across. Watson was a man who went to a Cary Grant movie and for a week after spoke in a light, slight, cocky English accent. He also did a weary, sneery Richard Widmark and – his favourite – a lean, mean, sinewy Dane Clark. Watson was a bit like a snake – the comparison is not really a good one for it suggests malice – but he was like a snake in his ability to continually shed his skin. Louis nods, and I hesitate, remembering that Louis too is a man who has shed his skin.

No, not like a snake, I correct myself, but like an actor who plays a number of roles one after the other, roles which he takes up energetically but later, with a kind of wilful amnesia, shakes off and denies. Louis looks puzzled, and I try to explain. Watson's first incarnation I can only theorize about: he must have been a sort of child prodigy hatched into an otherwise undistinguished Scarborough family, bringing home to his bus-driver father and seamstress mother miraculous report cards and brimming with a kind of juicy, pedantic, junior-sized zeal. But by the time I met him, he had left that scrubbed good-son image behind and transformed himself into a studied, lazy dreamer of a student, tenderly anarchic, determinedly bumbling and odd. Oh, very, very odd. A structured oddity, though, which both thrilled and terrified him; he needed someone, me, to bring reality to the role. Later, as a married graduate student in Vancouver he had stunned me with a whole new set of mannerisms and attitudes; he literally fought his way into all-roundedness – he boxed, he ran for elections, he wrote articles on alfalfa, he signed petitions, he played softball, he even forced himself to attend chamber music recitals and read up on the history of ballet. And I had adored his earnestness, his determination, his rabid certainty which completed, it had seemed to me, some need of my own. I had not quite loved his Young Professor Self, his two year retreat – it seemed longer – into piped and bearded tolerant middle-class academe, his almost British equanimity, the completely unforeseen manner in which he began to utter whole networks of archaisms, words like vouchsafe and gainsay, words strung together with a troubling catgut of hitherto's, wheretofor's and whilst's; once, completely unabashed, he began a sentence with a burbling I daresay. It had been during that period that we actually bought a house with a garden. And actually conceived, with brooding deliberation, a child. House, wife, child, all he needed was the ivy. But already he was on his way to his next creation: rebellious young intellectual. For a while he did a balancing act between the two roles: one Sunday afternoon, sulky and depressed, the three of us had taken a walk around the neighbourhood. Seth, who must have been two years old at the time, walked between us, holding on to our hands. He was a little slow and unsteady, and Watson yanked him now and then angrily. But then we happened to pass by a house where an elderly couple were taking the afternoon sun. Seeing them, Watson had smiled gaily; he had swung Seth merrily to his shoulders in gruff fatherly fashion, crooning nonsense into his startled ears; this extraordinary display of affection had lasted until we were out of sight of the couple. Watching him, I had been sickened; that was when I knew he was a man without a centre.

As he careened toward thirty, he seemed to dissolve and reform with greater frequency, and each reincarnation introduced a new, more difficult strain of madness. Watson seemed unable, psychologically unable, physiologically unable, to resist any new current of thought. He was the consummate bandwagon man. Yet, I had loved him through most of his phases. Riding off to Vancouver on the back of his motorcycle, my face pressed for thousands of jolting miles into the icy smooth leather of his shoulders, hadn't I thought that I would be safe forever? And for most of the eight years we were together I tried to be tolerant, sometimes even enthusiastic. But what I could never accept was the way in which he coldly shut the door on his past lives. The fact that he so seldom wrote to his parents was a troubling warning; I could sympathize, but still it seemed heartless not to acknowledge the birthday gifts of knitted gloves and homemade fruitcake. Friends, abandoned along the way, wrote imploring letters – what is the matter with Watson, why doesn't he write or phone? The *Journal* which he founded in a burst of professional ardour became another dead end. He and Doug Savage quarrelled irrevocably over the definition and degree of scientific responsibility. And he refused to have anything to do with the Freehorns after they once teased him about his intermittent vegetarianism. Seth he regarded as a kind of recrimination, a remnant of a former, now shameful, life which he wanted to forget. Of course I saw that eventually I too would have to go.

'So it wasn't such a shock,' Louis says, 'when he . . . when you separated.'

'It was still a shock,' I tell him. 'I knew it was coming, but I couldn't believe it when it actually happened.'

When I look at snapshots of myself taken during that period I am amazed that I am not deformed by unhappiness, that I am not visibly disfigured, bent over and shredded with grief. In fact, except for my bitter, lime-section mouth, I look astonishingly healthy. In the first months I was so weighted with sorrow and relief that I slept twelve hours every night. I was so emptied out that I ate greedily and constantly, buying for myself baskets of fruit as though I were an invalid. My eyes in those photographs gleam like radium;

perhaps I was crazed by the cessation of love, still disbelieving, always certain that Watson would return in another guise.

And in an entirely hopeless way I know I am still half-expecting him to turn up, remorseful, shriven, redeemed. Why else am I keeping Eugene waiting if not for my poor bone of expectation? Waiting has become my daily religion. Tomorrow I must remember to ask Brother Adam why, after all these years, I am still wearing my four-dollar wedding band.

When Louis speaks again, he asks with phlegmplugged caution the perfect question. 'Where is your Watson Forrest living now?'

One lives for moments like this. 'Here,' I pronounce solemnly, feeling my tongue cooling in delicious irony. 'Watson lives right here. Isn't that amazing, Louis? Can you believe it? He lives here in this very town.'

Louis shows perhaps a lesser degree of astonishment than I would like, but nevertheless he shakes his head in slow, grinning wonder.

And both of us, sitting in silence over our coffee cups are stewing in the rarified, blood-racing excitement of knowing exactly what will happen next.

The Whole World Retreat is two and a half miles south-east of Weedham, reached by a neglected section of secondary road. The young brown-eyed waitress at the Wayfarers' Inn is pleased to give us directions. 'We buy all our lettuce and onions from them,' she dimples, 'and I don't care what anyone says about them, they make the best whole-wheat bread you ever tasted. Sort of nutty like, you know what I mean. Crunchy. All our customers ask where we get it.'

We take the road slowly, swerving here and there to avoid potholes still glittering with yesterday's downpour. The country-side is green and rolling like calendar country; and the farms, though small, seem prosperous with good straight fences, herds of healthy cows and cheerful country mail boxes: The Mertins, Russell K. Anderson and Son, Bill and Hazel Rodman, Dwayne Harshberger, and, at last, a mail box that announces in blocky, green letters, The Whole World Retreat. Louis pulls the car to a stop on the shoulder of the road.

Back at the restaurant we agreed that we would simply drive past the place. It would be fun – I had emphasized the word *fun*, while despising the sound of it – it would be fun, out of curiosity, to drive by and see what the place looked like. I had proposed this to Louis in my lightest, most floating accents, as though this were no more than a crazy whim, a mad impulse, as though I were one of those programmed eccentrics who love to do mad, mad, mad things on the spur of the moment. Like Greta Savage who spends her life crouched on the contrived lip of unreason with her: *who else does crazy things like eat sardines for breakfast, who else is mad enough to take a holiday in Repulse Bay, who else is demented enough to tune in every day to the Archers*. I have long suspected that her insanity is partly an affectation; now I adopt her shrill cry – 'I know it sounds silly, Louis, but let's, just for the fun of it, drive by.'

An act of adolescence, for don't high school girls in love with their math teachers furtively seek out their houses so they can cycle by, half-drowning in the illicit thrill of proximity. I hate Louis to see this undeveloped, irrational side of my personality which hungers for cheap drama, but not enough to pass up the opportunity of seeing the Whole World Retreat. And besides, hasn't something more than chance brought me this close? Isn't there at least a suggestion of predestination in this afternoon's events, and hasn't Louis with his surprise revelation introduced a note of compelling, almost mystical significance? This day clearly has not been designed for rationality. Even though it is almost four o'clock, it does not seem right to turn back toward Scarborough where the tunafish casserole awaits, no doubt about it, already browning in my mother's oven, and where my mother herself waits with her contained, wordless questioning. Something entirely unforeseen has been set into action; I can feel the piping tattoo of my pulse in my throat, and, looking sideways at Louis's suddenly brightened eyes, I can see that he shares at least a measure of my excitement.

Beside the mail box a sign in heavy lettering announces: Green onions, Rhubarb, Homemade Bread, Fresh Eggs, Nursery Plants. And at the bottom in larger letters: Absolutely No Chemical Fertilizers. Louis and I sit, thoughtful for a moment, reading the sign and thinking our thoughts.

The house itself is set well back from the road. It is a top-heavy house, late Victorian in old-girlish brick, and its porch skirt of turned, white spindles gives it a blithe knees-up-Mother-Brown gaiety. Red and yellow tulips, not quite open, stand cheerful in a curved bed. The sloping front lawn is exceptionally beautiful with its twilled, gabardine richness and its fine finish of new growth.

There is no one in sight.

'They sell nursery plants,' I remark to Louis.

'Yes,' he says, 'they do.'

'I wonder what kind of things they have at this time of year.'

'Hmmm.'

'Actually,' I take a deep breath, 'actually I'd thought of buying some nursery plants.'

No response from Louis.

I try again. 'For you, Louis, the two of you. Something for the backyard. I thought it might make a good wedding gift.'

More silence, and then Louis says cheerfully, 'The perfect thing.'

'We could just see what they have in stock.'

352

'Are you . . . that is . . . are you sure?'

I pause. Then lunge. 'Yes. I'm sure.'

We leave the car – Louis checks both doors to make sure they are locked – and walks up the loose-gravelled drive toward the house. He stumbles slightly, then catches himself, but I don't even turn my head. I can feel excitement leaking in through my skin and for an instant I feel I might faint.

Up close the house looks slightly less picturesque. There is an old wringer washing machine on the porch, a pair of men's work gloves hanging on a nail (Watson's gloves?), two rain-sodden cartons of empty pop bottles. The screen door, rather rusty, has been inexpertly patched.

I knock.

'Hang on a minute,' a woman's low voice calls from the shadows behind the screen, 'I'm coming.'

From inside the house we hear a young baby wailing. Baby! It takes my brain an instant to decode the message: a baby, oh God. Then plunging grief – Watson's baby. And in another instant I will be seeing Watson. He will come striding through that screen door and see me standing here with my old, grotesque vulnerability hanging around me like a hand-me-down raincoat. What am I doing here?

A young woman, plumply tranquil, wearing granny glasses, pushes open the door. She wears a dirty, pink shirt over her jeans and on her hip rides a screaming, naked baby of about fifteen months. 'Sorry to keep you waiting,' she says in a flat but friendly southern Ontario voice. 'I had the baby on the pot.'

'That's all right,' Louis says wheezing.

'What a lovely baby,' I half moan. 'Is it –' I peer closely, 'Oh, it's a little girl.'

'Faith,' the woman says.

'Pardon?'

'Faith. That's her name.'

Louis receives this information silently. He is searching his pockets for a handkerchief. Automatically, never missing a beat, my kindness act uncoils itself. 'What an interesting name.'

'My husband calls her Mustard Seed.'

'Oh!' The word husband pierces me. 'Oh?'

'Just a joke. Faith of a mustard seed. From the Bible.'

'Oh, yes,' my head bobs.

'Well,' she says smiling and shifting the still wailing baby to her other hip, 'is there anything I can help you with?'

'We saw your sign,' Louis says indistinctly. His asthma is threatening; he is alarmingly tired. I should never have dragged him here; we should never have come.

'Nursery plants,' I say, clearing my throat. 'We were interested in nursery plants.'

'Terrific,' the young mother beams. (Young! she can't be older than twenty-five. I am shaken by a shower of dizzy shame for Watson, this is too much.)

'I wanted to buy something for a wedding gift,' I say. 'A shrub, I thought, something like that.'

'Just a sec,' the woman says. She peers over her shoulder into the kitchen. 'My husband can show you what we've got. Of course, it's early, there's not much, but he can at least show you what we've got.'

'Look,' I say, taking a step backwards, 'we'll come back another time. When you've got more in.'

She won't stop smiling at me; her yeasty good cheer glints off her glasses, making creamy Orphan Annie coins of her eyes. 'You might as well have a look,' she says. 'He's right here. He'll be glad to show you what we've got.'

Footsteps across the kitchen floor, a man's footsteps, a man's muffled pleasant voice saying, 'I'm coming.' *Watson.*

But the face that appears in the doorway isn't Watson; it is younger, leaner; it has blue eyes. And this man is taller. Not only that but he has straight, straw-coloured hair hanging to his shoulders and a muscular chest moving under his T-shirt. 'How do you do,' he says, stepping onto the porch.

'How do you do,' Louis and I chorus. Louis gives me a quick, quizzing look, and I manage to flash him the smallest of smiles.

'Hey,' the young man says, squinting at me, 'hey, aren't you Charleen Forrest?'

Run, I cry, *bolt. Now. Make for the road. Leap in the car, run.* 'Yes,' I say, 'I am.'

'Well, for Pete's sake,' the smiling girl says, showing a place in her lower jaw where a tooth is missing.

'Can you beat that,' her husband mutters with awesome gentleness. The baby stops whimpering and holds herself suddenly rigid. Then she wets herself; a surprisingly wide stream of pale baby pee creams off her mother's hip and splashes to the porch floor.

'Oh hell,' the girl says with equanimity, stepping sideways out of the puddle.

'Charleen Forrest,' her husband murmurs again. He sends me a warm, slow smile.

'How do you know who I am?' I ask, thinking: Watson, he must keep a picture of me, imagine that, who would have thought it of Watson?

'I've got all your books,' he says. 'And your picture's on the back. I would have recognized you anywhere.'

'Oh,' I say, disappointed.

'And then, of course, knowing Watson –' he shrugs and smiles, 'not that that matters. We really dig your stuff. Cheryl and I.'

'That's for sure,' Cheryl says.

'Thank you,' I say absurdly. Sweetly?

'Don't suppose you've seen Watson lately?' he asks me.

I stare.

'We sure miss him,' Cheryl says in tones soft with regret. 'It's just not the same here without Watson. Is it, Rob?'

'He was a beautiful guy,' Rob says mournfully. 'One real beautiful guy, that's all I can say.'

'But look,' I say to the two of them in a sharply raised voice, 'he still lives here? Doesn't he?'

'Gosh, no,' the gap-toothed Cheryl says. 'Gee, it's been – what Rob? – two years now?'

'Yeah. More than two years. He split – let's see – it was round the end of March, wasn't it, Cheryl? Two years ago March. We haven't had a postcard from him even.'

'But that's impossible,' I tell them firmly. 'It can't be true.'

A look of concern passes between them, a look which firmly shuts me out, and I feel a nudge of suspicion. Are they trying to protect Watson, pretending he isn't here, trying to fool me like this?

'You see,' Rob says, taking the baby from his wife, 'Watson sort of, well, I guess you could say he got disenchanted. You know, with the whole scene, the whole group thing, what we were trying to do here.'

'And the others,' Cheryl prompts him.

He nods. 'That was part of it too, I guess. There were about eight of us, Cheryl and me and the others. All of them younger than Watson. Mostly kids who'd dropped out of the whole city thing. Younger kids. Watson kept saying they were getting younger and younger all the time. He finally got to thinking, I guess, that it was time to move on to another scene.'

'He was forty,' I tell them abruptly. 'Two years ago he had his fortieth birthday. In March.'

'Gee,' Cheryl says, 'Forty!'

'But he must be here,' I insist, 'because every month he sends me a cheque from here. The child support money. For our son. He sends it every month. Always right on the fifteenth and it comes from here. Weedham. I know because I always check the postmark.'

They laugh softly as if I'd said something outlandishly amusing. 'That's Rob,' Cheryl explains grinning. 'Rob's the one who sends off the cheque.'

'You mail me the cheque?' I ask dazed.

'It was the one thing Watson wanted me to do. He left, Christ, I don't know how many postdated cheques. Enough till the boy's eighteen, I think, isn't it Cheryl?'

'And enough money in the bank to cover them. That's what's important, I guess, eh?'

Rob continues, 'He wrote a note, left it on the back door, this door here. All about the cheques, like where to send them and all. And I haven't forgotten one, not so far anyways.'

'That's very kind of you,' I say, feeling my mouth freeze with etiquette and sorrow.

'But you know,' Rob rambles on, 'I might forget sometime. Memory's not my strong point, ask Cheryl here. What I should do, since you're standing right here, is just give you the whole bunch of cheques. Right now. That way you'd have them right with you and you could just cash them as the dates roll round.'

Cheryl nods enthusiastically at this piece of logic, and I feel suddenly flattened by confusion. Something inside me twists, something sour, something sharp, but I manage to smile and say, 'Sure. Why not? While I'm here I might as well take them with me.'

Cheryl goes into the house and comes back in a minute with a large brown envelope. 'They're in here. You can count them if you want.'

'That's okay,' I say. 'I don't have to count them. And thank you.'

'No need to thank us,' Rob says. And then he adds wistfully, 'We sure miss Watson. It's not the same.'

Should I ask them? I have to. 'Where's Watson living now?'

'East,' Rob says. 'He went east.'

'You mean the Maritimes?'

He laughs again. 'No, not geographical east. Philosophical east. He was into the mysticism thing. Hindu mainly.'

'Buddha too,' Cheryl offers.

'You don't know where he went?' I can hear a shameful bleat in my voice. 'Geographically, I mean?'

'No. Like I said, we haven't heard anything from Watson. Not in two years. Just that note stuck on the door. He didn't say where he was going, just that he was going East. With a capital E. East.'

'And that's all?'

'That's all. The others, they kind of drifted off one by one too. After the baby was born. Some of them couldn't really ride with the baby thing. So now there's just Cheryl and me. And Mustard Seed here.' He blows a noisy kiss into the baby's fat neck. 'We're just kind of a family now, you might say. We still do some farming but not like when Watson was here. But our bread baking operation is going along pretty well.'

'And the nursery plants,' Cheryl adds.

'Oh, yeah, the nursery plants. That's what you folks were looking for, wasn't it?'

Behind the greenhouse in the spilled, late afternoon sunlight, Louis and I pick out some good healthy shrubs: six mock orange with their roots bound in sacking. And a flat of petunias, white and pink mixed. I pay Rob with a twenty-dollar bill, and he helps Louis put them in the trunk of the car. Then we shake hands all around and head for home.

I sit beside Louis with the brown envelope on my lap and it occurs to me that I will never again receive a message from Watson,

Watson my lapsed-bastard, first-love, phantom husband. The last link – a smudged, treasonous postmark – has just been taken away from me. It wasn't much, but it was better than nothing. The arrival of Watson's cheques – the regularity, the suppressed silence – offered me something: not hope, certainly not hope, I am not such a fool as that, but a pencil line of connecting sense in the poor tatter I'd made of my life. A portion of renewal. And a means by which the worth of other things might be tested. Damn you, Watson.

'There, there,' Louis is saying. 'There, there now.' The curving kindness of his voice – what a good man he is – makes me conscious of the tears falling out of my eyes.

Chapter 6

It takes us a long time to get back to Scarborough. For twenty minutes we're stalled in traffic. An accident maybe; it could be anything. So many people in this city. Louis's cautious driving style, so reassuring earlier in the day, is an irritant now that it's five-thirty, five-forty-five, six o'clock. A heavy rug of sky pushes down on the streaked sunlight; my head aches. At exactly six-thirty my mother will be placing her Pyrex casserole on the blue, crocheted hotpad in the middle of the kitchen table. I twitch with nerves. Doesn't Louis know how punctual my mother is about meals? Well, he'll soon learn.

Louis tries to cheer me up by talking about his favourite poet, Robert Service. I wish he wouldn't. *Please, Louis, don't.* His voice cracks with strain and it's disappointing to hear he hasn't read Hopkins. But his lips smack with pleasure over a stanza of 'The Shooting of Dan McGrew', and I chide myself for expecting more than I deserve.

At last Scarborough, the shopping centre, the school where I went to kindergarten (I was the one whose socks were always sliding down), the grid of streets so minutely familiar but whose separate names now seem cunningly elusive. At seven o'clock Louis pulls up in front of the house, and from the living room window a face (whose?) registers our return.

'Aren't you coming in, Louis?' I ask. 'Aren't you staying for supper?'

'I'm a little tired,' he says weakly. 'This chest of mine.'

'Are you sure you won't come in? Just for a minute?'

'I think I'll have an early night,' he says. 'You'll explain to your mother, won't you?'

'Sure.'

'I'll bring over the shrubs in the morning. Put them in first thing in the morning.'

'Fine. And Louis . . . thanks for everything.' I emphasize the word everything; suddenly I'm tired, too.

'Good night.'

'Good night.'

I'm late. Will my mother dare to scold me. Yes, she won't be able to help herself. This in itself is alarming enough, but something else is even more frightening, something unnatural about the crouched, waiting house, or is it that strange car parked in front? Or perhaps there are such things as psychic waves, perhaps Greta Savage is right after all about telepathic electricity, perhaps tense, waving vibrations actually penetrate my skin as I walk around to the back door. I don't know. But coming into this house alone at this hour makes me suddenly and ridiculously weak with fear.

The first thing I see in the kitchen is my mother's tunafish casserole. Its tender breadcrumb crust is unbroken. A serving spoon lies tentatively by its side, but the table hasn't been set. How odd.

Eugene. What is he doing here? He is supposed to be at the Orthodontists' banquet eating warmed-up roast beef and hard little scoops of mashed potato. He crosses the kitchen and presses me in his arms. Eugene, not here, really, can't you see my mother's standing right here?

My mother is standing by the stove. Her hands can't seem to

361

find a resting place. They're not clutched behind her back, they're not clenched at her hips, not folded across her chest, not nervously laced beneath her chin; they are floating freely in a frightening pantomime of helplessness.

Martin and Judith. They are standing in the doorway. How curious, they aren't actually touching each other, so why do they seem to swim before me in blurry tandem unison like synchronized dancers. Married people grow to look alike – it must be true – just look at those two twin jaws slung in the same attitude of guarded concern. Concern? What is the matter with them?

And then there are the two policemen. Why do policemen wear that dispirited shade of blue, snow-shovel blue, looseleaf notebook blue? Two policemen sitting at the kitchen table. Sitting there. But when I come in the door, they shuffle politely to their feet. A dream, of course.

'Charleen,' Eugene holds me close.

'Thank heavens you're home,' Judith's mordant contralto escapes in a gasp.

'Now don't get excited, Judith,' Martin says. 'Give her a minute, everyone.'

'Are you Mrs Forrest?' one of the policemen demands.

'Wouldn't you like to go into the living room?' my mother frets.

'You must be calm,' Eugene says into my shoulder. 'You must try to remain calm.'

'And your regular domicile is Vancouver?'

'Just take it easy, take it easy now.'

'Keep things in proportion . . .'

'You'll find the living room more comfortable.'

'We have one or two questions for you, Mrs Forrest.'

'Here, Charleen, sit down. Martin, get her to sit down.'

'You'd better sit down; you must sit down.'

362

'There, that's better isn't it?'

'And when was your departure from Vancouver, Mrs Forrest?'

'Leave her alone for Christ's sake, can't you see she's confused.'

'Take it easy, Char, take it easy –'

'. . . if you'll just answer a few questions . . .'

'The living room is cooler and you could . . .'

'Keep your balance, that's the important . . .'

'Your exact arrival in Toronto was . . . ?'

'Hey, give her a chance . . .'

'You tell her.'

'I'm only trying to help.'

'I think Eugene should be the one. He's . . .'

'We understand this is upsetting, Mrs Forrest . . .'

'The living room . . .'

'. . . unfortunately they expect a complete report at headquarters.'

'Charleen, listen to me. Are you listening?'

'Yes.' Was that my voice? Was it?

Eugene is sitting next to me with both my hands in his and he is saying the most preposterous things. Incredible things. How melodramatic – I wouldn't have thought it of Eugene. Seth has disappeared, Eugene is saying that Seth has disappeared. What a joke. Is it a joke? It can't be, because these policemen are writing things down and besides my mother doesn't like jokes. And neither, I realize for the first time in my life, neither do I.

Seth has been taken somewhere by Greta Savage. Taken away. Several days ago. No one knows for sure when. Or how. But they have both been missing for several days. Now don't get excited. No one knows where they are at this precise moment, but in all probability they are safe. Greta Savage has disappeared with my

363

son and Doug Savage has called in the police, that is what has happened, Charleen.

'Say something, Charleen,' Eugene commands.

'Is she going to faint?' Judith's arm is on my shoulder.

'It looks like it. Someone get some water.'

'Are you going to faint, Charleen?'

'Darling.'

'No,' I say distinctly. 'No, I'm not going to faint.'

All I have to do is hold on to consciousness. Nothing is more important than that, for the moment nothing more is required of me. But if I shut my eyes for even a second I will never see Seth again. I must sit still, I must pretend I am composed of dry, unjointed wood, if I move one inch from this table there will be an explosion.

I must try to understand. Slowly, perfectly like a child memorizing the Twenty-third Psalm, *He restoreth my soul for his something-or-other sake*. Certain facts must be absorbed.

Doug Savage has been trying to reach me all day. The last call came from Parry Sound. He phoned at least four times today. Finally he agreed to talk to Judith. Judith phoned downtown immediately and had Eugene paged at the conference. Eugene came home at once and since then he has been trying unsuccessfully to reach Doug Savage. But Doug Savage promised Judith he would phone back at eight o'clock. That's less than an hour, Judith says, only fifty minutes now, and until then there is nothing anyone can do.

Seth and Greta have been missing all week. While I was eating English muffins on the train, while I was kissing Eugene in the back of a taxi and, Oh God, while I was chasing around the countryside with Louis Berceau on a foolish, pointless, private, childish quest Greta and Seth disappeared; they took the Savages' car in the middle of the night – there is some confusion about which night it was, Sunday? Monday? The Vancouver police think – there is reason to believe – that Greta may have given Seth some sleeping pills. Sleeping pills!

For the first two days Doug thought he could avoid calling in the police. He had a hunch that Greta might have taken Seth to a cottage they own in the mountains in Alberta. He borrowed a car and drove all night, but when he got there, he found only rumpled beds and tyre tracks. They must have spent the first night there. After that, he thought they might have gone to Winnipeg where Greta has old friends, but when he got there, twenty-four hours later, he couldn't find any trace of her. So he phoned here last night – Can that possibly have been only last night? – hoping Greta had made some kind of contact; after that he phoned the police. There had been no alternative.

The police: they are looking right across the country, but they have to move cautiously (are they dealing with a mad woman?). They don't know. I don't know. The situation has been judged too risky for public appeals, but they are making all sorts of inquiries. It seems Greta is driving mostly at night. A gas station attendant just outside Thunder Bay is almost certain they stopped there: a woman and boy resembling the police description stopped for gas and a hamburger. Did the woman appear dangerous? No. Had the boy appeared intimidated or drugged? No one had noticed. Which way were they headed? The attendant wasn't sure. All he could remember was that they were in a hurry.

There is nothing to do but wait until Doug calls again. The two police officers wait courteously in the living room. My mother frets about whether or not to offer them coffee. Eventually she decides against it. She is more confused than alarmed; her six-thirty supper has been disrupted and in some indefinable way the untouched casserole precludes the making of coffee. As always she is just outside of events, hovering – ghostlike but demanding – at the perimeter. 'How could you leave him with people like that?' she scolds me sharply. 'What kind of friends are they?'

Judith tries to soothe her, but Martin flushes with anger. Martin is convinced that what I need is a stiff drink, but of course there is nothing, not in this house. 'I've got some Scotch in my suitcase,' he says, suddenly assertive. He brings it out, and my mother, her hands still flapping wildly, finds a juice glass. But my stomach leaps and dissolves; I can't even look at it; Martin picks up the glass, regards it mildly, and then drinks it off neat.

Judith's voice floats over my head in a sort of chanting reassuring descant. 'Look at it like this, Charleen, they've both been seen alive and well. Yesterday. So they're okay. Maybe she's a bit on the crazy side, but she isn't dangerous, that's what Doug Savage said on the phone. He said try not to get Charleen upset because Greta wouldn't hurt a fly, it's just a matter of hours before they find him.'

Martin pats me awkwardly on the crown of my head. 'Look here now, Charleen, she's a little unbalanced maybe, but, God, who isn't, and you've known her for years. You know she wouldn't do anything to hurt him, nothing *really* crazy. You've got to keep thinking what she's really like.'

Eugene sits wordless beside me. He's not a wordy man, he never was a wordy man. He's still holding on to my hands, and I'm grateful to him. There's nothing to say. And nothing we can do.

I think of the huge distance between Toronto and Vancouver, the blending agricultural regions, the mountain ranges, river systems, squares of acreage, contours, city limits, county lines, townships and backyards with chickens and shrubs and children. I try to hold that whole terrain in my head; it is a numbing exercise, though it shouldn't be all that difficult, for haven't I just crossed that country myself? Haven't I touched every inch of it? I think of all the people strung out over that distance, imbedded in their separate time zones. Seven-thirty: they're washing dishes. I can hear cutlery right across the country dropping into drawers. They're bathing children, playing bridge, reading newspapers, all of them magically sealed in their preserving spheres of activity. Out there in all that darkness is Greta's car, a blue Volvo – it has to be there – cruising past apartment houses and suburbs and farms; and these people, shutting their windows, watering their lawns, walking their dogs, they just *allow* her to go by. Maybe they even wave to her. Maybe she waves back, she has always been so friendly, so pathetically friendly. She would do anything to help a friend; she is so kind, she wouldn't hurt a fly. Remember that, above all remember that; she wouldn't hurt a fly.

Eight o'clock. We wait in the kitchen. The silence is minutely detailed like a blueprint for a piece of immensely complicated machinery. The minutes are sharply cornered and pressing, and each one hangs rigidly separate.

Eight-fifteen. Why doesn't Doug call? Something has happened. One of the policemen asks if he might phone in a report.

'No,' I gasp.

Eugene shakes his head, 'Better not tie up the phone here.' The policeman nods politely and asks if he might use the next-door neighbour's phone.

At this my mother looks up, horribly alarmed, and I see her mouth twist into its tight diminishing shape. I know that shape, its denials, negations, interdictions, the way it closes to inquiries, the way it forbids, the way it ultimately blames and refuses. Now. She is going to do it now, going to give one of her terrible, unforgiving no's.

But she doesn't. Bewilderment – or is it fatigue? – makes her thin lips collapse. She nods a shaky assent. Then she rises and puts the kettle on.

In a moment the policeman returns; there are no further developments, he tells us. We will have to wait a little longer, that's all.

My mother is moving around the kitchen putting her trembling hands to work. (What have I done to her, what have I done to her this time?) Now she is making tea, now she is arranging jittery cups on a tray. Judith gets up to help her and together they begin to make sandwiches. How extraordinary, my mother actually has a package of boiled ham in the refrigerator. And cheese. Sandwiches are disaster fare; who would have thought my mother had a sense of occasion. She and Judith stand with their backs to us buttering bread. They are exactly the same height; I never noticed that. Their elbows move together, marionettes on a single lateral string. Abstract kinship suddenly made substantial. But why am I thinking about ham and cheese and kinship? Why am I not thinking about the centre of this disaster; why am I not thinking about Seth?

Because I can't bear to.

Seth dead. No, that's not possible. It's not possible because my life isn't possible without him; it's not possible when I'm sitting here, wired with reality. Pulse, heart-beat, nerves, breath, sudden sweating, hurting consciousness, all the signs of life failing me now by *not* failing. In this kitchen every small sound is magnified; my mother's half-invalid, half-despairing shuffle, the policemen laughing in the living room (laughing!), Martin crashing into his ham sandwich, the sugar spoon which strikes with dead neutrality on the formica table. And my eyes: suddenly I can see with wolfish clarity. I can see the neat hem on my mother's sheer kitchen curtains, her tiny over and under and over stitches, and through the curtains a glittering, mocking, glassware moon is coming into view. Evening. Nine o'clock. Doug Savage, why doesn't he phone? Seth dead. No, it's not possible.

Sleeping pills. Greta stuffing Seth with sleeping pills; she is so small, such a weak, wiry woman, something dark about her face, always a sense of shadow. But Seth is quite strong for his age, well developed, remarkably healthy. His health is startling; something godlike nourishes him despite his inheritance; I've never been able to understand it. I picture his strength against Greta's weakness, and a tiny flashbulb of hope goes off under my skin; she can't possibly harm him.

Then I remember how clever she is, how she is veined with a wily unaccountability. Her secrecy about Watson's letters; she hints she has heard from him but says nothing more. And her sudden, piercing, illogical bursts of purity. Madness? Not really madness. How did Doug once put it to me? 'Greta is rational enough, it's just that her rationality is not as evenly distributed as it is in more balanced people.' Certainly she is not a fanatic, not in the accepted sense of that word, but she suffers from blinding pinpricks of virtue. The way, for instance, she once burned Doug's thesis on the diseases of short ferns because she believed it had been conceived to fill an artificial academic requirement. (Only by good fortune had she overlooked the carbon.)

Her weaving too is girded by purity; the way she refuses to touch synthetics and swears to give up weaving altogether if she is forced to work with wool that is chemically dyed and treated. Then there is her violent anti-smoking stance. And her contempt for Eugene and what she considers his crass profession. Her leaps into various systems of the human potential movement. Her bright, birdlike fixations: the insistence (I suddenly remember) with which she had determined to pick up Seth at school last week. Then there is her refusal to have children; here perhaps her fanaticism is grounded on objectivity, for she would have made a shocking mother for all her devotion to Seth. But most painful to me has always been her clinging admiration for Watson; she once confided in an orgy of tactlessness that she 'reverenced' Watson's decision to alter his life. She keeps track of him with passionate persistence, long after everyone else has given up, smothering him with letters, forcing him to acknowledge her existence, coercing him by her indefatigable energy to keep her supplied with news of his latest incarnations. Ah, Greta, poor Greta, poor, twisted, buggered-up Greta, where are you? It's nine-thirty and I'm going crazy, where are you?

In the living room the policemen have turned on the television. Hawaii Five-O. Screams, sirens, the sound of bullets, throaty accusations, weeping, all so bearably unreal. What a poor tissue fiction is, how naively selective and compressed and organized, justice redressed in exactly sixty calculated minutes, the violence always just marginally tolerable, the pressure just within the bounds of human acceptance, tragedy in an airtight marketable tin.

Martin paces. My mother and Judith wash plates and cups, and Eugene goes next door to phone a car rental firm. He has decided that the minute Seth is located we must have a car to get to him.

I think bitterly of Watson. Wherever he is, he is being spared this hour. Of everything he has left undone as a father this seems the worst.

Even Louis – I think of him with a flash of envy – even Louis in his furnished room, so wonderfully protected from all this. So innocently unaware. What peace not to know.

And Brother Adam, you with your abstract wisdom, your fire-escape view, you know nothing of what I'm suffering, you are a dream, you don't even exist for me now.

And Seth, what are you thinking, wherever you are? Are you safe?

*   *   *

Judith, always compulsive, is tidying the kitchen. She covers the tunafish casserole with a dinner plate and puts it in the refrigerator. Then she swirls a wet cloth over the table, picking up my purse and putting it on top of the cupboard.

'What's this?' she asks, picking up an envelope.

I am slow to react; am I losing consciousness after all? Then I say, 'Oh. That's mine.'

It is the envelope containing the child support cheques, my last connection with Watson. A business envelope, eight-by-eleven in business-coloured brown. Closed with a huge paperclip.

I open it idly, and the cheques slide out on my lap. What a lot of cheques, twelve for each year, and yes – I count them – enough to last until Seth's eighteenth birthday. And a stack of addressed envelopes with a rubber band around them. There's even a sheet of postage stamps. How wonderfully organized of Watson, beneath his many layers he must still be in touch with that boy prodigy of his youth and with his dull parents who always paid their bills, in touch too with his unknown, sober ancestors who never ran away from their debts.

There is something different about the final cheque: it is dated for Seth's eighteenth birthday, May 21, and it is made out for five thousand dollars. Five thousand dollars! I feel my breath harden; how had Watson managed to save five thousand dollars? He must have been exceedingly careful over the years to save that much money. But how pointless, how useless, a piece of paper for a son who is missing. A son who can't be found.

I can't help it. I'm starting to cry. I can't help it. This piece of paper, this five thousand dollars – it isn't enough. It's so futile, it's just like Watson to make a gesture like this, so stagy, so impressive and so utterly useless.

But there's something else in the envelope. Still crying I pull it out. It's another piece of paper, a page raggedly torn from a notebook. But the message on it is carefully typed.

I have to read it twice before I realize what it is. It is Watson's farewell note, the one he must have stuck on the screen door before he left the Whole World Retreat. Rob and Cheryl, those two good children, had been more than worthy of the trust he placed in them, guarding not only the cheques but his final words of good-bye. How absurd, though, to write a farewell note on a typewriter, how somehow incongruous, how like Watson. The note he once left me, the one I burned in the barbecue, that note had been typed too. I had forgotten Watson could type; I had forgotten a lot about Watson. But I had not forgotten his embarrassing penchant for prophecy; reading his words of good-bye, it all seems suddenly very familiar.

Dear Brothers and Sisters,
These words are written in love and sadness.
The life of the spirit is love
but it is also containment and peace.

It is time for me to leave you.
Time to go East.
You will understand.
Understanding is all.

Two things I ask of you.
First, care for the land which
We have made green.
It will feed you purely.
But the grass will give you
Peace and delight.
Care for the grass before the grain.

Secondly, I leave an envelope of envelopes.

Please mail one each month for me.
I put my faith in all of you.

Remember
There will be other lives
Other Worlds.
   Watson Forrest

At last the telephone is ringing. Eugene leads me to the hallway, holding my arm as though I were a thousand years old. Everyone – Martin, my mother, the two policemen – gather around me.
   'Hello.'
   'Charleen.'
   'Doug.'
   'Are you all right?'
   'What's happened? Have you found them?'
   'No, but I think we're onto something now.'
   'Where are you?'
   'I'm out at Weedham, Ontario with the cops. At the Whole World place.'
   'Yes?' I breathe.
   'They said you were here –'
   'Yes, but –'
   'They're not here. But we haven't given up.'
   'Tell me,' my voice bends with pleading, 'do you think they're . . . all right?'
   'Oh, God, Charleen, if you knew how terrible I feel about all this. You and Seth and . . . if you only knew. But I think it's going to be all right, I think we're going to find them.'
   'What happened? Do you know what happened?'
   'I just don't know. I thought Greta was okay on Sunday. A little edgy, but no worse than usual anyway. But as near as we can figure

out, she overdid the meditation thing. She rounded. That's what we think. She just rounded.'

'Rounded?'

'Went over . . . you know, over the top. It happens sometimes. She lost touch with the real world, what they call rounding. But I know she'll come around. You know Greta, she wouldn't hurt a –'

'But why did she take Seth?' I am crying into the phone. 'Why did she have to take Seth?'

'We're not sure. That is, the police can't figure it out unless she was just crazy to have a kid of her own. But I tried to tell them I don't think that's it. I've got a crazy hunch – this sounds really crazy – but I think maybe she's trying to take Seth to Watson.'

'Watson?'

'I know it sounds insane, but you know Greta. She might take it into her head that Seth would be better off with Watson. You know how she idolized the guy, always has. And she was, well, a little uneasy in her mind about Eugene and all that, you know how she is sometimes . . .'

'You really think . . .'

'It's just a guess, that's all. That's why I came out here, out to Weedham. But the kids here haven't laid eyes on him for a couple of years.'

'Greta is taking Seth to Watson?' I repeat this numbly.

'That's all I can think of. I'm going crazy trying to think. That's why I'm two hours late calling you. I turned my watch back instead of forward when the time zone changed, I just found out, that's how mixed up I am. I've just been looking and looking all week and I'm just about out of my mind.'

'We'll find them,' I say falteringly, unbelievingly.

'Look, I'm sure Greta knows where Watson's living. I mean, I know she writes to him now and then.'

'Yes. I know.'

'Look, Char, I don't suppose you've got any idea yourself where Watson might be.'

I think for a quarter of a minute and then I say, 'Yes.'

I give Doug the address very slowly so he will be able to write it down.

Standing in my mother's crowded little hall, we make hurried plans. Eugene and I and one of the policemen will go to the meeting point and wait for Doug Savage. The police will send reinforcements immediately.

The other officer will stay here with the family. He has just received a message, he tells us; a motel operator near Parry Sound reported renting a room last night to a middle-aged woman who was driving a dark coloured Volvo with B.C. plates. Was she alone? The report is not entirely clear, the officer explains. It was late at night, very dark, and no one is sure whether she was alone or not.

'We can take my car,' Eugene says.

'Your car?' Martin asks.

'A rental,' Eugene explains shortly. 'They've just brought it over.'

'God,' Martin says, 'that was quick.' He says this with mingled surprise and admiration, and for a moment all of us turn and regard Eugene who is checking his wallet for his licence. Such a simple thing, renting a car; Eugene would never be able to understand why my family stands in awe of such simple acts. I pick up my purse in the kitchen, and Eugene and I follow the policeman out the back door.

It is a big car, hugely clean, and the three of us fit in the front seat easily, Eugene driving, I in the middle, the policeman enthusiastically giving directions from the right. Eugene turns the car south toward the lake.

For me every passing car takes on extraordinary significance; each one must be checked off against Greta's blue Volvo. *She is sure to be in the city now.* I strain in the dark to see.

Vancouver, Calgary, Thunder Bay, Parry Sound, what could it signify? Perhaps a straight meaningless sweep across the whole country. What if they kept going, across Quebec, across the Maritimes, what if they dropped senseless into the sea like lemmings?

Then suddenly I am overcome with flooding despair. A moment ago, hearing the gassy zoom of the rented car, I had felt temporarily buoyant. Now, from nowhere, comes the knowledge that Seth is dead. The certainty arrives in the middle of a breath. I had inhaled with hope and by the time my breath left me I was certain he was lost forever. This dark road, this silence.

It was a night like this when Seth was born. A spring night, the streets dry and dark with only a cold knot of a moon in the sky. Watson was out at a peace rally and I, drinking coffee in the apartment and, feeling the first kick of pain, had been shocked and frightened and then, suddenly, for no reason, I had become serenely confident, packing quickly and neatly, phoning the doctor, locking the windows, calling the taxi, and then riding down the tree-arched Vancouver streets, sucking in the cool, friendly darkness as though it were somehow edible, exaltation knocking inside my heart. This was it, this was the beginning of my life, the only life that was going to matter.

'You want to take a left here,' the officer advises Eugene after a mere ten minutes. 'This is a one-way.'

'Okay.'

'Now, you want to jog right at the stop sign. I know this neighbourhood pretty well.'

'Parking?'

'Anywhere now.'

Eugene slows the car. 'Maybe we'd better not park right in front of the building,' he suggests.

'Squeeze in there by the hydrant, what the hell. Anyway there it is, that's the house. That big bugger on the left.'

This is a certain type of Toronto street – narrow and, despite the streetlights, deeply shadowed. Cars park all along one side. The houses are tall and narrow and old; wooden porches hang on to their blackened brick fronts. It's a warm night, and here and there people are sitting out on their front steps; I can see the glowing red tips of their cigarettes. The front yards are small and, though I can't see in the dark, I know they are made up of packed earth and clumps of weeds; this is the kind of neighbourhood where there are always too many children and where it is shady even on the brightest days.

The blue flicker of television sets fills most of the front windows. Eugene turns off the ignition and says, 'Let's go.'

The policeman stands outside for a moment checking the other cars on the block. 'That's one of ours,' he says pointing to an unmarked Ford. 'And those two guys are ours too.'

'Let's go in,' Eugene presses.

'But Doug Savage isn't here,' I say, suddenly confused.

'They'll be a few minutes yet,' the policeman says, checking his watch, 'all the way from Weedham. Even in good traffic that's a fair run.'

'No sign of a Volvo,' I hear Eugene saying.

'She could've ditched it anywhere.'

'I'll go in,' I tell them.

'I wouldn't advise that,' the policeman says, 'you never know about these characters.'

'I'm going in,' I tell him again.

'I'll come with you,' Eugene says.

'I think it would be better if I went alone, Eugene.'

'We could back you up,' the policeman says, thinking hard.

'If I could just talk to him alone. For a few minutes.'

The policeman ponders a moment and then asks, 'Is he, well you know him, he was your husband. What I mean, is he a dangerous guy?'

'Is he, Charleen?' Eugene turns to me.

'No,' I almost smile. 'He's not dangerous at all. He's like a . . . like . . . like a baby.'

The policeman checks with his friends in the parked car. When he comes back he nods at us and says, 'Okay. We'll have a go.'

It's a large house, one of the largest on the street, a three storey with jutting bays and ugly round-topped windows. Even in the dark I can see that it's in shocking condition. A few of the windows are broken, and most of them, except for two or three at the top, are dark. The front steps are shaky. The open porch is garishly lit by a naked bulb and it's filled with dirty plastic toys, a wicker chair with a rotted cushion, a dead plant in a pot. I'm frightened now, reluctant; perhaps I've made a crucial error in coming here.

The three of us stand on the porch for a moment, and for some reason the policeman is telling us about himself. His name is Bill Miller, he says, and he doesn't usually come out on jobs like this. He's filling in, he tells us, because this is a special case. Of course, he says shrugging, every case is special if you think about it. 'We'll back you up,' he says again in what sounds to me like Dragnet dialogue. 'If your boy's up there, we'll get him out.'

There are six doorbells stacked in a wiggly line on the door frame, but the name we want isn't there. A man appears in the doorway, a short, scrawny man, neither young nor old, with a rabbity neck and a small, sharp nose. He is so drunk he has to lean on the door jamb to keep from falling down.

'Yeah?' he challenges us.

378

I explain who we want to see.

'Sure, sure, he's up there,' he tells us. 'Lives at the top. I told him I'd put up a lousy doorbell for him, but what the fuck for, no one ever comes to see him.'

'Is there anyone up there with him now?' Eugene asks.

'Naw. 'Less they come up the fire escape. I been here all night.'

Bill Miller says, 'Look, mister, what we want to know is, did a woman come in here tonight?'

'Woman, eh?' he winks obscenely. 'I always tell him that's what he needs, a good roll in the hay to straighten him out. He's a real nut.'

'A woman with a boy?' Eugene asks carefully.

'Search me,' he shrugs. 'Why don't ya go up and have a look for yerself. Third floor. Name's on the door, ya can't miss.'

Eugene and Bill Miller position themselves on the dark second floor landing. The stairway to the third floor is narrower and there is no railing, but a dim lightbulb shows the way.

I am at the top of the house standing in a tiny hall; there is only one door and it is clearly marked in blocky, hand-painted letters, The Priory, Bro. Adam. (The diminutive 'Bro.' is a warning.) Silence. Then the sound of my own breathing rushing out into the silence. I knock smartly on the door. Twice. Three times.

No answer, but through the old cracked wood I can hear something stirring. Like cloth being moved. Like someone sighing. Someone moaning.

I knock once more and wait. And then I turn the knob. It opens easily, a wide swinging, and I call out, 'I'm coming in.'

Afterwards I could hardly believe that I spent less than five minutes in that room. A small square room under the eaves, and yet my first impression was one of blinding, dazzling space. It was the mirrors, of course, huge mirrors mounted on two facing walls and lining the sloping ceiling, so that the small space seemed endless and unbelievably complex, like the sudden special openings that sometimes occur in dreams.

It was like stepping into the warm, glowing, artificial interior of a greenhouse with its combination of plant life, glinting glass and stillness. The air, after the reeking hallway, was deliciously fresh and smelled of earth and new growth. A narrow window let in the fragrant early spring air and on the other side a door stood open to an iron fire escape.

The room was alive with tiny lights. They were strung on wires and they beamed like miniature suns on the wooden flats of grass. The whole room, except for a neatly made-up army cot, was carpeted with grass. In the rebounding arrangements of mirrors and lights, the grass stretched endlessly, acres of it, miles of it; it was like coming upon a secret Alpine meadow, like a pocket of perfect and perpetual springtime where there was no night, no thought of cold or death. Even time seemed to fall away from me, as though the endless grass lived in another dimension altogether, where growth and fertility took the place of hours and days.

Watson sat on the bed in a lotus position; I was conscious first of his gleaming skull and then of a certain bodily heaviness under his robe of dull red cloth. A book lay open on his lap. 'I was afraid you might try to come,' he said after a moment.

My throat closed soundless over his name: Watson, Watson, Watson. Still there, still there, that tender – no, no, more than tender – sliver of pain and youthful love lodged in the centre of my body. A twisting breathlessness like a rising funnel-shaped cloud of anguish pressed on my lungs, robbing me of speech and, for a moment, of coherence. What was I doing here leaning on this doorway, gasping for breath and for that portion of love that had surely died?

'Why are you here?' he asked again.

Then, like a stone sinking, I regained the powers of speech and thought.

'Brother Adam.' I pronounced the words with finality, as though they were a summation. He gazed at me with detached calm.

'Brother Adam,' I said again, deriving a curious energy from the flat sound of those two words. I couldn't summon surprise. I couldn't pretend surprise even to myself; nor could I distinguish the moment in time when I'd begun to know who Brother Adam might be. It seemed to me at that moment, standing in that incredible room, that I must always have known.

'You shouldn't have come,' he said. (No, I shouldn't have. I had wanted a holy man with a bright prophetic eye and a tongue threaded with psalms, not this squatting, middle-aged would-be-sage grunting his way into being.) Of course Watson's vision of himself had never been less than apocalyptic: It occurred to me that the name Adam was just slightly substandard in its patent simplicity. A swindle really. Adam, king of his rooming-house Eden.

'There's something I have to ask you,' I said firmly.

'I'm leaving tomorrow.'

'Where?'

'East. I'm going East.'

I came close to smiling, for there was a central, unnourished innocence in the way Watson pronounced the word East, and I saw that I would have to be careful or run the risk of destroying him entirely.

'Tell me exactly where you're going,' I persisted.

'India, Japan,' he waved vaguely.

'Alone?'

'Of course!'

'You're not taking anyone with you?'

'No one.'

'Something's happened, Watson. Something you should know about.'

'Is it really so important? I'm sure you can look after whatever it is.'

'Seth is missing.'

I watched his eyes; they blinked once, that was all. I remembered once years ago when Watson had seen a dwarf tapping his crutch by a bus stop; he had come close to weeping; something should be done, he had said. But the compulsion to relieve suffering was an abstraction for him, a folk belief in husk form. (Later I realized that outrage was only another form of innocence.) For a missing son he could only blink.

'I said Seth is missing.'

'Missing?'

'Have you seen him, Brother Adam? Just tell me if you've seen him.'

'No. Why would I see him?'

'Greta Savage has taken him. Taken him away.'

'Greta Savage.'

'We think . . . the police think . . . she's going to bring him here.'

'Why would she do that?'

'Are you sure they didn't come here?'

'They wouldn't come here.'

My throat closed with helplessness. Why did he have to speak in these dead, ritualized negatives? This convoluted room with its lights and mirrors and riotous grass was just another dead-end. I bent down for a moment and touched the tops of the grass. 'You're leaving all this behind?' I asked.

'I'll take seed,' he said, pointing to a suitcase beside the bed.

I stood up abruptly, and at that instant Watson's face took on a startled expression. For the first time I became aware of a commotion down below on the street, a screeching of brakes, car doors slamming, people running on the road, some of them shouting. We heard too the sound of footsteps on the stairs of the house. Brother Adam rose with haste; the folds of his robe sighed around him.

Then, quite clearly, I heard Eugene's voice calling me. It seemed to come from the street. Or was it echoing up the stairwell? He was shouting something. It sounded like, 'We've got Seth, Charleen, we've got him. We've got Seth and he's okay.' I stood completely still. I had never, it seemed, listened before with this degree of intensity. There were more voices. And again there was the sound of running on the stairs.

Brother Adam picked up his suitcase, and with a sweep of his robe, he moved toward the fire escape. But he stopped there, staring at me for a moment as though waiting to be released.

'Charleen,' was all he said. A question or a cry? Even afterwards I couldn't decide. Who was it who said that the sounds of our own names are the only recompense we have for the difficulties of living? I am certain, however, of one thing: that Watson didn't actually step out onto the fire escape until I nodded across at him. Then without a sound he dropped into darkness. I never even wished him good luck.

The next face I saw was Seth's. He burst into the room with Eugene behind him, absurdly offhand in his tan windbreaker. My arms around him, his tumbled hair smelling of potato chips, his familiar face laughing at me above the brilliant jungle of living grass.

Late Wednesday night. Some days are too long; it seems too much to ask of mere human beings that we live through them. What we need, what I need, is release from today. I need sleep, darkness. But I can't sleep. Consciousness is flaking away, but I'm still absorbing the various levels of unreality that have suddenly invaded my mother's Scarborough bungalow; I'm breathing them in, examining them, puzzling over their intricate folds and, like a classic insomniac, reliving all of it.

The policemen – they've all gone home now. How do policemen manage to get to sleep after a night like tonight? Of course, it's probably nothing to them; line of duty and all that; a ho-hum affair really; wouldn't even make the papers, one of them had told us.

Doug and Greta. It has been so simple in the end, so completely unspectacular. (Greta had simply driven up to the house and opened the car door. She never even suspected she was being followed.) How tender Doug had been with her. In the middle of the street with the searchlights and the beginning of a curious crowd, how gently he had held her, crooning into her hair, 'It's okay now, baby, I'll take care of you, there now, don't cry like that.' But she had cried. A small, animal weeping perforating the quiet neighbourhood, her thin shoulders shaking, 'I don't know what I was doing. He was going to India. I wanted Seth to see him. I didn't know what to do. All I want to do is go to sleep.'

'I know, I know,' Doug had said. 'You need to sleep. I'll take care of you now. You don't have to worry about anything.'

Watson. No one had seen him come down the fire escape. No one knew where he went. 'Too much confusion,' one of the officers had said, rather embarrassed. 'Anyway, it looks as though he wasn't involved.'

'He was moving out anyway,' the scrawny man told us. 'Paid up his rent yesterday, but the bugger left all his goddamn garbage behind. Lived there two years and you oughta see the goddamn junk he's got. A real nut, one of yer hopheads, oughta be in jail.'

Watson living alone for two years! Watson, a crouching ascetic! How extraordinary really, considering his terrible need for an audience. (Then I remember the mirrors.)

Louis Berceau, another solitary – but his time is coming. What a lot he's giving up, the enormity of the sacrifice! Why? Why? His blissful detachment is ending; now he will be assaulted by all sorts of troubling concerns; his life will begin to overlap with others in ways which are not casual but responsible and which may throw into jeopardy his springy step and his childish good faith. Ah, Louis, sleep well tonight.

My mother who will be married the day after tomorrow: she has taken a sleeping pill. As soon as we came home with Seth, she announced that she was going to take a sleeping pill and go to bed. She explained that she does not normally indulge in such drugs. The doctor had given her these, but she takes them very sparingly. Only for pain and anxiety, she explained. Pain and anxiety: she pronounced these two words absently as though they amounted to nothing more than a case of indigestion, a stomach cramp, a twinge of heartburn. Judith and I exchanged wry looks. Only pain and anxiety? Was that all?

Judith and Martin. They are sleeping together in the back bedroom off the kitchen. Judith has been offhand but tactful. 'Look, Char, it's not that I don't love you and all that, but as long as Mother's dead to the world – if you don't mind – the fact is, I just can't sleep soundly unless Martin and I are . . . you know . . . you get used to the feel of someone, and Eugene probably –'

Eugene, yes. Lying in my mother's veneer bed, his arms around me – he is sound asleep now, but he has thought of everything: he has set his travel alarm for six-thirty so we can be sure to switch back before morning. He has also driven Greta to a hospital, found Doug a hotel room nearby, bought Bill Miller a bottle of rye. And checked Seth over for damages: 'Of course I'm not a doctor, but there's nothing wrong with him that a good night's sleep won't fix.'

And Seth is here in this house. Still a little baffled, a little confused – 'I know it sounds crazy but she said you and Dad were getting back together again and she was supposed to take me to Toronto and I was too mixed up and half asleep. I guess I even believed her for the first day or two. It sounded like a dream, you know . . . like a wish come true.'

'A wish? You mean you wished – ?'

'Well, not exactly a wish –' He stopped, smiling suddenly, a self-mocking grin, but I could tell he was smiling at something else too, smiling at that swelling intangible that the 'pome people' refer to as fate and others simply call life. It was a dazzling smile.

He was glad to see Eugene. Eugene is going to get him a plane ticket so we can fly back together Friday night after the wedding. The concert is Saturday; with luck they'll let him play even if he did miss a few rehearsals. He's in good spirits and went to sleep almost immediately.

And that's the most extraordinary thing of all: Seth is asleep in this house and he's sleeping where no one else has ever slept before, not my father, not Cousin Hugo, not Aunt Liddy, not Eugene, not anyone. Wound in a sheet and topped with a single blanket – for it is surprisingly warm tonight – he is sound asleep in the living room on my mother's sacred chesterfield.

The whole house, in fact, is asleep.

Chapter 7

F riday. My mother's wedding day. I wake up early and
something whispers to me: get this right. Remember every
detail. Be accurate, be objective, be thorough. Make a
Chronicle of this, make a Wedding Album, get it Right. Begin
with the cloud-crammed dawn, the sky oily-blue and unsettled. A
heavy dew, a choking, webby haze. Around noon the sun nuzzles
its way through, making the day exceptionally humid. A little
cooler late in the afternoon. At six there is a brief downpour, at
eight a swollen, streaky-eyed sunset, but by that time Eugene and
Seth and I are on our way back to Vancouver and it's all over.

We start the day by eating breakfast together, my mother and I,
Eugene and Seth, Martin and Judith. Since there are only four
kitchen chairs, Eugene carries in two from the dining room. It
occurs to me that this is perhaps the largest number ever to gather
in this room for breakfast.

We drink coffee – my mother allows for exactly two cups each –
and eat buttered toast. 'Margarine is cheaper,' she reminds us, 'but
the day hasn't come when I can't afford a bit of butter in the morning.'

There is a great deal of conversation around the table; the six
of us are surprisingly comfortable together. Eugene, laughing, tips
his chair back slightly and fails to respond to my mother's sharp
disapproving glance.

387

My mother speaks to Seth – this grandson she scarcely knows, this grandson whose arrival has occasioned embarrassment and chaos but whose presence has somehow enlivened and restored the household – 'I suppose you'd like some cornflakes for breakfast?'

'Yes,' he answers, 'if you have any.'

'Well, I don't,' she returns. 'I refuse to spend good money on rubbish like that.'

At this Seth laughs uproariously, as though his grandmother has said something exceptionally witty.

'What *you* need is a good haircut, that's what you need,' she continues.

Seth claps his hands over his ears in mock horror. Or is it mock horror? I refuse to meet his eyes.

'Maybe you're right, Grandma,' he says amiably, demonstrating his instinct for the inevitability of things. 'I'll give it some thought.'

'If I were you I'd give it more than thought,' she retorts with spirit.

'I think there are some hedge clippers in the basement,' Martin says.

We linger over our coffee with the languor of passengers on a steamship, the last leg of the journey in sight. The wedding looms ahead – three-thirty in my mother's living room – but even that event is overshadowed by the liberating awareness of our separate departures, the return to our other lives which, like real sea voyagers, we view with a mixture of reluctance and anticipation.

'Martin,' Judith says after breakfast as she tidies my mother's kitchen, 'did you see that thing in the *Globe and Mail* about the judge?'

'No,' Martin answers, 'what judge?'

388

'You know, that Supreme Court judge, old what's-his-name. Seventy-six years old and getting married.'

'Oh yes,' Martin says, 'I think I *did* see the headline.'

'And he's marrying a woman about the same age. Second marriage for both of them.'

'Hmmm,' Martin comments.

'So it's not so odd really, people getting married in their seventies.'

'Who ever said it was odd?'

'Maybe it's the coming thing.'

'Maybe.'

'It's logical, when you think of it,' she says thoughtfully. 'There's a nice – you know – economy to the whole thing. In fact, it sort of fits in with the recycling philosophy.'

'Oh?'

'After all, here's Mother getting an escort and chauffeur. And Louis is getting a cook and housekeeper.'

'Is that all?' Martin looks up amused.

Judith scours the sink with energy.

'Is that all?' Martin asks again. Then he starts to laugh.

'What's so funny?' Judith asks turning around.

But Martin is laughing too hard to answer.

My mother spent almost all morning at the hairdresser's.

It had been Judith's idea: 'Look,' she had reasoned with her, 'you don't even have a hair dryer. And it's so damp this morning your hair will never dry. It would be a whole lot easier if you just went down to that little beauty place next to the Red and White. Eugene could drive you over, couldn't you Eugene? And you can have it washed and set and be back by noon.'

'It's such a waste . . .'

'I'll phone right now and see if they can work you in. I'll explain . . .'

'There's so much to do here . . .'

'Charleen and I can tidy up the house. You have a nice restful morning under the dryer. I'll phone . . .'

'I don't know . . .'

'I'll ask if they can take you at ten-fifteen.'

She had gone. Judith had won. It was in every way a sensible plan, but I had been appalled by my mother's quick surrender, her willingness to be led. This weakness is something new; she *is* getting old.

'She's getting old,' I say later to Judith.

'Yes,' Judith nods briskly. She is plugging in the old vacuum cleaner, and I watch as she attacks the living-room rug. How realistic Judith is, how offhandedly she deals with the externals of life. She knows how to manage our mother, how to persuade her against her will, and she accepts her victories with stunning ease.

The vacuum cleaner is thirty years old, an upright Hoover with a monstrous black bag, and the sound of its roaring motor fills the house.

I picture my mother in the hands of a bullying shampoo girl in platform shoes, I think of the painful plastic rollers and the chemical sting, the scorching heat of the hair dryer, the futile aggression of *Harper's Bazaar*, and suddenly I am swept with a desire to rush out and find her and protect her. That is when it strikes me that I must . . . love . . . her in a way which Judith would never comprehend.

'It'll do her good to get out of the house,' Judith yells over the roar of the vacuum cleaner.

Yesterday morning Louis came to put in the shrubs I had bought. He worked slowly but with pleasure.

'Good healthy roots on this one,' he said, patting the soil around a mock orange.

'I don't know why you thought I needed more bushes,' my mother called to me crossly from the back door. 'There are already more than I can look after.'

'I like the smell of a mock orange,' Louis said to me. 'When it's in bloom it's the most wonderful perfume in the world.'

After my mother went back into the house, Louis whispered to me, 'Remember what we were talking about yesterday?'

'Yesterday?' I blinked.

'About that friend of yours. The priest.'

I stared.

'You were going to ask him to come to the wedding.'

'Oh,' I breathed, 'oh, yes, I remember.'

'I've been thinking it over. And on second thought maybe it wouldn't be such a good idea after all.'

'Oh?' I said.

'I appreciate it, I really do, but you know, a stranger and all,' he paused and nodded almost imperceptibly toward the house, 'maybe it wouldn't be such a good idea.'

Later, when he had finished the planting, he went inside the house. He and my mother sat at the kitchen table talking a little and drinking coffee, Louis stirring in sugar, and my mother primly, awkwardly, perseveringly sipping. Seeing them sitting there like that I had a sudden glimpse of what their life together would be like. It would be exactly like this; there would be nothing mystical about it; it would be made up of scenes like this.

Not that I understand the complex equation they teeter upon, or the force that brought them together in the first place. It occurs to me that there are some happenings for which the proper response is not comprehension at all, but amazement and acceptance.

*   *   *

Eugene drove my mother to the hairdresser's, and Seth, feeling restless, went along for the ride. While they are gone Judith and I vacuum and scrub, dust and polish. Martin, whistling, helps us wash the windows with vinegar and old newspapers. Then we stand back and regard the living room with its old, slipcovered chesterfield, its bulky armchairs, dark tables, heavy curtains and the rounded archway into the even gloomier dining room. It is scrupulously clean, but for all the crowding of furniture it looks barren, pinched and depressing.

'We'll put the lace tablecloth on,' Judith decides. 'That should help a little.'

Martin takes the tablecloth down from the top of my mother's linen cupboard, and throwing it over his arm, begins to tap out a soft cha-cha-cha. 'Ta ta tatata, ta ta tatata,' he sings as he whirls and swoops in the narrow space between the china cupboard and the dining-room table. The tablecloth swirls and circles, cascading to the floor as he steps deftly and lightly around the chairs. 'Down, down, down South America way,' he hums to the lacy folds.

Judith smiles at him lazily. 'You'll tear it, Martin, and then you'll catch it.'

'Then I'll catch, catch, catch, catch it,' Martin sings, dipping gracefully past us.

Judith takes the cloth from him and opens it on the table. 'Well,' she eyes the yellowed edges, 'you can't say it looks exactly festive.'

But then Eugene comes in the front door carrying armloads of spring flowers.

'Flowers!' I exclaim.

'I never thought of flowers,' Judith marvels.

'Voila!' Martin cries, and, slowing to a cool elbow-spinning, shoulder-dipping softshoe, he shuffles into the kitchen to look for vases. For an instant – it couldn't have been more than a second really – I wish, feverishly wish, that I could dance away after him. I wish Judith would stop frowning and tugging at the edge of the tablecloth, and most of all I wish Eugene would stop standing there in the doorway, heavy and perplexed, with the tulips slipping sideways out of his arms.

Then Judith cries, 'You're a genius, Eugene, I love you.'

Then something happens: I look at Eugene in a frenzy of tenderness and begin to be happy.

Yesterday afternoon Louis offered to cut the grass.

'It's too much work,' my mother told him, 'especially after putting in all those useless bushes.'

'I'll cut the grass,' Seth volunteered.

My mother considered, 'Might as well keep busy,' she said. 'Idle hands . . .'

Seth laughed; he seems to find his grandmother's sayings shrewd and amusing. He carried the old hand mower up from the basement, oiled it carefully and began cutting back and forth across the tiny back lawn.

Watching him, I suddenly remembered the box of grass I had left behind in Vancouver, Brother Adam's grass. I had left it on the window sill, abandoned it without a thought, when I might easily have arranged for a neighbour to come in and water it. By the time I get home it will probably have turned brown; in all this heat it might even have died. How, I demanded of myself, had I been so neglectful?

The idea came to me that there may have been something wilful in my oversight, that I may unconsciously have conceived a deathwish for my lovely grass, hating it while I pretended to love it. (The mind is given to such meaningless mirror tricks.) Had I subconsciously recognized Watson in those lengthy, grassy letters, had something about them touched a vein of familiarity, a flag of memory. Toying with these thoughts, I couldn't decide, but my aptitude for self-deception pressed me closer and closer toward belief. Poor Brother Adam, his love of grass which I had believed was prompted by an Emersonian vision of oneness, was only one more easy commitment, an allegiance to a non-human form, a blind and speechless deity. And poor Watson, his life hacked to pieces by his endless self-regarding; every decade a ritual pore cleansing, a radical, life-diminishing letting of blood. (After he had disappeared down the fire escape, after the excitement of seeing Seth had died down, I had picked up the book he had been reading; it was titled *The Next Life*.)

It is a good thing Eugene kept the rented car because it turns out to be quite useful. At noon he picks up my mother from the hairdresser's and brings her home. Seth arrives a few minutes later by foot; he has had his hair trimmed and, smiling sheepishly, he allows us to admire him.

We eat sandwiches standing up in the kitchen, and then Eugene drives Martin and Judith to Union Station to meet their children who arrive on the one o'clock train.

I hardly know Meredith and Richard, and Seth has never seen them. Richard is shy, somewhat sulky, and, after three hours on the train, wild with hunger. Meredith at eighteen is beautiful. Judith has told me that her daughter's beauty has made her own ageing bearable. 'It's an odd consolation, isn't it?' she said. 'You'd think I'd be jealous, but I revel in it.'

Meredith kisses her grandmother with surprising force. 'Well, how does it feel to be a bride again?' she bursts out.

'I was just going to lie down for my rest,' my mother says in a wavy-toned way she has.

'Right now?' Meredith's eyes open wide.

'Just for an hour. I always have a rest after lunch, you know that.'

'Hold it for five minutes, Grandma. I've got a surprise for you.'

'A surprise?'

'You wait here. I'll set it up in the kitchen.'

Meredith, shopping bag in hand, races into the kitchen opens her blue umbrella on the kitchen table, balancing it carefully on two spokes. Underneath it she arranges a dozen small parcels wrapped in silver paper and tied with pale pink ribbon.

'Okay now, Grandma. You can come in.'

'What in the world . . .'

'It's a shower, Grandma, a kitchen shower.'

'But I've got everything I need . . .'

'I know, Grandma,' Meredith dances around the table, 'but you're a bride, you've got to feel like a bride.'

There is a new set of measuring cups in copper-tinted aluminum.

'But I have some measuring cups . . .'

'But they're all dented and ancient. I noticed last time we were here.'

There is a new ironing-board cover.

'Now you can throw that old rag away,' Meredith chortles.

There is a little needle-like device to prick the bottoms of eggs with.

'So they won't break when you boil them,' Meredith explains.

'But all you have to do is add some salt . . .'

There is a wooden spoon. A new spatula. A twisted spring for taking lumps out of gravy. Two tiny soufflé dishes in white china.

'For you and Mr Berceau,' Meredith tells her joyfully, 'and you can put them right in the oven.'

There is a miniature ladle for melted butter. A painted recipe box made in Finland. And a beautiful, new streamlined egg beater with a turquoise plastic handle and whirling, purring, silvery gears.

'Lovely,' everyone agrees.

'Just what you needed.'

'Meringues, cakes . . .'

'– a beauty –'

'But I have an egg beater . . .'

'Grandma, smile. This is your wedding day, you're a bride.'

While my mother rests we set up the presents on the buffet. There aren't many. Judith and Martin are giving bedspreads.

'Two bedspreads?' I ask.

'Well . . . yes. One seemed sort of, you know, suggestive. I mean, that's the way she might see it. Two sort of cancels out the whole thing. One for the guest room and one for her room, more like a general refurbishing. God, I hate all this delicacy, but you know how she is, and the fact is, we couldn't think of anything else.'

Eugene has bought them a kitchen radio which we think was rather an inspiration, a trim little model in white plastic with excellent tone and a year's guarantee. And since my shrubs hadn't been very successful, I decided yesterday to buy something else, something small but personal: I decided to give them my complete works, my four books of poetry.

Curiously enough my mother has never read anything I've written. She has, in fact, never expressed the slightest desire to do so, and a species of shyness has prevented me from ever sending her a copy. Furthermore, though she is not an astute reader, it has always worried me that she might comprehend something of the darkness in my poetry. It might wound her; it might remind her of something she would rather forget.

But now seemed like a good time to make a presentation. Like

Judith, I had begun to know that I might never be able to talk to her. Who knows? Perhaps this was a way.

I had to buy the books retail by going to a bookstore and paying the regular price instead of getting them directly from the publisher as I normally do in Vancouver. Eugene and I went downtown yesterday to a very large bookstore, and there, in the poetry section, I found all four of my books. (They have recently been re-issued as a rather attractive set.) My picture in rainbow hues smiled happily at me from the back covers.

It was an altogether surreal experience to be buying my own books; I felt as though I were participating in a piece of cinema vérité. I felt, in fact, extraordinarily foolish placing those books in the hands of the cashier at the front of the store.

She checked the titles and then she turned the books over to check the price. Now, I thought, now she's going to suffer a brief instant of confusion; then her mouth will fall open in astonished recognition.

But none of this happened. Instead she took my twenty-dollar bill, slapped it down on the cash register, sighed sharply, and snapped at me, 'I suppose this is the smallest you've got.'

'Yes,' I said weakly, faintly, 'I'm afraid that's all I have.'

Meredith and Judith and I make three bouquets, one for the dining-room table, one for the mantel of the artificial fireplace and a tiny one to set on the telephone table by the front door.

'Shouldn't we save some for Grandma's bouquet?' Meredith asks. 'Or is Mr Berceau bringing that?'

Judith and I stare at each other; neither of us had thought of a bridal bouquet. 'Damn it,' Judith bursts out, 'I should have ordered something.'

'Maybe Louis *will* bring one,' I say, not very convincingly.

'Hmmmm,' Judith says, 'I doubt it.'

'I don't suppose she could carry some of these tulips?' Meredith asks.

'Not really,' Judith says, 'tulips aren't quite the thing for a bridal bouquet.'

'Maybe if we phoned a florist right away . . .' I begin.

'Lilacs!' Meredith says. 'They'd be perfect.'

'I don't know,' Judith says doubtfully.

'They'd make a perfect bouquet,' Meredith assures us, 'and there are tons of them in the backyard. And they're at their best right now.'

'Well,' I say, 'why not?'

'The only thing is,' Judith hesitates, 'well, you know how Mother always was about lilacs. They're just weeds, she used to tell us. Remember that, Charleen?'

'No,' I reply, 'I don't remember her ever saying that.'

'We were always wanting to take a bunch to school – you know – flowers-for-the-teacher sort of thing. And she'd never let us because she said they were just weeds.'

'I don't remember that,' I say again, and saying it I am conscious of a curious lightening of heart. It is somehow wonderful and important to know that at least part of the burden of memory has been spared me.

'But lilacs are beautiful,' Meredith protests, 'they're heavenly flowers; I can't think of more gorgeous flowers. I'll make a bouquet for Grandma, just leave it to me,' she says.

Eugene, who is not normally introspective about his profession, just as he is not particularly critical or adulatory about it, once told me that he occasionally has moments when he is visited by a sharp sense of unreality. It happens most frequently when he is delivering to his young patients lectures on the importance of brushing their teeth. For a moment or two he feels himself undergoing a dizzying separation: suddenly he is the farmboy from Estevan eavesdropping on a solemn, middle-aged professional in a white jacket who is piously pressing for dental hygiene as though it were a system of morality. He is invariably self-amused when this occurs and at the same time awed by the transcendental experience of seeming to overhear himself.

I had something of the same feeling myself yesterday talking to my mother about Greta Savage; I had replied to her questioning with a calm I hadn't known I possessed, and hearing myself I had felt very close to being the person I would like to be.

'What are you going to do about that woman?' she asked.

'What woman?'

'That crazy woman. That kidnapper.'

Without really intending to, I heard myself defending Greta, explaining to my mother that Greta had taken Seth as an act of love. She loves Seth, and, in a neurotic, labyrinthian way, she loves me too.

My defence of Greta was all the more surprising because I defended her instinctively. Like the kind people of the world – like Eugene-the-orthodontist – I had judged with instant charity; like the good folk in fairy tales I had performed magic, spinning gold from straw, transforming apples to golden guineas. Kindness, kindness – a skill which I have nourished and rehearsed and worried into being – had jumped out and taken me by surprise. Without thinking, without laborious reflection I had fallen into its easy litany.

Even more surprising, it had given me a temporary ascendancy; my mother had been silenced; perhaps kindness and bravery have a common root.

'Greta acted out of love,' I told my mother again, and, overhearing myself, I knew it was true.

*　　*　　*

'Here comes Louis Cradle,' Martin calls from the front window.

'Louis who?' I ask.

'Louis Cradle. And he's all zooted up.'

Judith, setting out teacups, explains, 'Berceau is French for cradle.'

'Oh,' I say, for an instant stung by my ignorance – how spotty my education was – was I going to spend a lifetime meeting such voids?

Louis Cradle, Mr and Mrs Cradle. Mentally I thrust about for the symbolism, cradle of a new life, no, too pat, the sort of pearl the 'pome people' dived after – the 'pome people' could never leave a paradox unturned, seeing life as a film strip jerking along from insight to insight, a fresh truth revealed every three and a half minutes – better forget about symbolism; yes.

Louis coming into the house looks no more dressed up than he was when he took me for lunch; indeed he wears the same old navy blue suit which does, however, look as though it has been brushed and perhaps even pressed.

But he is wearing a hat, a soft cloth cap in a fine wool, rather a strange choice for so warm a day. Yet, the effect seems not unsuitable. I've often noticed that men who cover their heads, sweetly and solemnly concealing the tops of their heads with turbans, hoods, fezzes and skull caps, seem to be putting on a spiritual covering which announces piety and humility and which, in the shorthand of costume, declares that life is perishable, vulnerable and worthy.

At half past two my mother has her bath; then she retires to her room again in order to get dressed. The house is ready. Martin and Eugene have even managed to pry open one of the living-room windows, long ago painted shut, and a breeze drifts in. The cake has been delivered, and there is a box of tiny, paper-thin cookies too. Judith and I arrange them on a tray; we put out milk and sugar, and I even set out a circle of lemon slices on a glass plate.

The only thing missing is a scene which I half-imagined might take place, the scene where my mother takes Judith and me aside and asks us if we object to the fact that she is remarrying, if we have any sensitivities about our father being more or less supplanted. Some faint, quivering, awkwardly delivered apology, a seeking of approval or even permission, at the very least a fumbling for consensus or a simple explanation: she is lonely, she needs someone to look after the furnace, see to the insurance, someone to talk to. But now it's almost time for the wedding. The missing scene is clearly not going to take place; thank God, thank God.

'Where's Grandma?' Meredith asks us.

'Getting dressed,' I say nodding at the closed door.

The minister has arrived, a young man, no more than twenty-five, with a prominent bridge of bone above his eyes; his face gleams with sweat. 'Hot day for May,' he announces nervously.

'Wonderful, isn't it?' Judith says a little defiantly. She has changed to a striking sleeveless dress in rough, lemon-coloured cloth.

'Perhaps you'd be more comfortable if you took off your jacket,' suggests Martin, who does not intend to wear a jacket.

'My mother will be out in a minute,' Judith says. 'She's just getting dressed.'

'This really is a happy occasion,' the young man remarks.

Louis, supremely relaxed and almost dapper, invites him to sit down by the window. 'It was very good of you to agree to come.'

'Do you think I should see if Grandma needs a hand?' Meredith whispers to me.

'No. She'll be out in a minute,' I answer.

'It's half past three.'

'Really?'

'On the dot.'

'Not like her to be late.'

'Especially for her own wedding.'

'. . . really should check, don't you think?'

'Give her a minute or two.'

'You're sure she's all right?'

'Maybe we should . . .'

'Ah, there she is now.'

'Mother.'

'Mrs McNinn?'

'Oh, Grandma!'

'My dear.'

The ceremony, a shortened version of the traditional marriage service, is performed in front of the artificial fireplace (symbolism?) and, since it is short, we all remain standing. Judith and Martin stand in the archway to the dining room, Eugene and I by the window, and the three children beside the television set.

My mother's voice repeating the vows is exceptionally matter of fact. She might be reading a recipe for roast beef hash, and curiously enough, I find her lack of dramatic emphasis reassuring and even admirable. Louis, on the other hand, seems quite overcome. He chokes on the words and once or twice he dabs at his eyes, though this may be the result of asthma rather than emotion.

From where I stand I can see only their backs; my mother leans slightly to the left; perhaps her operation has unbalanced her. And Louis stoops forward as though anticipating an attack of coughing. They look rather fragile as people always do from the rear; it is after all the classic posture of retreat. Retreat from what? Age, illness, loneliness? Louis slips a ring on my mother's hand and they stand for a moment with hands joined. Two is a good number, I think, and like a chant it blocks out the remainder of the service for me. Two is better than ten; two is better than a hundred; two is better than six; when all is said, two is better than one; when all's said, two is a good number.

'That's a lovely bouquet you're carrying, Mrs McNinn. Oh, I'm so sorry, I should have said Mrs Berceau.'
   'Well, lilacs aren't my favourite, but my granddaughter here . . .'

'Won't you have some tea, Louis?'
   'Yes, please, Judith, that's just what I need.'
   'And a piece of cake?'
   'A nice cake, isn't it?'
   'You weren't a bit nervous, were you, Louis?'
   'Well, to tell you the truth –'
   'Welcome to the fold, Louis.'
   'Well, well, thank you, Martin, very kind of you.'
   'Great institution, marriage.'

'Do you think she's holding up okay, Char?'
   'She looks a little tired. But not bad.'
   'Considering . . .'

'Nice you could come east with Aunt Charleen, Eugene.'
   'I wouldn't have missed it, Meredith.'

'You're just being polite.'
'No, really.'

'What do you think, Judith, should I bring out the champagne?'
'I don't know, Martin. You know Mother. What do you think?'
'I don't know. Oh, hell, why not?'

'And that woman over there? Mrs Forrest? She's your aunt, is that right?'
'Yes, she's a poet. Most people think we look alike.'
'And the man with her? Dr Redding? In the grey suit?'
'That's Eugene. Her lover.'
'Lover?'
'You look so shocked. Are you really shocked?'
'Of course I'm not shocked. Why should I be shocked?'

'You must have been scared getting kidnapped like that.'
'Scared?'
'I mean, did you think she was going to try for ransom or something like that?'
'Naw, it wasn't like that. It was – I don't know – it was kind of fun, the whole thing.'

'You look beautiful, carrying that bouquet.'
'Have some more cake, someone has to eat all this cake.'
'It's good cake.'
'A little dry, if you ask me.'

'May I propose a toast . . .'
'Good idea.'
'I've never had champagne before.'
'Neither have I.'

'Really?'

'Delicious.'

'Like ginger ale, only sour.'

'Ah, look at the bubbles rising.'

'You're supposed to *sip* it, Richard.'

'Here, have another glass, Judith.'

'If you're sure there's enough . . .'

'Lovely.'

'Tea is plenty good enough for me.'

'Here's to marriage.'

'Here's to the bride and groom.'

'Here's to the future.'

'Happy days.'

'I love you, Eugene.'

'Charleen, Charleen.'

Nothing is what it seems. Our plane flying west is defying a basic natural law which says that on any given day the sun sets only once; but here it is setting over Lake Superior, again over Winnipeg, over the prairies, over the mountains. We're diving into its fiery, streaming trail, we're chasing it down to its final, almost comic, drowning. *Don't tell me about the curve of the earth*.

Eugene, peering down through grey mist, says, 'What we should do is buy a farm. A few acres. For weekends, you know. Maybe grow some vegetables, have a horse for the kids. Might even be a tax advantage there . . .'

My childhood is over, but at the same time – and this seems even more true – it will never be over. Say it fast enough and it sounds like a scuttling metaphysic of survival. *Who ever said you can't live without logic*.

'Ladies and gentlemen,' a voice says, 'this is your captain speaking.' *But how do we know it is our captain?*

'We've just been told there's a light rain over Vancouver –' *A light rain, a light rain, the beginning of a poem, a light rain.*

'But visibility is excellent –' *Watch out for symbolism now.*

'We hope you have enjoyed your flight. This is your captain wishing you a good evening.' *Good evening, good evening.*

All Fourth Estate books are available from you local bookshop.

For a monthly update on Fourth Estate's latest releases, with interviews, extracts, competitions and special offers visit
www.4thestate.com

Or visit
www.4thestate.com/readingroom
for the very latest reading guides on our bestselling authors, including Michael Chabon, Annie Proulx, Lorna Sage, Carol Shields.

London and *New York*